R. Lee

The African Wanderers

The Adventures of Carlos and Antonio

R. Lee

The African Wanderers
The Adventures of Carlos and Antonio

ISBN/EAN: 9783743393363

Manufactured in Europe, USA, Canada, Australia, Japa

Cover: Foto ©Andreas Hilbeck / pixelio.de

Manufactured and distributed by brebook publishing software (www.brebook.com)

R. Lee

The African Wanderers

The Bird-Thief at Sierra Leone.—*Page 62.*

THE

AFRICAN WANDERERS;

OR,

The Adventures of Carlos and Antonio,

EMBRACING

*INTERESTING DESCRIPTIONS OF THE
MANNERS AND CUSTOMS OF THE TRIBES, AND THE
NATURAL PRODUCTIONS OF THE COUNTRY.*

By MRS. R. LEE,

AUTHOR OF 'ANECDOTES OF THE HABITS AND INSTINCTS OF ANIMALS,'
'TREES, PLANTS, AND FLOWERS,' 'ADVENTURES IN AUSTRALIA,'
ETC.

Fully Illustrated.

GRIFFITH & FARRAN,
SUCCESSORS TO NEWBERY AND HARRIS,
WEST CORNER OF ST. PAUL'S CHURCHYARD, LONDON.
E. P. DUTTON & CO., NEW YORK.

PREFACE.

'WHERE we have suffered much, we love much,' is a saying verified by the undying interest which the Author of the following story takes in the western coast of Africa. To call the attention of the wise and good to a part of the continent (the river Gaboon) but little known, has been one of the chief objects of her present undertaking; and in order to gain credit for her assertions, it is necessary that she should briefly state how far the fiction in her pages extends.

With the exception of the field of battle, the finding of the two boys, the journey to Santander and Liverpool, the history of Carlos has been invented as a vehicle for carrying the reader into scenes which have hitherto been but faintly described. Antonio is only an imaginary personage after he lands in Africa. Every production, every character is true; and most of the circumstances are drawn from the personal experience of the Author or her friends. Among the latter she has to thank Captain William

Allen, R.N., for allowing her to extract materials from his graphic description of Fandah; also Mr. Freeman, whose conversation and reports (the latter supplied by the kindness of Mr. Beecham) have afforded her useful statements. One kindly impulse, one mite added to the exertions made in behalf of this magnificent land, will indemnify the Author for her labour, and the anxiety which necessarily attends publication.

R. L.

CONTENTS.

CONTENTS.

CHAPTER XII.

CHAPTER XIII.

CHAPTER XIV.

THE

AFRICAN WANDERERS.

CHAPTER I.

THE moon was sailing through a cloudless sky of that deep blue colour which is peculiar to the south, and illuminating the beautiful mountains and valleys of Spain. Glancing above and afar, the eye rested on none but the images of peace, and the bounty of the Almighty; but on looking immediately around him, the spectator might receive a painful proof of how much man does to deface this fair creation. His strife and contention had been there, and the plain was strewn with the dead and the dying; for it was the evening after a fearful battle, which had taken place between the two struggling parties, called the Carlists and the Christinos.

On the occasion to which these pages refer, the Carlists had remained masters of the field, and the Christinos had fled in all haste, leaving their dead upon the ground.

A fatigue-party, commanded by an English officer who had entered the service of Don Carlos, and formed chiefly of men of his own nation, was searching amidst the slain for those who might, though wounded, be still alive, and was followed by carts, in which straw was laid to receive the sufferers. Strangers to the vengeance which men of the same country feel towards each other in civil war, the soldiers indiscriminately sought for both friends and foes, and, carefully filling the vehicles, were about to return, when a low, wailing cry met their ear. 'Surely that was the cry of a child,' said Captain Lacy to his sergeant; 'how can it have come here? Look for it, Brown.' The man obeyed, but his search was fruitless; the sound had ceased, and nothing but the faint moans of those in the carts was heard, as even the slow motion at which they were going increased their pain. The wounded men were placed in a barn near the camp, where the surgeons were waiting to administer to their relief; and when the fatigue-party had rendered all the assistance that lay in their power, they returned to quarters to eat their scanty meal. The English captain, wrapping himself in his large cloak, tried to rest from the exciting labours of the day; but it was a vain effort, for that wailing cry still rang in his ear. At length, starting from his rude couch, he exclaimed, 'I can bear it no longer; that child's cry haunts me, and I must find out whence it comes.' On leaving his tent, he again summoned his sergeant, and both once more went to the field of battle.

It was no delusion; that plaintive cry had been borne through the stillness of the night to the camp, and now guided the steps of the Englishmen to the spot whence it proceeded. Under a small clump of tall bushes, apart from the rest of the plain, lay the body of a noble-looking Spaniard. A ball had pierced his heart, and his death must have been immediate. The countenance, though pale, had therefore resumed its natural expression, and seemed to tell how worthy he had been of the love of that wife who, also dead, lay stretched across him. By their side sat two little boys, one apparently three, and the other two years of age : the latter, exhausted with crying and hunger, had fallen asleep upon that mother's arm, which had so often formed his resting-place when in life ; while the other, leaning his head upon his father's motionless form, and grasping the hand of his little brother, convulsively sobbed, and at intervals uttered the cry which had arrested the attention of the Englishmen. For a few moments the soldiers paused, and the tears of the brave men rolled down their cheeks. 'This is a sad sight, sir,' said the Sergeant, who first broke silence ; 'she must have looked for him in the field, and then dragged him here in order to try and recover him. Seè, she has torn open his jacket and found the wound, and then her heart must have broken with grief,' he continued, as he gently raised the young woman from her husband's body. 'They were a beautiful couple, however, and well off, I should say, by the woman's dress.' 'What shall we do with the children, Brown ?' said Captain Lacy, speaking for the first time ; 'are both alive ?' 'Yes, sir,' replied the Sergeant, 'one is asleep, and the other is too frightened at us to cry any more.' 'We cannot leave them here,' observed the officer ; 'they must go to the camp with us. Give one to me, and you take the other.' The sleeping child was safely laid in his arms, and the Sergeant hugged the brother closely to him. Both then proceeded to Captain Lacy's tent, where these two rough men, like tender nurses, tried, by a little broth and kind words, to assuage the fear and hunger of the elder; while the poor infant was warmly wrapped in a cloak, and laid upon his benefactor's mattress.

'Now we have done what we can for the poor little things,' said Captain Lacy, 'we must go back to the plain before our camp-women have stripped the bodies. I would not have the remains of those two rudely touched for the world. Follow me with the tools.' They proceeded to the task. The grave was dug; the few ornaments and some gold coins belonging to the unfortunate pair were secured; and Captain Lacy, taking his prayer-book from his pocket, by that bright and silvery light read the English Service for the dead. The bodies were then laid side by side; the earth was heaped over them, some of the branches belonging to the bushes above fastened down over it, both to protect and conceal the mound; and the soldiers slowly and sadly resumed their way to the camp. Before they reached it, however, Captain Lacy stopped, and said to his companion, 'Brown, my good fellow, take half the money and the ornaments which belong to those whom we have just interred; they are your share.' 'No, no!' vehemently exclaimed the Sergeant; 'no such plunder for me; I never yet stripped the dead, nor robbed the orphan. Keep all, sir, if you please, for the poor little boys; they may like to have them, for the sake of their father and mother. I am almost tired of fighting in this country, sir, for we see so many sad sights here, and this day has sickened me more than ever. I shall never forget that poor girl's face, nor the long black hair which shaded it. 'Tis true, she and her husband were not on our side, but they may be none the worse for that.' 'You are an honest man, Sergeant,' observed Captain Lacy. I hope I may be able to reward you some day for your good feelings; but, like you, I am weary of such a war as this. We cannot, however, as honourable men, retreat from it at present; and at this moment we must both see what we can do further for the children.' On their return the infant was awake; but after receiving some nourishment, again fell asleep from fatigue. His example was soon followed by his brother; but rest was banished from Captain Lacy's eyes. A soldier, and but little to depend upon beyond his profession, how was he to provide for the two helpless creatures who had thus been placed in his hands? Certainly he might find some one of the soldiers' wives who would attend to them at present; but the future was too full of uncertainty, hardship, and suffering, for him to dare to think of it without apprehension. Placing his trust, however, in that Divine Being who had thus selected him to save these orphan children, he determined to do all that lay in his power, and leave the rest to Heaven.

At daybreak Sergeant Brown was summoned to a consultation in Captain Lacy's tent, the result of which was, his strong recommendation of a good-natured Irishwoman, the wife of one of the British soldiers, who, for a mere trifle, would take care of the children. He sought her; and when the proposal was made, she willingly promised to watch over them as if they were her own, refusing any reward beyond the feeling of being useful; and she forthwith began to wash their soiled skins with a tenderness and vivacity which augured well for her skill. But her fair face and hair, and her blue eyes, in addition to the surrounding

scene, so bewildered the poor little things, that they
shrieked, clung to each other, and imperfectly called
for their parents. Kathleen, their new nurse, could
not speak a word of Spanish; but the Sergeant and
Captain Lacy caressed and soothed them in their
native tongue, so that they became gradually reconciled to those who were so heartily engaged in their
service. Too young to have received any lasting
impression, they, in a few days, were even attached to
their protectors; but as, notwithstanding Kathleen's
good-will, she could not give them her whole time,
they were necessarily left much to themselves. The
elder, therefore, who already appeared to be the
graver of the two, soon learned to assist his brother,
and to steady his tottering walk; and both progressed
much more rapidly than those children do, who have
only soft carpets to move upon, nurses to feed and
prevent them from falling down, and plenty of con-
trivances to procure them amusement. To their
benefactor they were an inexhaustible source of
interest, and beguiled him of many an hour's fatigue;
though afterwards, when he was personally engaged in
fierce strife with the enemy, he almost wished he had
not taken charge of them; for if he fell, what would
be their fate? In a few weeks the camp broke up,
and the troops marched to a distant station; when
the Captain's boys, as they were called, were either
seated on the top of the baggage, or travelled in the
arms of those with whom they were especial favourites.

The success of the Carlists was of short duration,
and they retreated from place to place with diminished
forces. At length their leader talked of quitting the
country to which he had been asserting his right; and

not till then did Captain or rather Colonel Lacy (in consequence of rapid promotion), turn his thoughts homewards, and, worn, harassed, and dispirited, long for that rest which wounds, hardship, and fatigue rendered absolutely necessary. The children had all the while been cherished by him with increasing affection; and although they chiefly lived in his tent, there was scarcely any one in the camp who was not ready to sport with or assist them. They throve surprisingly; and at the end of two years, when they appeared to be about four and five, they were as sturdy and hardy as children who were double their age, were friends with every individual in the camp, and were perfectly doated upon by their generous benefactor, Sergeant Brown, and Kathleen. Poor Kathleen! death bereaved her of the husband whom she had followed with such toil and danger; and thus stricken, she clung with still greater affection to her young charges. They spoke both Spanish and English, the latter with a strong Irish accent, imbibed from their nurse; but any instruction during their wandering and uncertain life had been perfectly out of the question.

Writing to Madrid, and obtaining assistance from the English Ambassador there, to whose family he was distantly related, Colonel Lacy gathered together his arrears of pay, as well as the little property which he had been able to save from the wreck of the service, and, furnished with passports for himself, the two boys, Sergeant Brown, and Kathleen, he prepared to cross the Peninsula to Santander, a small seaport town in the north, where he hoped to find a vessel which would convey them to England. The country was in such a state that no party was safe; the Carlists robbed the

Christinos, the Christinos plundered the Carlists, and
the banditti stripped them both. For greater security,
those who were obliged to travel generally assembled
together in numbers, and hired waggons, in which a
portion rode at a time, while the rest, marching on foot
formed a sort of guard. Adopting this only chance of
safety, slight as it was, Colonel Lacy and his followers
joined other travellers bound for the same place, and
in this manner reached Santander. On one occasion
they had a very narrow escape from the bandits, who
poured from the mountains into the narrow passes in
such numbers, that it was impossible for a small force
to make much stand against them. A waggon had
been attacked by the ruffians only an hour or two
before that of Colonel Lacy passed over a certain
spot; and his party probably owed its safety to a
necessity on the side of the robbers to secure their
spoil and prisoners, which took them off the road.
The remains of the broken vehicle, and the bodies of
one or two who had perished in defending themselves,
or others, told but too plainly the history of the
struggle; and the succeeding passengers used all
possible speed to reach a place of security before the
marauders had time to return and overtake them.

At length the cavalcade reached Santander without
any serious disaster; and there a scene presented itself
which can scarcely be described, or even imagined.
Numbers of British soldiers who had been serving in
the Spanish armies of either party, without pay, and
rendered utterly insensible to every good feeling by
the lives of bloodshed, rapine, and cruelty, which
they had been leading for several years; without any
one to superintend them, under no kind of authority;

generally speaking, in rags, and even these, in many instances, gradually bartered away for food,—they crowded to the port in order to obtain shipping for their native country. Some, who had not a single article of clothing, had taken the parchment manuscripts which had been carelessly scattered far and wide as nothing worth, when the convents had been plundered, had cut them into something like shape, and transformed them into jackets and trousers. What would the poor industrious monks and learned men who wrote these have said, could they have foreseen the fate which attended their labours? and who knows but that some precious document, some brilliant effort of intellect, may have thus been lost for ages? Nothing could exceed the strange effect which this dress produced, unless it were the lawlessness and misery of the unhappy wearers. It was hardly safe to be in the same town with them; and when the vessels designed for their transport by the English government arrived at Santander, they flocked on board in such numbers that it was difficult to accommodate them. Colonel Lacy took a passage for himself and party in one which contained the least portion of this extraordinary cargo, and aided by the captain of the ship and the Sergeant, he contrived to keep his fellow-passengers in some sort of subjection. Finding a few of his former soldiers among them, they more willingly returned to proper discipline; and during the short interval occupied by the voyage, no disaster occurred. The independent habits of the children soon reconciled them to the novelty of a sea voyage, and they slept on a locker in the cabin, without a thought of discomfort. As they neared the English shore, and were standing together upon deck, the

Colonel asked the Sergeant where he was going, and what he meant to do with himself. The latter hesitated, coloured, and remained silent. 'What can I do for you, Brown?' inquired Colonel Lacy. The man's countenance brightened, and he then replied, ' If I may be so bold, sir, I must say I should be very unhappy if I were wholly to leave you and the children ; we have gone through so much together, that I feel as if I belonged to you, and so Kathleen thinks. Your honour says that you mean to settle in a house of your own, and you will want some one to wait upon you. We wish to make a match of it ; and if you would take us as your servants till you could get better, we would do our best and serve you without wages. I have a bit of a pension, you know, sir, which would keep us in clothes.' Pleased with such a proof of attachment, Colonel Lacy thought this would be an excellent arrangement for all parties, and replied, ' Be it so, then ; you and Kathleen shall remain with me, at any rate, for a time ; and the question of wages will be easily settled, by my giving you that which I would give to others.' Accordingly, as soon as the good-hearted soldier had settled all his affairs in London, the whole party journeyed together to Liverpool, where the Colonel's friends and relatives principally lived, and where he found, by the death of one of the latter, an inheritance awaited him which made him easy as to the future provision for his adopted children, who were looked upon by all with interest ; notwithstanding that there were several who thought their benefactor romantic in his devotion to their welfare.

CHAPTER II.

THE air of Liverpool, impregnated by the smoke of many chimneys and factories, did not agree with Colonel Lacy's health, accustomed as he had been for years to live almost entirely in the field; he there-fore took a house at Wavertree, within a walk of the town, and close to a day-school for boys, where his *protégés* commenced their education. Doubtful whether they had ever been baptized, and deeply impressed with the importance of this holy rite, he, soon after settling, had the ceremony performed, which admitted them as members of the English Church, under the name of Henry (which was Colonel Lacy's own) and Charles, in memory of that master for whom the soldier had fought and bled. However, as they were always addressed by himself and the Sergeant in Spanish, they retained the appellation of Henriquez and Carlos all their lives. They very early in life showed a great difference of character. Henriquez, the elder, was thoughtful, and would probably have been shy, had not the publicity of his life prevented it. His attachment to his benefactor was fervent and unceasing; but he evinced it rather by his perfect obedience to his will than by voluntary caresses, ex-cept, indeed, if the Colonel were ill, and then the anxiety and affectionate devotion of Henriquez were unbounded. He was called at school the grave Don, or *the* Don; while his quicker and more animated brother was nicknamed 'Little Don Carlos.' Never was there a greater contrast than that presented, in many respects, by the brothers; for Carlos was as idle as Henriquez was industrious; he was careless and noisy, though full of affection, which he demonstrated in the most vehement manner. His fun, his talent for mimicry, his sparkling vivacity, won all hearts on a first acquaintance; but he often tired even his best friends by his restless activity and love of change. Henriquez seemed rather to win affection gradually; but once obtained, it was never even momentarily withdrawn from him.

For a time the little household went on smoothly and regularly, as might be expected under the direction of two soldiers, who so much love order and obedience; but the marriage of Colonel Lacy wrought considerable changes. Two children had been added to the party by Kathleen; but as the Sergeant exercised his principles of discipline even over them, almost as soon as they were born, they had never troubled Colonel Lacy as long as he was a bachelor. To his lady, however, it was a very different matter, and to have the house already peopled by four children, she found to be past all endurance. As she made no impression on her husband when she tried to induce him to send the Browns away, and being determined to make a clearance of them, she tried to render their lives so miserable by petty annoyances, that they themselves would volunteer to leave the service. Still they loved their master too much to complain ; and he knew nothing of the system pursued by his lady, till one morning, after having been on the previous day tormented beyond all bearing, the Sergeant entered his study, and making his usual military salute, steadily and quietly announced the necessity which he was under to leave Wavertree. 'What is the matter, Sergeant?' exclaimed the Colonel. 'Why should you wish to go away?' 'We could live with your honour till death,' was the reply; 'but it cannot be expected that your lady should think of us as you do, and it is very natural that she should not like our children. It is therefore much better for you, sir, and for ourselves, that we should go.' The Colonel was surprised; but the whole of Mrs. Lacy's plan seemed to be revealed to him in a moment, and he wondered that he could have been so long blind to her proceedings. 'What do you think of doing, Brown?' he asked. The Sergeant replied, that he thought of trying to procure a place as porter at some warehouse, and that he supposed Kathleen must take in washing. 'No, no!' hastily exclaimed the Colonel. 'I shall not ask you to stay, because I see clearly that this house is no longer comfortable for you; but you shall not go till I have made some arrangements for your future welfare. So saying, he reached his hat, and walked into the city, where he spent the morning in making inquiries for situations, and did not return till he had a prospect of procuring an advantageous post for his faithful followers.

On reaching his own gate, the Colonel found the whole establishment in a state of disturbance: little Don Carlos, with his eyes red and swollen, and his whole countenance bearing marks of having been in a towering passion ; Henriquez endeavouring to soothe and reason with him, though himself much agitated : the Sergeant and his wife only just succeeding in quieting their own children, who had been bellowing at the top of their voices ; and Mrs. Lacy still in a state of great excitement. On returning from school, the two boys had found the latter scolding Kathleen more than usual ; upon which the Sergeant, who had just returned from working in the garden, coolly taking his wife's arm under his own, said 'your ladyship need not be so angry with my poor girl, seeing that she will not be here very long to trouble you. I gave the master warning this day, and it is only because he wished us to remain, that we are to stay a little time longer.' The moment the boys heard this they flew to their friends, declaring that they should never leave them, that they were sure there must be some mistake, and that their dear papa would never suffer them to go after being with him through so many battles, and after living with him for so many years. The Sergeant tried to explain, but Kathleen sobbed as if her heart would break. This was too much for Carlos to bear, and throwing his arms round her neck, he exclaimed, 'That it was that woman there—that Mrs. Lacy who had done it; and go they should not, in spite of all her wickedness.' The latter, in much anger, tried to take the boy away from his nurse by force, and in her turn abused him ; but he resisted, and declared that he would protect Kathleen till he died. A scene of violence ensued, which had only just subsided when the Colonel approached his house. Carlos and Henriquez were waiting for him in the drive, when the former, jumping into his arms, in an agony of grief, entreated him not to send the Sergeant and his family away. Henriquez took hold of his arm, and looked imploringly in his face. 'My dear Carlos,' said the Colonel, 'you are not in a fit state to talk about anything ; but you may be sure that our friends shall not be ill-treated. Wait for me here, my dear boys, till I have spoken with Mrs. Lacy on the subject.

What passed between the husband and wife never transpired ; but in about half an hour the Colonel returned to the garden looking very grave, and said to Carlos, 'You have been rude to Mrs. Lacy, and have forgotten that she is my wife : therefore I expect you will make an apology. When you have begged her pardon I will talk to you.' There was no disputing the mild but authoritative tone of his benefactor, had the boy been so inclined ; and with his eyes cast down, Carlos suffered himself to be led into the presence of the lady, when he begged her forgiveness for whatever he might have said when he was in a passion. Mrs. Lacy did not receive the apology very graciously ; but she knew that her husband must be obeyed, and with some effort she restrained her feelings. The Colonel then told the boys that 'the Browns would not leave the neighbourhood, and not even the house, till they could be comfortably settled.' 'But then we shall not see them every day, papa,' said Carlos. 'No, my boy,' was the reply ; 'but you would not be so selfish as to wish for anything which would interfere with their welfare ?' This was a new view of the whole affair, and silenced Carlos. Order, though not contentment, was restored : the Browns looked sad, and the Colonel also, but he was, if possible, more kind to them than ever ; the boys lost their vivacity ;

Mrs. Lacy was stiff and cold to every one, and kept her room as much as she could, in order to avoid the sight of the offending parties.

After an interval of some days, Sergeant Brown and his wife were appointed porter and housekeeper to one of the public institutions in Liverpool, with a salary which enabled them to live with great comfort, and put their children to school. It was the best asylum possible for a worthy old soldier; but it was much more valuable in the eyes of Sergeant Brown, from the capability which it afforded of seeing his beloved master. frequently, as well as the boys, who generally paid their friends a visit every half-holiday.

All things in the family circle at Wavertree continued to be peaceful for a time, and the Colonel flattered himself that even his wife was satisfied; but he was unfortunately mistaken. The lady too often recollected that she had brought a fortune to her husband, to be moderate in her expectations. The lesson which Carlos had received was soon lost upon him; and he was so impetuous and noisy, that Mrs. Lacy declared he would cause the destruction of her nerves. When reproved, he would be more quiet for a day or two, but only burst afresh into still more uncontrollable spirits in consequence of the restraint. A whole holiday had given the lady so much of his presence, that she was completely tired of him, or fancied herself so; and she asked Colonel Lacy if he always meant to keep those boys at the school near Wavertree. 'No,' said her husband, with a significant glance, which plainly told that he penetrated into her motives for the question; 'at midsummer next they will go to Rugby. It is now March, and I expect that you will put up with Carlos' noise and thoughtlessness till then ; after that, you will be relieved of him for some time. I am sure Henriquez never gives you any cause for complaint.' Mrs. Lacy uttered no reply ; and knowing that she must submit, made up her mind, though unwillingly, to tolerate the boys a little longer.

When Colonel Lacy communicated his plans to his adopted sons, they were at first overwhelmed with sorrow, for the prospect of leaving him was heart-breaking to both ; but when he told them that it would be one of the steps which would lead to their becoming independent and providing for themselves, they were better reconciled. When in their room at night, however, Carlos said to his brother, ' I know why we are going away ; it is all that Mrs. Lacy's fault. I must not call her that woman any more, for it made papa so angry.' ' Pray do not call her anything,' said Henriquez, ' but Mrs. Lacy.' ' You will see,' continued Carlos, ' how I will plague her till we go !' ' You forget,' retorted Henriquez, who more steadily considered the matter, ' that when plaguing her, as you say, you plague papa also.' ' I did not think of that,' returned Carlos. ' Well, I will behave as well as I can ; but what do you think papa means to do with us when we leave school ? You are twelve, and I am eleven, I suppose ; you may depend on it Mrs. Lacy will not let us have any peace in the holidays.' ' She will,' rejoined Henriquez, ' if you behave properly ; you see she does not complain of me, or try to thwart me in any way.' ' But I know what she says of you,' continued Carlos. ' What does she say ?' asked Henriquez. ' She says you are sly,' answered Carlos. ' I overheard her when she told one of her friends; and I dared her before the lady to say so to papa, for it was false.' The colour rose into the cheeks of the noble boy, and with his peculiar disposition the accusation sank deeply into his heart; scorn and anger agitated his whole frame, the more violent because his nature revolted from it; he walked up and down his room, and opening the window, leaned out to cool his heated brow. At length, with a resolute effort, he subdued his passion, when Carlos, embracing him, told him it was not worth his notice. 'I know it is not,' said Henriquez, sighing; 'but I wish it were midsummer.'

At length the holidays were over, and Colonel Lacy, wisely sparing his lady the trouble of outfitting the two boys for a public school, with the assistance of Kathleen, performed the task himself. Very sad were his *protégés* to leave their only earthly parent, and for some days previous to their departure, even the high spirits of Carlos were subdued; even Mrs. Lacy's pet dog had a respite from him; he was gentle and attentive to its mistress, and seemed as if he could never leave the side of his benefactor. He took leave of Kathleen with a hearty kiss, and eyes full of tears. Henriquez could not speak. Each boy shook hands with the Sergeant, and gave the children a parting present. Mrs. Lacy was so glad they were going, that she bestowed a cordial farewell upon them; but the saying 'Good-bye' to the Colonel, from whom they had never been long separated, was the heaviest trial they had ever known. The excellent man pronounced a blessing upon them, faltered out an adieu which had little in it of the firmness of the soldier; and when he returned to his home to be no more cheered by their voices and sunny faces, he felt as if a blank had fallen upon his existence. Not so Mrs. Lacy; she was immoderately gay and happy, as if relieved from a weight of care; and the Colonel could scarcely forbear to observe, that he would have been better pleased with some degree of sympathy on her part.

Years passed away: the boys spent their holidays constantly at Wavertree; and Carlos, having become much more manly, laid aside a number of those provoking ways, which, though little in themselves, yet prove of infinite consequence in the daily intercourse of families. The characters, however, of the two were not altered, only further developed. Henriquez was a persevering, industrious boy; did not think he fully comprehended a thing until he had regarded it in every point of view, and when once understood, never forgot it; thus he excelled, for his years, in various branches of education, as well as in manly sports. As for little Don Carlos, as he was still called by his schoolfellows, though his rapidly increasing height rendered the first part of the epithet rather inapplicable, he was a universal favourite. Impetuous and violent, he constantly gave offence, but was afterwards so sorry for his fault, so generous in accusing himself, that he was instantly forgiven by those whose feelings he had wounded. He was thoughtless, daring, and active; but his was headlong courage, rather than that cool self-possession which Henriquez evinced. No boy in the school could vie with him in any of the agile sports there practised; his love of adventure betrayed him into many scrapes, but he always seemed to get out of them again in a manner which surprised every one, and which was so unaccountable to his companions, that they pronounced him to be the luckiest fellow in the school. He made a creditable figure at the periodical examinations; but how he obtained his knowledge was a mystery, he was so insufferably volatile. But while Henriquez took the highest rank, and gained prizes, Carlos was satisfied with that which alone was necessary in order to prevent him from disgracing his benefactor. 'He will never make a shining or a deep scholar,' wrote his master to Colonel Lacy, 'not from want of power, but from his unsteady character; and I should think him admirably calculated for a life of activity and enterprise.'

The vacation again came round; and four years spent at Rugby again excited the animadversions of Mrs. Lacy. Finding that hints met with no attention, she openly expostulated with her husband, on the continued expense which he was incurring for those who had no claims of relationship upon him; and, reasonably enough, reminded him that he had now three children of his own, who were higher objects of duty. The Colonel, however, turned a deaf ear to her suggestions; said, that 'when his two other boys required to go to school, their elder brothers (laying a stress upon these words which made the lady's cheeks tingle) would, in all probability, be able to provide for themselves, and there' was still plenty of time to look around him for the settlement of Henriquez and Carlos.' Finding herself thus thwarted, Mrs. Lacy, as a last resource, determined to express her opinion to the boys themselves. She told them plainly 'that they were now a burden upon the Colonel; that he had done more for them than he ought to have done, considering that he was a married man with a family;' and working herself up to a high pitch of excitement as she proceeded, she said, 'they ought to be ashamed of eating the bread of his real children.' A new light seemed to burst upon Henriquez and Carlos; their right to the kindness of Colonel Lacy had never before been questioned, but their position seemed now to be changed in a moment.

The high, generous feelings, the nice sense of honour which well-disposed boys imbibe at a public school, made the struggle the greater. Henriquez did not trust himself to offer any reply; and, seeing an approaching storm gathering in Carlos' whole frame, and agitating him violently, he dragged him out of the room before it could find vent. Scarcely knowing what they did, they rushed from the house, went into the fields, and wandered they knew not whither, uttering their feelings to each other in broken sentences. They did not return till Colonel and Mrs. Lacy had gone out to dinner; when, as if ashamed to look any one in the face, they sought their bedroom. 'We can never return again to Rugby,' said Henriquez. 'Where are we to go?' asked Carlos. 'Surely I could get a clerk's place,' observed Henriquez. 'I shall go to sea,' exclaimed Carlos. 'Nonsense,' returned his brother; 'you don't know what you say. Why should we not be always together as we have hitherto been, and try and get something to do near papa? I am sure when he gets old, he will want us to take care of him, though we are not his real children, as she says.' 'That's true,' resumed Carlos; 'but I hate that woman, and never wish to look at her again.' 'I hate her as much

C

as you do,' retorted Henriquez, 'but'.—— 'There are
no buts with me,' interrupted Carlos : 'I will not go
back to Rugby, and I will not stay here.   I detest
learning and writing ; and I vote that we should tell
papa what we feel to-morrow morning.'   The brothers
talked for some time longer, each defending his own
plan, when they heard the carriage drive up to the
door.   Never did the Colonel's voice sound so musi-
cally in their ears, as when, entering the hall, he asked
the servant if the young gentlemen were come home ;
and when told that they were in their own room, he
observed that they were gone to bed very early.   He
gently opened their door as he passed to his own, and
blessed his dear boys ; and grateful as that blessing
was to them, it wrung their hearts to agony.   In after
years, amid toil, suffering, danger, and wrong, it stole
upon their ear ; the recollection of it seemed to soothe
their sorrows, and more than once it preserved them
in the hour of temptation.

Morning dawned before the lads could go to sleep ;
and at breakfast their pale faces and silence betrayed
that something was wrong.   They declined eating ;
but, frightened at the consequence of her remarks,
Mrs. Lacy, with unwonted kindness, pressed them to
take food.   To oblige her, or rather to oblige the
Colonel, they complied ; but the toast remained un-
touched on the plate of Henriquez ; and Carlos, after
vainly endeavourig to swallow a morsel, hastily rose,
exclaiming, 'It chokes me !'   He then pushed his chair
from the table, and rushed out of the room.   'Something is the matter,' said Colonel Lacy.   'Henriquez,
go to my study ; take Carlos with you, and wait there
till I come.'   Henriquez obeyed ; and Mrs. Lacy, who

had no conception of the feelings attendant on generous and elevated minds, exclaimed, 'I am sure I did
not mean to hurt the boys. I only wanted to rouse
them to exertion; for you spoil them till they fancy
that they are for ever to live as gentlemen, at yours
and your children's expense.' 'What have you said?'
asked the Colonel, with unusual sternness. 'I insist
on knowing every word.' Thus urged, Mrs. Lacy
confessed the whole; at which her husband exclaimed,
'Poor fellows! I do not wonder at their distress.' He
left his wife to her own reflections, and, proceeding to
the study, told the lads that he knew all that had passed,
therefore no explanation was necessary; that they were
responsible only to him; that they must be aware how
very different his sentiments were to those of his wife;
and that they were quite as dear to him as his own
children. His intentions towards them would prove
this; for he had always destined Henriquez for a
learned profession, and Carlos for the army. After
thanking him with all the deep fervour of their affection and gratitude, the brothers respectfully urged
him immediately to procure some situation in which
they could maintain themselves. However small the
emolument, they would make it sufficient to live upon;
'for,' added Carlos, 'the thought of taking that to
which we have no claim, and injuring the children of
one who has been a father to us, is beyond our
endurance.' He again mentioned his earnest desire
to go to sea; but Colonel Lacy would not hear of it;
insisted on their remaining quiet at Wavertree, at least
for a time; made it a duty to him that they should
continue for a short period on the same footing as that
which they had held all their lives; and, in the mean-

while, he would try to provide for their future career in a way which would be satisfactory to their feelings of independence.

For the present, then, the lads were quieted, though it was impossible for them to be happy under Mrs. Lacy's roof; and they ardently longed for that which they called 'emancipation.' It was a severe lesson, but one which had the good effect of imparting a wholesome sense of humiliation on naturally proud spirits, marked in the one by an increase of thoughtfulness, and in the other by subduing his often boisterous mirth. Colonel Lacy had much interest among the wealthy merchants of Liverpool; and there was a general feeling of respect towards him, owing to his character and his conduct to the orphans. Consequently, exertions were immediately made; and the result was, that two clerkships were in a few weeks placed at his disposal for his boys, each with a salary of sixty pounds per annum to begin with, and an increase according to service. 'With this,' said Colonel Lacy to them, 'you must take a lodging between you in the city; and I shall make arrangements with Kathleen to look after and market for you.'

It was so sudden a change, however, from the careless and generous liberality of a schoolboy, that they committed many mistakes, especially Carlos. But Kathleen helped them out of their little embarrassments, they thought, by her good management; but, in fact, she had received orders from Colonel Lacy to apply to him in all difficulties; and he it was who supplied the deficiencies, often smiling at the perplexities of the novices.

Winter came, and the young Spaniards diligently

devoted themselves to their duties, thereby giving great satisfaction to their employers. They met in the evening in their own little sitting-room, and breakfasted together; but their Sundays were always spent with Colonel Lacy, by his particular order; for, besides the happiness he invariably felt at having them with him, he by it secured their attention to those religious duties which he knew formed the all-important part of their lives, and which were but too often neglected by those who spent the rest of the week immersed in business. The lads seemed to be happy and contented for several months; but when spring returned, there was evidently a restlessness and alteration about Carlos : he no longer expressed any satisfaction at his comparative independence; he no longer passed his evenings cheerfully with Henriquez, entering with zest into the books and drawings which formed the relaxations of both ; he no longer poured forth the numerous Spanish songs which he had learned, and sung as if by intuition ; he no longer whistled through his morning toilet; but, weary and dejected, he constantly, on his return from business, threw himself into a chair, and seemed to be brooding over some subject which he did not as yet care to communicate. 'I can bear this no longer,' said Henriquez to him at length, 'at least tell me what is the matter with you?' 'Do you not see?' replied Carlos ; 'do you not feel the glorious spring, the sun high in the heavens, the birds soaring in the sky, the leaves and the flowers expanding in the glittering rays, and everything inviting us to freedom? I hate the counting-house, I hate the desk, I hate the narrow dirty streets—I hate them all, as I hate Mrs. Lacy,' he added, lowering his voice, for he knew that Henriquez would scold him for these last words. 'Hush, Carlos!' said the latter; 'you told me you would not say that again. I know it is of no use urging upon you how thankful we ought to be for our present situation, but I now appeal to your affection for our dear Colonel, and for myself. What should I do without you, left alone as I should be, to struggle with what you know to be as uncongenial to me as it is to you? How should I be able to get through it all?' Ashamed of his selfishness, Carlos was silenced for a time, but again did his wishes assail him in an irresistable form. I was among his duties to visit the docks, where he saw vessels starting for all parts of the world; and in an unguarded moment, he involuntarily confessed to his master, who was very much interested in him, that he felt the most intense desire to be a sailor, and an utter aversion to a sedentary employment.

'You must send that younger boy of yours to sea,' said the merchant to his friend the Colonel, when talking of him after dinner at Wavertree, 'even if it be only one voyage by way of trial. He will never settle till he has had some experience in the disagreeable part of such an occupation. I have known many a lad cured of this common propensity in that way; but mind, he must enter as a common sailor, and have no indulgences.' Colonel Lacy sighed at this confirmation of what he had long foreseen and feared: he was disappointed and distressed, but he could not help feeling the force of his friend's suggestion; and after long deliberation, reflection, and consultation with others, he resolved that Carlos should be gratified. A ship was then in port, bound to the coast of Africa. The master was a gentlemanly person, who had been in the navy; and Carlos, to his great joy, was entered as one of the men. Accustomed to brave everything himself, Colonel Lacy never thought of shrinking from climate, and Carlos had no fear. 'You must rise from the lowest grade,' said his benefactor to him, 'if you would thoroughly understand your profession, and you must first be before the mast in order to learn how to command. At the beginning you must make up your mind to come in contact with all sorts of characters, which you must not suffer to contaminate you,—must witness much coarseness and vulgarity; and, educated as you have been for the station of a gentleman, I suspect these will be your greatest trials.'

The kindness, the generosity, with which Colonel Lacy met the wilful Carlos' wishes, made him almost repent of his wayward resolution; but the alternatives sickened him,—dependence, and living with Mrs. Lacy, or else the close, dark counting-house, and its accompanying routine. His sanguine temperament made him bound over the steps by which he was to rise; and in his fertile imagination, he saw himself standing on his own deck, his vessel freighted with the merchandise of his beloved Henriquez, spreading her white sails to a glorious breeze, the brilliant suns of southern climes bronzing his cheek, the dark blue waters sparkling around him, and the rich treasures of other countries poured out at the feet of his noble benefactor and his children. 'What a glorious picture! is it not, Henriquez?' said he; 'I only wish you could share freedom with me.' 'There is no such thing as freedom for us at present,' returned his brother: 'and much as I sigh after it, I would not purchase it at the rate you must do, for all the happiness which it confers.'

The parting scenes had better be passed over without description ; they served to convince all parties, except one, of the depth of their mutual affection, and she wondered why the Colonel should be in such low spirits about a wilful boy, who was nothing to him but an object of charity : this, however, she wisely kept to herself.

CHAPTER III.

THE vessel in which Carlos was to sail was named the
'Hero;' and as she was to start immediately, he was
ordered on board. Every hand was necessary for the
final stowing away of the cargo, which consisted of
bales of cotton goods, ammunition, muskets, iron
bars, brass rods, pigs of lead, hats, cheeses, salt, and
various etceteras. Although he had frequently super-
intended the shipping of goods in his capacity of
clerk, the novice was scarcely prepared for the scene
of confusion which a merchant vessel presents when
near her departure. The moment he set his foot on
deck, he was accosted by one of two men with,
'Avast, brother! lend us a hand to stow away this
chest in the hold.' 'A likely-built young fellow,' said
his companion, 'but somehow, he looks too much
like a gentleman.' 'I did not come here to be a
gentleman,' observed Carlos, overhearing him; and
as he spoke, helped the slighter of the two sailors.
This action won the hearts of his messmates, which
might otherwise have been prejudiced against him by
his appearance, and they never forgot it. 'Is Lacy
come?' inquired the first mate, who, in the absence
of the Captain, held the command. 'Ay, ay, sir,'
was the reply. 'Then send him aft for orders,' continued the officer; who, measuring Carlos with an

experienced eye as he obeyed the summons, seemed to regard him with peculiar satisfaction. Open, brave, and good-natured, Mr. Mortimer performed all his duties with cheerfulness, except one, and that was writing, which he detested much more than Carlos did; and accordingly, as he knew the history of the latter, he had determined, if he found him good-natured, to make him his peculiar *protégé*, and, inducing him to be useful in the capacity of his amanuensis, employ him as often as he could in the after-cabin. Satisfied with the expression of Carlos' handsome face, he desired him to go into the storeroom under the cabin, and help the steward to stow away the private stores which would be handed down to him by the latter; 'he is only a bit of a lad,' added he, 'and not to be trusted by himself, so some one must work with him.' Carlos cheerfully obeyed; and as he pushed his way along the deck, amid hampers, boxes, bags, lanterns, spare rigging, bolts of canvas, sails, water casks, dried provisions, pickle-tubs, and dozens of ducks and fowls tied together by the legs in bunches, he advanced to the cabin-door, where the surgeon, a tall raw-boned Scotchman, with difficulty poised himself, as he stood smoking his pipe. He had evidently been taking more than one farewell glass with his friends; but still had sufficient politeness to think that the fumes of tobacco might be disagreeable to some ladies within, who, being a farmer's daughters, had come from the country with cakes, fresh butter, eggs, milk, and huge cabbages, for their cousin the Captain. They were accompanied by their brothers, and were sitting on the locker across the stern, taking tea amidst candlesticks, mugs, compasses, log-glasses, lamps, dishes, etc., looking very rustic and demure. Carlos involuntarily took off his hat when he saw them, but proceeded below to perform his task. This was barely ended, and he was looking round at the contents of the room, when he heard the blast of a trumpet, resounding from one end of the vessel to the other, and succeeded by an order to turn up all hands and clear away, which made him spring from the depths below, in expectation of at least a visit from the owners of the vessel. He aided in thrusting the unhappy ducks and fowls into their coops, rolling the casks to the side, and piling the other things one upon another; when, pausing for breath, he looked out for a boat full of dignitaries. Nothing of the kind, however, was to be seen, but the mate shouted, 'Silence fore and aft; the Captain does not come on board till to-morrow morning; and now, my lads, we'll have a dance.' A long roll upon the drum ensued, and then one of the country gentlemen took a violin from the corner in which he had hidden it, and began to scrape and tune his instrument. Carlos had never danced except with ladies and gentlemen, and involuntarily shrank from the romp which ensued; but a thump on his back, with an injunction to take his partner, if he meant to be good for anything, caused him to advance towards one of the rosy-cheeked damsels. He so far forgot himself as to ask for the honour of her hand, at which she at first stared, and then, thinking he was mocking a fine gentleman by way of a joke, laughed heartily. This recalled him to his actual position, and leading her out, he mingled with the dancers. So contagious is genuine mirth, that in spite of the heaviness of his heart and the novelty of the scene, he soon found himself joining in the laughter around him, and he became animated by the intricate mazes through which his lady led him. As he performed his part in so satisfactory a manner, he was evidently in great request, and was obliged to dance with each of the young damsels. Grog was handed round between the dances, mixed to the satisfaction of the female part of the company; and the gaieties were ended at twelve o'clock, by another loud blast of the trumpet, and another long roll upon the drum. A boat was made ready, the farewells exchanged, and the visitors were sent ashore. Overcome with fatigue, Carlos threw himself on a chest and slept; not, however, without considerable wonder that he should have danced for hours, after immediately quitting his brother and Colonel Lacy. Even the few who composed the watch resigned themselves to slumber, and the ship was quiet till the morning sun was high in the heavens. It was Sunday; and Carlos, starting from his hard couch, was the first to shake off the fatigues of the preceding evening. The scene around him was anything but encouraging, and his heart misgave him, when he looked back to the comforts and refinements of the home he had voluntarily quitted, and which were so particularly enjoyed by him on that day of the week above all others. The nine o'clock bells from the various churches, recalling such different and orderly habits, seemed to invite him to return to pray in the temples raised to God; and he almost longed to regain the shore for that purpose alone. But little time, however, was given him for the indulgence of his thoughts; for the first mate, half dressed, issued from the cabin, roused the ship's crew, and ordered everything to be put in proper order—'*made taut,*' as he called it, for the Captain's arrival.   In two hours a complete metamorphosis had taken place; breakfast was over, and the men, in their blue jackets and trousers, their white shirts, and shining round hats, with long ends of ribbon floating from them, appeared to belong to a well-conducted vessel.   The Captain came on board, prayers were read, and all present apparently listened with attention; dinner ensued, and then the pilot arrived.   A favourable breeze had sprung up, the anchor was weighed, the men cheeringly singing as they ran round with the capstan-bars, and the sailors' favourite plan was realized, viz. that of sailing on a Sunday.

As soon as the 'Hero' had well cleared the mouth of the Mersey, the pilot resigned her into the guidance of her commander; but before he took his departure, he inquired for Carlos, into whose hands he put a small parcel, saying, that he had promised a young gentleman to deliver it at the last moment; and before Carlos could inquire from whom it came, the man had slipped down the gangway into his boat, and pushed off.   The sailor's duties are, of course, heavy at first, and Carlos had no opportunity of examining the contents of the packet at that moment; thrusting it, therefore, inside his waistcoat, he waited for the hour of leisure.   He was not so violently assailed by seasickness as some are, but a faintness and dimness of vision occasionally crept over him, which made exertion very irksome; still he did not flinch from his allotted occupations, and was very angry with himself for the thought that would creep in, in spite of every endeavour to keep it out, that the sailor's life was not quite what he had expected. He was stationed in the first night-watch, and, approaching the binnacle, he contrived to open his packet, and read the following letter :—

'My beloved Carlos,—I know you refused all offers of money from our benefactor; I therefore, as your elder brother, insist on my right to supply you to the extent of my power, only regretting that my means are so far below my will. I have turned the little sum into gold, which passes everywhere, and I entreat of you to keep it till the hour of need arrives; then make use of it as the representative of myself, whose affectionate wishes you will follow by such a proceeding. To this I add, what I am sure will be a comfort to you, even when you least expect it. It is a small prayer-book (much more portable than that given you by the Colonel), which you will be always able to keep about your person; and can consequently look into it at any moment that may be snatched from more active duties. I was so afraid you would refuse my offerings, from fear of robbing me, that they will not be put into your hands till you can no longer communicate with the shore. Receive them with the fervent and incessant prayers of your loving

'Henriquez.'

It would be difficult to describe the emotions of Carlos as he perused this letter. Ashamed of his own wilfulness, wondering at what he now thought his want of affection, he paced the deck without exchanging a word with any of his companions of the watch; and more than one tear of repentance wetted his cheek. For what had he exchanged the society of such a brother as Henriquez? For that of a set of men, indifferent alike to his presence or his absence, inferior to him in education, and with whom there could be no exchange of intellect, which certainly affords the purest of all enjoyments. 'But then,' said he to himself, and starting from his reverie, 'it is the first step towards a life of enterprise and independence, and in it I shall surely become better acquainted with the wonders of God.' The shrill whistle which announced the change of the watch enabled him to go below, and he spent part of the time allotted to rest in securing his treasures in such a manner that they should never leave him; and into the bag which contained them, he put a ring which had been given him by one of his schoolfellows, thinking it ridiculous to wear it on his finger in the position in which he stood among his messmates.

Light winds detained the 'Hero' for some time in the Irish Channel, during which period Carlos became tolerably initiated into his nautical duties. No matter how dirty or how disagreeable the task, he was the first to begin and the last to leave off work. The agility for which he had been so famed in his schoolboy days now proved of infinite service to him: he was equally ready to go aloft and below; and although every one felt his mental superiority, even envy was obliged to acknowledge that that superiority did not stand in the way of his activity and obedience. At length the ship cleared the land, and dashed across the Bay of Biscay. 'Sail ahoy!' said a man employed at the mast-head. The glasses were out in a moment, and two homeward-bound Indiamen were discovered, bearing down full upon them. As they neared the 'Hero,' the three vessels backed their sails to speak each other; and Carlos had an opportunity, while the commanders were engaged in questions of latitude and longitude, names of vessels and ports which had been left and which were to be attained, etc., of contemplating the noble sight which the Indiamen presented. Their sails were set, even to the moon-rakers and sky-scrapers, in order to catch the light breezes aloft, and their hulls bent gracefully under the weight like a swan dipping its head into the waters as it swims along, now dividing them with its breast, and now gently expanding its wings as it prepares again to stoop. 'When,' said Carlos, 'shall I command such a vessel as that?' forgetting the hundreds of human lives, and the amount of wealth, for which such a command would render him fearfully responsible.

Seeing that the young sailor tried to understand all he saw, the Captain, who dared not show him any preference at first, at length asked Carlos if he would like to observe the sun every day in order to ascertain the latitude in which they might be, and being answered in the affirmative, offered to lend him a sextant for the purpose; but the Colonel had provided him with this instrument, and with it he daily took his station on deck by the side of the Captain and first mate, just before twelve o'clock. Besides this instruction, he was allowed to read some books on navigation; and on pretence of teaching him yet more, Mr. Mortimer often enticed him into the cabin when the Captain was asleep, but in reality employed him in keeping his log for him.

The beautiful island of Madeira, for which nature has done so much, and man so little, was passed at such a distance, that a mere glimpse was obtained of its sharply pointed, lofty mountains, studded half-way up the sides with lovely villas and gardens. The towering peak of Teneriffe, rising abruptly from the sea, was long in sight, and conveyed the idea of a painted scene at a theatre, rather than a reality. The calmer waters and beautiful weather gave less to do on board, and Carlos had an opportunity of becoming better acquainted with the characters of those around him, than when they were always busily employed. They formed a motley assemblage from various countries, each individual of which was, as sailors generally are, strongly stamped with his national peculiarities; although the frank, open-hearted manner, and mode of speaking, the childish simplicity with which every impulse is obeyed, was common to almost all.

The principal friends of Carlos were his two first acquaintances on board, whom he had helped with the chest. One of these was a Venetian, named Antonio. He had been a gondolier, then a sailor in the Mediterranean, and lastly had entered the English service. He was well versed in all the languages of the south; consequently was able to converse in Spanish with Carlos, which was a great tie between them. The two friends, when work was over, would often sit in the main-top, teaching each other the songs of their respective countries; Antonio telling romantic stories, or instructing Carlos how to carve bones and wood. He was one of the greatest mimics and best buffoons ever seen, and the favourite of the whole ship's crew. He was Carlos' washerman, for

D

this was an office to which the latter felt an uncon-
querable repugnance, and for the performance of which
he offered Antonio all his allowance of grog. This,
however, was not accepted, the Venetian being of the
same temperate habits as himself; and he therefore
distributed it among the others of the ship's crew.
Another perfection possessed by Antonio was that of
making canvas trousers, laying the material upon the
deck, and shaping it with his knife; he was also a
good mender and maker of sails; in short, he could
turn his hand to any and everything, and was the
merriest of the whole set, except, indeed, the Irishman,
Johnstone, whose voice and laughter might be often
heard in the hold, or aloft, in calm or storm,—in fact,
on almost all occasions,—but who was always ready to
help a friend in distress or perplexity.

The second favourite of Carlos was Hall, a sturdy
Englishman, whose curling, light brown hair, blue eyes,
gigantic form, and prodigious strength, showed unerring tokens of his Saxon descent. He more than
any of the other men felt the superiority of the young
Spaniard; his manner towards him was always respectful, and he even seemed to extend over him the protection which a Newfoundland dog does over his
smaller canine brethren. His great delight was to put
Johnstone into a furious passion (no difficult matter,
by the by), he himself never losing his temper. On
these occasions, the quick-witted Irishman would load
him with the most humorous abuse, and as Hall sat
laughing beside him, at last end the scene by finding
out the joke, and joining in the mirth at his own
expense; but this by no means prevented him from
being again deceived on the morrow.

It was the custom of the good-natured Captain to make his men leave off work at four o'clock every afternoon, and encourage them to play at various games, as a substitute for bodily sport. In hare and hounds, Antonio and Carlos were unmatched; only Johnstone ever being able to catch them when they personated the first of these animals : the wonder was to see them chased, for when their pursuers thought themselves sure of them at one end of the vessel, they had most unaccountably slipped to the other, almost gliding through the air; and when Hall was seeking them in the forecastle, they would be climbing up one of the masts. Hall, however, made the best bear, and constructing a den for himself with the spare spars which lay midships on the deck, he would throw a frieze coat over him, and with an occasional roar from his capacious lungs, await the blows of the rest of the men, who struck him as they rapidly passed by with knotted ropes-ends. When tired of his position, he would catch a leg of the enemy, and thère was no escape from that powerful grasp; down came the victim upon the deck, those behind tumbling over him in their headlong course, and he was then made to take the bear's part. It was observed that Hall never caught Carlos, and that Carlos either crawled from under the mass of forms, or leaped over it with his wonted agility. The whole vessel shook from stem to stern on these occasions, while the first mate openly laughed, and the Captain, half hidden by the cabin door, tried to conceal his enjoyment of the scene; and each secretly lamented that his dignity would not suffer him to join in the fun. On bright moonlight nights, Sandy, the Scotchman, a straightforward, cold-looking, quiet personage, was dragged from his hammock with his bagpipes, and made to play Scotch reels, while his messmates danced, and invented steps and figures which, for variety and intricacy, would have shamed the best dancing-master in Europe.

'Surely you'll get up and see the fleet we're passing through,' said Johnstone one morning to Carlos, as he lay sleeping in his hammock. 'What fleet?' asked Carlos, opening his eyes. 'They are Portuguese men-of-war,' answered the Irishman, 'cruising about in these seas; so make haste and get up.' Only half of Carlos' time for rest was expired; nevertheless he rose immediately, and was much surprised, as he ascended to the deck, not to see a single mast or sail. A triumphant laugh from Johnstone and others convinced him that he had been tricked; but the real sight was so pretty that he forgot to be angry. A slight breeze just curled the blue waters of the Atlantic, and the sun made every bubble glitter with his rays. Over the whole expanse were scattered a multitude of small, white, pink, and blue bladders, with curling tendrils depending from them, and about the size of a common butter-boat. They seemed to be come out to enjoy themselves; and yielding to every motion of the waves, they floated along, as if they had abandoned themselves to pleasure. Johnstone had made use of the English sailors' name for them when he summoned Carlos, who would not have missed seeing them on any account. He dipped a bucket into the water, and bringing up one, began to handle and examine it. The bladder was soon empty, for it contained nothing but water, and the animal lay like a number of strings in his hand; he was, however, very glad to throw it overboard again, for it stung him, as if it had been a bunch of nettles.[1]

The approach of the continent of Africa was made manifest by a quantity of red sand, which was wafted from the desert, and deposited on the larboard side of the sails ; and although out of sight of land, some curious insects more than once were discovered, which undoubtedly came from the same quarter.

Contrary winds detained the ' Hero' for some days in the bay of the Cape de Verde, and there it was that Carlos saw sharks for the first time. The cry of ' Shark ! shark !' was loudly given by the watch ; but all that could be seen was a small, pointed, black substance, coming towards them, just peeping above the surface of the waves, and which was the fin on the back of the fearful animal. ' He's a hungry one,' said Mr. Mortimer, ' he is bearing down so fast on us ; get the hook out, put a piece of salt pork upon it, hang it out over the stern, and let us catch the fellow.' The shark, however, was not hungry, or he was too cunning to be taken in ; he swam round the bait, and touched it occasionally with his projecting muzzle, but never attempted to take it in his mouth. He continued, however, to follow the ship, and was soon joined by three or four others, with whom all attempt at capture proved equally unsuccessful ; but their company was esteemed a bad omen by the superstitious sailors. Carlos, whose curiosity to see a shark was much excited, examined the hook every time he had an opportunity of going near it, in the hope of finding one of the sharks hanging to it ; but for several days

[1] This mollusca is called the *Physalis Holothuria*, *Physalis* of Linnæus.

he was disappointed. One afternoon, however, when in the cabin he cautiously peeped out of the stern window, and saw one of the huge creatures on its back, lying with its mouth open, just under the bait. Dexterously and suddenly he jerked the chain, and the hook entering the lower lip, the monster was caught. Down went the log-book, away went all idea of etiquette in the Captain's cabin. Carlos flew on deck, proclaiming his victory ; and all hands, except the steersman, throwing aside their employments, rushed off to haul the animal in, and before the Captain, who was asleep in his berth, could rise to inquire what was the matter, it lay floundering on the deck, having thrown the ship's boys down with the lashing of its thick fleshy tail. It was soon despatched with knives, and Carlos then had an opportunity of examining the formidable rows of teeth. It was a true shark,[1] and measured twenty-five feet in length ; had breathing-holes in the sides of its neck ; and its upper triangular teeth had double points, while the under had only one, which was very sharp, and proceeded from a broad base ; altogether forming an apparatus which made Carlos shudder to look at. The monster was white underneath, of a brownish grey on the back and sides, and the fins were black. It was soon cut up ; the cartilaginous arches which support the teeth were taken out, with the teeth attached to them, and hung up to dry, reminding Carlos of the men-traps set in gentlemen's grounds to catch poachers ; the backbone was given to Antonio ; and some steaks were cut off (for sailors will eat anything), a portion of which was consigned to the cook

---

[1] The *Squalus carcharias.*

to be dressed for supper, and the rest rubbed with salt, and placed in the caboose chimney, to be smoked. The remainder of the body was thrown overboard, where it was eagerly devoured by its brethren ; but the ship did not lose the smell of it for some days in spite of the scouring which the deck received. Carlos was prevailed on to taste the steaks, but one mouthful was sufficient for him, and took away all desire for another. Antonio, after dividing the backbone into four portions, made three walking-sticks, by thrusting an iron rod through them ; and separating and cleansing the rest of the vertebræ, converted them into rings, with which the men afterwards fastened their Sunday handkerchiefs. All, however, were first hung up to dry for some time, as the bones of sharks are softer than those of the generality of fishes ; the hard or bony matter contained in them being deposited in grains, instead of threads or fibres, and resembling cartilage.

CHAPTER IV.

THE 'Hero' at last weathered the point, or Cape de Verde, which runs far into the sea, completely verifying the geographical explanation of the term, and came to anchor close to the little island of Goree, which had been completely hidden by it. The latter was about six miles from the mainland; and here Carlos received a better impression of the natives of Africa than he had formed from the black cook on board, who was a native of Congo, and consequently no favourable specimen of personal beauty. The Jaloffs, on the contrary, are a handsome race, and some of their mulattoes may be termed beautiful; most of those who came alongside the vessel to sell their fruits and provisions were neatly dressed and well-behaved. The first order given on arrival was, that no person should purchase rum; and even punishment was threatened to those who should have taken any on board. The Captain then asked Carlos if he could row; and, being answered in the affirmative, he made him one of the boat's crew, and ordering his gig to be manned, proceeded to the shore. He did more; for, knowing Carlos' abilities, he took him with him wherever he went as his clerk, and thus gave him an opportunity of seeing the interior of the merchants' houses, and rapidly surveying the tiny fortress on the hill, with the batteries below, which defended the island. Chairs, stools, cane-sofas, and matting, formed the principal furniture; but the dress of the higher classes of women struck Carlos as peculiarly graceful. It consisted of a handkerchief twisted round the head in a conical shape, and frequently ornamented with gold; a full skirt of cotton, and a large piece of the same material, or of muslin, thrown over the shoulders. The trade was soon accomplished; being only the sale of iron bars, powder, shot, and some Manchester prints, which were selected on board in the evening by the merchants themselves. Most things are supplied to this settlement by the French, to whom it was ceded by the English.

Passing the entrance to the Gambia, on leaving Goree, the vessel steered for the Isles de Los, those little fairy specks of earth which lie like sparkling gems upon the ocean. The main object of the voyage was to trade in the Bight of Benin, therefore time would have been lost had the 'Hero' touched at all the places on the way. In this part of the passage some degree of alarm was felt at the sight of two waterspouts not very far from each other, which seemed to be rapidly approaching the ship. The enormous black clouds above, with their long descending funnels, forming deep abysses in the sea, and whirling the waters round with prodigious force, were fearful to behold, but inexpressibly grand. Orders were given to load two small guns which stood on deck, and which were placed there for the purpose of signals in case of distress; and as soon as the 'Hero' showed by her motion that she was feeling the influence of the phenomenon, they were fired through the spouts, as they are called, and the latter were immediately dispersed. They were succeeded by a dead calm, and, as a current was setting in towards the shore, some apprehensions were entertained that the ship might drift too near the land; therefore, to keep her head right, the boats were manned and fastened to her bows, and the crew took it in turns to tow her along. The sun was scorching; there was but little air—that little seemed only to add to the heat, and the men evidently suffered from their exertions. The next morning several of them complained, and were placed on the sick-list; but their symptoms were such that the surgeon, Mr. Fraser, suspected there was another cause for their illness. On communicating his suspicions, the Captain ordered a search to be made, which but confirmed them; for several rum bottles, both empty and full, were found secreted in the men's chests and hammocks, and which, in spite of orders to the contrary, and vigilance to enforce them, had been secretly conveyed on board at Goree. Nothing can be more injurious to the constitution than new and bad spirit; and it has laid the seeds of many a fever which has been attributed solely to climate. With such warnings constantly before their eyes, it is surprising that English sailors will persevere in drinking it; for, if questioned, they will most of them own how pernicious it is, and that they thus take away their best chance of escaping from a climate which in itself is so baneful to European life. As the surgeon had predicted, several of the crew were disabled, but none of them died. Carlos himself felt

indisposed, in consequence of his exertions in the
boat; but his temperate habits soon enabled him to
shake off his malady. Antonio was not attacked; but
poor Hall, who could not practise the same forbearance, was sadly reduced. The Spaniard and the
Italian waited on the sick, comforted them as much
as lay in their power, and endeavoured to cheer their
spirits. Carlos frequently, instead of sleeping, would
read to them, thereby exciting much astonishment
that such a scholar as he should be a common sailor
like themselves. One of the men, who was by far the
most ill, always refused assistance, and never would
be sponged with vinegar and water, as the surgeon
had ordered; but having fainted one day as he attempted to rise, the doctor desired Carlos to strip
him, that cold water might be thrown over his body.
Carlos obeyed, and then exclaimed, 'I see why the
poor fellow would never suffer his shirt to be taken
off.' The back of the wretched man was covered from
one end to the other with deep scars, which crossed
each other in various directions, and which told too
plainly of the punishment which he had undergone.
'He must have been flogged through the fleet,' observed Mr. Fraser, who had been in the navy; 'I
have seen more than one man made wholly good-for-
nothing by such means; and I never liked the expression of this fellow's countenance.' Gray (for that was
the sailor's name) recovered his senses, and when he
became aware that his secret was discovered, was
frantic with rage. 'This is your doing!' he exclaimed
to Carlos; 'but for you this would never have been
known.' Mr. Fraser explained that Carlos had undressed him by his orders, and both promised secrecy;

but the man, collecting all his remaining strength, struck a furious blow at Carlos, which made him reel. The blood of the latter rushed into his cheeks, his naturally impetuous temper was roused, and with flashing eyes he was about to retaliate, when Mr. Fraser caught his arm, and said, 'Stop, Lacy, the man does not know what he is about.' Carlos' uplifted hand fell passively by his side; and after a momentary struggle with his feelings, he thanked Mr. Fraser for his interference, and owned that he had been very wrong to give way to his passion. Gray had again sunk down; but his eyes rested on Carlos with so malignant an expression, that the surgeon shuddered, and sending his assistant away, hastened to tell the Captain what had happened. 'I have long had my eye upon that Gray,' said the master of the 'Hero,' 'and I suspect he was the chief agent in conveying the rum on board. He is ripe for any mischief; and I have such strict orders to take care of Lacy, without showing any preference, that, even if I were not inclined to do so of my own accord, I should think it my duty to separate him from Gray.' Then, turning to the first mate he told him to order Lacy's hammock to be in future slung in the steerage, instead of the forecastle. This was in all respects a happy change for Carlos, and the removal to a more airy sleeping-place had perfectly restored him to strength, when the ship dropped her anchor opposite Crawford's Island, and between those of Tamara and Factory.

After breakfast the next morning, the usual party for the boat was summoned, and all proceeded to the islands. The Captain dined ashore at Crawford, during which time, as there were only two or three native houses, besides that of the English merchant, he gave his men leave to roam about as they pleased, hoping that the ramble would prove beneficial to their health. Carlos, Antonio, and Hall went together, and were delighted at the beauty of the finely-cut foliage of the mimosas, the broad leaves of the bananas, the lovely flowers, and the exquisite plumage of the birds as they darted from bough to bough. Among them was a splendid oriolus, covered with black and yellow feathers. The walking party were much annoyed, as they ascended the grey rock, by the number of millipedes, which lay so close together, that they could not avoid frequently stepping upon and crushing them. They at first fancied that they were venomous, like the centipedes; but these thick brown creatures, with their multitude of legs, were perfectly harmless.

Having explored the whole of Crawford in a very short time, Carlos, in his own name and that of his companions, asked permission to take the boat and go to Tamara and Factory; all pledging themselves that there should be no repetition of the misdemeanour committed at Goree. Leave was granted, and on landing at Factory, they visited the native monarch who resided there in a thatched house, and who, with all the shrewdness of his race, detected Carlos' superiority, and presented him with two white beans and a red one in token of amity; at the same time giving him to understand in English, that, had the latter colour predominated, it would have been a declaration of enmity. He took them to see the schools, where a Marabout—for they were all Mohammedans—was teaching the children, who, for want of boards or slates, were writing Arabic on the sand with pointed sticks. The king gave them all some oranges, and they returned to fetch their Captain. On coming close along shore, the boat's crew perceived a turtle lying fast asleep just under the surface of the water. Of course this was considered as a fair prize, and they secured it; but as they lifted it in, the boat was nearly swamped by its enormous weight and size. 'This will be a capital present for the Captain,' said Carlos, 'but what shall I do with this large dead lizard, which the old woman gave me just now, when we came away from Tamara?' 'It is a monitor,' said Hall; 'and when I was in the West Indies I used to see such things eaten, but I never tasted them myself.' 'You may take my word for it they are very good,' observed Antonio, 'for I have often heard so; therefore you may give it to me, Lacy, if you do not like it yourself.' 'You are quite welcome to it,' rejoined Carlos, 'for I do not fancy a supper of lizard.'

The next day the English merchant from Crawford went on board the 'Hero,' where he was regaled with the salted beef of England, and some turtle's eggs, of which the reptile had been full, and which she had probably gone to the shore to deposit. The flesh had been generously yielded to the ship's crew, in order to afford them a fresh and strengthening mess after their late illness. The lizard was skinned and roasted, and Carlos was prevailed on to taste it. To his surprise, he found it to be like the most juicy, delicate chicken; and he was equally astonished at the agreeable, wholesome flavour of the turtle, when cooked without the rich and stimulating condiments which are lavished upon it when served at European tables. In the afternoon the Captain returned with the mer-

chant, who promised to send him back to the vessel
in a few hours in his own boat, and this gave all his
men time to make everything ready for a fresh start
the ensuing morning.

Tea on board ship is often accompanied by such
viands as serve to render it a substantial meal; and,
in pursuance of this custom, the first mate had ordered
the turtle, which had been left by the men, to be served
for the cabin table. Work was over; and Carlos was
standing quietly by the side of the vessel, watching
the broad shadows cast by the cocoa-nut trees on
shore, when the steward hastily summoned the cook.
The man obeyed, muttering something which could
not be understood, and in a few minutes he was seen
again, retreating backwards in an attitude of defiance.
Mr. Mortimer followed, and ordered him to the
caboose in a loud voice; the cook aimed a blow at
him with a long knife, which had gone so far as to
tear his waistcoat, when Carlos pulled the man's hand
back, and seizing the knife, threw it into the sea.
At that moment Carlos felt himself forcibly pulled
behind, and four of the crew dragged him towards the
fore part of the ship. He would have been carried
down into the forecastle, had not Hall come up just
at the time, and rescued him with his vigorous arm.
'I will keep them at bay,' said he to the astonished
Carlos, 'while you retreat to the after cabin. I will
join you there in a minute. I do not want any help,'
he added, seeing that Carlos still lingered near him;
'run to Mr. Mortimer; Antonio is there.' Carlos
obeyed, though without knowing why, and found the
officers, with the Italian, the steward, and one or two
others, defending themselves against a large portion

of the crew, and trying to prevent their entrance into
the cabin.   He attacked them in the rear, which
made a division in favour of the weaker party; when
Gray, who was the ringleader, aimed a furious blow
at Carlos with an iron bar, which would probably
have been fatal, had not Hall, who then joined him,
felled the ruffian to the ground.   Taking Carlos by
the arm, he rushed with him through the assailants,
and, standing by the side of the officers, caused a
cessation of hostilities.   Thus reinforced, Mr. Grant,
the second mate, had time to get to the firearms, and
reappearing with a brace of loaded pistols, fired one
of them into the air.   Johnstone, who had been held
back by superior force, now made his escape to the
officers, and the numbers began to equalize.   Not,
however, till some blood was shed were the mutineers
overcome; they were then put in irons, lodged in the
forecastle with closed hatches, and an armed guard
placed over them till the Captain should arrive.
Signals were made to request him to return immediately; and it was with great satisfaction that he was
seen, very shortly after, to enter the merchant's boat,
and steer for the vessel.

'Do tell me, sir,' said Carlos to Mr. Mortimer, when
things were somewhat quieter, 'what all this means?'
'A mutiny, I suppose,' was the answer; 'but what the
cause may be I really cannot imagine. The turtle was
burnt and smoked, the potatoes were dried up, I now
think on purpose to provoke me; and when I sent
for the cook to tell him of it rather than find fault
with him before the men, the fellow was insolent. I
ordered him out of the cabin; he refused to stir, and
stood there abusing me; but I drove him forward

with my fists. I am afraid, however, that this is only
the beginning of some preconcerted plan, for the man
began to bawl for help as if I had been murdering
him; the others then rushed at me in a body, intend-
ing, I have no doubt, to get into the cabin and take
possession of the chest of small arms. Fortunately,
Mr Fraser and Mr. Grant were on their guard, and
defended them till we could muster sufficient force to
get the better of the rascals. You do not know, Lacy,
what a horrible thing mutiny is. I cannot think that
our men, who have hitherto been so orderly, can have
willingly engaged in it; and therefore I suppose they
must somehow have been tempted. I suspect that
that fellow Gray is at the bottom of it; but when the
Captain comes, we shall hear the rights of the story.'

'What is the matter?' said the Captain, as he
stepped on deck.

'I can hardly tell you, sir,' returned Mr. Mortimer.
'There has been a row with the men, but what they
want I don't know. They have never been themselves
since they took the new rum.' When Mr. Mortimer
had described the foregoing scene, the Captain ordered
the men to be released from their irons, and brought
to him under a guard. The mandate was obeyed, but
the looks of the culprits said nothing in their favour.
They had evidently been drinking too much; for it
is the custom with many sailors to save their grog
for days, and then take it at one sitting. They
said they had started up in defence of the cook,
who, although black, was their messmate, and they
would not stand by and see him murdered; that
they were half-starved, and worked almost to death;
that they would bear their wrongs no longer, and

E

were determined to have justice in some way or other.

These men had always been indulged with the best salt provisions in considerable quantities; had been allowed coffee, cocoa, rice, oatmeal, treacle, potatoes, fish, soup, puddings twice every week, etc.; and their hard labour was no more than being obliged to get the goods out of the hold. There were twenty-five men to work the ship, and therefore none could be called upon for much exertion in that respect; in short, the mischief more probably lay in over-indulgence, rather than privation or extraordinary toil. Stung with their ingratitude, the Captain ordered them back into confinement till they came to their senses; upon which Gray sprang upon him, and would have knocked him down, had not Mr. Mortimer interposed. As it was, the Captain reeled under the blow; but soon recovering himself, although very gentle on most occasions, he became like an enraged lion, and dealing his strokes right and left, soon silenced all the mutineers; their irons were again put on, and they were taken back to their prison with an allowance of biscuit and water. The first mate was sent to them the next morning to know if they showed any signs of repentance for what had happened; but their only answer to the appeal was a petition, which some of them had drawn up, asking for more and better food, and less labour. Of course this could not be complied with, and they continued sullen and obstinate.

Most inconvenient were the consequences of this disturbance, for the duties of the ship fell so much more heavily on the well-disposed; and in such a climate it was dangerous to tax them with extra labour. It was therefore madness to sail while matters remained in this state ; and the Captain made up his mind to continue where he was till his rebellious men should be tired of their position, and consequently return to their former good conduct., While thinking over their perplexities one morning, the first mate saw a long sharp canoe issue from a small creek in the island of Tamara, and come in the direction of the vessel. She was filled with those industrious and valuable natives of Africa, whose home is the Kroo country, and who, from their fidelity, activity, and power of speaking all the languages of the coast, almost always accompany the African traders in their outward-bound voyage. They generally make their appearance for this purpose at Sierra Leone ; are slight in form, bear excellent characters, are quiet, obliging, and intelligent ; and, with few exceptions, return in their fragile conveyance the moment the vessel to which they have been attached starts for home. On some occasions, however, they have been prevailed on to go as far as England, of which expedition they are always very proud ; and they then get back by another trader going to the coast. They eat scarcely anything but rice, a stock of which is generally placed on board for their use ; and they spend their gains in their native country, rarely, if ever, preferring to live away from it. Their canoes may often be seen like minute specks upon the ocean, paddled by from five to ten men ; and though a larger wave than usual will often swamp their fragile conveyance, they right it again, jump in, and paddle on as if no disaster had happened.

It was a providential circumstance which had

brought the Kroomen as far north as the Isles de
Los, or Los Idolos, more properly speaking; but they
said there were very few traders just then on the
coast, and they had come this distance in the hope of
meeting the first new arrival. Their chief, Ben Liverpool, so named because he had once visited that city,
presented what he called his books, and which, in
fact, were the testimonials given to him by the various
masters under whom he and his men had served.
These were all so much in their favour, that the Captain gladly struck a bargain with them, and he was in
this manner relieved from his painful dilemma.

All was made ready for sailing; the disaffected men
still refusing to come to any terms short of their
demands; the island of Factory was passed; the point
rounded; and, on the other side, to the great joy of
the Captain, lay a brig-of-war. 'Ah, my lads!' exclaimed Mr. Mortimer, 'this will soon bring you to
your senses;' thereby alluding to the rebels. Com-
munications took place between the vessels, and the
commander of the war-brig, Captain Hamilton, promised to interpose his authority. In the evening
he went on board the 'Hero' with some degree of
state; his boat's crew dressed in blue jackets,
white trousers, and straw hats; and a midshipman
took the helm. He was received with all the ceremony possible: each man present had put on his
best clothes; the Captain and his mate stood in
the gangway with their hats off; and he was ushered
into the cabin, where he was informed of all that
had passed. He ordered the offenders to be
brought on deck, where he addressed them; told
them they had no excuse for their conduct; and

when he concluded his lecture, he said, 'If they did not immediately return to their duty with cheerfulness, and promise to behave well in future, there were plenty in his brig who would be glad to exchange places with them ; and he should draft them into his own crew. They well knew what would await them there if they misbehaved themselves ; that he should never be many hour's sail from them, as the track of the trader was that of the "Flora," and that his eye would be always upon them, with full power to punish as he thought proper.' A slight shudder passed over Gray's frame at these words, and he was one of the first to submit. The others, after a few moments' hesitation, followed his example ; said they were sorry for their conduct, and professed a strong desire to return to their duties. Thoughtless and fretful from fever and rum, they might perhaps be excused ; and they spoke heartily and sincerely, except Gray, who uttered his apology with so many more words than were necessary, and so rapidly and eagerly, that fear, not conviction, had evidently influenced him. Carlos good-naturedly assisted in taking off his irons ; but the wretched man whispered in his ear as he knelt by his side, 'I hate you !' pronouncing this with a bitterness of tone and look which but too well vouched for its truth. The expression went to Carlos' heart ; he recollected that he had but too often made use of the same against one whom he had considered as his enemy, but never till it was directed towards himself did he feel its full and unchristian force. He determined to write to Mrs. Lacy as soon as he should reach Sierra Leone, and ask her forgiveness for this and all his other misdemeanours. He felt for the first time how often he must have provoked her beyond endurance, and the only thought which soothed him was the hope of making reparation.

Tranquillity being restored, the merchantman at length sailed for Sierra Leone; but at about a day's distance from the island, a slight disaster occurred. The cabin-party was at dinner, and Carlos below in the steerage, when all at once there was a reeling motion in the ship; she was taken aback, one of her yards was shivered to pieces, and fell with much noise, and the sails were split to ribbons. A general rush was made for the deck; the Captain shouted forth his orders, each man obeying instantaneously, and the ship wore round. In an equally short time the whole sea was as perfectly tranquil as if nothing unusual had happened. Carlos looked bewildered, when Mr. Mortimer shaking him by the arm, said, 'There's a white squall for you. Look aloft at that little round cloud whizzing away in the sky; it's that which caused all this commotion. They do not often come as far north as this; but we shall have plenty of them below the Bight.'

The vessel proceeded; but as there was a probability of her having been rapidly and imperceptibly taken out of her course by the squall, just as she neared the mouth of the river of Sierra Leone, the Captain stood anxiously watching the colour of the water. Suddenly he gave orders for sounding, and Antonio stood in the chains with the lead in his hand. Swinging it round, he, in melodious tones, sang, 'A quarter less ten;' meaning thereby, in ten fathoms all but a quarter. In about twenty minutes he heaved again; then it was 'a quarter less seven.' 'Heave again

directly,' exclaimed the Captain. 'By the mark six,'
sang Antonio. 'All hands put about ship,' was the
next order rapidly given, and as rapidly executed—
the Captain himself, in the emergency, lending a helping hand. 'Now heave, Antonio,' shouted he. 'By
the deep nine,' was the song. 'All's well now,' said
Mr. Mortimer, 'she's in deeper water;' and he seemed
to breathe more freely. Carlos asked Hall for an
explanation, and was told that the ship had nearly
come upon a shoal which lies outside the river. 'Perhaps,' said he, 'the squall sent us on faster than the
Captain thought; or perhaps the shoal may be laid
down a mile or two out of its right place, as these
things often are. One minute more, and we must
have struck.'

CHAPTER V.

As the Krooman had stated, but few vessels happened at that time to be lying in the beautiful port
of Sierra Leone, and the 'Hero' came to anchor just
opposite to the principal landing-place. Fair was
everything to the eye. Freetown, with its regular
streets, steepled church, white verandahed houses,
warehouses, and lovely looking villas, placed on the
rising ground; the whole interspersed with beautiful
trees, and backed by mountains; the exquisite foliage,
the gay birds, the glorious sun, adding brilliancy to
every hue; the fleecy clouds, which every now and
then rested on the tips of the high points of land (for
the light rains had just passed away),—all presented a
scene so attractive, that no one would have thought
anything injurious could lurk underneath it. But this
lovely river brought with it the most pernicious gases,
from the decayed vegetable matter which floated on
its surface; and the swamp beyond, covered as it was
with the most luxuriant verdure, cast its baneful influence over the lovely city, till it had become the
inevitable grave of hundreds of victims. As usual,
Carlos accompanied the Captain on shore, and while
waiting in the ante-room of one of the merchants'
houses, he heard a rushing and pattering noise, with

now and then a gentle squeak, behind him. Turning round, he saw a door which led to a storeroom, and which did not quite touch the floor. Through the aperture left, a number of little feet showed that a regiment of rats were passing by; and he was not at all sorry that they had chosen another apartment for the peregrination. Tired of standing, he seated himself in a large chair, and leaning back his head, his eyes naturally rested on the roof, for there are no ceilings in these countries, on account of the insects and reptiles which they would harbour; and on the white-painted planks he saw a spider, the body of which was the size of a shilling, but its long legs extended over a surface as large as a pudding-plate. As he did not know the habits of these insects, and that they remain torpid, as it were, for weeks at certain periods, he fancied that it would immediately fall upon him, and shifted his position. This, however, was of no use, for another and another, in the same state, made it impossible for him in so small a space to get out of their way, and he began to feel quite uncomfortable. He knew that spiders have numerous eyes, and he could not help fancying that, though invisible at that distance, they were fixed upon him, ready to let themselves down when they had settled where to drop. He was at length relieved by the entrance of the Captain and the owner of the house; but in vain did he cast uneasy glances upwards. Neither took the hint; or if they followed his looks above, they thought there was nothing uncommon to be seen.

Having been commissioned by the Captain to get some fresh fish for his table, when one or two of the merchants dined on board, Carlos went through the market-place with the purchase he had made in a basket hung over his arm. He was thinking whether it could be a salmon, it so much resembled those which he had seen at the fishmongers in Liverpool, when suddenly he felt his basket much lighter, and looking into it, perceived that the fish was gone. Turning suddenly round, in order, if possible, to catch the thief, he saw Hall convulsed with laughter, and who, unable to speak, pointed to a large bird of the stork kind, called a Jabiru, whose crop betrayed that he was the offender. It was a tame pet, which was suffered to walk about where it pleased, and thrust its long beak into everything—the natives regarding it with superstitious reverence, and the Europeans tolerating it for its dexterity, and the droll incidents which it occasioned.

On reaching the ship, Carlos found his friend Antonio enjoying a bathe in the river, and expostulated with him, saying, that the Captain had warned them not to go into the water, on account of the numerous sharks which invested it ; but Antonio only laughed at his fears, said that 'the sharks were such cowards, they dared not come near him,' and continued his amusement. Carlos went into the cabin to give an account of his purchases, when a loud cry of 'Antonio ! Antonio ! swim for your life ; he is coming fast upon you,' met his ear. In a moment he was on deck, and saw the Italian striking out with his utmost strength to try and save himself from the murderous jaws of a huge shark. Most of the men stood breathless by the side, but two were in the chains, each ready with a rope, by which to haul up their companion as soon as he was sufficiently near to catch hold of it. All, however, seemed to be in vain; Antonio was becoming exhausted, and his speed consequently slackened. He stretched out his hand; he was still a yard from the rope; the monster all but touched his legs, and was about to turn on his back in order to seize his feet, when Carlos, who had snatched up a harpoon lying on deck, darted it with unerring aim, and the waters were instantly tinged with blood. Sick and dizzy from agitation, he could not at first tell whether the blood flowed from his friend or the shark. A warm embrace, however, soon convinced him that his blow had been effectual. Antonio had seen the movement in his favour, and receiving new energy from it, again struck out, reached the rope, and was immediately hauled up in safety. A loud cheer bade him welcome, and all the sailors crowded round Carlos to shake him by the hand. There was only one exception to the general feeling, and only one pair of eyes that malignantly scowled upon him. 'How dreadful is hatred!' said Carlos to himself; 'I am glad I have written to Mrs. Lacy.' The Captain took the opportunity of again pointing out the necessity of prudence; but thinking that Antonio had· been sufficiently punished by fright, he imposed no further chastisement on him than to forbid his again going on shore, some privation being necessary for the sake of example.

At the end of a week, sail was again set, and the ship dropped anchor for the night just outside the river. It was a glorious evening, and as the men had but little to do, they put out several fishing-lines. A pull at one of them showed that the bait was taken, and it was accordingly hauled up. The prize proved to be a large silurus, or cat-fish; so named from its fancied resemblance to that domestic animal, the mustachios of which are represented by the barbs of the fish. The men had been treated to fresh provisions while in port, so they let the silurus, which is not a tempting morsel, lie neglected on deck, till one of the boys, nicknamed Paul Pry, on account of his superabundant curiosity, supposing it to be dead, seated himself close to it, in order to examine it more thoroughly. Presently he gave a violent shriek, and exclaimed that he was stung. The blood flowed even through his sailcloth trousers, and showed that he really had been wounded in the thigh. 'Poor fellow!' said Hall, 'the beast has struck him with his back fin; and they say, in other parts where I have been, that its wounds are poisonous. The piece should be cut out directly, or he will be sure to die.' 'Carry him to the doctor,' said those who stood around; and they accordingly conveyed him to the surgeon, laying him upon the cabin table. Mr. Fraser, who had already retired to his berth, instantly arose, and after examining the wound, took out his instrument-case, and producing a sharp scalpel, rapidly passed it round the incision, then drawing the edges together, fastened them with adhesive plaster, put on a bandage, gave the boy a composing draught, and desired that, as he was agitated by terror, he should be carried to his hammock. He was lifted with the utmost tenderness and care, undressed, and gently laid in his bed by those very men who, but an hour before, would have buffeted and kicked him about as nothing worth; for the heart of the sailor is full of feeling and compassion to others in the moment of suffering. Carlos lingered behind the rest, under pretence of helping the surgeon to put away his instruments; and the latter, seeing that he wished to say something, encouraged him to speak. 'I should like to know, sir,' said Carlos, 'if the fin of the cat-fish does really contain poison, as Hall says.' 'No,' replied Mr. Fraser, 'its bad reputation arises from the first spine of its back fin being toothed like a deeply-notched fine saw. It strikes with this fin, having the power of raising and depressing it at pleasure, with much force; and when it is drawn back from the wound, the flesh is so torn by the teeth, that it becomes quite ragged, and is apt to fester, especially in warm climates. There is no other foundation for the story of poison; and as there is nothing like a clean wound for healing, you saw me scarify that of the boy.'

As daylight dawned, the mate of the 'Hero' saw with pleasure that the 'Flora' was hovering about in the offing; he made a signal that all was well, and then steered towards the leeward coast. The progress of the ship was arrested for a few days off St. Anne's shoals, close to what are called the horse latitudes—a name which arises from an old story of a vessel, with a cargo of horses, being becalmed in that spot so long, that the crew were obliged to eat these animals. The 'Hero' made no voluntary pause till she arrived at Cape Mount, which forms the northern extremity of the flourishing American colony of Liberia. A couple of bullocks were there taken in for the use of the ship; fresh provisions being thought one means of securing health. They were full-grown, but not larger than English calves. The American governor sent off a canoe, to ask the Captain ashore; but the latter, anxious to proceed, declined the invitation, and went on to Cape Palmas, where there was also a very flourishing settlement, equally unvisited by the 'Hero.'

On reaching the Dutch settlement of Elmina, Carlos and the Captain went ashore, in order to visit the king of the town, the son of a former Dutch governor and a native woman. He was a large, dark man, who had been educated in England, and was then a lively, intelligent boy; but a long residence in his own country, and the rare intercourse which he held with polished Europeans, had completely changed him; and when, in the days of his wealth (which was reported to be very considerable), he revisited the scenes of his youth, he found no enjoyment in them. Most of those whom he had known were dead or dispersed, and, unable to accommodate himself to the forms of English society, he changed his intention of remaining for some time, and suddenly returned to Africa, where, surrounded by a multitude of children and servants, who would have been slaves before the days of abolition, it was difficult to suppose that he could be the rich man he was reported to be, and yet feed so many mouths. The castle was situated not far from the mouth of a river, celebrated for the enormous white mullet caught in it, and which are of a remarkably fine flavour. Carlos was invited by the king to stay to dinner with the Captain, and placed at the lower end of the table, with the sons of the house; and when one of these delicious fishes was brought in, which had been caught that morning, about a mile from the estuary, he could not help thinking of all he had read at school concerning the famous fish named

by the Romans *Mullus*, after the sandals worn by the
kings of Alba, and which it was supposed to resemble
in colour. The Elmina specimen was as large as a
cod-fish, and would have fetched an enormous sum in
those ancient days. It was fortunate for Carlos that
he liked it, and could make a meal of it; for all the
other viands were so strongly impregnated with the
small capsicums called bird or Chili pepper, that
they almost took the skin off his uninitiated palate.
In the evening the visitors walked out to the country
or garden house; a snake rushing across their feet as
a matter of course, and in the building itself, multitudes of lizards playing at hide-and-seek. In the
garden were naturalized many West Indian fruits,
such as the delicious cherry, the sugar-sop, sour-sop,
etc. Bearing with them a basket full of these delicacies, presented to Carlos by the royal sons, he and
the Captain rejoined the 'Hero' just as she was getting ready to drop down to the next settlement on
the Gold Coast, belonging to the English.

The vessel let go her anchor in the open roads
before Cape Coast Castle; which, though larger than
that of Elmina, also presents a long range of white
buildings. It is more imposing, because these are
placed on a rock called Tarbara, rise from the spur in
front, and occupy two sides of the quadrangle. They
are regularly fortified with bastions, curtains, ramparts,
etc., and the walls are gun-proof; but it would be
difficult to hold them long against European troops.
They are commanded by neighbouring heights; but
on these Martello towers have been erected, and form
the outworks. The native town is interspersed with
merchants' houses, which are also seen straggling for

some distance into the bush.   There was no landing
there in boats, on account of the violent lashing of the
surf against the low rocks and sand.   The ship's
boats, therefore, either approached as closely as
possible, and their contents were emptied into canoes
which took them ashore, or canoes were hired expressly for the use of each ship.   The Captain of the
'Hero' adopted the latter plan, and, going to town
with him, Carlos was much struck with the chorus
kept up by the canoe-men, who form a caste by themselves.   It resembled chanting; and when he looked
at them, he could not help laughing at the hideous
faces which they made, and with which they try to
intimidate strangers.   On nearing the shore, they
leap out of the canoe, watch for the incoming wave,
and run it up the sand with the water; but even then
the passengers are constantly obliged to be carried a
short distance, if they would escape a wetting.

Wherever there are Englishmen there are luxuries;
and the dwellings at Cape Coast were superior to
those of Elmina; the apartments were well furnished,
and even decorated, and generally faced with veran-
dahs or galleries running along the first floor.   That
next the ground was devoted to stores, and frequently
a large hall, where the numerous male servants sat
and slept on the bare floor, while the women were
admitted up-stairs, and lay upon matting.   Among
the former were always a multitude of boys who had
lived with Europeans, in order to 'learn sense,' as
they called it; that is, they were not paid any wages,
or fed, but had the run of the house, in order to learn
how to become servants in their turn, and to pick up
what they could.   The kitchens, or cook-houses, as

they were termed, were generally detached from the main building, and often at one end of the gallery. Those belonging to the castle occupied the lower part of one wing, and faced the sea. In its vicinity a number of vultures, called Turkey buzzards, were always to be seen, either hovering about to pick up the offal thrown out, or thoroughly gorged, sitting upon the neighbouring guns, in so stupid a condition that it was easy to knock them over with the hand.

Carlos was pleased to find a church within the walls of the fortress, and a school in the town, to which numbers of children daily repaired. At Cape Coast were the headquarters of the Wesleyan missionaries, who at that time had also begun their labours in the neighbouring countries. The Fantees, who form the native population of Cape Coast, had themselves asked to hear the word of God; and the cause seemed to be prospering, inasmuch as the conduct of the natives was better; many of them had, of late years, risen to great respectability, and warmly encouraged the spreading of the gospel.

It was, however, with the merchants that Carlos had most to do; and he was surprised to find the native women among the keenest traders. Their objects were chiefly ornaments; Manchester prints for themselves and their children, and India cottons for their followers. Coral they bought with avidity; and one of them gave gold dust for some strings of it, which amounted in value to the sum of sixty pounds. This was to be placed round the loins, under the skirt, to support an enormous cushion, which all wore on their backs. Beads, unless new and fanciful, were bestowed upon their servants; and nothing delighted

F

them more than European jewellery, unless it were too strongly alloyed with copper. The mulatto women, some of them quite fair, were often remarkably handsome, and all extremely well-conducted. On going one morning to the house of one of these, who was the chief woman in the country, from her birth and wealth, she called Carlos into the room where she was dealing out the provisions for her people and household. For the former she had selected two fishes of tolerable size, which he had not seen before, and which struck him as so disgusting, that he thought he never could have eaten them, for he still retained all his European prejudices concerning food. They were two young hammer-headed sharks, so called from the peculiar development of their heads on each side, and which the poorer classes esteemed as a delicacy. The mulatto laughed at his abhorrence, and asked him many questions about himself. She shook her head when she heard he was going to the Bight of Benin; told him to take care of himself, for that many persons died there; cautioned him against eating too much fruit, or going out into the sun; and above all, told him, if he were taken ill, to keep a good heart, and feel sure that he would get well again, for he was slight in figure, and lively in disposition, and had not too much colour. Then taken out a little box from a large chest, which was carefully locked, she opened it; and among a number of exquisite articles of delicate gold workmanship, lay several curious-looking beads. One of these she presented to Carlos, telling him it was an Aggry bead, and that some thought there was a charm in them. For herself she did not believe it; but at all events,

she would give him that as a curiosity, and to remind
him of all she had said. Carlos questioned her still
further about the bead, which looked as if composed
of various substances, was very hard, and had evidently
passed through the fire. She informed him that these
precious relics were dug out of the ground, generally
with a quantity of gold, and were found by chance;
the natives said that smoke always issued from the
place where they lay, but this she did not credit; that
many were thought worth one or two slaves, and he
that possessed most of them was esteemed as rich and
fortunate.[1] Carlos thanked her exceedingly, not only
for her present, but for the kind interest which she
took in him: the former he put into the little bag
which contained his prayer-book, at which she seemed
much pleased; and when he took his leave of her, she
watched him with her eyes full of tears till he entered
the canoe, thinking what might probably be his fate
in such a climate; for she had seen many, equally full
of youth and vigour, fall among the foremost.

One afternoon, as Carlos was copying out some
accounts in the cabin, and the Captain was dining
ashore with one of the principal merchants, the first
mate summoned him on deck, saying, 'Come and tell
me who these black fellows are, each paddled along
in a five-handed canoe. I think they must be kings at
least, by the manner in which they sit in their chairs,
and the large umbrellas held over their heads.' Carlos
pronounced them to be two gold-takers, one in the

---

[1] These curious beads are many of them fac-similes of those
found in the tombs at Thebes, etc. *Vide* 'Essay on the Superstitions, Customs, and Arts of the Ancient Egyptians, etc.,
Bowdich.'

service of the governor, named Cracon, and the other
in that or the merchant where the Captain was engaged. These men are always of the highest respectability and acknowledged fidelity, and their office is
to separate the adulterations from the real gold dust
which passes into the master's hands in the way of
commerce, and is so frequently mixed with brass and
copper filings. They also weigh it, and superintend
its melting into bars, in which form it is sent to
Europe. Each was accompanied by a servant in a
handsome cloth, who took charge of the fancy silk
umbrella. The men came on board with a grace and
dignity which would have shamed many a minister of
state. They had fine persons: one slight and pliant,
the other looking like a black Jupiter; their heads
were entirely shaved, with the exception of a small
patch a little on one side, from which hung a very
handsome gold ornament. They had no European
beads on, but round their wrists were bracelets of
Aggry beads, mixed with strings charmed by the
Fetish man or priest; also heavy gold manillas in the
form of snakes. Round each ankle was a string of
golden ornaments, made in the shape of little bells,
stools, musical instruments, weapons, etc.; thick
gold rings were upon their fingers; and their sandals
were made of leather of various colours, beautifully
worked in narrow stripes, and the straps of which
had a large tuft of many coloured silks. An ample
cotton cloth of native manufacture, striped blue, white,
and red, was wrapped round them like a Roman
toga, and this was decorated at the lower edge
with a fringe of cowries, which rattled with the
slightest motion, and made the cloth so heavy, that

it was difficult for the wearer to walk when he had
it on.

On reaching the deck of the ' Hero,' the gold-takers
lowered their cloths from the left shoulder, which was
the most respectful salutation they could give; and
then said they were acquainted with the Captain, who
had sent them to trade with the first mate. Carlos
presented Mr. Mortimer to them, upon which they
each snapped their fingers within his as a sign of
friendship, and then followed him into the cabin,
where he set before them the best things which the
ship afforded. One very freely partook of the good
cheer; but the other scarcely touched the drinking
part of the entertainment, saying, that a blow on his
head from a fall made rum or wine too strong for
him. When the repast was over, the guests inquired
for hats. The mate could scarcely forbear to utter
his accustomed 'Whew!' when anything uncommon
occurred. Carlos and Mr. Grant, the second mate,
with difficulty suppressed a laugh, but, concealing
their mirth, brought the article for the inspection of
the traders. It was no common hat, however, which
these gentlemen required; each must have one decorated with gold. Several were produced; and at
last, one with gold binding, band, and rosette, was
chosen by the slighter man; while the Jupiter preferred that which had gold strings from the sides,
fastening at the top of the crown with a golden button,
on which he looked with great satisfaction. It was
scarcely large enough for his thick and round head,
but he could not resist the trimmings. Carlos could
not forbear smiling, as he held a looking-glass before
each, that they might see if their purchases were

becoming; and when the larger customer was obliged to stick his a little on one side to keep it on, he burst into a shout, which was followed by Mr. Mortimer and Mr. Grant, and at last joined in by the good-natured creature himself, who seemed to regard it as a sign that he 'looked handsome.' Both natives were so pleased, that they paid the high price asked by the mate without hesitation, and on going away, asked him to visit them the next day. He promised to do so, if he could obtain permission from the Captain; for, said he to Carlos, in a whisper, 'It must be high fun to dine with these fellows.'

Poor Mr. Mortimer! the leave was granted, and in his best sailor's garb he went ashore. He did not drink too much, but he partook of the black soup, made chiefly from fresh palm-nuts, and which, when they have once tasted, few Europeans can resist, and ate too freely of the delicious fruit placed before him. He returned with a quantity of the latter, which the gold-takers had *dashed*, or given him. He had exposed himself to the sun, and afterwards to the night-dews, and the next morning all the premonitory symptoms of fever and dysentery appeared. These rapidly increased; and for three days he revived and sank alternately, and at the end of that time was so reduced that there was not the least chance of his being able to do duty for many weeks. The surgeon was of opinion, that if he proceeded further along the coast, to where the climate was even more prejudicial, there was no chance of his recovery. It was therefore with deep regret that he was left in the hospital at Cape Coast, scarcely conscious of what was doing for him, and his mind so prostrated, that he did not

understand what was meant by the heartfelt adieus
which his messmates gave him. He was laid in a
canoe and conveyed to the shore; the second mate
was promoted to his place, and Carlos at once
installed in that of Mr. Grant. This promotion was,
in some respects, the most judicious that could be
made, and in others not equally so, for it increased
the envy which several had felt at his being always
in attendance on the Captain. The latter, in telling
his men that they must consider Carlos as their officer,
attributed the advancement to his scholarship, at
which no one could reasonably grumble; and certainly the young mate bore his honours so meekly,
that no one could justly complain of him. Antonio
and Hall were less familiar when they addressed him;
but he soon convinced them that no estrangement on
his part was likely to take place, as far as they were
concerned.

The loss of Mr. Mortimer made a sensible impression on the Captain, who, from that moment, evidently
became restless and anxious, watched every symptom
in his men with intense interest, rose several times
during the night to prevent them from sleeping in the
open air, which they were apt to do during the great
heat, and redoubled every precaution. He hastened
to finish his business at Cape Coast, and sailed from
it as soon as possible, determined not to touch anywhere else till he reached his ultimate destination, the
Calabar river. He hoped that by getting into the
open sea, he should destroy any germs of fever which
might be lurking in the constitutions of the sailors,
little knowing how insidious they are, and what a
grasp they frequently take before they openly declare

themselves. He was strongly advised to go to Accra for a time, which is decidedly the healthiest spot in the whole country, and called the Montpelier of the leeward coast, with its open savannahs and fresh breezes. His fears, however, prevented him; and anxious to shorten his stay as much as possible, he steered direct for Calabar, while all his crew were apparently in good health. He did not think of himself, and every effort was made to preserve the very men who had even threatened his life. Carlos could not help being struck with this lesson of forgiveness, and seconded him in everything. Among other preservatives invented and practised by Mr. Fraser, bitters, as they were called, were given out every morning to the crew instead of grog. They were made of quassia, and other bitter drugs, steeped in sherry; and at eleven o'clock each man came aft, and was made to drink a wineglassful in presence of the surgeon. Those who appeared to be less robust had strengthening things administered in the shape of food; while the strong and full of habit had cooling draughts administered to them. For himself, the doctor declared that he had no fear, for he had been inured to a West Indian climate.

CHAPTER VI.

THE expectations of the Captain were so far realized, that, for the first few days, the whole crew seemed to revive, and cheerfully perform their allotted duties; the favourable symptoms increased as the ship stood out to sea; and when, after a short period, they again steered for land, the men continued to be active and happy. The weather, however, soon became intensely hot; there was scarcely a ripple upon the waters, and the chief way made by the 'Hero' was owing to the current. At a little before ten a dead calm generally took place, the sea became like glass, and the sails flapped listlessly round the masts; but at half-past eleven a slight breeze set in from the sea. This lasted till a little before ten at night, when, generally speaking, the calm again took place. Then the land breeze blew till the next morning; and this was the usual routine of the twenty-four hours. The latter, however, was much the colder of the two; and those who could scarcely bear their linen clothes on during the day, were glad to wear their warmest woollen garments at night, and even then shivered. There was not much to do on board; but sails were mended, awnings made, casks were prepared for holding palm-oil, and fishing was much encouraged. When in deep water, it was a frequent amusement to watch for the spermaceti whales, which frequent the whole range of these seas. Their spoutings, as they are called, certainly did not resemble the fountains which are often represented as issuing from them in prints ; nevertheless they do eject water from the vent at the top of their heads to a great height, which, spreading out like a fan of fine mist, glitters in the sun, and has an exquisite effect. They would play frequently round the ship in numbers, but their presence did not banish a multitude of fishes, which were to be seen at a great depth in the clear liquid. Among them was the moon or sun-fish,[1] for it bears both names, which, looking as if half of it had been cut off, lay stupidly on the surface of the water, and was easily taken, but was only good for making glue. Then there was the pilot-fish, with its bright blue stripes ;[2] and one vulgarly called a dolphin,[3] which has been so often mentioned by the poets for its beautiful changes of colour when dying. On first leaving the water it is of a bright silvery hue, and dark bluish grey on the back ; but as it expires, every colour of the rainbow is seen on its surface, all most exquisitely passing one into the other, and becoming brighter as the agony of the animal increases. These hues, however, cease at its death.

One inhabitant of the deep, of the tribe of Mollusca, was of an extraordinary shape, and excited much curiosity ; the sailors called it the devil-fish, and it certainly was ugly enough to justify any evil name which might be bestowed upon it. Its shape was triangular, in consequence of a fleshy fin on each side, which appeared to be continuous with the body. A number of suckers issued from its head, placed on the

---

[1] Orthagoriscus.   [2] Centronotus ductor.   [3] Coryphæna.

side of a fleshy appendage; and some processes like
enormously long arms, with what appeared to be a
hook at the end, seemed to be thrown out in search
of prey. The Congo cook and Kroomen told mar-
vellous histories of these animals, insisting on it that
they threw these long arms into the canoes and
dragged men out, who became so enveloped in them
that they could not escape; that they even fastened
themselves at the bottom of small canoes and pulled
them down, men and all, and that there was no
remedy on such occasions but to chop off the arms.
There was probably some exaggeration in these
stories; but no one could see the animal without
feeling sure that it had great powers of destruction.
One of them, on being struck with violence, sent forth
a dark liquid which coloured the water all round, and
which let Carlos into the secret of its being a sepia,
or species of cuttle-fish.[1]

The sea had occasionally appeared to sparkle in
several parts of the voyage, but the hopes of seeing it
on fire, to speak like a sailor, had never been realized
according to the notion which Carlos had formed from
reading accounts of it. He was, however, completely
gratified one night when the ship came into what the
men called the heel of a storm. The clouds had
cleared off, but the water was still agitated by the
previous wind, so that a white foam crowned the
surface of the ocean in every direction; and this
glittered with a light unlike that of any other luminous
appearance. It was not deep, nor orange enough for
fire, but it was pale and sparkling, seeming to be
constantly renewed as every bubble rose over its

[1] Sepia octopodia.

neighbour; at a distance it looked like one broad sheet of light, and was much increased in the ship's track, from which a bucketful was drawn up astern, in order to try and ascertain the cause of the appearance. The liquid soon lost its brightness when stationary, but it was renewed every time it was shaken; and on taking some up in his hand, Carlos perceived several small animals of a red or brown colour, from which luminosity evidently proceeded. They were of various shapes, but chiefly that of a wheel, and were accompanied by a quantity of very minute shining particles, which Antonio assured him were the remains of decayed fishes.

With all these beautiful phenomena around him, Carlos was never weary of looking out; but he was sadly disturbed one evening by a very ghastly spectacle. The Captain and he were leaning over the side of the ship earnestly conversing, when the former suddenly ceased speaking, and by the bright moonlight Carlos saw him turn excessively pale. On being asked what was the matter, he pointed to a dark object lying below, close to the ship. A heave of the latter soon sent it to a short distance, and both saw with horror that it was a dead human body with the face uncovered. It was evidently that of one who had died at sea; and having been imperfectly fastened in its wrapper, the shot put in to sink it had escaped, and it had floated along with the current. Some efforts were made to push it to a distance, but it rose again and again, and continued to follow the vessel for several days, rendered still more appalling by the numbers of sea-birds which preyed upon it. 'The men will think this a bad omen,' said the Captain,

'for we are all more or less superstitious;' and he
was right. The crew shook their heads; were evidently impressed with an apprehension which they
could not lay aside; and as for Carlos, that distressing countenance haunted him day and night, and
even he felt it impossible to get rid of an indefinable
dread of the future. He thought that he should
never again look upon the birds with patience; but
he could not help feeling interested in one which
seemed to attach itself for several days to the ship,
and which would, under other circumstances, have
afforded him much diversion. It was called a Booby[1]
in common language; belonged to the genus of pelicans; and constantly hovered in the immediate vicinity
of the 'Hero,' darted into the water two or three times
in the course of the day, came out again with a fish
in its beak, and then perched itself on the yards,
especially those of the studding-sails, which are set to
catch the light winds of the tropics. After this it
appeared to be quite stupid, and suffered itself to be
taken by the hand. It was much more amusing when
it settled itself in one of the open stern-windows,
twisting its head from side to side, apparently listening to the conversation of those within. Then a gull
was caught, and Carlos tried to tame it. It was one
of the rarer species with black legs, termed the Ivory
Gull; was very gentle, and allowed him to caress it;
but after about a week it refused to eat, though he
tried to tempt it in many ways, and it died a few days
after.

These innocent enjoyments were soon to have an
end; grief was near; and fever again manifested

[1] Sula.

itself. ' I am sorry to tell you, sir,' said Carlos to the Captain one morning, 'that two of our men have sickened during the night, and are now quite unable to get out of their hammocks.' 'Summon the doctor!' exclaimed the Captain mournfully. The usual remedies were skilfully applied, but the disease proved the strongest·; and on the fourth morning, Antonio was called upon to sew the poor fellows up in their hammocks. The service for the dead was read over them by the Captain with an unsteady voice ; and long was it before Carlos forgot the plashing sound with which the mortal remains of his companions were consigned to the deep. The effect of these deaths on all the survivors was most striking, for each thought them but the beginning of new misfortunes ; and the gloom which ensued, although but a natural consequence, was the worst feeling for the health which could show itself. On Mr. Grant it took a strong hold ; for his quick, lively temperament was peculiarly liable to receive impressions. He had hitherto laughed at all fears ; and although he considered his promotion to be first officer as dearly purchased by the loss of Mr. Mortimer, he could not help feeling a little proud of the elevation. From the moment, however, that these two men died, he sank both in body and in mind. The ensuing morning he stood by the side of Mr. Fraser, who had not yet risen, and said, 'My turn is come, doctor. I have got the fever. I am now going to lie down, never to rise again in this world.' Mr. Fraser started up in alarm, felt his pulse and head, examined his tongue, questioned him as to his symptoms, and could not perceive anything to apprehend 'Nonsense,' he cried, 'your pulse is healthy, your tongue clean; you say you have no pain anywhere, and there is not a sign of fever about you. A dose of quinine will set you all right by to-morrow.' 'Of course I shall take what you give me, sir,' observed Mr. Grant, 'but I know it will all be useless; fever or no fever, I feel that I shall die.' 'Of course you will die,' rejoined the surgeon, 'if you are determined to do so; but rouse yourself, man, you have no more fever than I have, and don't be afraid.' 'I am not afraid,' said the mate calmly; 'but for all that, nothing can save me.' Then turning to Lacy, he continued, ' Brother, take care of my things, and see them delivered at the place to which I have directed them; go yourself, if you can, to the house when you get back to Liverpool, and tell them there all about me. I awoke last night suddenly, and felt that the hand of death was upon me; and I have done all I can to settle my mind ever since.' So speaking, he went to his berth, from the side of which the doctor scarcely stirred the whole day, putting everything in practice that medicine or reason could devise. At night, seeing that his patient was in a tranquil slumber, and that his pulse, which had become more and more depressed, was again stronger, he himself went to repose. About four o'clock the next morning, Carlos, who was lying awake in the adjoining berth, heard a groan, and hastening to the sufferer, found him dead. This sad occurrence formed one of many instances on that fatal coast of the consequences of mental depression; as if the vital force were weakened by the inhaling of some deleterious gas, and was naturally followed by a prostration of the mind.

The death of Mr. Grant obliged the Captain to

take a more active part in the duties of the ship than he had hitherto done ; and trembling for him also, Mr. Fraser urged him to abandon the rest of the voyage, and steer immediately for England, adding, that he would give him a certificate for its having been absolutely necessary. ' It is madness,' said he, ' to go up a river while your men are in this condition ; not one of you will be left alive.' ' I cannot answer it to my conscience,' replied the Captain, after some reflection, ' not to perform that which I engaged to do. The ship is loaded for the Calabar trade, her papers are made out for that place ; I cannot return with her cargo unsold, and I am not justified in going anywhere else.' ' That may be,' rejoined the surgeon, ' but at any rate stand out for Prince's Island, and remain there some little time to get your men into proper order.' ' What is the use ?' again returned the Captain, ' they were all quite well soon after we left Cape Coast ; but, although this is the healthiest time of the year, directly we approach the shore they sicken again, and I question if any of us live to take the ship home. Hall, you say, is sick, and several others ; and if it were not for the Kroomen, we should not have hands enough to go through the work. Even now I shall be puzzled to get the goods out of the hold.' ' Surely these reasons,' persisted Mr. Fraser, ' speak louder for Prince's Island, or St. Thomas' even, than for Calabar ;' but the Captain shook his head, and remained fixed in his intentions.

Poor Hall was no more ; another and another sickened ; but Gray seemed to bear a charmed life, and to walk unconcernedly amidst the dead and the dying, as if nothing but health and vivacity were around. The shore began to open upon them by a long flat line of coast; the breezes became unsteady; they entered a wide estuary, and land covered with wood was seen at a distance. Preparations were made for barter with the natives, and the goods required for that purpose were very gradually brought on deck; and as no rain was expected, a tarpaulin was quite enough to protect them from the dew at night, which became profuse on nearing the land. No extra fatigue was given to the men who still continued unscathed; and at night the anchor was let go, that almost all might rest and avoid exposure. The Captain constantly stood on deck in the sun, to superintend his arrangements, while Carlos gave orders in the hold. One day eight bells (twelve o'clock) were rung, and dinner was shortly after announced. The cabin trio assembled, but, to the great consternation of the surgeon, the Captain pushed his plate from him, saying that he had a violent headache, and could not eat. Every suggestion that his skill could furnish was immediately put in practice by Mr. Fraser, although there was but one set of remedies; and for a while the naturally strong constitution of the patient gave a hope that he would recover. In the meanwhile, Carlos was in the sole command of the vessel, and his energetic mind seemed to rise to meet the occasion, or rather he received strength from above to fulfil his duties. He carefully concealed the ensuing deaths from his kind-hearted master, for fear of depressing him further. He kept the ship at anchor, that she might not be still more surrounded by the vapours of the shore, and himself saw all Mr. Fraser's commands executed.

G

Antonio was invaluable to him, and seemed almost to anticipate his wishes. The Kroomen were orderly and attentive, but appeared to be used to such scenes. The few white men, besides Antonio and Gray, who could work, performed their allotted tasks with listless indifference, as if they felt themselves doomed; and even the latter was quiet.

Having seen the ship made snug for the night, and given the last orders, after an absence of three or four hours from the cabin, Carlos returned to it to rest himself; but as he passed the Captain's state-room, he there saw Mr. Fraser on his knees, his face buried in the quilt thrown over the sick man, and his hand grasping one which was no longer able to return the pressure. The frank, gallant sailor, who had cared for every one but himself, had breathed his last without a struggle; not, however, unconscious of his approaching fate, for his Bible was found open where he had been reading the 17th chapter of the Gospel of St. John, and his emaciated fingers lay upon it, as if it had only fallen from them when they had no longer the power to hold it. Inexpressibly grieved and shocked, Carlos stood for a moment perfectly appalled. He then sought to raise Mr. Fraser from his knees. 'Take me to my berth,' said the surgeon; 'I shall be the next victim. I have for some days felt that I too was stricken; but I kept up as long as there was life in the noble-hearted creature just gone. I hoped it would be a slight attack; but I am certain there is that within me which says it is impossible I can survive, and I must make use of the little time in which I may remain conscious. Let me have an hour to myself,' he added, as he lay down, 'and then come to me again.' Carlos tottered rather than walked up the companion-stairs in an agony of distress, which threatened to overwhelm him. At first every consideration was lost in the grief he felt at parting with those who had become dear to him, during long intercourse in that narrow space which so tries the tempers of men, and in the afflicting scenes which had of late so heavily crowded upon every individual; but as the hour wore away, he became sensible to the danger of his own position, and if he were to escape the fever, he felt that he was now in the uncontrolled power of a fierce and bitter enemy. One friend alone seemed to be at hand, and that was Antonio; but as he sat mournfully brooding on all this, he recollected that he had a Friend who was even then watching over him, and who was able to save from all danger and suffering if He pleased. Lifting then his heart to that Friend, and seeking His aid through the only true medium, he became sufficiently composed to return to the surgeon.

As Carlos asked how he felt himself, Mr. Fraser took hold of his hand, and said, 'I grow weaker every minute, and shall not be here long; therefore all I have to say must be told now. Don't cry, my poor fellow,' continued he, seeing the tears streaming down the cheeks of his young friend. 'Your lot is perhaps the worst. I have been beaten about the world from early childhood, and have few left who will lament my death. I have been wild and reckless, and have estranged those who would otherwise have loved me, and I know it to have been my own fault. But this voyage has brought me to a sense of my errors, I hope; and I had determined to lead a very

different life if it had pleased God to spare me. Now
I have but one thing left, which is to seek the mercy
of that God, through His Son, and humbly to hope,
that although late, my repentance may be accepted.
But, my dear Lacy, time and strength are passing
away, and I must talk to you about yourself. An
awful responsibility will fall upon you ; but there are
three or four who will surely stand by you. Antonio
is wholly your friend ; the Scotchman is getting better,
and will be faithful ; and Johnstone also—but he is
in a very precarious condition still. We are in sight
of land, therefore you are bound to take me and the
Captain ashore to be buried. Lay me under some
tree, for I have often thought of late that I should
like to have a grave under one of the palms.' Mr.
Fraser paused, his mind evidently beginning to
wander; but after a quarter of an hour he made
another effort, and said, 'As soon as we are provided
for, you had better take the vessel to Fernando Po,
which is the nearest place where you will meet with
Europeans. You must not attempt to go on to
Calabar, for the natives there, when they see your
condition, will probably board you in numbers, murder
you all, and take possession of everything ; therefore
get away as fast as you can to a place of greater
safety. Perhaps you may meet with the " Flora," and
she will render you assistance.' The dying man again
sank back upon his pillow, his hand locked in that of
his friend and sole attendant. After a few minutes
had elapsed, he asked Carlos to read him some of the
prayers of the church, and first of all the confession·
Carlos obeyed, and Mr. Fraser feebly repeated it after
him. He then joined his hands, as if in fervent

prayer. He requested to hear the 51st Psalm, and evidently followed it, for his lips moved as if he were saying the words to himself; but as Carlos paused, in order to find another passage of Holy Writ, he turned round and saw that his auditor had sunk into a stupor. From that stupor he never awoke, and about midnight he passed away to that land from which there is no return.

Frequently during the night had Antonio visited the cabin to request Carlos to take some refreshment, and see if he could be of service; and now, when all was silent, and had been so for some time, he crept softly in again. Unwilling, however, to disturb the mourner, he seated himself on the companion-stairs to be ready if he were called. Morning began to dawn, and as it shone on the cold faces of the dead, Carlos burst into a paroxysm of grief. This in some measure relieved him; and when it had subsided, Antonio endeavoured to rouse him to action by asking if he had any orders to give. 'You have passed the night in the open air,' said Carlos, 'you are quite cold. Why did you run such a risk? recollect your are now my only friend.' 'Never fear for me, sir,' said the faithful Italian, 'my Venetian blood does better in these countries than that of the English, and so will your Spanish; but what must be done now?' The two consulted together, and agreed that it would be best to follow Mr. Fraser's wishes and advice in everything. Carlos therefore ordered the anchor to be weighed, and with the little breeze which remained, endeavour to get the ship somewhat nearer to the island. In about an hour he thought he was at a distance from it which might easily be attained by the boats, and the anchor was again dropped. Calling the carpenter to him, he said, 'You must put some planks together as well as you can, so as to make two coffins.' 'Two, sir!' said the man, with an air of consternation. 'Even so,' said Carlos, striving to subdue his own emotion; 'the Captain and the surgeon are both gone.' The man perfectly reeled, and hiding his face with his rough hands, burst into tears. 'My good fellow,' said Carlos gently, 'get to work immediately, for we must be quick in what we have to do; the sun will get high, and we must be under weigh and out to sea before night.' 'I should think so,' said a deep low voice in Carlos' ear; he started, and turning quickly round, saw Gray with his eyes fixed upon him, expressing what he felt, and which look Carlos afterwards recollected through life. Spite, defiance, and treachery, were all there; and there was a security of villany about the man which must have put Carlos on his guard, had he not been in too distressed a state of mind to be capable of observation.

The last offices for the dead were performed; they were laid in their narrow houses, and brought on deck. 'Man the boats to go to the island,' said Carlos; but Gray stepped forward and exclaimed, 'I suppose Mr. Lacy, you mean to kill us all by sending us ashore in the heat, and asking us to stand in the sun and dig graves.' 'If the men are afraid,' observed Carlos, 'although it is not my place to leave the ship, I must go. I know one who will help me. Come, Antonio,' he continued, 'put the tools into the boats, and we will take the Kroomen. You shall have Mr. Fraser, and I the Captain.' Upon this

Gray offered to take charge of one; said that he had no objection to be of use if the Kroomen rowed, and as he was the strongest and healthiest of all the crew, he should best perform the work. Carlos was surprised, but declined his services. Saying, however, that he would at least take one boat, and lifting one of the coffins down the side, with the assistance of the Kroomen, he seated himself at the helm, and was ready before Carlos and Antonio had procured the spade and some ropes. There was nothing to be done then but to permit him to go, and the three started with their melancholy freight for the point of land, which looked like an island at high water.

That island was lovely to behold; some tall trees stretched their arms over it, as if to protect it from the fierce rays of the sun; and under their shade grew a multitude of bushes, which still glittered with the plentiful dew of the preceding night. The gay birds fluttered through the branches, and the most gorgeous flowers now and then peeped from between the openings. No perfume, however, was there; for as the place was approached, a rank odour was perceptible, which proceeded from some low mangrove-trees, whose roots and under-branches were slimy, and which encircled the spot so as to make access difficult. The boats rowed round in order to find an opening, which, after a little search, was accomplished. The coffins were landed, and leaving them in charge of Gray, Carlos and Antonio penetrated into the interior to find a suitable spot. Some little time was spent in choosing a place which they thought would correspond with the wishes expressed by Mr. Fraser; and as they wandered about, Carlos suddenly stopped, and exclaimed, 'I fancied I heard a shout. There again! there certainly was a voice.' 'I did not hear it,' said Antonio. Both stopped again to listen, but all was quiet, and they with some difficulty found their way back to the landing-place. Great was their astonishment when they saw the coffins abandoned; and hastening through the bushes, perceived that only one boat was there, and that without its crew. 'How very extraordinary!' said Carlos; 'where can they be? we can never haul these up alone.' They called, but no answer was returned; when Carlos, suddenly seizing Antonio's arm, exclaimed, 'Look there!' and he beheld all the men in the one boat, rowing as fast as they could towards the vessel. Even as they spoke, such was their speed, that they appeared like a mere speck upon the waters. 'That cowardly rascal Gray,' said Carlos, 'is frightened at being out in the sun, and has taken all the men away that he may get back the faster. It will be impossible for us now to take the coffins to the spot we picked out, and we must put them into the ground as near the first tree as we can; it is lucky they have left us the ropes and the spade. We, at least, can perform the most important part of our duty.'

Digging a hole in the sand, the two Europeans laid their dead side by side, and Carlos, taking the prayer-book of Henriquez from the bag in which it was suspended round his neck, read the burial service; then covering the coffins, the two took the way to their own boat, in order to get back to the ship as speedily as their strength would permit. On arriving, their thirst was excessive, and Carlos said, 'Look in the locker; I ordered a small cask of water to be put into it, for I knew we should want it.' 'What's this?' exclaimed

Antonio, as he lifted up the lid, and saw a large bundle wrapped in an old sail. They opened it, and found that it contained a woollen dress for each, and spare linen trousers; some biscuit, powder, shot, bullets, a hatchet, and two or three pieces of salt pork and beef; and instead of one, two casks full of water. Upon the clothes were pinned a paper, on which some trembling characters were traced. With the greatest difficulty they read these words : ' It's a' we could do for ye ; there are guns under the planks.' Raising some planks which lay at the bottom of the boat, they saw two guns with bayonets, the locks of which were carefully wrapped round with woollen stuff to keep them from the wet. A horrid suspicion came over the mind of each, to which neither of them seemed to dare to give utterance. They looked into the vacant space for some minutes, and then Carlos exclaimed, 'What is to become of us, Antonio ?' ' They have abandoned us,' returned his companion, 'that's pretty clear. Let us get into the boat, and push off ; perhaps we may still see the vessel, and there are surely some on board who would not consent to such a thing, though we do not know who are Gray's accomplices ; perhaps, if they see us, they may stop that wretch from fulfilling his intentions.' They rounded the island and stood out for the ' Hero ;' they made signals ; they tied a handkerchief on to one of their oars, and held it as high as they could ; they shouted ; they roared with all the strength of despair—but it was of no use. A light breeze sprang up ; the ' Hero' spread her sails, and was soon out of sight. ' It is all over with us,' said Carlos, and threw himself at full length in the bottom of the boat.

CHAPTER VII.

UNABLE to afford any comfort, wholly unable to offer any advice, in the dangerous and forlorn situation in which they were placed, Antonio allowed his fellow-sufferer to remain quiet for some time, and strange to say he slept,—ay, and slept for some hours; and Antonio, seeing that he did not wake, securing the oars, and throwing the sail over both, lay down beside him and slept also. It was one of those periods of suffering when the calm of despair creeps over the mind, and soothes even by its intensity. The over-wrought energies are tired out; nothing can be done; and the spirits sink for a while under the weight of bodily exhaustion. The night was far advanced before either of them awoke, and then Carlos was the first to rise. He looked around him with astonishment, and it was some little time before he could recollect all that had passed, or understand how he and Antonio should be in an open boat on the ocean; but, refreshed and invigorated by that rest which he had so long required, he felt more calm, and he prayed for strength, while he coolly contemplated their probable fate. Hope, however, which is always strong in the youthful heart, and which, even in some old ones, is undying, whispered a vision of the future; and he said to himself, 'Why should I have been pre-

served in the battle-field,—why should I have escaped
the fever when all were dying around me, to perish
here in the open sea? No, it surely is not the will
of my Father in heaven to destroy me now, and He
will give me courage and resources by which I may
get through even this trouble. Antonio,' continued
he aloud, seeing his companion gradually becoming
conscious, 'look about you, man, and tell me what
you think of our prospects?' 'I see very little in
the prospect, sir,' answered Antonio, turning himself
completely round. Don't call me sir any more,' said
Carlos; 'there is no difference of rank here; we are
brothers in misfortune, as we are brothers in the sight
of God, so give me your advice.' After a pause,
Antonio exclaimed, 'All I can think of is to get to
Fernando Po.' 'But I am afraid,' returned Carlos,
'that while we slept we have got off our course, and
we cannot tell, without instruments of any kind,
where we are.' 'Well, then,' rejoined Antonio, 'suppose we take it in turns to pull for five or six days
in the direction in which you suppose it may lie.'
'Five or six days!' observed Carlos; 'how shall we
get food for all that time?' 'Let us see,' continued
Antonio, 'how much biscuit there is in the bundle.'
The deserted men again examined their little store;
found, besides what they had already seen, some cold
boiled rice, a little tub of oatmeal, a few herrings, and
some fishing-lines and hooks. 'This, with management, may do,' said Carlos; 'the water will be our
greatest difficulty, for the casks are small.' His heart
again sank within him, and he sat a long time considering their unhappy position. At length, he added,
'I know that the current sets very strong to the south

all along this coast, and we must have drifted a great way; therefore we are far from the latitude of Fernando Po, and we shall never fetch it up again. I really think the best way would be to steer south-east at once, and try to make the land. That once reached, we can coast along, and may meet with human beings, although they may be only savages. Moreover, the Captain told me that vessels often touch at Cape Lopez, and we may fall in with them either there, or on their way to it.' 'Besides which,' observed Antonio, 'we can go ashore and look about us for water, and can always stop during the great heat; we will haul the boat on to the sand, turn it keel upwards, get under it, and be sheltered from the sun. Carlos could not help smiling; and Antonio continued, 'To be sure it is a great many miles for two men to accomplish in a little boat, but there are no heavy seas here to swamp us; and if we find food ashore, we need not be in a hurry, and can rest as often and as long as we like.' 'I wonder,' observed Carlos, 'who put those things into the boat for us! It could not have been Gray himself, for he evidently had no good-will towards us; yet it must have been some one who knew what was going to happen. The writing is that of the Scotchman, and if he did it, he must have befriended us slyly; but then, why did he not warn us of it? Perhaps Gray, whose plot it must have been, intimidated the rest, and they were too weak to resist him. I am certain now that one of the Kroomen shouted to us; but I dare say Gray silenced him. We must be as sparing as possible of everything we have, and not mind a little hunger. We must also save our powder and shot as much as we can for occasions of self-defence, or great emergency. Now, I think we ought to recruit our strength by obeying our appetites; it is rather unfortunate that this is the first time I should have been hungry for many days.'

The two friends ate some of the rice, and drank a small quantity of water; then took it in turns to row, according to the best of their knowledge, in the direction of the shore. Observing, however, how strong the current was in their favour, they unhesitatingly husbanded their strength, by resting during the great heat of the day. Their only guides, like the navigators of old, were the heavenly bodies, and these enabled them to make even more way by night than by day. They pursued their plan for several revolutions of the four-and-twenty hours, and still saw no signs of land. Water was getting scarce; and then Carlos suggested that they should steer direct east; 'for,' said he, 'we do not seem to come to anything by going on in this manner.' On they went, but still they were in the open sea; the last drop of water was drained from the cask, and no land appeared. They rowed the whole evening—the whole night, the expanse of waters still surrounded them; their parched tongues refused to move; and, giving themselves up to the fate which seemed to await them, each locked a hand in that of the other, their heads became confused, and creeping under the sail, they lay down to die. In a short time they became insensible; but a heavy, and to them refreshing, dew fell, moistened their covering, restored them to a little animation, and they were roused to complete consciousness by the boat striking against something hard. They rose and for a time a new energy seemed to inspire them ; to get ashore had been their object, and now it was accomplished for them. They were too weak, however, to haul the boat up out of the reach of the surf; but she had a kedge, and with this they contrived to fasten her so that she could not get adrift. They then landed, and, by the dawning light, saw nothing but dreary waste. 'Let us dig,' said Carlos ; 'perhaps the water may be less salt after filtering through the sand.' They tried it, but it was not drinkable ; they went some yards farther inland, and it was only brackish ; they went still farther, and did not procure any. They sucked their wet sail, sopped some biscuit in the best water which they had found, and swallowed it as well as their swollen throats would permit, and, in a little time after, were able to crawl to the top of a hillock of sand, which was at a little distance from them. 'Joy ! joy !' cried Carlos ; 'I see some trees not very far off; and where there are trees in this country, there is most probably water. I am younger than you are, Antonio ; therefore I will go in search of it.' 'There is not much difference between us,' replied his companion ; 'nothing shall separate us. But before we go, had we not better dig a hole in the sand, take our things out of the boat, and bury them, that no one may find them ?' · 'I do not see a sign of anything but ourselves in human shape,' returned Carlos, smiling at his friend's useless caution ; 'and I really think that we shall exhaust our little strength by the exertion. I should say that they are quite safe in the boat.' Antonio yielded, and, with their guns in their hands, they started, slowly proceeding towards the trees. Frequently, however, were they at first obliged to stop and rest; but as they approached, the verdure seemed to give them new life, for there is nothing so dreary or disheartening as a waste of sand. When near enough to ascertain what the trees were, and that they were cocoa-nuts, they absolutely bounded forth in a state of delight; they rushed through the tall, rank grass, and in a few minutes found themselves on the banks of a stream. They lay down flat, and putting their lips to the water, drank a long deep draught, heedless of what the hidden dangers might be around them. The effect was almost intoxicating, and they now felt that they could conquer every difficulty. Just then Carlos heard a rustling and crushing of the grass and reeds close to him, and seizing Antonio by the arm, turned sharply round, exclaiming, 'Run! run! there is a huge beast!' The huge beast, as he called it, pursued them; but the instant the travellers ascertained what it was, they ran in a zig-zag direction, and thus gained ground upon it. They escaped unhurt; and when the danger was over, could not help laughing at the adventure. They concluded, however, that they could not be far from some large river; 'for,' said Carlos, 'crocodiles do not constantly inhabit such small streams as that, though we have proved that they make snug retreats in them, when they communicate with a larger body of water.' 'How do you know?' asked Antonio. 'I have read a great deal about natural history,' answered Carlos, 'as I have always been very fond of it, and I expect that I shall find my little knowledge useful now. That tells me that crocodiles turn with difficulty; and that is why I pulled you first one way and then the other, till, I suppose, you thought me mad.' 'What is the difference, if any, between a crocodile and an alligator?' inquired Antonio. 'Alligators,' replied Carlos, 'have wider and blunter muzzles, some of the lower teeth lodge in holes in the upper jaw, their feet are only half webbed, and they are more slender in their proportions than crocodiles. None have been found in Africa or India, although travellers often mention them. I suppose they think that they are the same as crocodiles.' 'Let us go back to the boat,' said Antonio, 'and now we know where to get water, take some rest. I feel as strong as a lion, and shall certainly be able to get down some cocoa-nuts by and by, that we may have a feast for supper.'

The boat was hauled up high and dry, and as soon as the sun began to decline, the forlorn men took their sail, their water-casks, their ropes, and their hatchet to cut down the trees. On arriving at the spot, however, Carlos said, 'It is a pity to cut down these beautiful trees. I watched the negroes, both at Cape Coast and Sierra Leone, as they climbed the palms; and I dare say that I could do the same, for they say that sailors are like cats. A rope will do as well as a hoop;' so saying, he formed a loop of one of the ropes, put it round himself and the tree, set hands and feet against the trunk, and slipping the loop which supported him at every step, in the manner of the natives, he reached the top. There he found a large spatha, or sheath, full of cocoa nuts, and having had the precaution to put his hatchet into his waistband, he soon separated it from the tree. 'Avast there, below!' he called out to his companion, 'take care of your head; and Antonio jumped aside just as the enormous weight

Carlos climbs a Cocoa-nut tree.—*Page* 100.

11

fell to the ground. It was easy enough for Carlos to descend; and when he had done so, both set to work with their knives, cleared away the thick, fibrous, green rind of several of the nuts, and boring a hole at the top with the point of one of their knives, took a draught of the sweet milk, which appeared to them the most delicious thing they had ever tasted; then, chopping open the nuts with their hatchet, they scooped out the pulp by way of more solid food, and putting the remainder into the sail, dragged them to the boat. 'What glorious things,' said Antonio, 'we can make out of these shells with our knives! We must lay in a good stock of them; but, perhaps, we may find some other treasures here, so we had better make some stay in these parts; there is no need for us to hurry.' 'Agreed,' returned Carlos, 'and before we start again we must lay in a regular stock of provisions.'

The friends slept in the boat that night, and, guns in hand, set off the next morning before sunrise for the stream. 'If we could see something useful to shoot,' observed Antonio, 'it would be as well, for that would frighten the crocodiles also; but I do not like to waste my powder and shot on them alone.' They had not proceeded far along the banks before several guinea-fowls and speckled partridges flew from the jungle, almost touching them as they passed. Firing at random amongst them, they killed several. 'Now,' exclaimed Carlos, 'we will have a roast! But let us load our guns first, for fear we should encounter a panther, or a lion, who might dispute with us for our prey, and think we are poaching in their preserves. I only hope we shall not eat too much, for we are not used to such luxuries.' Lighting some branches and leaves by firing a little gunpowder over them, each plucked his bird, and setting it upon a stake, roasted it in the embers before it had become cold, and consequently tough. They then cooked others, which supplied them with food that would keep for several days ; and after this they proceeded farther, to explore the banks of the stream, and the neighbouring jungle. At a little distance they saw some broad green leaves floating gracefully over the water's edge, and hanging from them were bright scarlet flowers, and large bunches of oblong fruit. They proved to be plantains and bananas.[1] 'This is indeed providential,' said Carlos ; 'the plantains are not ripe, and will supply us with bread, which is the staff of life, and keep for months when roasted.' They returned to their fire, cooked their prize, and, heavily laden, were returning to the boat, when Antonio exclaimed, 'A thought has just struck me ; and he immediately began cutting down the tall leaves of some young cocoa-nut trees which were springing from the ground. 'You can never carry everything,' said Carlos. 'Then I shall drag it,' was the reply. So, tying the leaves into a bundle, and lashing them, as he termed it, round his waist with a rope, he proceeded with his train, which now and then bade fair to drag him backwards, as it caught against some obstacle, and the purport of which was no further explained by him, than by a mysterious shake of the head, when Carlos endeavoured to guess. On reaching the shore, he begged his friend to take care of the rest of the things, for he was going to be very busy ;

---

[1] Musa Sapientum.

and with his knife began to strip the leaflets off the large middle rib of the leaves, till the latter resembled slender poles. These he stuck at certain distances into the sand, tied them together at the top with cocoa-nut fibres, and spreading the sail over the whole, clapped his hands with delight, and exclaimed, 'There; did you ever see such a beautiful hut? Here we will sleep, and sit when the sun is high, and carve our cocoa-nuts, and '—— 'Stop, stop!' said Carlos, laughing, 'we are not going to live here for ever.' 'No,' returned his companion; 'but while we are here, we may as well enjoy ourselves.'

The shelter thus afforded during the ensuing night was pronounced to be the perfection of comfort; and in the morning, as much refreshed as if they had slept amid the paraphernalia of a European bedroom, they repaired to the stream. 'The bush, as the people of Africa call the wild wooded country, is not such a bad place after all,' said Antonio; 'everything you want is found there ready-made.' 'Yes,' rejoined Carlos, 'and that is one reason why the natives are so indolent. Those who have only to stretch out their hands to gather their food will never work for it; and then they want so little clothing. Thus, with many of these nations, wants must be created among them before they will become thoroughly active and industrious. That is also one of the reasons why they persist in the slave-trade, for it gives them much less trouble than tilling the ground, or carrying on manufactures.'

'If there are guinea-fowls,' said Antonio, as he and Carlos walked to the bush next day, 'there must be eggs. Would it not be a good thing to hunt for their nests?' 'I should have no objection to some roasted eggs,' replied Carlos; 'but I am afraid, in seeking for them, we should find much worse enemies than even a crocodile, and I have no fancy for firing our guns on that which will not do for food. As we must not stay long in any one spot, we had better get our provisions in as quickly as possible; and I wish we could contrive something to hold more water than our casks will contain.' 'We can fill the empty cocoa-nut shells,' observed Antonio. 'Yes,' rejoined Carlos, 'till we sink the boat, for there are plenty to be had here.' The friends wandered on, carefully looking around them at every step. They saw multitudes of the most beautiful lizards, some of which had large orange crests on their head, and which chased each other through the grass, and up and down the trees, gliding along so noiselessly that they did not frighten the gay birds in the boughs above them. They were never weary of admiring the latter, some of which were so tiny, and so jewelled in their plumage, that Antonio called them humming-birds. Carlos, how-ever, told him that naturalists are pleased to say, that there are none of these fairy-birds in Africa, their sub-stitutes not having the same arrangement of pen-feathers. They were fortunate enough not to meet with many serpents; and those they did see slunk away at their approach. One, it is true, rushed across Carlos' naked foot, which made him pause for a minute; but as he did not irritate it in any manner, it did not molest him.

'Hush!' said Antonio, suddenly, 'there is such a strange beast looking at us on the other side of the river. Do you think it will come across?' Carlos turned round, and saw a most extraordinary animal,

directly opposite to them, lying upon the grass, with
two of the same kind, much smaller, close to it. 'Are
they whales?' asked Antonio. 'No,' said Carlos,
laughing; 'whales do not come ashore to graze, and
these are eating the herbage around them.' 'They
have whiskers,' observed Antonio, 'and the largest is
evidently the mother, and suckles her young; yet her
body ends in a large oval fin. She has no teeth in
front, and her short fore-legs are just like fins with
nails at the end.' 'It must be a Manatus, or Sea-
Cow,' said Carlos. 'I don't think she will hurt us,
so we will not try to kill her. Let us see if she will
be frightened if we roar.' The two began to make as
loud a noise as they could; upon which the animal,
pushing one of her young into the water, and taking
the other up with her two fore-fins, plunged into the
river and disappeared.

After this adventure, the travellers separated, in
order to make further discoveries; and presently
Carlos shouted, 'Here's a treasure, Antonio, just what
we want!' 'A nest of eggs, is it?' asked Antonio.
'No,' said Carlos, 'nothing to eat or drink, but tend-
ing towards the latter, for it is a calabash tree; and
here we may have vessels of all sizes for holding
water.' They gathered a number, but found them too
heavy to carry; so they, on the spot, scooped out the
inside, and then tying them together by the stalks
which they had left on, slung them across their
shoulders, and went back to the shore. Here, as
they sat under their hut, during the mid-day heat, they
found ample employment in preparing the calabashes
for their purposes. The first, however, which they
put into the sun to dry, cracked all to pieces; and,

taught by experience, they filled the others with wet sand before they exposed them to the scorching rays, and the moisture was gradually abstracted with that of the sand. After two days' work of this kind, they were possessed of bowls, dishes, and several hollow vessels for holding water; and Antonio carved two excellent spoons out of the cocoa-nut shells. They then prepared their stock of provisions for a further voyage; they roasted their plantains, and packed them into calabashes; and each guinea-fowl that was cooked, was enveloped in plantain-leaves, and laid in an empty cocoa-nut shell. They climbed some more trees, and had a large stock of the cocoa-nuts themselves; they cut off bunches of bananas, procured as much water as they could carry, took down their hut carefully, laid the sail, poles, and cords in the boat, and, after stowing everything away in the most commodious manner, they launched their bark once more into the wide ocean, cheerfully saying, 'Now for Cape Lopez!'

At first the boat was leaky, but they baled her out and she swelled again. They did not land for many days, continuing to pull as incessantly as their strength would permit. After a very hot night, however, they required rest, and again went ashore. 'This is not at all encouraging,' said Carlos, looking around him; 'there is nothing to eat here, except some crabs. I never before saw so many collected in one spot; there must be something close by on which they feed, but I do not see it. They gave us a capital dish one day when I lunched with Mr. Williams at Cape Coast; he called it by its native name of "Kuttakim Kicky," and said it was a stew made of crabs.

We have neither the butter, nor the eggs, nor that deliciously glutinous vegetable the Encruma,[1] to concoct such a thing here; but we might roast some of the crabs.' 'You catch them then,' said Antonio, 'while I look for some weed and drifted wood for a fire; but take care that they do not pinch you with their claws. We may as well cook enough for several days.' While the crabs were on the fire, Carlos observed, 'I must own that it is very cruel thus to roast these poor creatures before they are quite dead.' 'Yes, I know that,' rejoined Antonio; 'but they boil lobsters alive in England. I have seen them put into the saucepan with the water quite cold, and heard them crawl about as it becomes warm.' 'If they had plunged them at once into the boiling water,' resumed Carlos, 'they would not have suffered more than a moment; but it is said, that such a plan makes the flesh flabby, and of bad flavour, which, however, is often an excuse for various acts of cruelty in the kitchen, such as crimping fish, etc.; but I hope our necessities justify us, for we could not eat them raw.' 'I am quite astonished,' continued Antonio, 'to find that everything agrees with us, and we keep up our strength with that which is often sour,—not to say worse,—and drink water which would not be suffered to come near our noses elsewhere; yet we are perfectly well, though rather thin and baked.' 'I suppose,' returned Carlos, 'it arises from taking so much exercise in the open air, and from our being so abstemious.'

They set up the hut that night, and had several hours of sound rest; but, towards morning, Antonio started up, saying, 'What is that walking over me?'

[1] The Okroe of the West Indies; Hibiscus esculentus.

and shaking Carlos, whose slumbers were heavy from fatigue, they both rose, and perceived that they were covered with crabs of all sizes; the hut also was invaded by them, not only inside, but outside, in great numbers, crawling in every direction. They examined their boat, but this also was full. They had no alternative, therefore, but to throw them out, and pushing off a little way into the sea, and letting go the kedge, finish their nap once more upon the ocean. The kedge dragged, and, as the boat drifted, they were awakened by a rushing noise; and hastily rising, they saw a large, glittering bluish fish, of considerable size, leaping out of the water into the midst of a shoal of flying-fishes, which fluttered in the air in order to escape from its voracity.[1] 'That's a Bonita,'[2] cried Antonio. 'What a breakfast we will make to-morrow of these flying-fishes which have fallen into the boat, and escaped the jaws of one enemy to enter those of another! I know how sweet they are; for we caught some, one watch, between Sierra Leone and Cape Mount, by hanging some lanterns about the masts, when they flew on board and dropped down dead on the deck. We ate them the next morning while you were asleep. Let us lie here quietly a little while longer, and then we shall perhaps get a larger number. We will cut off their long fins, split them open, roast some upon sticks, and dry the rest in the sun.' After waiting some time, another shoal made its appearance; and loaded with their prize, the sailors went ashore.

It was the custom of the travellers, when they left their boat for any length of time, to empty it of everything, in case it should be taken from them by any

---

[1] Exocetus volitans.   [2] Scomber pelamys.

unexpected party; for although they had not as yet
met with any signs of human beings, they knew not
how long this might be the case. Fortunate for them
was it that they pursued this practice, for, after spend-
ing the whole day in cooking and drying their fishes,
and the night in sleep, they awoke to the painful consciousness that their only mode of conveyance was
destroyed. They had pulled down the poles of their
hut, folded the sailcloth, and packed up all their possessions, when Antonio exclaimed, 'Where's the boat?'
She was nowhere to be seen ; but, far out to sea, they
beheld a dark substance, now and then rising above
the waves ; and soon after, some planks were washed
ashore, which they recognised as having belonged to
their boat. They stripped and swam to fetch her in,
hoping to be able to mend her ; but the wreck was
too complete ; and without wood, without nails, or in
fact any of the proper implements or materials, it was
in vain to think of ever floating in her again. The
frequent dragging ashore, the lying in that fierce sun
for days at a time, had completely worn her out, and
shrunk the wood ; and, instead of repining, the deserted men had every reason to be thankful that she
had not foundered at sea : this was their first feeling,
but the next was the total frustration of all their hopes
of getting to Cape Lopez by her means. The dreary
sand lay on one side, presenting, as far as the eye
could see, not a sign of vegetation, and on the other
were the gently-heaving waters, equally lifeless for
their purposes. Not the slightest shade could be
found ; food there was none, except what such a
chance as an emigration of crabs, or a shoal of flying-
fishes, presented to them ; and they seated them-

selves by the broken planks in the deepest dejection. 'I don't think that anything can help us now,' said Carlos; 'and we shall soon be food for those large vultures which are even now wheeling about over our heads, in anticipation of a meal; they have picked our fish-bones, and most probably will pick ours before long, for we shall die of starvation.' 'That little book round your neck does not teach you that, Lacy,' observed Antonio. 'Did you not, only last night, read that "they went astray in the wilderness, out of the way, and found no city to dwell in; hungry and thirsty, their soul fainted in them. So they cried unto the Lord in their trouble, and He delivered them from their distress?"[1] 'You are right, dear Antonio,' said Carlos; 'by God's help, we shall yet be preserved.' 'Not if you let your foot bleed in that manner,' observed Antonio. 'What have you done to it?' Carlos looked down, and beheld a stream of blood flowing from a wound on the outside of his foot, and, on examining it, found a sharp piece of the shell of the worm-like serpula,[2] so common on that coast, still sticking to the flesh, and which he supposed had adhered to the sunken rocks on which he had stepped when he went in search of the boat. The wound was bound up with a shred of sailcloth; and both then reviewed their stores, preparatory to a walking expedition and they were convinced that they could not have remained much longer at sea, for their last cocoanut was eaten; almost everything else was getting extremely low, and, what was of still more importance, they had very little water left. 'We have plantains, and fish enough, however,' said Antonio, 'and you

[1] Ps. cvii. 4, 5, 6, Prayer Book version.   [2] Serpula vermicularis.

must not walk for a day or two. You shall stay here in the hut, while I go in search of what we want.' 'No, no,' said Carlos, 'you must not leave me ; you know not how long it may be before you find water. In the meanwhile, we can gather some of the shell-fish we see here, and which we have hitherto overlooked. I do not suppose they will poison us as mussels often do; at any rate we must try them ; and when they have been spread out in the sun, we can add them to our fish : so let us go to work, and take out the animals. If we had any great stock, we could not carry it; for we shall now have to bear everything on our shoulders, and the lighter our baggage is the better. We can smoke these creatures over a fire, made of the pieces of the boat.' ' But I don't like to burn the poor old thing,' said Antonio. 'Oh ! we've no business to be sentimental,' observed Carlos.

Antonio strolled up and down the shore, gathered together several shells with their inhabitants,[1] at the same time remarking how little the variety there was in them, and how few of any size ; whereas, he had heard that in some countries the most beautiful kinds lay thickly strewn upon the shore. The greater part of the ensuing night was spent in making arrangements for a land journey. Antonio cut the sail into square pieces, to which he fastened strings, made by untwisting one of the ropes, and so contrived knapsacks, into which he put their clothes, spare powder, etc.,—in short, everything which would go in such a compass ; and Carlos made bags to sling across the shoulders, containing their dried mollusca, and the

[1] Purpura, Donax, Venus ; Arca senilis ; Oliva nana and Cypræa, Buccinum, Murex, etc.

remainder of their crabs and fish; and each was to take a water-cask. Carlos carried the axe, and Antonio took charge of the spade. Some powder and shot were distributed round their waists; and their guns, which were their heaviest burthens, remained in their hands. 'It costs me more to leave the hut than anything else,' said Antonio; but we cannot load ourselves with the pole. I'm thinking that if we meet with natives, they will take me for a monkey of some sort. Your hair, Lacy, is hanging over your shoulders, and your mustachios are very respectable for your age; but your beard does not trouble you much; whereas mine reaches to my waist, and, joined to my hair, whiskers, and mustachios, must produce an effect which may be serviceable, for I am sure it would frighten the fiercest enemy.'

CHAPTER VIII.

At about four o'clock in the afternoon, the two friends cast a long and lingering look at that beautiful ocean which had for so many nights cradled them on its surface, and lulled them to sleep with its gentle undulations. 'Shall we ever see the sea again?' said Antonio. 'Nay,' said Carlos, 'you are taking my part now, from which you roused me so lately; if we do not see it, we shall never behold our friends any more.' 'I have been on it,' continued Antonio, 'ever since I was a child, and it has been like a mother to me; no wonder that I am sorry to lose sight of it, and feel depressed.'

Carlos' foot was still very painful when he walked; and the morning was far advanced while they were still upon the burning sands. They now verified the poetical description often given of 'Afric's burning clime.' They thought, however, that in the far east they saw something like the dim outline of trees, and accordingly directed their steps towards it. They had put on their shoes, thinking that their feet, now unused to much exercise, would be protected by them; but they were soon obliged to take them off again, for they could not bear their chafing pressure. They therefore tied them up in their knapsacks, and proceeded barefooted. Carlos' wound, however, was

not benefited by this arrangement, and before nightfall it had become so inflamed with motion, and the
heat of the sand, that he could not go any farther.
He lay down, but the sand scorched him, and he
hastily rose again. 'Let us sit upon our knapsacks,'
said Antonio ; and they untied them from their backs,
and converted them into seats. 'The sun is hottest
at the top,' continued the Italian ; 'I will dig a deep
place, and you shall cool your foot by putting it into
the hole.' This was repeated several times, which
gave great relief to the sufferer. 'Is there any water ?'
said he. 'Yes,' replied Antonio, 'plenty for to-day :
take a good draught ;' so saying, he filled a cocoa-nut
shell with it, and Carlos drank it eagerly. Scarcely,
however, had he swallowed the last drop, when he
perceived that he had taken all there was. 'You
have given me all !' he exclaimed. 'You wanted it
most,' answered his companion. 'We shall get into
the forest to-morrow, and there find plenty. We must
be in the neighbourhood of some large river, I am
sure ; for there seem to be hills at a great distance,
and all here is flat.' Carlos slept, and Antonio soon
followed his example ; both rising refreshed after a
few hours' rest. The former limped onwards, supporting himself by his musket ; and as the dew was heavy
towards morning, both put on their woollen clothes to
protect themselves from what they knew to be injurious ; but they had become inured to damp, and
only felt its cooling effects. At length, about noon
the next day, they reached the outskirts of a forest ;
and worn and weary as they were, they could not help
admiring the extraordinary beauty of the foliage, so
unlike anything which memory recalled to them as

existing in Europe. Huge trees, wholly unknown to civilised man, spread their enormous arms over those of lower stature, while at every interval the tall and stately palms gracefully waved their enormous plumed heads, almost to the semblance of a breeze. 'Who would think that those bending leaves were so strong,' said Antonio, 'and that their mid-ribs should be useful for so many things? Ah, my dear hut! you were made of them, and I shall never see the like again;' upon which he assumed a very pathetic expression. Carlos burst into a laugh, and rejoined: 'I do think, Antonio, if ever we get back to England, instead of living in a house, you must ask my dear Colonel to give you a corner of a field, and let you build yourself an African hut for your abode.' 'No such thing!' returned Antonio, 'unless you will give me the African climate; the cold, damp ground of England would lay me up with a rheumatic fever. But do you see those broad leaves, Lacy? they look just like mallows (Hibiscus); and I am sure if you applied some of them to your foot, they would cool you and relieve your pain.'

The application recommended by Antonio was most serviceable; but the absence of the sea breeze began to be felt by both, and they were more oppressed by the heat than they had ever yet been. 'I suspect,' said Carlos, 'by the position of the sun at this time, just over our heads, that we must be close upon the equator; do you not see that it is nearly vertical?' 'To be sure I do,' exclaimed Antonio; 'and what is more, I feel it too. But look here, I have something which will cool our mouths.' So saying, he displayed a pine-apple, which he had just cut from beneath its

l

tuft of long, sharp-pointed leaves. It was neither very large nor very finely flavoured, and not to be compared with those enormous golden pines which Carlos had tasted at Cape Coast; nevertheless it was very grateful, as well as several others which they gathered. They then penetrated farther into the forest, where the closeness of the atmosphere became more and more intolerable, and both sank down as if they could not get any farther. Antonio rested upon a heap of leaves and branches, and Carlos upon what he supposed to be the fallen bough of a tree. He leaned his head upon his hands, and for a few minutes neither of them spoke; but then the poor fellow started up as pale as death, and catching Antonio by the arm, dragged him some yards from the spot. Surprised at this sudden movement, the latter could not at first speak; but recovering himself, he exclaimed, 'Are you mad, Lacy? or what is it,—a lion?' seeing how alarmed his companion was. 'No; worse!' was the answer. 'As I was sitting I felt something tremble under me, and looking both to the right and left, a sort of shivering motion was visible among the leaves for a great distance. I put my hand down to examine the wood, as I thought, and felt the scales of what I now perceive was a huge snake.' Antonio was almost as much frightened as Carlos; but after a pause said, 'It must be sick, or else it would have come after us. Shall we go and look at it?' 'Not yet,' replied Carlos, 'I have not quite recovered from my fright.' 'The sooner the better,' resumed Antonio; 'and we cannot go away from here too quickly, for I don't like such neighbours; so let us pick up our bundles and start. Besides, I think I see a path yonder; and we had better follow it, for that must have been made by man.' They approached the enormous reptile, and saw, indeed, that it was one of the largest boa-constrictors. Finding that it was still immovable, they ventured to examine it, and following it in all its length, they saw a pair of antelope horns sticking out of its mouth, while its swollen body showed that the rest of the animal had been swallowed by it. 'The secret is out,' said Antonio; 'the beast has eaten so much that it cannot move. I shudder to think that he might have chosen us.' 'Let us shoot him,' proposed Carlos. 'No, no!' returned Antonio. 'I know how to manage it better than that. I'll show you how I learned to kill snakes in Barbary;' so saying, he proceeded to the tail of the animal, and giving it a blow with the hatchet, broke its spine. 'It will never move again,' continued he. 'Perhaps some time or other we may be driven to eat one, for I have heard say that they are just like veal; at present, I am not reduced to dining off snakes.'

Thanking God for their deliverance, and with renewed energy in their hearts, they pushed on through the jungle till they came to a somewhat closer space. 'Oh, Giove!' cried Antonio, 'here's meat and drink for us at once. Look at that fruit above our heads!' 'Custard-apples!'[1] exclaimed Carlos; 'I saw some at Cape Coast. You must climb the tree, Antonio, for I cannot with my lame foot.' The fruit was gathered, and some saved for another meal. Antonio, however, would have eaten more, had not Carlos repeated the caution he had frequently received on his way along the coast, not to eat too much fruit at first; adding, 'for although we have lately had plantains, and cocoa-

[1] Anona.

nuts, and bananas, we have always had flesh or fish ; and these latter fruits, especially the banana, are not as mischievous as others. By the by, do you know that the Portuguese never will cut bananas with a knife, and always bite or break them?' 'No,' answered Antonio; 'why?' 'Because, when the fruit is cut, its cells or divisions appear in the shape of a cross; and then they do not like to eat it. But it is getting late, and I want to know where we shall pass the night.' 'Ah, my dear hut!' cried Antonio, with a sigh, 'how I miss you!' 'You are quite silly about your hut,' said Carlos; 'but as I see no better place, suppose we sleep under this large tree. We can wrap ourselves up in our jacket, scrape a heap of leaves together, and lie down. There are no snakes here, as far as I can see.' Forming as good a bed as they could, they lay down, and were presently asleep. How long they had remained so, they could not tell; but they were roused by a heavy tread and crackling noise near them. 'What's that?' said Antonio. 'Keep still for your life!' answered Carlos, in a low voice. 'I am sure it is a wild beast, and our only chance is not to move a finger—scarcely to breathe.' It was a noble lion, who, as he approached them, seemed to sniff the air, as if scenting his prey, erected his magnificent head, lifted one paw from the ground, and paused as if to listen. However, he passed on, lashing his sides with his long tail. Not till even the echo of his footsteps was no longer heard, did either of the travellers venture to move, when Antonio whispered, 'Are we safe, Lacy?' 'Yes, for the present,' replied Carlos. 'Had we not better get our guns ready? continued Antonio; 'for if he should come back this way, we may find it necessary to shoot him.' 'He probably will return by the same path,' observed Carlos, 'and the wisest thing is to get out of the track. I have had sleep enough for to-night.' Retiring therefore to some little distance, and sitting with their loaded guns in their hands, they anxiously waited till day should appear. 'The lion,' observed Carlos, 'was most probably on his way to the water-side to drink, and if we follow his footsteps, we also shall find water.' Carlos was right. As soon as it was sufficiently light, they cautiously pursued the track, and came to a small stream, at which they drank, filled their casks, and refreshed themselves with a bathe, fearless of crocodiles. This was of infinite service to both, and hopefully they again went their way along the path which they had previously discovered.

The chief adventure of the ensuing day was finding the body of a negro, who appeared to have recently died, and which Carlos proposed to bury; but Antonio dragged him away, saying, 'We had better attend to ourselves, and he is past any good that we can do for him.' 'From appearances,' said Carlos, 'I should think that a slave kaffle had passed this way not long since, and we are lucky to have escaped.' 'Why?' asked Antonio; 'are we not white men?' 'Certainly,' replied Carlos; 'but such inhuman brutes as slave-dealers would not hesitate ill-treating two defenceless men. However, the danger is over now, and by keeping in its track, we shall probably be led to some town.'

As they journeyed on, their suppositions respecting slave-traders were confirmed by several indications, such as the breaking down of bushes, the fragments of corn-meal where the party had evidently rested; and soon they stumbled over something which lay in their path. 'Another body?' asked Antonio. 'It is a child,' said Carlos, stooping to raise it. 'He is not dead, and perhaps we may save him. He must have been abandoned by the unfeeling wretches, because he could not keep up with them. Give me some water.' He poured a little down the throat of the insensible sufferer, and bathed his face with it. 'He lives!' cried he, exultingly. 'Have we any plantains,—any food?' Antonio produced their scanty store; but the poor child, when he opened his eyes, seemed frightened and bewildered, screamed, and, after one look at his preservers, obstinately hid his face in his hands, not daring to glance at them again. The voice of kindness, however, will, sooner or later, find its way; and when, as the child sat rocking himself backwards and forwards, Carlos gently pulled away one hand, and put a piece of plantain to his mouth, he raised his eyes, and stared with astonishment, but some degree of confidence. On seeing Antonio, however, he again screamed, and clung to Carlos as if for protection. 'It's my beard and whiskers,' observed Antonio; 'I told you so. What shall we do with him? We can never sleep in a tree with him as we did last night, and we have very little food. Stop! I have it,' continued he, after a pause; 'he can ride upon my back.' 'Evening draws on apace,' said Carlos; 'let us have our supper, and then find a way to secure the child. One thing is certain, that we must take him with us wherever we go.'

The Europeans divided their slender meal into three

The Deserted Slave-boy.—_Page_ 120.

portions, one of which was eagerly devoured by the little negro. They then sought for a tree which might be easily mounted, and having found .it, Carlos first ascended, and Antonio, fastening the ropes together, tied one end round the body of the child ; the other was held by Carlos, who gently drew the little thing up to him ; then lashing both himself and the boy to the most convenient bough which he could find, with Antonio on the other side, they all three slept soundly. They let the child down the next morning in the same way, and then sought for food. He soon became accustomed to them, appeared to be about six years old, and very intelligent. When they showed him their empty provision bags, he instantly comprehended what they wanted ; and as they went on, searched on all sides for something to eat. After some time he stopped, clapped his hands, began to try to clear away the bushes, and to scrape the ground up with his hands 'I do not see anything,' said Antonio ; 'but he must mean that there is a root to be had where he is seeking ; suppose I try with the spade.' This made the child stare ; but when Antonio, with little difficulty, turned up an irregular, brown-looking tuber, he laughed with delight ; then hastily collecting fuel, he made it into a large heap, procured sparks by rubbing two sticks quickly against each other ; and thus setting light to the mass, he waited till the flames had subsided, and in the ashes placed the tuber, which he turned frequently. It proved to be a yam (Ignamia), and was soon cooked and devoured by the party. They dug up others, and prepared them in the same manner to carry with them. On these, with more plantains and custard-apples, which they occasionally found, they subsisted tolerably well for several days. Of small animals there were none, and the birds did not penetrate into that thick part of the forest. 'Who would have thought,' said Antonio, 'that that delicate little flower, like brown velvet, and that slender creeping stalk, should have such a large root?' 'It is not the root,' replied Carlos, 'but a swelling of the stem which contains nourishment for the whole plant, in the manner of bulbs. The wild yam found here is not equal to those introduced upon the coast; it is not so farinaceous, is darker in colour, and I believe is called the hog yam.'

As the poor child walked with difficulty in consequence of over-fatigue, ill-treatment, and swollen limbs, the young men took it in turns to carry him on their shoulders. From his elevated position, he told them which way to go, for he seemed perfectly to recollect the path; and as he saw objects before they did, he more than once gave them notice of approaching danger. As they proceeded in this way, he one day made signs for them to stop; and he himself, descending from Carlos' shoulders, took a hand of each, and hastily dragged them behind some trees. As they stood there, something appeared to be forcing its way through the jungle, which would have crossed their path had they remained in it. It was a huge rhinoceros, advancing with a slow step, grunting as he walked, rubbing himself against the trees, and occasionally whetting the horn which came out of his nose. He seemed to perceive the party; but they did not provoke him, and he did not offer to molest them; for as these animals do not eat flesh, they are very seldom the first to attack man.

At the end of a few days, the cries of delight which were uttered by the child, led them to suppose that they were near some place which he recognised. He pointed to some smoke which curled up between the trees; the forest gradually became thinner, and a native town, with a broad river flowing about a quarter of a mile from it, burst upon their gaze. The trio proceeded by the directions of the child, till they found themselves opposite the entrance of a small bamboo house, neatly, and even tastefully constructed, and where an old woman was pounding maize with a long-handled wooden pestle, in a mortar made from the hollowed trunk of a tree. The instant she caught sight of the travellers, she uttered a yell which resounded through the whole town, and so roused the inhabitants, that with spears and knives in hand, many of them rushed to the spot. On seeing the extraordinary appearance of Carlos and Antonio, astonishment at first kept them silent; but this soon gave place to the most violent gestures, shouts, screams, and exclamations. Some threatened and rushed up to the strangers with their knives and shook them close to their faces; others just touched them with their spears, and all pressed round with such eagerness, that the white men thought they should be killed, either from suffocation, or by the weapons levelled at them. They scarcely dared to make an effort to save themselves, for fear their movements should be construed into defiance; and they knew that resistance was hopeless from the disparity of numbers. During this time the boy was sitting upon Carlos' shoulder, and did all in his power to keep off his countrymen, by signs, and by crying out to them ; but the former were unheeded, and his voice was too feeble to be heard amidst the clamour; in fact, they did not even seem to see him.   A woman, however, shrieking with all her might, rushed through the multitude, who, checked by her cries, parted in order to give her a passage.   With wild gestures she threw herself at Carlos' feet, who, instantly comprehending that it was the mother of the child whom they had rescued from death, placed her lost one in her arms.

All was now changed : instead of threats and insults, the Europeans were in danger of being suffocated from joy and gratitude ; but they were at length conducted with triumphant shouts to one of the principal houses in the town.   As they went along, her son appeared rapidly to relate to his mother how he had been saved by the strangers, for they saw him act the whole ; and she, making them enter her dwelling with many gesticulations of joy, instantly endeavoured to provide for their comfort.   In a short time, the father, as they supposed, made his appearance.   He had not been in the crowd ; but some of the natives having gone to him, to announce the arrival of his child, he united his efforts to those of his wife in order to honour and welcome the deliverers.   There was no communication, however, except by gesture, and this was sooner comprehended by Antonio than Carlos ; and interpreting the signs made to them, he and his friend followed the man to a separate room, across a small court, where he gave them matting and soft cushions to sit and lie upon.   In a short time after, he brought them a meal of stewed goat's flesh, fowls, cassada-break, sweet potatoes, and salt, and gave them some fresh palm wine to drink. Their host, by taking them to the back of his premises, kept off the multitude; and fastening a door with a rude wooden latch on one side, and letting down a curtain of bamboo cloth over the aperture through which they had entered, left them to repose.

'We have got into good quarters here,' said Antonio. 'I should think so too,' observed Carlos; 'if the teeth of these people were not filed to a point, and if there were not a strange and sullen expression about most of them.' 'What do you suppose then?' asked Antonio. 'I have always heard a bad character of those savages,' returned Carlos, 'who file their teeth; but as it may be only fable, we had better not think about it. At any rate, we seem to have some claim to their gratitude, by having saved the child; but I see you can scarcely keep your eyes open, and I am nearly in the same condition.' 'Here goes then for a nap,' exclaimed Antonio; 'but I shall sleep upon my arms; that is, I shall hold my gun fast, and shall tie the strings of my knapsack round my wrists; and I advise you to do the same.'

The feeling of security from wild animals, with a dry bed of matting from which they could not fall, as they might from the boughs of a tree, was so delicious to the travellers, that they slept soundly for the rest of the day and the night. They were awoke early the next morning by a tremendous shouting, yelling, and screaming, mingled with a noise of drums, the ringing of metal, the clash of various substances, the sounds of which they could not recognise, and bursts of a wild sort of chant. They were about to rise and gratify their curiosity, when their host brought them water in large brass pans for ablution, with cotton cloths by way of towels ; and not long after reappeared with a breakfast of broiled fowls and millet paste.   Their little friend also came, placing himself close beside them, and trying, by his devoted attention, to convince them of his good-will.   They asked, as well as they could, the reason of the noise which they had heard ; but as they did not comprehend the child, when his father had left them, he led his friends through the wooden door to a back part of the town, where, in a sort of temporary shed, they saw a number of men who were evidently prisoners ; for they were bound with cords, not only to each other, but their feet were so tied that they were unable to walk.   They sat upon the ground in the deepest dejection ; and a sullen sort of despair seemed to have taken possession of them, which bordered upon apathy.   On seeing the two white men, a glance passed rapidly among them, accompanied by a sort of scowl ; but their heads quickly sank again upon their breasts, and they appeared to take no further notice of anything.   ' These are slaves,' observed Carlos, ' and they suppose we are come to buy them.   The noise we heard was, doubtless, in honour of their arrival.   But as some of them are wounded, there has evidently been a fight of some sort ; perhaps the poor creatures resisted capture.' But turning to the child, who made some intelligible gestures, he gathered from him that there had been a war, and that these were prisoners brought in by the conquerors.

On entering the town, the Europeans found the whole place in commotion, preparing for a *fête* in the evening.   The huts were decorated with large boughs

of trees and palm leaves; bowls and calabashes full
of palm wine were set in the sun to ferment; the
pestles and mortars were going incessantly, in order
to make the heavy dough used as bread; wooden
platters were being washed; fruits and vegetables
were heaped in piles, while handfuls of capsicum pods
were collected, and everything bespoke a feast upon
a grand scale,—even the presence of the newly-arrived
white men seemed to be secondary to the impending
gaiety. 'But I do not see what animals they are going
to roast,' observed Antonio. 'I wish I did,' returned
Carlos; 'perhaps they will not slaughter them till the
evening, for meat turns in a few hours in this hot
country.' They attempted to stroll into the forest in
order to pass the scorching noon-tide heat there: but
they were met on all sides by some of the natives
who, with vehement gestures, immediately turned them
back again. 'This looks very like being prisoners,'
exclaimed Carlos: 'I am not sure that our lives are
secure till to-morrow morning; and I think we had
better go back to the hut, where we may be safer,
and, at any rate, we can attempt to defend ourselves
with our guns.' They accordingly returned to their
apartments, and had just taken the bayonets off to
clean their weapons, when their host came in, and
courteously requested them to give them up to him.
They pretended not to understand him, when he tried
very gently to take them out of their hands; but this
they firmly resisted, and he left them. Presently, however, he returned with several persons, who appeared
to be a chief and his suite,—if a diadem of parrot's
feathers were a mark of dignity, and if a number of
ivory and brass rings round the arms and wrists, and

rows of beads covering the neck of one, bespoke a high station. His countenance bore strong marks of sullen ferocity; and commanding those who followed him to wrest the muskets out of their hands, the Europeans suddenly found themselves defenceless. To attempt to prevent this would have been perfectly useless; and when search was made for their powder and shot, they quietly resigned that which they had about their persons, only too glad to save the rest of their things. Their host apparently told them that the guns should be restored; but as they were apprehensive of further robbery, they remained close to their knapsacks the whole day, except, indeed, when one at a time, led by their little friend, went cautiously to peep at what was going forward.

A meal was brought to the white men by the child about sunset, and in half an hour the light of numerous fires and torches was blazing all round. The clangour of metal and the occasional firing of the guns were heard, mingled with loud cries; while shouts of human beings, frantic screams, loud recitatives, as if a narrative of exploits, and the noise of many feet passing and repassing, all saluted their ears. Now and then a tremendous shout was heard, as if every inhabitant of the place had yelled at the same moment, and was succeeded by a dead silence for about a minute, and which was again broken by the same succession of noises. After about two hours of suspense, the curtain before the entrance to their room was suddenly pulled aside, and a party of natives rushing in, bore the Europeans irresistibly along with them, to what appeared to be the principal group of the place, who were seated round a large fire in the middle of the street. The man with the diadem was there, and the father of the child whom they had saved. The child himself, with his mother, who, as a female, was not permitted to eat with the men, hovered round and helped to wait upon the party; often, however, putting a morsel or two into their own mouths as they performed their offices. Large pots of coarse earthenware were placed upon the fire, the contents of which were distributed in wooden platters or bowls; each was first offered to the chief, who picked out the pieces which he liked best, and then sent the remainder round to the rest of the circle. The meat was torn to shreds with the fingers, and then conveyed to the mouth with wooden spoons. All was greediness, noise, and uproar. Many rose, and drawing their triangular knives out of their brazen sheaths, struck them together, and flourished them in every direction as they danced; others threw their long spears into the air, and leaping up, caught them in their descent. Only a few muskets were fired; those of Carlos and Antonio were in the hands of the chief's followers. Food and drink were offered to the strangers, which Antonio was about to accept, when Carlos said to him, ' I have the most horrid suspicions about the flesh ; and if we drink we shall get intoxicated, and then it will be all over with us. Only pretend to accept what they give us, and when they are not looking, let us throw it away.' 'We shall perhaps be the next victims,' observed Antonio. 'Very likely,' returned Carlos ; 'but we must not hasten our fate.' The two sat uneasily watching the progress of the feast, and nothing could exceed the filthy excesses which were committed ; but repletion and intoxication soon

K

mastered men, women, and children : the noise gradually subsided, consciousness diminished, and the whole populace seemed at length to be involved in a general stupor. When all had been quiet for some time, the Europeans heard a slight noise behind them, and their little friend gently touched the shoulder of each.

As they turned round, he made signs to them to be silent and follow him, they thought to their room ; but he led them in another direction. Unwilling to abandon their knapsacks, they endeavoured to go back and fetch them ; but the child so earnestly implored them to proceed with him, that, as his intentions towards them were likely to be good, they obeyed his request. Striking through an angle of the forest, they reached the side of the river, and there found a lad seated in a canoe, the mother of the little boy on the bank, and all they possessed in the fragile bark, with the exception of their muskets ; their bayonets, however, were quite safe. The woman made signs for them to enter the canoe ; and at once comprehending that she was favouring their escape, they followed her orders. She, with the utmost volubility, rapidly gave directions to the lad ; then pointing to her child, tossing her arms up in the air, and bowing herself to the ground as the strangers seated themselves, she hastily disappeared with her son through the forest.

CHAPTER IX.

THE canoe, dexterously paddled by the lad and assisted by the current, rapidly passed every object; and by morning's dawn it came to a spot where another river appeared, and both uniting, formed a large body of water which flowed to the west. There was more difficulty in proceeding through this; and seeing that the lad was tired, both the Europeans took it in turns to assist him. Their awkwardness was at first amusing, and several times they were in danger of upsetting the canoe; but they soon became more expert, their strokes were more regular, and they made rapid way through the noble sheet of water, which increased in beauty as they went along. On one side was an open country; and, standing up, they saw mountains in the distance, sharply cutting the deep blue sky, and almost white with the intense flood of light which the sun poured upon them. 'Those hills,' said Carlos, 'cannot be volcanic, for their outlines are not pointed enough. I should say that they have been there as long as the country has been created. What beautiful savannahs, with here and there a noble clump of trees! Look at it well, Antonio; for if it should please God to lead us back safe to our own land, we shall like to think of what is more beautiful than anything I ever heard or read of. Look again, see that mighty, dark

mass moving slowly along; now it separates into
several portions, and speckles the plain.' The lad,
who saw the direction in which their heads were
turned, exclaimed, 'Elephant!' 'Ah, you speak
English,' cried Antonio; but the negro shook his
head, and it appeared that he only knew a few words.
'I shall never be tired of looking at this magnificent
country,' said Carlos; but the negro making signs to
him to sit down, he was forced to obey. The canoe
went swiftly on, and, as the sun was high, shot across
the river, and passed under the shade of the lofty trees
which entirely clothed its banks on that side.

'Look, Lacy,' said Antonio, 'look at those people
in white, sitting in a row along the water's edge; do
you think they are waiting to catch us?' Carlos for a
few minutes gazed at them with some apprehension;
but he burst out laughing as they approached, and
saw a row of pelicans, some of which, however, were
of the most delicate rose-colour. Each stood still as
if made of stone, with its eyes fixed upon the water
beneath: suddenly one, and then another, darted
their heads into the river; and as they did so, the
enormous bag· which proceeded from their lower jaw
became distended; and when it was quite full, most
of them slowly flew away across the forest. 'They
are going to feed their young,' said Carlos; 'and now
you know, Antonio, what has given rise to the fable
of the pelican ·feeding her children from her own
breast.' 'Ah!' said Antonio, 'I suppose this is one
of the wondrous stories which those who travel are
able to contradict; but I know that people sometimes
do not like to be told that that which has been
believed for many years is not true. You have heard

of that beautiful shell called the Argonaut, have you not? They say that the first idea which ancient people had of sails and rowers was taken from the animal of that shell, which was reported to stick up a little sail, and row along with its arms; but they have no sail to set, and the oars or arms are nothing but a number of suckers which lie out of the shell in order to procure food, and not to produce motion.'

At about two o'clock, before the sun began to decline, they came to an opening in the forest, caused by a creek, which the lad entered; but the canoe soon became so entangled in the bushes which grew under the water, or just peeped their heads above it, that all hands were required to effect a passage. The barrier once passed, they steadily pursued their course, and saw on one side of them a high hill, covered with trees and jungle; and the other side was flat, although equally covered with forest. A cry of admiration and astonishment burst from both the travellers as their eyes first took in the whole view. 'These myrtle-like trees,' said Antonio, 'grow in the water, under the water, and out of the water; and those that are out have long things like pieces of coral hanging from them. Look, Lacy, these berries open at the bottom, and leaves come out of them; they are growing in the air.' 'Ah, then,' cried Carlos, 'I know what they are, for I have read about them; they are the scarlet-berried mangroves (Rhizophora). The seed drops out of the berry when ripe enough, but still remains attached to its covering; the first leaves and fibres of the root spring forth, and it does not fall till the young plant is strong enough to support itself in the mud below; otherwise, it would sink and become rotten.' 'How beautiful!' exclaimed Antonio; 'I wish we could know all that God does.' 'It would be too much for our minds if we could,' resumed Carlos; 'but let us, placed as we now are, in the midst of His wonders, observe all we can; and the more we see, rely on His goodness, which has provided for the meanest of His creatures with as much love and care as He has bestowed on those who are called reasonable. See what brilliant fishes, wholly unknown to us, are playing in the waters; observe those flashing insects, hovering over the surface; behold those exquisite flowers hanging down the bank; watch those splendid birds as they whirl through the air! All we have suffered is amply repaid by witnessing such glories as these.'

As the travellers advanced, their admiration was changed into wonder; and both were struck with the admirable beauty of the scene on one side, and its awful grandeur on the other. To the high rocks of sand, streaked red, orange, and yellow, were attached innumerable creepers, some of which hung in festoons and ropes, covered with blossoms, or occasionally floated into the air; and among them lizards, like sparkling gems, darted along, creating a flash of light; butterflies of every varied hue sported in the life-giving sun, now with long feathery fringes to their lower wings, and now with pieces like glass and silver set in them; while innumerable tiny creatures, sparkling with jewelled throats and breasts, pursued them from twig to twig. On the tops of the largest trees were grey parrots, screaming and flying at each other, or defying the numbers of monkeys which climbed the trees in pursuit of them. Sometimes the latter succeeded in snatching the red feathers from the parrots' tails, in order to suck the quill part, and they in their turns pecked at the droll animals with their strong beaks; and then ensued such a squeaking, chattering, and screaming, as to deaden all other sounds. But what a contrast was offered by the opposite side of the creek! It was a forest in a swamp; immense trees, bare of branches to a great height, stood in a thick, black, stagnant liquid. Nothing else seemed to be alive in it; even the trees themselves appeared to be pillars of stone; and as their naked trunks became gradually lost to sight from the gloom and the distance, they looked like the receding columns of an edifice too vast for human hands to have erected. And truly so it was: those glorious trees, in their silent majesty, bespoke the matchless power of the Creator, and reared their gigantic heads as if to say, We live in splendour and beauty, where man cannot even breathe.

The silence of the Europeans was broken by an impediment in their way: it was a tree which had fallen from the sunny bank directly across the creek; and such was the carelessness of the inhabitants, that they stepped over it each time that they passed, rather than be at the trouble of removing it. 'More wonders, Lacy!' exclaimed Antonio; 'there are oysters growing on that tree.' 'Yes,' said Carlos; 'and on those branches along the bank close to the water's edge.' So saying, he broke off one of the boughs, and each taking out his knife, opened the shells, and ate their contents, not forgetting also to supply their companion. They were small, but very delicate in flavour, unlike the huge rock oysters which they had seen on the coast; one of which, cut in pieces, made an ample stew, and whose shells resembled a large stone.

Stepping over the tree while the canoe passed underneath, they proceeded till they came to what was evidently a landing-place. 'Naängo !' exclaimed the lad; and jumping out, fastened the canoe to the stump of a tree. The others also stepped ashore; they took their knapsacks, and other possessions, on their backs; and when their guide said, 'Come, come !' they followed him through an ascending path in the forest.

At the summit of the hill they suddenly emerged from the trees, and beheld a large, wide street, composed of well-constructed houses of bamboo, thatched with palm-leaves, and most of them decorated with carved doors, painted with red and yellow ochre, which the travellers afterwards learned came from some large pit at a distance from the town. These houses consisted of several rooms, and most had gabbled points. The forest all round was cleared for a considerable space; but here and there some huge trees threw their vast shade across the street, and afforded a cool retreat from the sun. The trunks of several were enwreathed with Ipomeæ in full blossom, varying from pale blue and pink to the deepest shade of red and violet. With these was mixed the yellow Thunbergia ; and all were for a time lost in the foliage, but appeared again from between the branches, and spread their vivid colours before the sun. There was an air of comfort and neatness pervading the whole, which augured well for the reception of the strangers ; and the natives, who saw them, though they looked upon them with curiosity, and suspended their labours in order to have their fill of gazing, did not press upon them with that savage inquisitiveness which they had experienced on the former occasion.

Advancing to one of the houses, evidently the residence of no common person, the lad motioned to the Europeans to stay outside while he went in; but he very soon returned with a native in a European hat and a handsome tunic, who gravely saluted them in English, and asked them to come into his house. Astonished at this reception, they bowed, and descending two steps, found themselves in a large room, with an earthen floor and two windows. It was furnished with several chairs, and a table of European manufacture, mingled with those of native workmanship. 'Are you hungry?' said their host; and on their replying 'Yes,' some excellent cassada-bread and some fish were set before them. On their refusing to take rum, a drink very like chocolate was offered; and they were served in earthenware, both of African and European workmanship, calabashes, and wooden bowls, some of which were tolerably carved. When they had made a good repast, their entertainer said, 'The sun is still high up in the sky; will you sleep?' They gladly accepted the offer, and were conducted to a room in which were two beds, with four posts, entirely surrounded and ceiled by cloth made from the bamboo. The same material covered the pillows, and, being finer, looked like brown holland; the sacking was of a coarser material, and formed of a different kind of grass. Besides these were two large, old-fashioned, white and gold arm-chairs, the seats and backs of which were covered with blue and silk

damask, and looked like French furniture ; the floor
was covered with iron bars. 'Sleep here till the sun
is quite down,' said their kind receiver. 'I will
then send you water to wash ;' and, closing the door,
retired.

'Well,' exclaimed Carlos, as he undressed and prepared to stretch himself upon the bed, 'this is true
hospitality ! This man receives us, poor, defenceless,
lestitute wanderers ; never asks whence we came,
how we got here, or whither we are going ; gives us
the best of everything, and suffers us to go to rest
without a single inquiry. It is sufficient for him that
we are strangers, and in need.' 'I do not know how
to get into a bed,' said Antonio, dwelling so much on
his safety and comfort that he took but little notice of
his companions verbal reflections ; but lying down at
full length, a murmur of satisfaction issued from his
lips, and before Carlos closed his eyes, he heard it
gradually decrease, and the tranquil breathing told
that the sleeper was perfectly at ease. The most
refreshing slumbers invigorated the two young men,
and enabled them to start up with alacrity, when two
youths appeared, each carrying a large brass pan full
of water, some native soap, cotton towels, a small
cupful of a white greasy substance with which to
anoint their skins, and some aromatic leaves to impart
perfume. 'I wish I could get rid of some of this
hair,' said Antonio ; 'I do think that a shave would
be a great comfort; but all in good time, and we
must be thankful for having hitherto escaped so many
dangers.' 'Depend on it,' returned Carlos, 'the last
was the most fearful.'

Having dressed themselves in their cloth suits,

which, from having been so little worn, were still
good, the travellers went to the sitting-room, through
a long passage which had rooms on each side, and
which they afterwards learned were the apartments of
the men of the family. The passage itself led to the
dwellings of the wives, female slaves, the cooking-
houses, and the court, where every household labour
was carried on. The evening meal was ready, consisting of fried goat's mutton, plantains, fowls, maize
bread, some sweet beans of delicious flavour, fried
bananas, peppers, large and well-flavoured nuts called
Kolla, the size of an Orleans plum, and a fruit named
Incheema. This was like a small melon in shape and
colour, and possessed a thick orange rind, within
which was a quantity of greenish pulp, containing
some hard dark-brown seeds. The pulp alone was
eaten, and in flavour resembled a green-gage. Carlos
requested his generous host to eat with them; he
complied; and all were attended by male and female
slaves, who frequently changed their platters and
offered them palm-wine. Good water, however, was
such a treat to the Europeans, that they were satisfied with this beverage.

The repast finished, native pipes, made of red clay,
were brought in, and tobacco was offered. Carlos
refused, but Antonio delightedly enjoyed the narcotic
with the master of the feast, who now asked for their
history. As Carlos narrated it, he every now and then
tossed up his chin and shook his head, particularly
when anything very dangerous was related, but made
no comment till Carlos had finished. He then said,
' Those people whose child you saved were Kaylees.
Lucky for you you took that child, for without that

they would have killed you. They have had war lately, and taken those prisoners whom you saw in the shed : one part will be sold as slaves, one part you saw eaten, and the rest will be eaten soon. Very bad people those; they don't care for goats, pigs, or fowls when they can get man. You would have been saved to the last, and then eaten too. They eat father, mother, children, who die in sickness,—anything to get man's flesh. That lad who brought you back belongs to some people below here, and was trading up the river when the Kaylees came to the place where he was, and took him prisoner with the others ; your coming away saved his life. Now you must not go from here till English ship comes to take you. English sometimes trade with us, and they will carry you home. Mostly French people seen here.' 'But how, then, do you speak English so well?' asked Carlos. 'We all speak English,' was the reply; 'because we like English, and English ships used to come in plenty, but now they fear sickness ; and one ship's crew was killed close by. But come now and see my brother the King, for I am only the Governor ; he will make bad quarrel with you, and me too, if you do not go to him ; he is sick and cannot move, but he knows all that happens.'

The Europeans expressed their desire to do that which was proper. The Governor immediately rose, and led them to a house not far off, of the same dimensions as his own ; but the sitting-room was raised, and reached by three steps. Here they found his Majesty reclining on a mat, his paralytic limbs covered with a cloth, and his head and shoulders supported by cushions. His wives fanned away with grass fans the minute sand-flies which came in myriads, stinging the

exposed parts of the person, while they themselves are
almost too small to be perceived. The head wife had
on a scarlet and yellow petticoat, fringed with little
bells, which jingled with every movement, and she
seemed to consider herself the great lady of the place.
Her royal husband, in very tolerable English, lamented
his inability to rise and receive his guests; held out
his hand to them and insisted on hearing their history;
then calling to one of his wives, he ordered her to
bring two mats, which were beautifully woven in
patterns, with grasses of different colours, and presented one to each of the white men. Carlos, after
thanking him, said he was sorry that they were too
destitute to have anything to give in return; but if
ever they should reach England, they would send him
a present which should mark their gratitude.

When the party returned to the Governor's house,
they saw a very fine young man, with the most agreeable expression of countenance, standing at the door.
He welcomed them with much grace and openness of
manner; and the Governor told them it was his son
Wondo, who was just come from an expedition into
the bush. He spoke English remarkably well, and
though a little cautious at first, before the evening was
over he seemed to consider the strangers as friends.
On entering, they were agreeably surprised at finding
some excellent coffee ready for them. Antonio said
it was as good as any he had ever tasted in his own
dear Venice, and was told that it grew wild in some
parts of the neighbouring forests. The next morning
they were regaled with a sweet, whitish, compact-look-
ing butter, which they recognised as the cosmetic presented to them the night before, and which they found

proceeded from the seeds of a large tree. 'If you would like to see the tree,' said Wondo, 'we will go to one which grows a little way in the bush.' They accepted the proposal, and accordingly started before the great heat came on, hatchets in hand, to clear the way. 'You must not let the King see that you have a hatchet of your own,' said Wondo, 'or he will expect you to give it to him; he likes presents too well.' 'I have been thinking,' said Antonio, 'that we shall never want shoes again till we can get another pair, and mine are much too heavy to wear in this country; suppose we give them to the King.' Carlos agreed to this; and they went on, thrusting long poles into the grass before them to frighten away the snakes, till they came to a tall tree with broad leaves, from which hung green pods, having a contraction near the middle. On picking up some which had fallen to the ground, they found they had a white, tasteless pulp inside, surrounding several large, flattish brown seeds. 'We break these seeds,' said Wondo, 'and boil them in water, when the butter rises to the top; we then take it off with a flat spoon and let it grow cold; but some people squeeze out the butter from the seeds by beating them a great deal, and then it is dirty, and not so good to the taste.'[1]

The more the young men saw of Wondo, the more confidence did they feel in him; his character appeare l to possess a rare solidity, and a truthfulness, which is by no means frequent among black men, and which made them rely on everything he said. They therefore frequently sought information from him on various points, and he was generally able to satisfy them, for

[1] Bassia Parkii (Bowdich).

he had often travelled into the neighbouring countries
to trade. 'Where did the Kaylees get those large
knives, Wondo?' asked Carlos one day, 'and their
cotton dresses also?' 'They make them both,' was
the reply, 'for they have plenty of iron and cotton
in their country; so have we, but we make nothing.
Something they trade a little with the ships, where they
get brass rods and beads. But when they come here,
we watch them very closely; and they do not like that,
for they are great thieves. They make plenty of things
with wood and iron, for they are clever; while we are
stupid, and do nothing but trade, and buy what others
make.'

Two new guests joined the Governor's party in the
course of the day; one named Nando, who, according
to Wondo, was his cousin, a very good fellow, and
always laughing; the other was Roölaï, the great
hunter. He had just killed several animals in the
bush, and on returning with the spoil, said he would
make a great feast to do honour to the white men.
Accordingly, the preparations were immediately commenced; but as the sun was getting high, Wondo led
his friends into the house, saying, 'Now you shall
see one of cur white men; there he stands,' and he
pointed to a strange figure close to the door. 'He
belongs to my father,' continued Wondo; 'and he
says there are plenty more like him in his own country
far away.' To the astonishment of Carlos and Antonio, a white negro was before them. The projecting
muzzle, large mouth, flat nose, and retreating forehead,
the characteristics of his race, were much exaggerated
in him; but his crisp, woolly hair was almost yellow
in colour, his eyes were of a dark blue, and from

seeing imperfectly in the day-time, they were constantly blinking, and had a vacant expression. His skin was of a reddish-white, and when his cloth fell accidentally from his shoulders, a number of blotches were seen in various parts of his body. He slowly retired as the party entered the house, where they had not been long seated before the inner door opened, and Antonio involuntarily started. The white negro issued from it, carrying a small harp; the frame-work was of a yellowish wood, with a carved head on the upright; the strings were made of the runners of a tree; and when the man struck the first few chords, it gave a deep rich tone. He seated himself, and began a low recitative, as if to preface what followed. At length he burst into a song of defiance, which Wondo said was the war-cry of his native land. He rapidly passed his fingers over the strings, and all seemed bustle and activity; the notes then changed to a mournful air, accompanied by a low wailing. 'Those are the prisoners lamenting,' observed Wondo. The negro then shouted sounds of victory, and at that moment he appeared to be perfectly frantic; he put the harp upon his foot, tossed it up and down, stretched out the arm that was free, and performed a number of gestures; the sounds then gradually died away as if they were retreating to a distance, the whole having a highly dramatic character. 'How very extraordinary!' exclaimed Carlos; 'it is perfect inspiration. Where did he get that harp?' 'He made it here,' replied Wondo; 'but he tells me there are plenty in his own country. I took him prisoner in a war which we had with '—— 'Hush!' cried Antonio, 'he is beginning again.' The musician recommenced by imitating the voices of birds; and to this succeeded a soft measure which again changed into a lively strain, as if for dancing. In the midst were heard the names of some of those present. 'He is praising us,' whispered Wondo, 'and he will end by describing a hunting party.'

When it became dark, cleft sticks were stuck into the floor of the Governor's room, and torches placed in the slits. These were composed of palm-leaves, tied together at each end, and filled with a sweet-smelling gum. A deputation, however, shortly arrived, inviting the whole party to the *fête*, and they sallied forth into the street. The houses were decorated with flowers and branches, and before them were placed benches, covered with country-made cloth. On these the guests sat a short time, which was considered as equivalent to a visit. A slave stood by ready to pour out palm-wine, rum, and brandy for the party. 'You must pretend to drink,' said Wondo, 'for I see you do not like it; pour the whole upon the ground as secretly as you can; but take especial care of the palm-wine, it is stronger than either of the other spirits.' The whole street was in a blaze with the large torches. Rings were made, in which the dancers performed numerous evolutions. The men were frequently bois-terous, but the movements of the women were in-variably slow and measured; some of them had their legs so covered from the ankle to the knee with brass rings, that it was surprising to think they could dance at all. Their chief perfection seemed to consist in keeping one leg constantly in the air, while they slowly hopped, or jumped, on the other; and when this had lasted some time, the performer received immense applause from the bystanders. Men and women never danced together, and not the smallest deviation from propriety and decency could be detected. The two principal female dancers were the wives of the King, who imperiously made all give way before them. Bowls of fruit, such as the Europeans had never seen before, were handed round with pieces of toasted plantains, and then choice morsels of mutton and fowls. Many shook hands with the white men, others touched their clothes, and then ran away laughing. A broad full moon in a cloudless sky far outshone the torches, and was of a brilliancy which is only known in such latitudes. One custom appeared perfectly ludicrous to the travellers, which was, that whenever the Governor drank, his son, or nephew, Nando, held something before him, that his inferiors might not see him swallow the liquid ; and when Carlos inquired the reason, he was told that at such a moment the enemies of a great man had the power of imposing a spell upon him, and therefore they must not know when he drinks. An old song, made on the first appearance of white men, was universally sung, the burthen of which was : ' Like the leaf of the fat tree, true I say.' As the strong drinks began to elevate the spirits of the multitude, the Governor advised the young men to retire ; and long before the entertainment was concluded, they were asleep upon their bamboo beds. `-

CHAPTER X.

THE residence at Naängo, salutary as it was to the travellers, was differently felt by them. As to Antonio, tossed about from one country to another till he had wholly lost sight of the ties which bound him to his native land, he could have been contented to have passed the remainder of his life with his two friends, Carlos and Wondo. But not so Carlos; every thought of home made him long still more ardently for the arrival of the vessel which was to convey him to those shores he had so wilfully abandoned. An intellectual educated person will for a time readily accommodate himself to any circumstances, and be happy even amongst savages; but he is sure, sooner or later, to become weary, to sigh for communion with spirits like his own, and to feel sad, even in his superiority over his associates. If, besides this, his affections are strong, he becomes restless and impatient; and when deprived of the excitement of danger and difficulty, it is impossible to describe the yearnings of his heart for his real home.

After playing the part of an honoured guest for a week or two, Carlos felt the most painful *ennui* creeping over him; and on talking of it with his friend, they both agreed that the only antidote would be some sort of employment. 'We want clothes terribly,' said

Antonio; 'our canvas suits are torn almost to pieces, and cloth dresses are so hot, that we cannot often bear them. We could make ourselves some, if we could but get the material. I saw a bale of canvas in the Governor's storeroom, and have longed for it ever since; but of course I cannot ask for it.' 'I should not have the least objection to turn tailor under your instructions, Antonio,' rejoined Carlos, 'and you have already taught me how to make trousers; but, as you say, the materials are wanting; and besides the canvas, where shall we get the needles and thread?' 'Here are some, and sail-makers' thimbles too, which I found in my blue jacket pocket,' replied Antonio; 'and these people must have thread, and be able to supply us when ours is exhausted.' 'I have a few sovereigns left in the little bag with my prayer-book,' added Carlos; 'but the natives here do not value gold; in fact, they seem quite to despise it; we must find some other means.' Wondo, however, in a day or two, met the difficulty. He had given his friends two panther skins; and wishing to take the old sailcloth for mending their white trousers, Antonio cut these skins into a proper shape, properly fastened strings to them, and thus made new knapsacks. Wondo watched their progress with great interest, and, struck with the convenience of such a contrivance for the bush on his hunting expeditions, ventured to ask if he could have one also. Of course the reply was in the affirmative. He produced the skins, and some cord of the excellent native hemp; the knapsack was made by the two friends, and was an improvement on theirs, inasmuch as it had some broad straps added to it, of the same skin, lined with cotton cloth to prevent friction, as they passed over the shoulders. It was shown with pride to all who came to the house, and Nando hinted his desire to possess one. Roölaï looked very wistfully; but the white men thought Wondo might be jealous it they extended the convenience to others. They, however, were mistaken; and two more knapsacks were completed accordingly (the skins having been supplied by Wondo), presented, and received with the utmost gratitude. Then it was that Antonio began to patch his trousers with the old sailcloth; and Wondo, with the utmost quickness, recollected the canvas in his father's stores; he asked for it, and bringing it in on his shoulder, threw it at the feet of his friends, saying, 'Make new ones.' The Europeans, with much satisfaction, spread the cloth upon the ground, shaped the garments with their knives, and set to work; but their thread began to diminish. 'We can give you plenty,' said Wondo, on being told of their perplexity; and running to the women's apartments, returned with handfuls, made from various plants, resembling hemp, and the leaves of the aloe and pine-apple. 'This is a treasure,' said Antonio; and both set hard to work, in a few days producing a jacket and trousers for each, using the old buttons for the new dresses, and, as Carlos said, making themselves gentlemen again.' 'We shall,' said he, 'be much more respected now; for these people, and I suppose all savages, are influenced by appearance. Even our friend Wondo takes much pains with his toilette; and as to Nando, he is a complete puppy. In short, I believe that the whole town of Naängo is inclined to foppery.'

As Carlos predicted, Wondo was enchanted with the appearance of his friends, and, when dressed, made them parade before the King, whose deference was evidently increased by their better covering; but when they offered to decorate Wondo in the same manner, he was in an ecstasy of delight. They took especial pains with his suit; and Carlos contrived to cut some buttons out of wood, even ornamenting them with his knife; and, instead of a shank, boring two holes in the middle with a red-hot needle for the thread to pass through. When finished, the tailors felt a positive pride in seeing how well they had fitted their finely-formed friend. Finding that the Governor also would have no objection to 'look handsome,' as he called it, they secretly prepared a suit for him, and presented it to him on the morning of a native *fête*, together with a small curved cup of wood, executed by Carlos. He had procured some old knives from Wondo, ground them to the shape he required, and his talent for drawing, or rather his eye for form, converted him into a good carver. The admiration with which these were received, and the increase of good-will which they seemed to create, were most gratifying, and gave the Europeans a pleasing feeling of independence. 'We cannot quite stop here,' said Carlos, 'but we must confine our practice to the men of rank, or we shall not have a moment for any other employment, or even exercise; and I cannot say that I particularly desire to establish myself as the fashionable tailor of Naängo.' 'It is all the same to me,' rejoined Antonio, 'what I do, as long as I am employed. Suppose you keep to the carving, and I to the tailoring line.' 'Agreed,' said Carlos; 'but if I do not find enough to do in my way, I shall return to the needle.'

Accordingly Carlos prepared more wood, of which

he found new and valuable sorts, and set to work. With much meaning the King one day hinted that he could not wear trousers; and laughing at the artfulness of the observation, both white men began their task for him—the one a jacket, and the other a wooden bowl. When finished, permission was asked to present them, and most graciously accorded. They had, however, some difficulty in keeping their countenances when they first entered the royal presence; his scanty, though long whiskers, and his side locks, were braided afresh, and newly tipped with beads, according to the fashion of the country; but he was painted with white, red, and yellow; his neck was covered with beads, and rings of metal and ivory were on his arms and wrists; his wasted legs were concealed as usual with a cloth, but this cloth was turned up, and his feet were stuck upright into Antonio's shoes, which, being too small for him, were slip-shod. His head wife had taken possession of those of Carlos, which were even smaller. This woman helped him on with the jacket, and the bowl was filled with rum and water, which he drank with the greatest satisfaction. Rapacious by nature, and rendered still more so by the promptings of his chief wife, who coveted everything she saw, he made a long harangue; told the Europeans that, 'Although he lay there unable to walk, he had power over everything, and he should be ashamed it he did not have all the same as the Governor.' On leaving the house, Wondo and Nando shrugged their shoulders, and turned away as if they were ashamed of the conduct of their relatives; and in the evening, they seemed perfectly disgusted when the wife came 'to see what next the white men were going to make for the King.' When she was gone, and the house was shut up, Wondo said, 'Nobody can hear me now, and I can tell you that that woman will come again to-morrow, and plague you always, and there is no satis-fying her.' 'I would rather work for your head wife, Wondo,' said Carlos, interrupting him. 'That Queen of yours is a most impertinent, troublesome, bold woman; and I turn perfectly sick when I hear the jingling of the bells upon her best petticoat, for then I am sure she is coming to get something out of you or your father. As to your wife, she is very good, very quiet; does all she can for us; and when I gave her the skin yesterday, with the cloth border and lining to throw over her children at night, with the wooden bracelet for herself, she seemed to think them almost too good for her.'

'Ah!' said Wondo delighted at the praises be-stowed upon his wife, 'she passes all; but I think we had better go into the bush to-morrow with Nando, Roölaï, and some slaves, to hunt, and that will stop the mouth of my uncle's wife for some time; besides, it is a long while since we cut any wood.' 'What do you cut wood for?' asked Carlos. 'To load the ships with,' was the answer. 'So then you do not deal in slaves?' said Antonio. 'No,' replied Wondo, 'neither I nor my father will have anything to do with that. But my uncle and the Queen, as you call her, will always trade in them; and those long, low houses behind theirs are the barracoons, where they keep the slaves to wait for the ships. Some will come before long; we buy as many as we want for servants, but we never sell them again. Come, let us go and ask Roölaï if he will go with us, and then get ready.'

The Hunter's Parrot-room.—*Page* 153.

The three friends proceeded to the hunter's house, and found him busy among his storerooms, which were filled with sweet potatoes, nuts of various kinds, corn, plantains, bananas, etc. etc.; and in his parrot-room were some of these birds, each fastened by one leg to a stake driven into the ground. They were awaiting the arrival of vessels, the crews of which eagerly bought them; giving perhaps a knife or an old pair of stockings for a bird, and corn enough to feed it all the way home, and then selling it for two guineas. The noise of these captives was so deafening, that Wondo beckoned Roölaï away from their vicinity, and then proposed an excursion to him. He readily consented, said he would take some of his men with him; and all parted for a time, in order to make preparations, first, however, settling the hour and place of rendezvous.

The packages were made, and the native hunters put on their proper dresses. Antonio and Carlos had fixed their bayonets to two long, tough, but light poles, which converted them into capital spears; these were cleaned and sharpened. The bows and arrows, with which they had long been practising under the guidance of the Naängo people, were made ready; the knapsacks were filled with comforts, the slaves carried water and provisions, a hatchet was slung across the shoulder of each, and the cavalcade departed while the other inhabitants were buried in slumber. Their path through the forest was guided by certain landmarks, consisting chiefly of trees and small risings in the soil; and, secure from danger and uncertainty, the Europeans for the first time fully enjoyed the beauties of the forest. They now had leisure to remark the epiphytes, or parasitical plants, which attached themselves to the trees, sometimes hanging from them in festoons, or in large waving clusters, forming the richest draperies ; the climbing plants frequently twisted into chains, by which the loftiest boughs may be attained, occasionally clasping the body of a tree, and uniting their stems, entirely enveloping it in their embrace, or else merely leaning against some mighty trunk, becoming of equal size, and growing with it in twin greatness ; the silk cotton trees, with their pods bursting, and scattering their short-stapled, cream-coloured, and silky substance on everything around, while roots from the tree, in the exuberance of nature, sprang many feet from the soil, and descending like buttresses, formed low walls along the ground ; the runners, which, dropping from the boughs, took root in the ground, and again ascended as trees, making parts of the forest one maze of vegetable matter, through which it was impossible to penetrate except by means of the hatchet.   Then, wherever there was the smallest opening, the loveliest flowers raised their heads ; the aromatic jessamine swept the ground from the tops of the highest trees, and scented the air for miles around ; and numbers of useful fruits and plants appeared.   Looking up as he passed, Antonio exclaimed, ' There is a cabbage growing on that tree ; I never saw such a thing before !'   ' I grant you,' said Carlos, ' that it looks very like one.'   ' You shall have it,' said Wondo ; and giving the order to one of the slaves, the man was up the tree in a minute.   No sooner, however, had he reached forth his hand to pluck off the parasite, then he drew it back again, exclaiming that there was a snake coiled up and asleep in it. 'Tickle its tail,' said one of his companions. Accordingly, pulling off a small twig, the man in the tree gently rubbed the reptile's tail, which immediately uncoiled itself, and after twisting about for a little while, stretched out its shining neck, and reaching the bough above, disappeared. The plant was brought down, and found not to resemble the cabbage except in the manner of its growth; and Carlos exclaimed, 'Well! I have heard of tickling the tails of fishes, but this is the first time I ever heard of a snake being treated in that manner.'

The party was provided with several guns, which were always kept loaded in case of attack from man or beast; but as they did not like to waste their ammunition, their principal shots were made with bows and arrows, and the spears served for nearer prey. As yet, however, they had seen nothing formidable; and at night they slept on the ground wrapped in skins, close to a large fire, which the slaves took it in turns to watch and feed. On the second night, Carlos awaking, found that the fire was nearly out, and rising to tell the men to renew it, he saw a huge pair of eyes glaring at him through the bushes, and glistening from the light of the dying embers. He instantly shouted with all his might, and the eyes disappeared. All starting up, joined him, and as they paused, they heard the rustling and crackling of leaves and boughs at a distance, which they knew must arise from the step of a lion or a leopard. That morning, as they journeyed on, they saw a large black snake lying on the ground, just across their path. 'Fire!' said Wondo, pointing to it. 'Fire! for it is fierce and venomous.' Carlos obeyed, and shot it, at which the slaves jumped with delight, and they carried it on their shoulders to their resting-place at night, for they considered it a rich treat when roasted.

On the second evening the party arrived at a cleared space, where two rude huts were erected in one corner. 'This is our home in the forest for the present,' said Roölaï; 'but when we have finished what we have to do in this spot, we shall go to some other. We leave our things here in charge of some of the slaves, and go round it in all directions. Now we will have some supper, and rest for a few hours; but while the cooking is going on, we will set the parrot-traps. I shall want a great many before next year, for I have known a ship take three hundred at one time.'

As Carlos and Antonio turned into one of the huts to lie down, the latter exclaimed, 'This is not as good as our hut by the sea-shore.' 'It is much larger,' said Carlos, 'and much better; so hold your tongue, and go to sleep.' The next morning all were on the alert, and first proceeded to fell some trees, which were to lie till the ships came, when they would be split, chopped into logs, and carried to the water's edge by the slaves. Some noble trunks were overthrown by the wood-cutters, both of ebony and red wood; and Carlos saw others, which he recognised as the African mahogany and teak. Here were some of the most valuable kinds, which were wholly unknown to Europeans, and which would prove incalculable treasures to builders, cabinet-makers, and dyers, etc. There was one species which the natives particularly avoided, because it was so hard, that it turned the edge of their tools. The red wood was with them used in medicine as well as dyeing, for they reduced it to powder, and rubbed their children with it to make them strong.

After passing three days in cutting timber, the party devoted themselves to hunting. 'We have not seen any large animals,' said Carlos, 'except on the second night.' 'No,' returned Wondo, 'they are too cunning to come near when they hear the strokes of our axes, which sound very far; but we will catch them now, in order to have their skins. I heard some jackals last night, and there must be larger beasts near. There are some pits not far from the hut, which we will cover with branches and leaves; and over these we will hang baits, at which they will spring, and so fall into the pit below. But look there! do you see that large rat? He lives among the sugar-canes; so let us mark which way he went, and get some of his food for ourselves. He is prowling about here to pick up what he can of ours.' 'Rat, do you call it?' observed Carlos, 'he is as big as a large cat.' They searched for the canes, and in an open space in the forest saw some twelve feet high, which they cut down, and tying them in bundles, conveyed them to the huts.

'Do you make sugar?' asked Carlos. 'No, we are not clever enough; we only suck the canes,' was the answer. 'It seems to me,' continued Carlos, 'that there are a great many things which you are quite clever enough to do, if you were not so idle.' 'True,' rejoined Wondo; 'and since I have known you, I have thought a great deal about it, and wish that somebody would teach us.'

The pits were cleared of fallen branches and leaves. A young kid, which had been brought by the slaves as part of the provisions, was killed, cut in pieces, and

hung on poles over them; and the hunters, returning
to their forest dwellings, found some of the men with
two beautiful genet cats, which they had just caught,
and whose skins they presented to the Europeans, in
order to make hunting-caps like those of their masters.
'Hark! I hear a grunting noise,' said Carlos; 'what
is that?' 'A porcupine,' replied Wondo; 'let us
catch him before he gets back to his hole, for he is
very good eating.' 'I saw his nose just peeping out!'
exclaimed Antonio. 'Here, here!' cried the Africans;
and Roölaï's spear transfixed him before he could make
any resistance. 'He is quite fat,' said the latter, 'from
feeding on the sugar-canes, and we will have him for
supper.' The largest quills were plucked out and laid
aside to be taken home, though it did not appear that
they were made useful in any way. The skin was
stripped off, and the body formed an excellent repast
of the most delicate flavour; superior to that of the
domestic hog, which is reared in numbers in various
parts of Africa.

The next morning the pits were inspected, two of
which were empty; but the third contained two enormous leopards, who were furiously trying to leap up
the sides. The hunters fired, and soon despatched
them with their bullets; and when they were quite
dead, they were dragged out of the pit with hooked
sticks cut from the neighbouring trees; and the slaves
were desired to take them to a distance, strip off their
skins, and leave the flesh for the cats, etc. 'Pull out
their teeth,' said Roölaï. 'What for?' demanded
Carlos. The man looked down, hesitated, and then
said, 'To help to make fetish.' 'I thought such a
good man as you are,' returned Carlos, 'with such a

hard head, knew better than to make fetish.' 'Why, you fetish yourself,' observed Roölaï. 'I!' exclaimed Carlos with astonishment. 'Yes,' added the man, 'with that bag and book round your neck.' Carlos smiled, and said, 'No, Roölaï, that book teaches me to pray to the great and only true God.' 'Will it teach me?' asked the African. 'I will teach you from it,' answered Carlos, eagerly; and before they slept that night he had begun his lesson of love. Wondo begged to be included in the instruction, and the careless Nando also; but he fell asleep in the midst of the lecture. At length the whole party lay down to rest; but Carlos, although fatigued, was very long before he could compose himself. He thought of the awful responsibility of the task which he, not an ordained messenger, had incurred; and how earnestly did he wish that he had profited more by the blessed words which he had so often heard in the land of his adoption! But he silently lifted up his heart to an all-seeing Judge, who would appreciate his endeavours, and asked for assistance, trusting that, even through his humble means, the word of God might find its way to the hearts of these children of the wilderness; and that the wretched, debasing religion, or rather superstition, of the fetish might be abolished. He at length fell asleep with a prayer upon his lips. Ample were his future opportunities, and the impression which he made exceeded his best wishes. But the greater his success, the more did he feel his own deficiencies; and he determined, should he ever return to England, to try and induce some pious men to go among these attentive, well-disposed natives, who would more effectually enlighten them, and bring to maturity the seed which he endeavoured to sow.   Example works wonders with untutored minds; and when his sable friends saw the serious and heartfelt devotion of the two wanderers, they involuntarily partook of the feeling, and always, after this period, gladly joined them in prayer.

The next morning the hunters started on their return, and as they wound through the forest they heard a plaintive cry. 'Where does that come from?' asked Antonio. 'Look up,' said Nando; and on the boughs above was a strange-looking animal, with long fore-legs, lazily dragging itself along upon its elbows, and stripping off the leaves by way of food.   As neither its skin nor its flesh was of any value, the party left it to its indolence; and Carlos imagined it to be a sloth.   Of monkeys, as they went along, they saw plenty; but they were too nimble to be easily caught, and peeped and chattered over their heads out of reach, and pelted them with small branches, or pieces of bark.   No sooner, however, did the hunters stop and make a show of spearing them, than they all rushed further up the tree, screaming with all their might.   There appeared to be several sorts; and one little lion monkey fell, and was stunned, so that Antonio easily secured him, and took him home inside his jacket as a present for Wondo's children, with whom he was a great favourite.   The travellers were surprised to see so many different colours among the animals,—black, yellow, grey, and various shades of brown were there; and one species especially attracted their attention, which had red hair, and a bright blue face, and which, in almost all instances, was carrying two or three others on its back with the utmost gravity.

The party in its progress roused a wild boar, which at first tried to escape them; but, separating and forming a sort of circle, they hemmed him in, so that whichever way he turned, he met the spear of one of his enemies. Finding himself thus in their toils, he made a furious rush in order to get free; and in doing this he knocked over one of the slaves, and made for Wondo, threw him to the ground, and would have gored him perhaps to death had not Carlos and Antonio appeared and made a diversion in his favour. The enraged animal paused for an instant, and then rushed at them; but standing firmly with their spears ready, he was pierced to the heart. Wondo warmly thanked them for his rescue. The four legs of the beast were then tied together, and he was slung upon a pole, and carried between two men. The heat now became intense, and they rested for a time. When about to start again, Roölaï exclaimed, 'Stay! I hear that which will show us something better than boar's flesh.' So saying, he led them to the spot, where a bird like a cuckoo, but with a conical beak and forked tail, was sitting on a bough, and, to all appearance, asking them to follow him; for as soon as they drew near, he flew slowly away, and again waited for them. He repeated this artifice several times, till at length he stopped and ceased to cry. 'It must be hereabouts,' said Roölaï, and looking round, saw a large old tree, in a hollow of which was an immense bees' nest, full of the most delicious wild honey. Fortunately for them, it was deserted, probably because the hole would not contain any more; and the hunters took peaceable possession of the treasure, filling their empty gourds and bowls with it. 'We sell plenty of wax to the ships,' said

Wondo ; 'and this honey is very good to eat.' 'Do
not these birds get stung sometimes?' asked Antonio,
as Nando left a portion of the spoil on a tree for their
feathered guide. 'They can only be stung about the
eyes,' was the answer, 'their skins are so thick ; but
they sometimes are driven almost mad when the bees
fasten on them there.'

Thus, with their honey and wax, their skins, their
wild boar, their monkey, their parrots, their capsicums,
their large limes, their coffee, a quantity of gum copal,
and various fruits, etc., they regained the town ; and
no sooner were they in sight, than the wives and children of the respective parties ran to meet them with
joyous shouts, relieved them of their burthens, and
heralded them triumphantly into Naängo. The next
morning they resumed their more peaceful occupations,
and remained quiet for several days ; then Wondo said
to his friends, 'You sit too much, I want you to play
at ball with us ; but we cannot find our balls, so come
with us and help us to make some.' The white men
instantly complied, and took the way to another part
of the forest, Wondo observing, as they went along, that
he and Nando had been shaving themselves, in order
to be ready. 'Shaving yourselves!' inquiringly ejacu-
lated Antonio, who did not see any diminution of
hair upon their heads. 'You shall see,' said the
Africans, with a smile. They walked on till they came
to a large tree, with thick, dark, leathery, and shining
leaves. Going up to it, Wondo and Nando each made
an incision in the bark, and taking off their jackets,
and giving their knives to their friends, exclaimed,
'Now, quick! quick! before it gets hard! spread it
all over our breasts and arms.' Highly amused, the

Europeans obeyed, and with their broad, flat instruments, plastered the cream-coloured juice over the
bodies of the black men; then, when this coating was
sufficiently hard, they took it off, rolling it into the
shape of balls as they went on. Now and then the
Africans winced, as a stray hair, which had escaped
the razor, was dragged out, and the utility of the
shaving operation was thus made manifest. 'This
is caoutchouc,' said Carlos; 'I wonder you do not
make water-bottles of it, boots, anything you please.
You can spread it over your bowls, your legs, in short,
whatever you choose; it will take their shape as it
dries; and thus you can have all sorts of vessels and
coverings, which will not admit, or which will hold
water; they can be carried to the bush, and never
broken.' Clapping their hands with delight at the
suggestion, the natives exclaimed, 'We never thought
of that; let us come to-morrow without telling any
one, and then go back and surprise all the people of
Naängo.'

That evening, as the caoutchouc collectors returned
home, Carlos asked why a house which they passed
had been shut up so long. 'Because,' replied Wondo,
'although we bury our dead two or three days after
death, we close our houses for seven; but I do not
know why.'

The game at foot-ball was played; and the next
morning the same party started early for the bush,
with slaves carrying an ample stock of provisions, and
moulds for the utensils which they intended to make.
They chose their trees, procured a flow of juice, covered
their models with it, and at the time of taking their
repast, and just before the great heat of the day, they

covered their legs, and patiently sat on the ground till the substance had taken its form; then, when sufficiently hard, they dragged it off, though not without difficulty and much laughing. Each, however, had his pair of boots; and Antonio suggested that the Queen ought to be asked to the bush, in order to submit to the same operation, and obtain the same treasure. Wondo and Nando were enchanted, and enjoyed the fun of appearing before their townsmen in these mysterious coverings, and with these novel utensils. They presented themselves at Roölaï's door, and enjoyed his comments; but he was much too great a friend to be kept long in ignorance of the contrivance, and the next day they aided him in procuring these new conveniences.

On returning from the bush, the party saw one of the Governor's slaves enjoying himself exceedingly with a vessel which had contained the honey. He was cleaning it out with a lime which he afterwards sucked; and when the Europeans laughed, Nando exclaimed, 'You do not know how good it is;' and jumping forwards, took the calabash out of the man's hand, and presenting a fresh lime to Carlos, asked him to taste. The mixture of sweet and sour was delicious; and after Carlos had taken a little of it, he gave it back to the slave to finish. The man seemed astonished, and would have refused it; but Carlos insisted on his receiving back that which had been taken from him. Nando looked thoughtful for almost the first time in his life, because it was the first time he had ever witnessed any consideration shown to a slave in little things. Carlos observed him, dived into his thoughts, and hailed them as a dawning of better feelings. Such trifles as these, of frequent occurrence, and the increase of comfort which those immediately around him derived from his advice and instruction, did an infinity of good, and had their bearing upon his more important labours. They began to listen to him as to a being of a higher nature than themselves—to believe that he was right in all things, because they found him to be right in a few. They loved both the white men—sported with both alike—shared their meals, their society, their labours with equal affection; but there was a feeling of respect and deference towards Carlos which they could not themselves define or understand. It was the power of education which thus told upon them; the spell which a superior and well-informed mind exerts over its inferiors, even though the influence may be unfelt by itself.

CHAPTER XI.

ON quitting the open space where they had one evening been playing at ball, the white men observed two young mulattoes in European clothes. 'These are Frenchmen,' observed Wondo. 'Where do they come from?' asked Carlos. 'From the French towns down the river,' was the reply. They saluted the white men with great politeness, and finding that they spoke French, tried to elicit the history of their appearance in Naängo, and the object of their visit. Having nothing to conceal, the travellers told all their adventures, and proceeded with them to the Governor's, where, after conversing for some time, the Frenchmen invited them to visit their settlements; said they themselves had been sent to France for education, lamented their absence from that country, added that they detested their own, and would give the world to go back to their fathers' land. When they took leave they went to the King's house, where they passed the night, and were gone before others had risen the next morning. 'Shall we go and see them, Wondo?' said Carlos. Wondo's countenance changed. 'What is the matter?' continued Carlos. 'If you go to see them,' said Wondo, 'you will never come back here; everything there like English; you will never live with black men again.' Carlos at once perceived the jealousy and susceptibility

of the negro character, of which he had had no suspicion, and taking Wondo's hand, instantly assured him
that he would not go, and that he was not so ungrateful
as to wish to leave them till he could sail in an English
ship. The tears started into the black man's eyes, and
he was satisfied.

As the Europeans were now very expert with their
bows and arrows, and also with their javelins, it was
proposed that they should go with their friends to the
other side of the river, and try to kill a buffalo. 'The
hump on the back,' said Wondo, 'is the best part, and
reckoned so good, that when we get it, we are obliged
to give some of it to the King. Two canoes full started
down that creek which the Europeans were never weary
of admiring, and had not proceeded far, when the foremost canoe, which contained Roölaï, Nando, and their
attendants, suddenly stopped close under the right-
hand bank, and motioned to the second to do the
same. The men in her complied, without knowing
why; but the cause was soon explained when they saw
a large black head above the water, fast approaching
them. There was no mistaking the squareness of its
shape, and Wondo exclaimed, 'That's what you call a
hippopotamus; look at his little eyes and ears, and
his big teeth : we must try to shoot him if Roölaï should
miss him; he often upsets the canoes in the creek.'
Roölaï and Nando each fired at him, but their arrows
struck him only in the body; he dived, but came up
again at a short distance from the second canoe. Wondo and Carlos let fly their arrows. 'Well done, Lacy,'
cried Antonio, 'you have hit him in the mouth.' The
hippopotamus disappeared, and lay at the bottom of
the water, but his blood tinged the liquid. 'How shall

we dislodge him?' asked Carlos. 'We must wait patiently,' answered Wondo, 'he cannot long remain below; but if we disturb him now, he will be in a rage and upset us, for nothing can then resist his fury. In a short time the wounded animal rose, and made directly for his enemies, but he was soon despatched by their lances. 'What shall we do with him?' said Nando, who, with the others, had now joined those behind; 'if we drag him ashore and leave him, the hyænas will eat him; if we keep him in the water, the fishes will do the same; and it will stop us too long to take him up to the town ourselves.' 'We are just under the town,' observed Roölaï; 'if I blow my horn it will be heard, and my people will come down.' A small elephant's tusk hung round his neck, and putting it to his mouth, the hunter blew a loud and well-known blast; and in a very little while some of his followers rushed down to the water's edge, and took possession of the huge carcase. Leaving it to their care, the hunters then resumed their way, and proceeded to the opposite bank of the river; no slight task, considering that it was fifteen miles broad.

After landing, the Naängo party then bent their steps to a spot which they knew to be frequented by buffaloes; the ground there was much trodden, and it was evidently the path followed by these animals when they came to the river to drink. There were several trees close by, which the hunters mounted, and there chattered and refreshed themselves with the food and drink which they had brought with them. 'No noise now,' said Roölaï after some time, and pointing to a little distance, where they saw a dark moving mass fast approaching them, and descending from a rising ground. 'All make ready to let fly your arrows,' he continued; but turning to the Europeans, he cautioned them to let the whole herd pass, and then to shoot the last, 'for,' said he, 'if you shoot the first, the whole herd will attack us; if you shoot one in the middle, those before will go on, and those behind will rush at us; but if you shoot the last, all the rest will go on.' 'They are very small,' said Carlos. 'But very fierce,' returned Wondo. The marksmen waited till nearly all the buffaloes were in the water, then shot their arrows into the hindmost. It immediately turned to face its antagonists; but not seeing them, stared wildly, and then rushed bellowing among it companions. They were alarmed, tossed up their tails, turned round, and immediately scampered across the plain. The wounded buffalo tried to follow them; but faint from loss of blood, the poor beast fell, and another shower of arrows appeared to despatch it. One of the slaves then descended, and went up to the prostrate animal, which, collecting all its remaining force, sprang up again. The man took refuge behind a tree; the buffalo pursued him; each ran round and round, the horns coming so near as occasionally to graze the man; but Roölaï stealthily got down from his hiding-place, stuck his knife into the nape of the beast's neck, and it fell instantly. The carcase was soon stripped of its skin and cut into pieces; the entrails and parts which were not eaten were left for the vultures, and the rest put into the canoes.

·The whole party embarked, and as they kept side by side, the natives sang in chorus. They paused, and then the two Europeans began one of the Italian songs which Antonio had taught to his companion, and in which he himself took the second. It so happened

that they had never done this since they had been at
Naängo, although they had often amused themselves
in this manner after they had been abandoned in the
Bight, and had beguiled many a weary hour by making an exchange of Spanish, English, French, and
Italian songs. The black men, who had never before
heard a harmonized air, were enraptured, stopped the
paddles, and suffered their canoes to float for a time;
and when it was finished, exclaimed, 'More, more!'
The Europeans complied, and again and again they
were asked to continue, the Africans behaving just as
children do to those who tell them stories; but as he
concluded a stanza, Carlos pointed to a small white sail,
which, glittering in the moonlight, was ascending the
stream. All eyes were turned towards it, and several
voices at once exclaimed, 'Gaston!' A look of intelligence passed between the three chiefs, and Nando
said, 'I was afraid he would soon be here.' The others
merely ordered their men to pull hard, and they shortly
entered the creek. 'Perhaps he is going past,' observed
Nando. 'I hope so,' returned Wondo, apparently relieved by the idea; but this hope did not last long, for
when they stopped at the landing-place, a gallant little
pinnace was not far behind. Roölaï waited while the
four other friends proceeded to the town, the white
men not failing to remark how suddenly the spirits of
Wondo had become depressed.

Tired with their expedition, Carlos and Antonio early
sought their beds; but they had not been long asleep,
when they were awoke by the most violent bursts of
thunder. The night having been so insufferably hot,
they had left their window, or rather shutter, open, and
presently a vivid flash of lightning illumined everything

in their apartment. It was immediately succeeded by
the loudest clap of thunder they had ever heard, and
they involuntarily started from their beds. They, however, retreated when they saw the lightning play along
the iron bars on the floor; and not till there was a
slight cessation, did Antonio venture to get up and
shut the shutter. He rushed into his bed even more
quickly than he had left it; and when Carlos asked
him what was the matter, he said, ' Look out and see.'
Carlos peeped out his head, and, by the light of the
palm-oil lamp which they always burnt, saw an immense
number of rats. ' What a commotion !' he exclaimed;
' see how they are running up and down the bamboos,
and in the thatch; here's a rascal scrambling up my
curtain; we had better act on the defensive.' So
saying, he sat up in his bed with one of his leathern
sandals in his hand, and Antonio followed his example.
With these they knocked off all intruders, and as the
storm subsided the rats became less and less agitated;
all were again quiet, and the white men finished their
slumbers in peace.

The next morning, when the Europeans entered the
sitting-room, they were surprised at finding a stranger
there to share their meal. Wondo still looked unhappy, and evidently watched the new guest narrowly.
The Governor was embarrassed, and even Nando was
not himself. The man was tall, slight, and remarkably
elegant in his proportions and movements; his complexion was dark and extremely sallow, but his features
were regular and finely cut. A mustachio covered his
upper lip; and his overhanging, dark brow shaded a
restless eye, which suffered nothing to escape his observation. His bow to the Europeans was graceful and

unembarrassed. He asked if they spoke Portuguese, and
Antonio answered in the affirmative. 'French?' continued he; to which both answered, 'Yes.' 'Spanish?'
he inquired; each nodded assent. 'And of course
you understand the natives around you?' was his final
interrogation; to which Carlos replied, 'Certainly.'
He then carried on a general conversation, and made
himself very agreeable, giving news of the French settlements below, to the natives of Naängo. He was
dressed in a shirt and trousers of the whitest linen,
and a jacket of chintz. Many rows of gold chains of
exquisite workmanship hung round his neck, and rings
were in his ears and on his fingers. His hat was large
and made of grass, and his feet were protected by
yellow morocco slippers. After breakfast, he went
away and took up his abode with the King, only coming occasionally to the Governor's. 'Who is he?' said
Carlos to Wondo. 'His name is Gaston,' replied the
latter; 'I think his father was a Portuguese; and on
the river he is called Yellow Gaston.' 'But what does
he do here?' inquired Carlos. 'No good!' was the
answer; 'but he trades, and I do not like to talk
about him.'

Two or three days passed very quietly. Carlos sat
over his carving, and Antonio at his tailor's work,
interspersing their occupations with the songs which
Roölaï came to beg of them, and which the whole
town would sometimes assemble round the Governor's
house to hear. There was, however, a dejection
about Wondo for which they could not account; and
when they inquired of him the cause, he constantly
replied 'Nothing,' and changed the subject. One
night, after retiring to their own room, Antonio said,

'I very much wish to finish this jacket before morning, for it is my own, and I do not like to appear shabby before that fellow Gaston. I tore that I have so terribly when we killed the hippopotamus, that it will never look well again. Will you help me, Lacy?' Carlos was most willing; and as they worked by lamp-light, an unusual sound met their ear. No word was spoken, but there was the tramping of many feet, with now and then the cracking of a whip. They paused to listen. 'What can that be?' exclaimed Antonio. 'You have seen those buildings behind the King's house,' said Carlos; 'I suspect that what we now hear, will, in a few minutes, fill them. This must be the slave Kaffle, which I am sure has been expected for some days, and that Yellow Gaston is concerned in the business.' On the ensuing morning, Carlos mentioned his suspicions to Wondo, who confirmed them, and said, 'that this man was one of the principal agents for slaves up the river, in each of its branches; that he sailed from place to place in his little pinnace, and he was now there to see if the coasts were clear of English cruisers; for there was a large ship expected, and he had already sent to her to say that she might approach in safety. Accordingly, she will be up tomorrow, or next day,' continued he, 'go first to Kaylee for the slaves assembled there, and then will lie-to off our creek.' 'Where does this man live?' asked Carlos. 'In one of the islands outside,' replied Wondo; 'but he has several homes, and wives and slaves of his own at each.'

That same evening Gaston called at the Governor's, and after some unusually friendly conversation, asked the Europeans if they did not find the weather very close and hot; and on their replying 'Yes,' he offered them his pinnace for a sail on the river, which, he said, would be cooler. They were about to reply, when they caught sight of Wondo, as he stood behind Gaston's chair, making signs to them to refuse. Carlos, therefore, politely thanked the Portuguese, but rejected the proposal, on the plea that he always found the air on the water below much more oppressive than that of the hill on which the town stood. A momentary expression of anger passed over the features of Gaston; but he recovered himself instantly, rose, wished them good morning, and went out. When the Governor had seen him enter his brother's house, he said in a low voice to the Europeans, 'Do not trust that man in anything,' and then suddenly began to talk of something else.

Carlos and Antonio asked to see the slaves; and taking advantage of Gaston's temporary absence, they went to the barracoons, and all that they had ever heard or read of, was only too sadly verified by the wretched condition of the unhappy creatures before them. 'One poor girl died last night,' said Wondo, ' and I have just bought another, who was chained to her; for perhaps they would not think of releasing her from the dead body till it was her turn to be shipped. All these have been chosen out of a lot by Gaston.' 'And what becomes of those whom he does not choose to have?' asked Carlos. 'Sometimes they are killed,' was the answer; 'sometimes they are let loose without food or shelter, and then they mostly starve. We have had them wander into this town, and drop down dead in the streets from weak-

ness ; sometimes the wild beasts eat them, and you
know what the Kaylees and some other people do
with them. But I mean this new girl to wait on my
wife Ahnda.'

In the course of the day the poor slave was installed in her new duties, in performing which she accidentally entered the room where the white men were
sitting. The moment she saw them she screamed,
and hid her eyes with her hands. 'She is frightened
at us,' said Carlos. 'I will cure her of that,' exclaimed Antonio ; 'at the second look she will think
me charming ;' and going up to her, he pulled her
hands down, and turned her face round to him,
saying, 'Look at me, my dear.' The poor girl again
screamed, and, fainting with terror, fell on the ground.
She was carried out of the room in strong fits, and
continued very ill the whole of that day. On the
next, when Antonio inquired how she was, and
expressed his sorrow for what had happened, Wondo
told them that she was better, but that she believed
she had seen evil spirits ; 'for,' said he, 'many people
here think that the devil is white. But,' added he,
'I want you to look at the ship in the river. She
arrived during the night, and Gaston will not be here
again for a day or two ; as soon as the sun is beginning to go down, we will start and look at her, and
row round her in the canoe.'

It was late when the two Europeans, Wondo and
Nando, went down the creek ; but before they had
reached the vessel, the moon had risen in the greatest
splendour. By her light, therefore, they saw one of
the most beautiful ships they had ever beheld ; which,
as sailors, they could well appreciate, and never be

N

tired of admiring. She was long and sharp in her hull, and in every respect formed for speed; her very planks seemed to be pliant, and yield to the pressure of the water; and she gave the idea that she could skim on the surface of the deep, and never sink below; her masts were long, and leaned a little back, or, to use the nautical term, were a little rakish, and were evidently capable of carrying a crowd of small sails aloft, to catch the light breezes. She was painted white, with a pale green streak; and they could plainly descry a long brass gun on the after-deck, mounted on a swivel, which would rake any antagonist from stem to stern. She was capable of holding at least three hundred slaves, and probably many more could be crammed into her. The friends remained a long time in the neighbourhood of the ship, looking at her in every point of view, conversing with the sailors on board in Spanish and Portuguese; but some of these men spoke each of these languages with a foreign accent, showing that they were not natives of either. 'What colours does she hoist?' asked Carlos. 'All,' replied Wondo, 'according to the moment; if she sees an English vessel at a distance, she hangs out the jack; if an American, she puts up the stars, and so on.'

The night was advanced before they could tear themselves away from the beautiful sight; and the moon had begun to decline, when Carlos, looking into the country on the other side, saw a pale yellow light far off, and which seemed to extend over a wide surface. On asking what it was, Wondo replied, 'That is a mountain which always shines, and, as you see is visible a great way off.' 'Were you ever there?'

inquired Antonio. 'No,' answered Wondo, 'it is a great fetish among the people who live there; and they will not let any stranger go near it. An uncle of mine was determined to find out all about it, and contrived to reach the place, and even to bring away some of the stones, which made a light in his hand; but the people found him out, and he was obliged to run very hard in order to make his escape, and he dropped the stones. But now we are again in the creek, sing to us.' The Europeans complied, and continued their melodious notes till they reached the landing-place.

Gaston returned; the slaves were shipped, and he again disappeared. But about two nights after they had seen him for the last time, while the white men were sleeping in their beds, they were awakened by a hasty knocking at the door. On inquiring who was there, Wondo, in a low voice, begged to be let in. They rose hastily and opened the door, which had a wooden lock both inside and out. He appeared to be much agitated, and at first could scarcely speak. Carlos begged of him to wait a little and compose himself; but the good creature shook his head, and said, 'There is no time to wait. I could bear to see you go to your own country, although I love you so much, but I cannot bear to see you go away to the bush; and yet you must go, or you will be murdered. We have no time to lose: I will walk a little way with you; but you must be quick and pack up all you have. Take everything—spears, bows and arrows,—you will want them; make up your knapsacks while I get some provisions for you.' He took the bags, which the poor wanderers had already used so often, and went away;

but to all their endeavours to obtain an explanation, they only received for answer, 'Not now, I will tell you all in the bush, but you must get out of the way of Gaston.'

Astonished and bewildered as they were, in half an hour all their wordly goods were on their shoulders, and, spears in hand, they waited for their friend. When he appeared with well-filled bags, Carlos said, 'I cannot leave your good father, and my friends, without some remembrance of them; and I have but little to give;' then taking three sovereigns out of the bag which hung round his neck, he begged of Wondo to give one to the Governor, another to Nando, and the third to Roölaï, requesting them to bore a hole in them, and wear them round their necks, in remembrance of those white men to whom they had shown so much kindness.

Besides the provisions, Wondo supplied them with a stock of arrows in deer-skin quivers, a couple of the large country knives, and two buffalo skins for them to sleep upon. Making signs for them to be as quiet as possible, he led them out at the back of the house; and taking a circuit outside the town, they stole silently into the forest. Feeling that there was some peril in their situation, the Europeans followed their guide without speaking, except now and then whispering to each other some caution to avoid any obstacle which might be in their path. At the end of two hours Wondo stopped, saying, 'I can go no further with you; as I must be back before day, or I shall be missed. Sit down for a few minutes on this old tree, and I will tell you everything. Those two Frenchmen came on purpose to find out who you were, and see

if you would trade in slaves, meaning to persuade you
to join them. Finding that this was not likely, and not
at all believing your story of having been left on the
shore, they were quite afraid you should know all about
them, for they sell a great many slaves themselves;
and they thought you were two spies, sent from the
English war-ships to find out all you could, and then
to tell the English where to come and find the slave-
traders. When Gaston came here to wait for the
slaves, he watched you himself, and set people to
watch you; and he asked you to go in his pinnace,
only that he might carry you away. He is a very bad
man; and when the crew of that English ship, which
I told you of, was murdered, he set the people on to
do it. The fever had killed a great many, so it was easy
to take the ship; he did not appear himself, but every-
body knows that he was at the bottom of the whole,
and had the greatest part of the plunder. When another
ship came here from London, and most of her men
were in the bush getting wood, and others were sick, he
brought down the Kaylees to murder them, and rob the
ship. He would have succeeded, had not some of our
people found it out, and fought along with the English,
and beat the Kaylees. I knew that some mischief would
follow when he came, and I was ashamed that you should
see the slaves. One of the King's wives is sister to my
wife, Ahnda; and she overheard Gaston settling with
the King's head wife that you must be killed, or you
would bring the war-ships here to blow up the town.
He said it must be by some trick, for fear my father,
I, Roölaï, Nando, and many here, who love you so
much, should find it out and be revenged upon him.
The woman then said she would speak to the fetish man

about it; and you know that he can do anything
secretly.   Ahnda's sister came and told all to her,
and she told me; but I must not seem to know it,
for if Gaston should think that I have saved you, he
will do me some mischief.   I must go back before
any one can see me.   Here are two little cups made
of rhinoceros horn, one for each of you · look at that
bright part when it is dry, and if you put poison in
them, that will turn black directly; so pour all you
are going to drink in strange countries into these
cups.   In the bags is all the food which I have been
able to get for you in a moment; of water there is
plenty in the bush; and you have arrows, spears, and
knives for hunting.   Follow the path which we took
before, but do not stay long at the huts, for fear the
fetish man should catch you, for he goes and sends
very far.   When you leave them, let it be in the
morning, and then go from the sun, keeping him a
little to your right; march on, and when you have
walked five days and nights, only sleeping when it is
very hot, turn still more to your left hand, and in one
more day you will come to some very good people.
They know me, and if you show them this horn,'
giving Carlos the small elephant's tusk which he
always used for signals when hunting, 'they will know
that you come from me.   They will lead you to the
big water, and put you into an English ship before
the rains come, for they will soon be here; and if
not, they will take care of you till they are over.   You
have taught me to know God, and you must ask Him
to bless me.   If you had gone away properly, I would
have asked you to take one of my sons with you to
learn everything in your country.   I will not forget

all you have told me. I will never trade in slaves,—
my uncle is made bad by that wicked wife.' Here
poor Wondo, who had been speaking in broken sentences, could not continue; and Carlos, who had not
been wearing his watch at Naängo, but put it on when
he started, took off his silver guard, and throwing it
over his friend's neck, bade him wear it in remembrance of him and Antonio. Actually sobbing with
grief, Wondo knelt and asked Carlos to bless him;
then suddenly starting up, he embraced both and tore
himself away. At a few yards' distance he stopped
to take a last look, waved his hand towards the path
which they were to pursue through the forest, and the
friends parted for ever.

CHAPTER XII.

LONG did the wanderers walk on in silence, for both were too sad to converse; at length Carlos threw himself down, exclaiming, 'I can go no further without rest or food; let us stop by this little river.   Antonio followed his example; and on opening their bags, they found not only an ample stock of provisions for some days, but india-rubber bottles, and several other things which their kind friend had thought would be of service, not even forgetting a pair of scissors wherewith to cut their hair.   After refreshing himself, Carlos said, 'Here we are once more without shelter in the wilderness; but do not be cast down, dear Antonio,' continued he, seeing his companion's miserable look; 'we are better off than we were before, for we have more means of defence with us; we are more expert in using those means; we know much better how to manage about provisions; we are better acquainted with the natural productions around us; we are more used to walking; and altogether know better how to provide for our safety and comfort, than when we were first deserted; so, as there is now light enough, let us read a prayer, seek the blessing of God, and then bravely set forward for the huts.'

At the huts they arrived without disaster, and there

they rested one whole night, in order to be more fit for their five days' march. 'I should like to stay here longer,' said Antonio; 'but I suppose we are not quite safe yet, for Wondo told us to be sure not to stay.' 'No,' replied Carlos, 'we cannot tell how far the fetish man's power reaches; for, after all I have heard of these men, I should say that the system pursued by them, in its secret influence, and unfailing vengeance, must resemble that of the Inquisition of our countries; but, before we go, I should like to leave some token for Wondo, which may convince him that we have come thus far without disaster.' Antonio suggested a lock of hair; therefore each cutting off one of his curls, tied it to the rafters of the hut in a conspicuous situation, in the almost certain hope that the hunter would see it and understand the sign.

Early in the morning the travellers collected their baggage, and sorrowfully left the last traces which remained of their excellent friends at Naängo; for the path which had been pointed out to them avoided both the wild beast pits and the clearings of wood. They struck into the forest according to the given directions, taking their start at sunrise, and observing that they should now be only five or six days before they came to the friendly town of which Wondo had spoken. At the end of that time, however, they were still in the mazes of the forest; but this did not give them any concern, for they could not be expected to follow the course with as much precision as a native would have done; and as their provisions diminished, they caught or shot both jays and pigeons, and roasted them over the fire, which they now knew well how to kindle. The former were of a reddish brown, with

bright blue feathers ; and some of the pigeons were
of a soft, rich green, with blue eyes.   Carlos often
thought what beautiful presents they would make for
friends at home ; nor was Mrs. Lacy forgotten among
the number.   But so he had often thought of other
things, and sighed over the impossibility of conveying
them.

The moon had utterly failed them for some nights ;
but as long as the forest continued tolerably open,
they marched on.   It now, however, became so thick
that they dared not try to penetrate through it when
wrapped in such obscurity, for it is impossible to con-
ceive anything more intense than the darkness of the
forest.   'We must already have lost our way,' said
Carlos, 'for the trees get more and more entangled.'
At last they found that they could not take many
steps without using their hatchets, which they knew
could not be right, and they turned back for a short
space, and then started in another direction.   This in
time ended in the same manner, even by day the
sun was obscured by the foliage over their heads,
and they became perfectly bewildered.   They proposed to mount a tree which appeared to be higher
than the rest, and in their perplexity, try to see something like sky, and a land-mark by which they could
steer.   Antonio, acting upon the suggestion, was the
first to ascend ; but as he laid his hand on one of the
lower branches, he gave a sort of cry and slipped down
again with the utmost haste, looking as pale as possible.   'What's the matter?' asked Carlos.   'As I
grasped that bough,' answered Antonio, 'I felt something cold and soft under my fingers, which moved
as I touched it ; and I am convinced it was a serpent

of some kind : if it had been a boa, we should have seen it from below.' 'Most likely,' observed Carlos. 'Come along then this way, it seems to be a little clearer hereabouts.'

At night they proposed lighting a fire upon the ground and taking it in turns to sleep. 'Far from a serpent tree though,' exclaimed Antonio, 'for a gentleman like that will see us from above, and perhaps glide down to warm himself before we know what company we are in.' 'We must incur that risk,' returned Carlos, and many others, thought he to himself, for he had naturally more reflection than his friend, and was possessed of much more information, which he had never failed to elicit at every opportunity. He would not, however, give utterance to his forebodings, for fear of dispiriting his more careless companion.

They lighted their fire, and as they sat by it they heard a loud sighing through the trees. 'That is like the sighing of the wind through the rigging of a ship,' said Antonio. 'It is the sighing of the wind through the rigging of the forest,' returned Carlos, 'if I may be allowed the expression.' This was followed by loud wailings, which seemed to proceed from animals, mingled with the plaintive cries of birds, the occasional roars of wild beasts, the hissings of serpents, the cracking and crashing of fallen boughs, and the rustling of leaves. 'We are going to have a terrible storm,' said Carlos; 'at all risks we must try again and get into a tree. If we remain here, the wild beasts will destroy us, and the rain will put out our fire. We shall be drenched wherever we are, for these tornadoes are but the beginning of the rains ; however, we must endure what we cannot fly from. I will mount first, for I have not had the shock which you felt at touching the serpent.' So saying, he sprang up, and knocking on all sides with the handle of his hatchet, to frighten anything which might be there before him, he reached the branches of a tree which he had ascended, and desiring Antonio to hand up all their property on the top of their spears, and then follow aloft, they again settled themselves for the night. It was well that they did so, for the whole forest seemed to be alive with creatures which hid themselves by day; and Antonio, as the fire shed its gleams on all around, could not help exclaiming, 'This puts me in mind of the plagues which beset my patron saint.' The serpents crept for shelter under the beds of fallen leaves, or disappeared among the bushes, hissing as they went, and coiled themselves up as closely as possible; the smaller animals crept into holes; the monkeys huddled together on the neighbouring trees; the sloth, unable or unwilling to move, uttered loud cries of distress; the rhinoceros grunted loudly as he forced his way into the thickest part of the jungle; the panthers, leopards, and hyænas crouched down; the lion walked uneasily from place to place; and all in the common danger, seemed to forget to be at enmity. 'I hope,' said Carlos, 'that we have not chosen the highest tree, for if we have, it is very likely that it will be struck, and we and our roosting-place fall together;' and as he spoke, a vivid flash of lightning made every object as clear as if the light of day had penetrated, or even more so, for it pierced through the thickest foliage. 'The flashes lasted long enough,' observed Antonio, 'for me to have threaded a needle by them;' and in the midst of this appalling scene, Carlos could not help laughing at this allusion to his friend's late employment. As they looked down they thought they saw, by the continuous lightning, a little old man striving to mount the tree where they were. 'There is some one coming after us,' said Antonio, 'up the tree; shall we spear him?' 'No, No!' hastily uttered Carlos, 'suppose it should be a human being; let us use the handles of our spears, and not the blades.' They pushed the intruder down, and neither saw nor heard him again, for the rain began to fall in torrents, and completely blinded them to everything. It seemed as if all around them were enveloped by one broad sheet of water. They grasped each other tightly with one arm, and with the other embraced the nearest bough; for their shelter rocked to and fro with the wind. Giants of the forest, which had stood for ages in stately magnificence, were torn up by the roots; the travellers could not hear each other speak, they could not hear themselves, for the one mighty and rushing sound seemed to occupy the whole sense of hearing. At length the lightning fell upon a tree not far from them, and a large portion of it was separated from the rest, carrying with it fragments of its neighbours, and scattering their and its own denizens all around. Some were crushed by the fall, others crawled or fluttered away. The poor Europeans had not a dry thread about them, notwithstanding their buffalo skins; and, thoroughly chilled, sat shivering on their perch, but not daring to leave it till daylight came, even though the tempest gradually passed away, and all was still below. 'I suppose,' said Carlos, 'the storm which we had at Naängo was

the first of the approaching rains, and that we shall
now have many of them. Then the rains will be
incessant night and day. We shall never be able to
stand them, Antonio, without shelter.' 'I have been
thinking so all the time the wet has been penetrating
into my bones,' observed Antonio. 'If you would
not laugh, I would propose something.' 'I know what
you mean,' returned Carlos ; 'you want to build a hut,
and live in it till the rains are over. So far from laughing at it, I think it would be a capital plan ; but-not
exactly in this spot. We shall, I believe, have incessant
rain for about a month ; but as the tornadoes have
only just begun, we may have time to find a better
place, and get a weather-tight roof over our heads
before they come.'

This prospect, and a faint gleam of sunshine, imparted new energy to the travellers ; they dried their
sodden provisions, put on the dry clothes which the
skins of the knapsacks had protected, wiped their
weapons, and with thankful hearts were about to resume
their way, when Antonio, who had first descended,
burst into a laugh. 'Here is our little old man of last
night,' said he, 'drenched to the skin ; had I known
who it was, I should certainly have admitted him into
our party. Hold up your head,' he exclaimed ; and
taking the poor shivering creature's chin in his hand,
he held up its face. It looked meekly at him and they
found it to be a Chimpanzee, about three feet high,
very broad in proportion, and very much resembling
an ugly, withered old man. It had very little hair in
the front of its body, which gave it a more disgusting
appearance. They presented a piece of plantain to it,
which it ate with avidity, and then looked at them

with a vacant, stupefied air. They left it to its fate,
and had not proceeded many yards, when they heard
a rushing noise behind them, followed by a shrill cry ;
and turning round, they saw that a huge leopard had
sprung upon the unfortunate Chimpanzee, and was
tearing to it pieces. 'What a providential escape !'
said Carlos ; 'surely it is the will of God to save us
yet,' and the wanderers raised their voices together in
thanksgiving.

The object of the Europeans was now to find a proper
place in which to erect their temporary dwelling ; but
it was very difficult to combine all the advantages which
they desired in one spot. The vicinity of a stream
was indispensable ; but this brought with it the more
frequent presence of wild beasts : they thought, however, that these animals would not require to drink so
often in wet weather, and they could every morning fill
their water-bottles, and leave their ferocious neighbours
undisturbed possession of it all night. After two days'
search, they fixed on a place where the forest was
rather more open than usual, not far from a small
river, and which seemed to be peculiarly desirable from
having a number of large bamboos growing close to it,
and of which it was comparatively easy to construct
their dwelling. They first of all felled four lesser trees,
as nearly as possible placed at right angles with each
other ; and then cleared the space between, trying
with their spades, as well as they could, to eradicate
even the roots, in which they succeeded tolerably well,
for the soil was a fine vegetable mould. They then
cut grooves in the four stumps, and laid beams across
from one to the other, which rested in the grooves.
This formed the framework for their floor, which they

made first of bamboo, then of earth, well knocked down, and then a layer of split bamboos and earth, smoothed and stamped down with their feet. The walls consisted of bamboo stakes stuck into the ground, and fastened to the frame with a sort of cordage, which was easily made from the runners of the neighbouring trees, and which was so strong and yet so pliant, that Antonio did not even regret his cocoa-nut fibres. In making knots they were of course expert. 'Why have we no cocoa-nuts?' asked Antonio. 'Because I believe they never grow so far from the sea,' answered Carlos. 'Nor have we any dates,' continued Antonio, 'except those poor little yellow things which we cannot eat; do they want sea air?' 'I do not know,' replied Carlos; 'but I never heard of those delicious dates which we buy in Europe, as coming from anywhere·except the northern and eastern part of this continent.

Having completed their four walls, with a raised floor inside, the builders cut open a door-way, and two windows, each as small as would be consistent with convenience, in order to be more sheltered from the wet. They then proceeded to the roof, which was made of a sloping shape, and projected over the sides. It was constructed of bamboo rafters, and a layer of palm leaves to serve as thatch; all of which were strongly fastened on with cordage. This took them a whole week to finish; but they had slept in their dwelling from the first moment that the sides had been raised, and their feeling of security was so great, that they seemed to themselves to be out of the reach of all dangers. The storms now became more frequent; but with their india-rubber boots on, they were able to work diligently between them ; frequently, however, stopping for a minute to observe how beautiful everything looked the moment the sun came out. Then the insects again took wing, the birds shook their feathers and chirped, and the leaves of the trees sparkled as if they had been covered with precious stones. The want of a door was very evident ; but as they could not contrive any hinges, they made a screen of palm-leaves, which, when inside, they fastened with a strong bar of wood, and which they closed after them when they were out, by loops and pegs. As their floor was three feet from the ground, they constructed a rude ladder of bamboo, which they could remove at pleasure.

The next care of the travellers was to lay in a stock of provisions which would not require cooking ; for they knew that there would be many days when they could not get out, and weeks, perhaps, when they would not be able to light a fire, and they had not time to build a hut which might serve for a kitchen. The honey-guide[1] stood their great friend, and, thanks to him, they found a large quantity of honey, which they stored away in calabashes which grew near the river. This made them search for limes, which they also met with in abundant quantity, not by way of a treat, but to counteract the sweet food. Numbers of plantains and cassada roots were roasted, and stowed away in rude baskets of palm-leaves. Of sweet potatoes they had but a small stock, for they would require cooking. The kolla nuts were one resource, and also some sugar-canes, which they knew to be very nourishing. Of custard and pine-apples they found only a few, as the forest was so thick around them. Not far

[1] Cuculus Indicator.

O

from the river, however, they procured a quantity of corn, which they parched, and laid up in a large pile at one corner of their dwelling. The heap began to look enormous, but they resolved not to touch it, till they were unable to go out to get food elsewhere. They shot birds of various kinds, roasted them, and laid some of them by, so that, whenever they took to their hut for a permanency, they would have animal food for a week. Their old woollen dresses were now invaluable, for they did not feel so chilled when they got wet in them ; and, in fact, they had not been much worn, on account of the heat. The skins which Wondo had given them made excellent beds, and they gathered some of the pods of the silk-cotton tree, the contents of which they stuffed into the legs of their old linen trousers, and so contrived pillows. The common cotton they procured in quantities, and filled the interstices between the bamboo stakes with it, pushing it in with their knives till they made their walls perfectly impervious to rain and wind; while the projecting thatch protected their windows and door. They only dreaded one thing, which was, that, in falling, some tree might crush their dwelling and them together; but this they hoped to be spared, as they were at some distance from those huge but stately ornaments of the forest, which sometimes rear their lofty heads to a height of at least two hundred and 'fifty feet. Every day some little improvement suggested itself, such as pegs to hang their things upon, etc. etc. ; but their chief attention, when they were able to go out, was directed to the clearing of a space all round the hut, that no enemy might secretly lurk in their immediate vicinity. This, however, was

a difficult task, for every hour's rain induced fresh
plants to spring up; and the portion which they had
left bare at night, was frequently covered again by the
next morning. They cut some stakes with sharp
points, and made a sort of fence of them all round
their hut, placing one end firmly in the ground, and
making them cross each other, so that the points were
outwards, and fastened the whole together with cords,
which they hoped would keep away small quadrupeds
and monkeys; but they knew that they could not
make any defence against the larger inhabitants of the
forest.

At length the time came when they dared not go
to any distance from their abode, for fear of being
surprised by torrents of rain; they every morning, as
long as they were able, stowed away a quantity of
water in their bottles and calabashes; but when the
rain came in earnest, the solitary men were obliged to
keep several days entirely under shelter. They were,
however, not a little pleased to find how perfectly
they had secured themselves from the inclemency of
the elements. At every slight cessation they sallied
forth and went to the river. 'It is lucky,' said Antonio, 'that we made our house so far from it; for it
is now swollen into a perfect torrent, and has taken
portions of its banks along it. Do you see those
floating masses of soil and vegetable matter?' 'Yes,'
answered Carlos; 'and the fall of a large tree shows
us something else; look on the other side, at those
birds' nests. I am sure those fruits to which they
hang must be tamarinds; and the birds who have
built there, must be weavers. They are as secure
from the rain in their nests as we are in ours.' 'It

looks like one large nest,' remarked Antonio ; ' they have so entirely matted it together with interlaced grass and fibres.' ' Yes,' added Carlos ; ' and yet beneath that common roof, each has its separate abode. I could not find it in my heart, if we could get at them, to wring the necks of any of these pretty creatures and eat them, though I should like some of the tamarinds. But take care, Antonio, there is a funny little animal with a sharp head and long ears peeping out of that hole ; stand still, and we shall have it—there are bands round its body, and it must be an armadillo. It is as good eating as pork.' He speared it, and nearly at the same moment Antonio speared another small animal ; but Carlos' was the best prize, for that of Antonio smelt so strongly of civet, that he threw it into the torrent. They con- trived to make a fire and eat their armadillo.

By one clear day they profited much, for they also killed a porcupine and a young boar, who, like them- selves, ventured to peep out and feel the sun. They dried and smoked their flesh, and hung it to the rafters of their hut, to be eaten when they were again prisoners. This moment was near at hand ; and then all they could do was to procure water. The time passed heavily, and the constant wet was unconsciously beginning to take effect. At the least cessation they opened their door and admitted the sun ; but the ne- cessity for going to the river exposed them very often. ' It must be confessed,' said Antonio, ' that we ought to have made something to catch the rain-water, and so have had a supply close to us ; if we had but that and something to do, we might live here like princes. But what is the matter, Lacy ? How blue you look,

and how you shake !' 'I do not know,' answered
Carlos ; 'but I feel very ill. I have pains all over me
—my head is so heavy that I can scarcely hold it up ;
and I have a constant desire to yawn and stretch myself. I hope I am not going to have the fever ; if I
should, it is much in my favour to have been so long
in the country without an attack.' 'Lie down, my
dear fellow,' said Antonio ; 'cover yourself up with my
things,—all the clothes you can find ; how I wish I
could get something hot for you ! That ginger which
we dug up last night might make some tea ; but then
we have nothing to boil it in : none of our vessels
would stand the fire, even if I could light one. What
shall I do ?' 'Never mind,' rejoined Carlos, 'I dare
say it is only a fit of the ague, after getting wet so
often ;' but he said this more to cheer Antonio than
from conviction, for he had too often witnessed the
first symptoms of this terrible disorder to be mistaken
in them. Antonio was distracted ; and all he could
do was to sit and pray by his companion, and the only
nourishment which he cared to take was a little parched
corn. As to Carlos, he never tasted anything except
water, for which he asked incessantly. His friend
tried to soothe him when he raved about his benefactor, his beloved Henriquez, Sergeant Brown, his
schoolfellows, his companions in the vessel—all the
distressing scenes which there took place seemed to
rise vividly before him ; and he constantly entreated
Antonio to send away that man Gray, for he would
kill them both. Then starting up, he would seize
Antonio's arm, and try to pull him away from the
wretched Gaston. Then he transformed Antonio into
Gaston, and defied him. In his lucid intervals he was

totally unable to raise his head; but he looked imploringly in his friend's face as he sat beside him, and
seeing its woful expression, he would beg of him not
to be too anxious, for then he would be ill also; and
he would end by saying, 'Don't grieve, my dear
friend, I shall get over it.' At length even these words
became inarticulate, and the last expressions which
were audible from his lips, were, 'Take care of yourself, my dear Antonio, for my sake.' But Antonio felt
that the injunction was useless. No care could save
him from the malady; for during the two preceding
days he had scarcely been able to crawl about, and
feeling that his turn was come, he made all the preparations he could for his friend's comfort, in case he
should recover. He placed water, corn, and plantains
within his reach; the door was already secured with
the wooden bar; he felt that all was done that lay in
his power, and, creeping to his bed, he lay down, as
he thought, to die.

For how long a period the sufferers remained in a
state of stupor, could never be ascertained; but Carlos
was the first to wake from it. As he gradually returned
to consciousness, he, in a feeble voice, murmured, 'Antonio.' Again and again he called; all was dark and
silent, and he thought his friend was asleep. He composed himself; he awoke a second time, and his first
effort was to call once more for his companion. It
was daylight. No one answered; therefore he thought
that perhaps he was up and out; but the door was
closed within. Still he murmured the name again,
and still no answer was returned. He raised his head
for an instant, saw the motionless form of his friend,
and exclaiming, 'He is dead!' again sank insensible

upon his rude couch. He lay unconscious for some time, but the pulse of life became stronger and stronger, and he tried to raise himself. Turning round, he saw the food and water-bottle placed beside him, and viewing it as the last act of love on the part of his faithful friend, he sank back upon his pillow, and, sobbing like a child, in broken accents murmured, 'It is all over with us both, and I no longer wish to live.' Then recollecting his dear ones at home, he tried with his trembling hands to take a draught of water and some plantains. These seemed to revive him; and after another night he was better. This period was passed partly in prayer, partly in a dreamy state, through both of which the painful consciousness of Antonio's death pursued him. He felt that the worst was indeed come, for he had lost his sole earthly support,—the kind, the untiring, the affectionate Antonio, whose vivacity and hopefulness had cheered him when in misery, who had protected him in danger, and who had always generously given up all to his friend. His thousand good and endearing qualities rose before him with renewed strength; all his little acts of devoted friendship, all his candour, all his usefulness, crowded upon him; and, stung with agony, he hid his face from the light. Suddenly a whisper came as if from heaven, that Antonio had evinced a sincere piety and deep sense of revelation, and Carlos was comforted.

Youth quickly rallies; and the Spaniard gained strength enough to crawl to his friend. Oh, joy! he still breathed, perhaps he would recover. The bare possibility gave Carlos new strength; fervently did he pray that it might be so. By degrees he moved his bed and pillow close to that of Antonio, and with his eyes intently fixed upon the sufferer, watched for the moment when the stupor should end, either in death or in life. Darkness came, and then clasping the dear rough hand, he lay in anxious suspense. A slight tremor took place in it, towards morning the limbs actually moved. 'These are convulsions,' thought Carlos. 'It is not to be,—none survive convulsions in this horrible fever.' But morning again came, a slight murmur issued from the bloodless lips, and Antonio, opening his eyes, fixed them on Carlos. He could not speak, but a faint tinge came into his cheeks; they returned, however, to their livid hue, and again his eyes closed. Agonizing was it to watch the changes which ensued; life seemed to flicker; and ever at the moment when Carlos' heart whispered, 'he rallies,' all became dark again. The open jaw, the distressed countenance, and the laboured breathing took away all hope.

At last Carlos thought Antonio might be faint; and, to his surprise, he was able to get up, and crawling on his hands and knees to the corner where the limes lay, he cut some open with his knife, squeezed the pieces into a small calabash full of water, and with one of the wooden spoons moistened the lips of the patient, who seemed to swallow a few drops; he bathed his temples with the same juice, rubbed the palms of his hands with it, and breathed upon them, and these endeavours seemed to revive him. He felt his feet; they were cold; and he warmed them with his own body, in which, it was true, there was not much vitality, but still there was more warmth in him than in Antonio. At length, it pleased God to second his endeavours, and his friend permanently returned to consciousness.

The first moment it was possible for the invalids to

venture out, they sallied forth, supporting each other's tottering steps, and leaning on their spears by way of staff. They, of course, went to the river to procure fresh water, and then returned, overcome with fatigue. 'The greatest violence of the rains seems to be over,' said Carlos; 'but perhaps we have another month of them yet to come, and then they will pass off with tornadoes in the same manner as they came on. Between these, however, I think we may make a little progress.' 'We must take care,' observed Antonio, 'not to leave this excellent shelter too soon, for with this ague hanging about us, a severe wetting might be fatal.'

A long and dreary month was it with the Europeans, notwithstanding their gratitude and resignation, which they felt ought to make them cheerful. The ague still tormented them, and as soon as they gained a little strength seemed to pull them back again; and their pale, sallow faces and wasted limbs, told but too truly how nearly they had fallen victims to this deadly disease.

An unusually heavy storm, which lasted many hours, succeeded by severe attacks of their cruel disorder, kept the friends close prisoners for nearly a week, when the sun shone gloriously. Again did the birds reappear; a general brightness seemed to come upon all things, and opening their door, the travellers enjoyed the cheerful scene. 'What notes are those?' said Antonio. 'Do you hear them?' They both looked out. 'Can it be those Love-birds?' exclaimed Carlos. 'What are Love-birds?' asked Antonio. 'Those pretty little green parroquets,' answered Carlos, 'with yellow and orange heads and throats.' 'No,' rejoined Antonio, 'they are just over our heads, and the sound does not come from thence. Hark! there it is again;' and listening, they distinctly heard a cry resembling the syllables, 'Toohoo,' three times uttered in descending and perfect thirds. 'See, Lacy,' said Antonio, 'it comes from those other three green birds above upon that bough. 'Yes! yes! look! as one sounds the note, the next pushes it off till all are gone, and now they sit close together once more, and sing it all over again. I must go nearer to them,' and he accordingly went out. Suddenly, however, he returned, his face expressing alarm and astonishment, exclaiming, 'Do you know that we have neighbours?' 'Neighbours!' repeated Carlos with equal surprise, 'where?' 'At the back of our hut is another,' rejoined Antonio. 'I am sure it must have been built while we were ill, for it was not there when we came; it is not as large nor as good as ours, but I saw some one moving in it.' 'We must be very cautious observed Carlos; 'but we will go together and reconnoitre.' Accordingly the two went out at the same time, made a circuit, hid themselves behind the trunk of a tree, and watched, spear in hand, for the appearance of some natives. Presently a female was seen with her young one, which she held with one hand, while with the other she dexterously mounted to the top of her hut, where she sat, seemingly to enjoy the pleasure of nursing her infant in the open air. 'That must be a wild man, or rather wild woman of the woods,' exclaimed Antonio. 'I think it may be the Inghĕna,' observed Carlos, 'of which Wondo has frequently told me such stories. These animals imitate men and women as closely as possible, but are worse companions than they would be, for they are extremely

The Inghena. —*Page* 200.

fierce, and one blow of their paw will kill a man. They build a hut and then live on the roof, as you see that one does now; they carry things about on their shoulders till they drop with fatigue; and none of them have ever been taken alive, their strength is so great. There must be another not far off, for they live in pairs; and the best thing we can do is to retreat as soon as we can, pack up our things, and go; for they are very cunning and treacherous. You know we have already been thinking of our departure, and this must decide us.' 'I shall be sorry to leave this,' said Antonio, 'before the tornadoes are quite over, for you know that we are scarcely able to move when that troublesome ague comes upon us.' 'Yes,' resumed Carlos; 'but if we wait for that, the fogs will be here, and they are worse for health than rain. The air then is generally more full of unwholesome vapours, and they last for about six weeks. Few escape illness at that period; and even those Europeans who have been for years in the country, and pass through other months with impunity, cannot resist their influence.' 'I recollect having the ague in England,' rejoined Antonio, 'about four years back; but it was not like this. It came always at the same hour, with regular intervals; but this cheats us; is very irregular in the return of its fits, neither keeping hours nor days; sometimes it appears even twice a day, suddenly takes away all our strength, and gives us pains in all our joints, especially our knees.' 'Yes,' added Carlos, 'I feel sometimes as if I should think anybody were performing a good office if they were to put an end to my existence; and I am most abominably cross and ill-tempered.' 'I can match you there,' added Antonio;

'but as I cannot complain of you, so I hope I do not try you too much.' 'Not at all,' answered Carlos; 'but it is very hard work not to answer sharply when the fits are upon me. I would fain stay here till the fogs are passed, but these Inghēnas may some day take it into their heads to be spiteful; and if they were to mistake this hut for their own, our door would not make any stand against their enormous strength.' So conversing, the friends reached their own abode, and began immediately to make their preparations.

The Europeans saw nothing of the Inghēnas for two or three days, and their packets were nearly completed, when one morning they were startled by the most fearful yell which had ever saluted their ears. Seizing their spears, they rushed to the door, and barring it, prepared to act on the defensive. Carlos looked out at one of the windows, expecting to see a whole body of natives pouring down upon them; but the noise proceeded from the female Inghēna, whom they saw bleeding and holding her young one, which appeared to be also wounded, close to her with one paw, while with the other she dragged the dead body of a leopard after her. 'There has been a fight,' said Carlos, 'and the leopard has had the worst of it. I think, however, that the baby is dead; the poor thing looks so piteously at it, tries to make it sit up, but it cannot support itself, and yet it is quite old enough to do so, for I saw it walking about. Now she will carry it along with her, according to Wondo's account, till it drops in pieces from her arms; but she herself seems to have been terribly torn in the struggle.' Some time after, the male Inghēna came home, bearing a large log of wood upon his shoulders; and seeing the leopard on the ground, examined it all over, turned it backwards and forwards, took his young one, inspected it, tried to make it eat, returned it to its mother's arms, saw her wounds, and caressingly seemed to try and comfort her. At length he took the little one up again, and looked about him as if for some enemy. Suddenly, a new thought seemed to strike him, and he came fiercely towards the house of the Europeans, broke the door at one blow, twisted out the wooden bar, and stood before them grinning with rage. His huge teeth and his ferocious appearance were most appalling ; but the travellers, weak as they were, dauntlessly stood with firm foot and steady hand to receive their antagonist. Strength was given by excitement. The fierce beast rushed headlong towards them, and fell on the point of the spears. One of them reached his lungs ; he seized it, snapped the handle in two, but that effort was his last. ' We must be off now directly,' said Carlos ; ' his wife may come after him, and although wounded, may yet have strength to tear us to pieces.' ' Shall we let him lie here, or toss him out ? ' asked Antonio. ' Let him lie,' replied Carlos, ' for fear the sight of him should excite her fury ; but now we have pulled the spear-head out of him, which I am sure we cannot afford to lose, let us shoulder our knapsacks and start as speedily as possible.'

Although somewhat overcome by the scene which had just passed, the wanderers gathered together all that they could carry, and, once more houseless, pursued their way. Their object was to get off unperceived by the remaining enemy, and, fortunately, they succeeded in their object.

CHAPTER XIII.

THE last danger was perhaps the worst and most imminent which the Europeans had escaped; 'But,' said they, 'God is everywhere with us.' On they went till nightfall, and then came the difficulty where to stop, for to climb a tree in their enfeebled condition was impossible. 'I am weary almost to death,' said Carlos; 'at all events let us sit and eat something, and we may surely light a fire. I must put a new handle to my spear; so, while you kindle the wood, I will cut down a pole.' They mended the weapon, took some refreshment, and again started; but then, overcome with fatigue, they were obliged to rest a second time. They once more tried to move, feeling how imprudent it was to remain; but their wearied limbs refused to stir, and completely enfeebled, they forgot everything, fell back, and slept. Carlos awoke with a sensation of weight upon his breast which impeded his breathing; and a slight quivering convinced him that some live creature must have lain down upon him for the sake of warmth. What to do he could not tell: if he spoke, it would rouse the animal as well as Antonio, and perhaps then his friend might be its victim; for what it was, he could not possibly form any idea. So there he lay, without stirring hand or foot,

scarcely daring to breathe, and in an agony of suspense. How long this lasted he could not tell; but
to him it seemed an interminable period. He, however, congratulated himself that Antonio did not
awake; for he thought he might, by a sudden impulse,
imprudently distrub the creature, whatever it was, and
both might be lost. Day at length began to dawn,
and then he soon felt a movement in the load upon
him. What was his horror when, between him and
the light, a head gradually arose, which, by its flatness,
he knew to belong to a venomous serpent I ' In a
minute its fangs will be into me,' thought he; but
he still had the presence of mind to remain quiet,
and the reptile in a short time uncoiled itself, and
slunk into the neighbouring bushes. Rising immediately, Carlos hastily awakened Antonio, told him what
had happened, and said, 'Let us get away as fast as
we can from this horrid place, and do let us try to contrive some sort of a ladder, which we can throw on to
the bough of a tree, and so manage to get up for the
night; for we can never sleep again on the ground
while we are in the forest. If we are not strong
enough to throw it over some projection, we may lift
it up on our spears.' They accordingly rested the
greater part of the day, in order to twist the pliant
stems of creeping plants into a means of ascending a
tree where they wanted to stop for the night. They
speared some of the quadrupeds which crossed their
path, and gained new strength from animal food; but
their agues tormented them extremely.

After many uncomfortable days and nights, to their
great joy the forest began to grow a little less dense,
and a portion of warmth penetrating into their poor

P

chilled blood, gave them a thrill of comfort. 'If we were now to stand before our friends,' said Carlos, 'I wonder if they would know us. As to you, Antonio, your long beard hides your thin face; but I have nothing to set off mine. I feel many years older since we left Liverpool; and, as far as I can reckon, it is only one since we set out. Such a life as we have led, brings with it more age than the lapse of time would warrant. I, however, lost all reckoning when I was ill; have no conception which may be the Sabbath, or even what the month may be; but I am sure every day ought to be a Sabbath with us, in praise of God for our deliverance.' 'Why is it,' asked Antonio, 'that we heard and saw so little of wild beasts while we were in our last hut? On other occasions the forest seemed to be filled with them.' 'I believe,' replied Carlos, 'that they retire into caves and secret places during the rains, and that many of the smaller quadrupeds remain in a state resembling torpor during that season.' 'I think we were torpid enough,' observed Antonio; 'but this is one of my worst days, Lacy. I can go no further while the fit is upon me.' Carlos, seeing his miserable condition, made him sit down, and while reclining beside him, was attracted by some bright yellow fruit, hanging from a wide-spreading tree, with dark-green shining leaves. 'How extraordinary,' he exclaimed, 'that these fruits should have hung through the rains; for they must have been nearly ripe when they came on! I shall see if they are good for anything.' So saying, he pulled down one of the boughs; and, as he did so, a very ugly-looking lizard clung to it to save itself from falling. It was so very different from any he had seen, that he left the fruit in order to show it to Antonio. The latter said, 'I know what it is, for I saw one in Italy in a cage : it is a chameleon ; it lives upon air, and constantly changes its colour.' 'I do not believe that it feeds on air,' rejoined Carlos, 'but on the minute insects which hover about, and are invisible to us ; see, even here, how cleverly it darts its tongue out to catch them, and coils it up again. Let us put it on to one of our knapsacks, and see if it will become orange and black like them, and then on our white jackets. Look it gets darker or lighter, according to the shade of colour underneath it, but its own colour does not actually alter. What numbers of fables are accepted as true in the world, and yet realities are quite wonderful enough! Now for the fruit,' continued he, and he procured a capful. 'Taste one, Antonio,' and he pulled one open for him. It had the most exquisite, rose-coloured pulp within, in which were many small yellow seeds. 'It tastes just like strawberries,' exclaimed Antonio. 'Then I am sure they are guavas,' said Carlos, 'and we must get plenty of them, for they are very wholesome.'

The ague fit over, the travellers again pushed forward, encouraged by seeing several clear spaces, for they were beginning to get weary of the confined view, and looked forward with much satisfaction to a more extended prospect. As usual in such parts, parasitical plants of new and bizarre forms seemed to live on every tree ; large clusters of golden-coloured blossoms waved about, and contrasted their rich warm tints with enormous branches of lilac or white flowers. There appeared some of a pale green, spotted with brown, having hairy long tails ; others sent forth long slender stalks, at the end of which floated vegetable butterflies. In several instances the lichens were most extraordinary, and equally beautiful, entirely clothing all the dead branches of the trees ; and one in particular seemed to be most abundant; it resembled a multitude of little clubs of every graduated shade of exquisite rose-colour. 'If we could but draw some of these,' said Carlos, 'to show to people at home, for they never will believe what we tell them ; but if I live to be a hundred years old, I shall never forget either these colours or forms.'

The fruits as well as the flowers augmented in number. They feasted on pine-apples, sparingly however, for they are said to be prejudicial ; but they were small, and of the red sort, not particularly fine in flavour. Aromatic creepers sent forth their delicious odours ; white and yellow Hibisci spread out their broad petals and splendid colours ; and all nature seemed, under the renewed sunshine, to be singing a hymn in praise of her Creator.

At length the Europeans emerged from the forest, and the most charming savannahs, interspersed with clumps of magnificent trees, opened upon their view. Numerous herds of antelopes were grazing on one part of the plain. Some were speckled, others were of a uniform light fawn-colour, with a streak of black ; and as Carlos sat to rest himself, he thought how differently they looked when stuffed and placed in museums— how that beautiful roundness of the back was then wholly lost, and how the carriage of the head was altered. As he mused upon this, a slight rustling close at hand made him look round ; when, laying his finger upon his lips to enjoin silence, he called Antonio's attention to the sight which ensued. It was a small antelope,[1] not larger than a domestic cat; it was of a slate-colour, and its proportions were so fairy-like, that the travellers could scarcely believe the reality of what they saw. Its legs were not thicker than the stem of a tobacco-pipe; its little hoofs, as they saw when it lifted one up, and paused to look at the strangers, were no larger than the tips of their little fingers; its eyes verified all that the eastern poets have ever said of the gazelle; and for a moment Carlos thought that it was some curiosity in nature, or that he was only dreaming of so tiny, yet so exquisite a form; but another and another made their appearance, bounding along; and at last one, more in advance than the rest, seemed to challenge the whole herd, and all galloped away with almost incredible swiftness. 'I heard of this pigmy antelope,' said Carlos, 'on the coast; but had no conception at the time of its beauty and diminutive size. But what can these hillocks be which are scattered like haycocks over the plain?' Now we are rested,' added Antonio, 'let us go and examine them. I feel rather uneasy, after our adventure with the boa, at remaining long on the immediate outskirts of the forest; only that I think those creatures might find here plenty of food without taking us.' 'They are not particular,' rejoined Carlos; 'and, I believe, seize the first that comes.'

The travellers then moved on, approached one of the hillocks, and saw some small holes in it, but nothing which could lead them to conjecture what it was. On presently arriving, however, at one in ruins, which displayed a number of chambers and communicating

[1] Antelopus Pygmæus.

galleries, Carlos exclaimed, 'These are the nests of the termite, or white ant.' 'Who would think,' observed Antonio, 'that so small a creature should build so large or so complicated a house?' 'He is cleverer even than you are,' rejoined Carlos; 'and you know you are a little bit conceited about your talents as an architect. There is one thing, however, for which he is much more celebrated, and that is, his destructive properties: he makes nothing of eating up a staircase in a week; and the cunning part of this is, that he leaves a mere crust on the surface, so that no one is aware of the mischief he is doing, unless he hears the little ticking inside, which marks the ant's progress. As Mr. Jackson was talking to me one day at Cape Coast, he leaned back upon the sofa, and down he came, sofa and all. I could scarcely help laughing; but after helping him to get up, we examined the legs of the furniture, and found that two of them were completely scooped out inside by the white ants; and he said that the only remedy against this was to paint the wood, and shoe the parts which stand on the ground with brass. But I wish,' continued he, 'I could form the slightest notion of where we are, and what direction we ought to take. We have walked many weary miles since we left Naängo, through a vast extent of forest; but how many weeks it is since that period, we have no means of telling. Still, considering our long confinement in the hut, we may not have made much way; but as to finding Wondo's friends, it is now out of the question, so we must even go where it pleases God to lead us. I see some enormous trees, not very high, but with rugged trunks, standing yonder; let us get into them and look about us.'

The friends proceeded, the antelopes flying from them as they passed, and when they came near the trees, Carlos exclaimed, 'These must be the mighty baobabs of which I have so often read, many of which, according to botanists, have stood since the creation of the world, and which Captain Clapperton described as having a number of green velvet purses hanging from them. Here they are. Look up, Antonio, at the fruit: it is full of a delicious, slightly acid, and farinaceous substance, in which the seeds are imbedded, and of which the monkeys are said to be so fond, that the tree is often called the monkey-bread. It is, however, named by botanists after the great French naturalist, Adanson, who was the first to describe it properly, after having seen it in Senegal, where he lived for some time. I have read a beautiful eulogium on him, written by the immortal Baron Cuvier. But now for the tree. It is easy to mount it compared to those we have been in the habit of climbing; and we may almost step up its trunk. I can well believe that its body is eighty feet in circumference. Now hand up the things; we will rest here for a time, as the horizontal branches form almost a room.'

The baggage was deposited, and the wanderers looked around. The same sort of scenery met their eyes in every direction, except on the side of the forest which they had left; and there was not a sign of a human habitation. Some hills, however, which showed their blue tops in the very far distance, they thought should be the point to which they would next shape their course. Towards evening they descended with their bows and arrows, and shot one of the antelopes, while the rest of the herd fled. It was fortunate that they killed it at once, for these animals often struggle violently, and are extremely strong and fierce. They skinned and roasted it, and this good food was most invigorating to them. After a time, when the travellers had returned to their tree, the frightened antelopes came back to the spot, and grazed peacefully under them; they then lay down on the thick grass to sleep. The moon rose, and all was still; but after an hour's repose, the Europeans saw an antelope from the outskirts of the herd approaching with a swift pace; head after head was lifted up, and then all, suddenly rising, scoured off, and were out of sight in two minutes. 'An enemy, I suppose,' said Antonio. 'I should think so,' returned Carlos : 'look there !' An enormous lion strode hurriedly past, apparently in a great rage, and pursued the herd. 'I cannot think how these beasts tell each other what they wish to be known,' said Antonio. 'It is evident that they do communicate events, perhaps thoughts,' observed Carlos, 'and it is a question which has often puzzled me. But I think we are in a bad neighbourhood here; so perhaps we had better be moving on with to-morrow's dawn. To-night at least we are safe, and have had enough to eat and drink, and that is all we poor wanderers can expect.'

According to their intentions, the travellers continued their journey; and thinking that they had made a great deal too much easting, they proceeded for several days in a northerly direction, through a country exactly of the same nature as that into which they had first merged on quitting the forest. 'Now is the time,' said Carlos, 'to see all the beauties of the vegetable kingdom, for the rains fertilize everything.

What beautiful flowers we are now walking upon, making the ground look like a gay carpet!' So speaking, he stooped, and with his knife dug some out of the soil. 'I thought so,' added he, 'most of these are bulbous. What would I not give to take them home to the Colonel, who is so fond of cultivating them, and who so much prizes those which he gets from the Cape! It appears that in this continent, wherever there are large plains, there are bulbs. What a rich harvest for the naturalist would this one spot afford! Look at the thousands of rich beetles and butterflies, wholly unknown in Europe, revelling in the flowers. But raise your eyes, Antonio, and behold that stately, magnificent tree, covered with red flowers, like tulips. Truly God is great!'

At night, as the friends journeyed on, the most brilliant light illuminated the plain for miles around: the fire-flies had taken their turn in displaying the glories of nature. But when the tired men mounted into a tree to sleep, they were disturbed by a loud, chirping noise, which increased rapidly to such a degree that they could not hear each other's voices without bawling. They descended in order to ascertain the cause, and as they stepped on the grass, all was silent in their immediate vicinity. They stooped down and picked up a large green grasshopper. 'This is one of the noisy little animals which spoil our night's rest,' said Antonio; 'there must be millions of them to stun us in this manner. Do they sting?' 'Not at all,' answered Carlos, 'but they are closely allied to those destructive locusts which infest Africa; and I only wonder that we have not seen a swarm of them. I suppose they at present find plenty to eat in their own habitations, among the young shoots which start up after the rains; but when they have exhausted them, they will set out on their travels, and perhaps in an hour or two destroy everything in this rich plain.'

The next day, as they were eating their scanty meal, they found themselves surrounded by cranes, who, with their beautiful plumage of grey, white, black, and red round their eyes, and their large brown tufts on their heads, approached them with the utmost familiarity. 'I saw one of these crown cranes [1] quite tame at Cape Coast,' said Carlos; 'and they seem to be almost as tame here, because, I suppose, they have not learned to fear man. Look at that pretty creature with his quick, restless eye, and one of his long slender legs lifted up as he listens to us. I cannot think where they come from, for they are, generally speaking, waders, and live in the vicinity of water.' Here Antonio laughed, and Carlos, looking round him, joined in the mirth; for several cranes of another kind were playing the most ridiculous antics before him, hopping first on one leg, then on the other, then on both legs, holding their heads on one side, and looking as affected as possible. They now and then struck their beaks together, as if to keep time to their dancing; stood still for a little while, and then began again. 'I know what they are,' said Antonio, 'for I used to laugh at them in the menagerie at Liverpool. They there call them demoiselles; [2] and I am sure no young lady ever gave herself greater airs in a ball-room.'

On approaching nearer to the mountains, which they had seen so far off, the appearance of the cranes

---

[1] Ardea pavonia.　　　　[2] Ardea virgo.

was accounted for; there the ground became more swampy, and at last a large lake appeared, on the borders of which lay an abundance of white lumps, which the travellers tasted, and found to be the alkaline substance called natron. Numerous little rivers seemed to meet in the lake, which probably did not exist in the dry season, but which now rendered the ground wet. They rather avoided these, for the fogs hung thickly over them both morning and evening. They, however, more than once refreshed themselves by bathing, taking care to get immediately into rapid exercise after leaving the water. Here was a quantity of rice growing wild, which would have been a feast to them, could they have managed to boil it. 'One principal thing our good friends in the ship forgot,' said Antonio, 'was to secure us an iron pot of some sort.' 'They did wonders for us as it was,' returned Carlos, 'and we have no right to grumble; but for them, we must have perished: and if ever I return to England I will find them out, and at least thank them for having helped us, probably at their own risk.' 'What are those black and white birds over our heads?' asked Antonio; 'they fly like crows.' 'They must be crows,' answered Carlos; 'and that huge brown bird above them is an eagle, I am sure. I dare say he now and then takes away a young fawn, perhaps one of those tiny antelopes; and his brother the crow finds plenty of worms and grubs in this rich alluvial soil. Perhaps, too, there are fishes in the lake we have just left. We must not, however, linger here, or we shall have to sleep in the swamp, and that will increase our ague, of which we have lately been getting so much better.' But do as they could, they found it impossible to extricate themselves from the marsh; and at night, when they could not walk any farther, they were glad to choose the driest spot, wrap themselves up in their skins, and lie down to rest. They soon found, however, that they were so tormented with mosquitoes, that they could not obtain a moment's sound slumber; and they began to think that there were worse places than the forest or the sea-shore. They turned upon their faces, covered up every atom of flesh that was exposed, and thus, in spite of suffocation, snatched a little disturbed repose. They arose as soon as their limbs had somewhat recovered their fatigue, and they walked in the direction which appeared soonest to free them from the damp and wet by which they were surrounded. 'Surely,' said Antonio, 'we shall soon meet with some inhabitants; we seem to have been weeks since we came out of the forest, where we left, it is true, the semblance of a human being, but more hideous than any other living representative.' 'To tell you the truth,' observed Carlos, 'I have heard such awkward stories of these natives of the interior, and their passion for human flesh, that I do not much covet falling in with them, especially after our experience at Kaylee. I think it would form a good rule, by which we might judge of the character of a people, if their habitations were or were not surrounded by plantations. If you recollect, there were none at Kaylee.' 'No,' rejoined Antonio, 'nor at Naängo, and there they did not eat men.' 'True,' resumed Carlos, 'but there they had plenty of everything in the forest, and were accustomed to white men. I grant you that my position may not, in all respects, be quite without exceptions; and yet

I think, if we were to see ground extensively cultivated round a town, especially in an open country, we might infer from that, that we were in no danger of being devoured by our fellow-men.' 'Perhaps we shall soon be able to verify your conjecture,' said Antonio, 'for, if I mistake not, yonder is a cluster of houses.'

Quickening their pace, the travellers approached the village. It was small and poor, and every inhabitant of it fled before them, taking refuge at a great distance in the plain and in the rice-fields, or in the trees which grew at a considerable space from their dwellings; mothers caught up their children and fled, screaming; and the men, though with spears in their hands, followed their example. Carlos caught one woman, but her terror was so great, that he let her go again; and finding that it was in vain to pursue them they walked on. 'You may depend on it,' said Antonio, 'that they think we are demons, as that girl at Naángo did. It was something of a mutual feeling, for I did not like their looks at all; but I wish we had got something to eat out of them. Our stock of arrows is so much lower than when we started, careful as we have been over them, that all food is doubly precious which we do not procure by their means. See, there are some stray fowls; shall we catch them and wring their necks?' 'Certainly not,' said Carlos; 'they may well take us for evil spirits if we rob them.' Antonio grumbled, and observed that they did not give them the opportunity of asking for them; but Carlos persisted in his opinion, saying, 'We have never yet trespassed on the property of any one, and let us not do anything which may weigh upon our consciences in the hour of trouble and danger, for we have much

before us.' Antonio seemed to think that a fowl
would not weigh very heavily upon him; but presently, brightening up, he said, 'You are always right,
Lacy; we must look for some reeds, of which we have
already seen plenty, and try and make some more
arrows. They are very good here, and will not want
barbs for small animals; and feathers we can easily
procure, for we now so rarely miss our aim that we
can always bring down a bird to get its plumage. I
wish we could find some poison. Wondo always
dipped his in the juice of that red-berried plant which
grew on the edges of the forest; but I see nothing like
it here.'

The Europeans passed on, subsisting well enough
on the productions of the flat country through which
they went. Besides antelopes, they speared wild hogs,
goats, and sheep, which now abounded, the latter of
which were covered with coarse and harsh wool; and
they always found dry grass and wood under the
clumps of trees, wherewith to make a fire, and roast
flesh enough to last for several days. With this
frugal living, constant change, and exposure to air,
they regained their pristine, or even greater vigour,
and wholly lost their ague. Of water they had sometimes too much; but their improved strength made
them less liable to be injured by its exhalations. They
stopped in its vicinity in order to gather the reeds
which they required for increasing their stock of
arrows. In seeking for feathers they shot a common
grey stork, which was flying lazily over their heads at
no great height; and when Carlos saw what it was, he
said, 'It is well this did not happen in Holland, for
the stork is almost a sacred bird there. Now, how-

ever, when we have plucked off his feathers, we will eat him.'

The sun began to incommode the travellers with his heat, and they were often obliged to rest in the middle of the day; but their complexions again became bronzed, and they seemed like two iron-sinewed men, walking amidst herds of buffaloes, elephants, and smaller animals, with a special warrant of safety. They saw enormous tusks of ivory lying upon the ground, some of which weighed at least one hundred pounds, and observed that the owners of these had much larger ears than those of the Indian elephants, which they had seen in zoological collections; and when they found the huge grinders, which the same animals had shed, Carlos saw that on the tops of them the enamel looked like plaited ribbons, instead of lozenges. The wonder to them was that they did not meet with ivory hunters. Occasionally they came upon droves of wild dogs, very much resembling jackals; but unaccustomed to man, none seemed to heed them, and there was only occasion for mere common measures of prudence, which chiefly consisted of abstaining from everything like provocation. The leopards, panthers, hyænas, and lions which they met with seemed to have plenty of other food; and of serpents they saw but few, and most of them were in the water of the swamps.

The country at length became a little more closely wooded, though it could hardly be said to amount to forests. There were little birds bearing a strong resemblance to blackbirds and thrushes; and when, in the evening, the wanderers heard notes resembling those of the nightingale, Carlos' schoolboy days rushed into his recollection so forcibly, that his heart ached. He scarcely slept that night, and was so saddened by the painful remembrance of what had passed since then, that he could scarcely rouse himself to cheerfulness again. Antonio perceiving this, during the next day challenged him to sing with him for the first time since their illness. Music seemed to restore peace; thankfulness for preservation thus far soon gained the ascendancy; and lightening their way with their almost inexhaustible stock of songs, their path became pleasanter and their future brighter.

On arriving at some huts under the trees, the Europeans prepared for a meeting with the natives, and entered the village with their spears ready for self-defence. It was, however, deserted : some of the dwellings were unroofed; of others the mud walls were crumbling to pieces; and they had evidently been abandoned in consequence of some struggle, for whitened human bones lay scattered around, and some ghastly skulls, tossed about here and there, showed that wild beasts and vultures had been at work, and separated the remains which man had left to rest upon the ground where they fell. 'There is another heap of bones here,' said Antonio, 'unlike those nearer to the huts. I see they belong to animals such as we ourselves have killed; therefore, I suppose that the natives threw their offal here; and the vultures, in acting the part of scavengers, must have had some fine feasts occasionally.' 'I wonder how long this place has been left desolate!' exclaimed Carlos; 'it does not take much time to strip the flesh from bones in this country, what with the climate, and the assistance of bird and beast. But what are you looking for inside that hut, Antonio?' The Venetian issued from the walls of one of the ruins, capering with delight, and crying, 'How lucky! I have found an earthen pot, which, by its look, must have been ·often on the fire; it is chipped a little, but is otherwise whole enough to answer our purposes; it seems to have been left expressly for us, as all the others are too much broken to be of any service. Now, Lacy, we will have such capital stews; boil our roots, and get some of those arums which we have met with, and which have hitherto blistered our lips, but which will be very good, after having been boiled in three or four waters.' 'But you forget,' observed Carlos, 'that you will have to carry it.' 'Oh! I do not mind that,' returned Antonio; 'I am quite strong now; and with some cordage which I have in my pocket, I can sling it at my back.' 'I will carry both spade and hatchet, then,' resumed Carlos; 'but if we go on accumulating as we do now, our march will be impeded. At all events, we must not leave our packet of skins behind us, considering that it is almost our only hope of barter when we do meet with inhabitants a little less savage than the last. Do you see that widely-spreading tree? It must be what is called a banyan; but which I believe is a species of fig. It would shelter a whole regiment, and evidently covers a space of many hundred yards. Let us sit under its shade and cook the goat which we killed this morning, and which is rather troublesome on my shoulder. As you say, we will stew our flesh and vegetables together; but I really am afraid, if ever we should reach England, that we shall never lose the habit of thinking a great deal of eating and drinking, to which we must now plead guilty.' 'Show me the man in the wilderness,' exclaimed Antonio, 'that is not. At all events, we cannot be accused of daintiness.' 'I am not sure of that,' added Carlos; 'we certainly contemplate a change of dishes with extreme pleasure.' 'Never mind,' rejoined Antonio, 'we have not many pleasures, therefore let us enjoy all we can.' The fire was prepared, the stew made, and as they partook of it, they contemplated the possibility of cooking rice and tomatoes, of the latter of which they had seen several new and curious sorts, hitherto left untasted, as well as the foliage which Carlos had seen cooked in imitation of spinach at Cape Coast, taking the sole precaution of changing the water once or twice in the boiling.

In the course of a day or two the travellers suddenly entered another village, which was curiously constructed, inasmuch as the houses appeared to consist of four mud walls, without entrance or windows. Several ladders, however, leaning against the sides, showed that those who lived in them ascended and descended by their means through the concealed roof. The moment the strangers appeared, men, women, and children mounted the ladders, which they drew up after them, and in a minute not a living soul was to be seen. The white men stared with astonishment; but Carlos, recovering himself, cried, 'Come away as fast as you can. Do you see those narrow slits in the walls? they are evidently for the discharge of arrows, which are probably poisoned;' and as he spoke, three or four whizzed past him. They retreated, and when out of the reach of the weapons, they discussed the reason of these strange proceedings. 'This evidently,' observed Carlos, 'results from fear of some powerful enemy, to which these people are exposed. Is it a neighbouring nation, or is it the slave trade? Perhaps both; and from one end of Africa to the other we find traces of that horrible traffic.' The same sort of thing occurred again and again, till the white men began to be almost heart-sick, and to think their journey interminable. Still these signs of slavery showed that there must be some outlet, some communication with more distant lands and the coast. 'Perhaps we were wrong,' suggested Carlos, 'to turn away from those mountains, where we might probably find men who are a little more civilised. We must surely have made *northing* enough, walking as we have done every day for such a time, though how long I know not, for the division of day and night is all we can keep up, because it is so visible to our senses. At all events, we must be hundreds of miles from Naängo.'

CHAPTER XIV.

AFTER proceeding for a considerable time through
alternate woods and plains, in which there was a great
sameness in both animal and vegetable productions,
the travellers began to find a few more sign of civilisation.   They now and then came to a clearing in the
bush, which was evidently the work of human hands,
and had principally been effected by fire, for the ashes
were scattered upon the ground by way of manure for
the next crop.   In others, maize was still standing,
and occasionally a spot planted with yams presented
itself, the slender climbing stalks of which were trained
upon poles.   Patches of millet had been reaped, and
the stubble alone was left.   'We must be near some
large place,' observed Carlos ; 'let us approach with
caution ; but first of all let us cut our hair with our
knives, and make ourselves look as genteel as possible.'
They accordingly rested that night, made their toilet
the next morning, and, with anxious expectations
proceeded on their way till they came to the outskirts
of the bush, where an assemblage of bell-shaped houses,
built of bamboo, and their projecting roofs thatched
with palm leaves, placed on the bank of a river, met their
view.   There was an air of ease and comfort, which
showed that this town was comparatively wealthy ; and
walking boldly on, the white men, without stopping

or heeding the astonishment of those whom they passed, threaded the intricate, crooked streets, till they came to a large open space, where they looked around them, in the hope that some one would accost them; but all seemed to be paralyzed, either by fear or surprise. One by one the natives first came to steal furtive glances; then more direct looks were given, and parties of them by degrees crowded together, till the strangers were in danger of being pressed to death. The moment, however, that the latter moved, the people fell back as if frightened, and suppressed groans were heard. The Europeans tried to make signs, by which their peaceable intentions might be understood; but these appeared to be of no further use than to amuse some of the little urchins, who seemed to think it high fun to mock and imitate the new arrivals, and who with difficulty stifled their laughter. Whispers began to arise which shortly amounted to clamour; when a man made his way through the mass, and authoritatively commanded silence. He was obeyed, and making signs in his turn to the strangers, he conducted them to a group of houses, fenced in with bamboo stakes, and a little apart from the rest of the town. He desired them to enter a hut and sit down, and telling them, as well as he could, to remain there, he left them. He, however, soon after returned, followed by a slave bearing a mess of rice and boiled goat's flesh. Carlos and Antonio ate of the proffered meal, and were then told to follow their guide, who conducted them into the presence of one who was evidently superior to the rest. This chief was seated on a mat spread upon the ground, smoking a pipe, the stem of which was a hollow reed, and the bowl of red clay, fashioned like a bird with its head turned over its back. He gave them a nod as they'entered, and after that tried to assume the most perfect indifference to their presence ; although his curiosity might be detected by the quick glances which he stole from between his half-closed eyelids. His attendants were apparently astonished, but dared not express their feelings. The Europeans stood before him in silence, and better specimens of the Caucasian race could scarcely have met his gaze. Their handsome, regular features ; their dark silken hair, which even the recent operation of the knives could not deprive of its large floating curls ; the straight, high forehead, bared as they saluted the chief by taking off their caps ; their perfect teeth peeping from their mustachios ; the short, rich beard of Antonio, with incipient signs of the same in Carlos, adding to the manly, yet benignant expression of their countenances in the eyes of the natives, who scarcely knew what a beard was ; their tall, muscular frames, divested as they were of superfluous flesh ; their well-shaped limbs, erect bearing, and graceful movements, seemed to command respect ; and there they stood, resting upon their spears, perfect models of the courageous, hardy European traveller. The effect which they produced among a race peculiarly susceptible to appearances was evidently imposing ; for the chief, after a time, fixed his large eyes upon them, and stared for several minutes without moving. He then looked around him, as if seeking for some one else, and gave an order. An attendant disappeared, and soon returned with another man, who give a slight start on seeing the strangers ; but immediately put out his hand, and

The Travellers introduced to the Chief. —*Page* 226.

shaking theirs, exclaimed, 'White man!' He then addressed the King, as if to explain who they were. Delighted to find an interpreter, Carlos told him an outline of their history, which he repeated to the chief, who afterwards ordered them to take possession of the hut to which they had already been shown, in the royal enclosure.

The interpreter led the way, left them in their dwelling, but soon returned with mats and cushions for them to sleep upon, and an attendant, who was ordered to sweep out the hut. Carlos endeavoured to make the man understand that they could not pay for what they had, nor could they give any present; but that when they got back to their own land, they would send a handsome reward to any one who would treat them well. The interpreter constantly nodded his head, but certainly did not comprehend more than half of what they said. Still, he was very useful, and seemed to take them under his protection, making signs to them that he would occupy the next hut, to which they saw his mats, cushions, and attendants remove in a short time. This vicinity kept off numbers who would have otherwise forced themselves into the enclosure to look at them, for as it was the first time the inhabitants of Assee had seen white men, their natural curiosity—of which the negro has an immense share—constantly urged them to beset the strangers. Two or three at a time were by favour admitted into the hut, where they sat with their eyes fixed upon the wonderful objects, and frequently bursting into a loud laugh; but whether the latter expressed approbation or contempt, the Europeans were at a loss to discover. Their persons were evidently discussed;

their clothes excited no little observation; and their every gesture produced a remark. At length, as the sun rose high, one by one the gazers disappeared, and the travellers themselves, glad to rest, sank into a slumber, resting upon their arms and knapsacks, for fear they should be stolen.

In a few hours the strangers rose refreshed, and each agreeing that it would be a capital opportunity of repairing their clothes, determined to remain there a few days, and hoped they should be allowed a torch, or a lamp, by which they could work at night. As soon as it was dark, however, they were summoned to the royal presence, where a *fête* was evidently in progress in honour of their arrival. They were about to obey the order· for their attendance fully equipped, but their friend, who told them his name was Ajimba, placed one of his men as a guard over their effects, and assured them they would there be perfectly safe. The King sat upon a raised seat covered with a mat, and he was himself enveloped in a number of cloths which were manufactured in the country. On his head he wore a high cap, and appeared to be a good-natured old man, but who was evidently ruled by a fetish man, who constantly stood close to him. All present, not excepting the King, had· two deep scars on their cheeks. The feast consisted of stewed fowls, some animal of a small size, rice, and a great deal of pepper, served in rude earthenware bowls. Fried bananas succeeded; palm wine was given to drink; and all helped themselves with their fingers, except the Europeans, who, taking the wooden spoons out of their girdles, ate with them, which created considerable astonishment. 'Do you think this is human

flesh?' whispered Antonio, whose suspicions were
always awakened when any unknown animal was presented to him. 'No,' answered Carlos, 'it is too
small.' The white guests, well knowing the intoxicating effects of palm wine, merely wetted their lips
with it, but found the dishes excellent. They were
then entertained with the usual amusements of music,
if such it might be called, and dancing. Among the
instruments was a sort of violin formed of a calabash,
with a piece of antelope skin stretched tightly over it,
a neck being introduced on one side. Along this
were some strings, evidently of animal substance, and
the whole was played with a bow. Antonio was
charmed with its resemblance to a Mandolin, and
begging to be allowed to look at it, he laid aside the
bow, struck the string with his fingers, and making a
running accompaniment of chords, began to sing.
Carlos joined, and their hearers appeared to be perfectly enchanted. They asked again and again for a
repetition of the pleasure, but the fetish man whispered
something in the King's ear, who from that moment
became restless and uneasy, and shortly after broke
up the assembly.

The next morning Ajimba, whose memory of English words rapidly improved with practice, took the
strangers round the town, in the centre of which was
a large banyan tree, under which all the debates of
the nation were held. Here three youths, with hands
tied behind them, were led up to the white men, and
the interpreter was desired to ask if they would buy
them. The surrounding crowd looked on with eagerness for the result; and when the white men turned
away with a look of disgust, and manifested much

disapprobation, a very significant look passed on all sides.

The houses consisted but of one room, with occasionally another, in which stores were kept ; but the cooking seemed to be carried on in the open air. In almost all was a hideous idol of some sort, variously decorated with a substance which looked to the Europeans like mother-of-pearl, feathers, beads, etc.; and there was a large edifice on one side of the town, at the door of which stood the scowling fetish man, who forbade them to enter, and thence they concluded it was the fetish house. All the people were decorated with pieces of stone, some substances sewn up in cotton, cloth, dirty strings, leaves, and teeth of animals of several kinds, which were charmed by the fetish, and which, from never being taken off, partook of the grease and dirt emanating from the bodies of the wearers. Here, as in every other part of Africa, the skin was anointed with vegetable or shea butter, palm oil, or some sort of grease, without which it would become whitish, crack, and peel off in flakes. Everything seemed to partake of the fetish, and consequently its ugliness and deformity were impressed on the minds of the Europeans in a painful degree. The idols seemed to represent the negro peculiarities in caricature ; and such characteristics exaggerated are hideous in the eyes of white men. As they walked through the streets, they met a man sneezing most violently, rolling his eyes about, twisting his head, making the most hideous grimaces, and practising all sorts of contortions with his body. All who saw him made way for him to pass, and looked at him with a sort of fearful respect. At last he threw himself on the ground near the fetish house, and appeared to be violently convulsed; and when the travellers asked Ajimba for an explanation, he told them that it was the fetish coming upon the man, who was always affected in this manner when the fit was present, and that he would soon be a fetish man.

Immense quantities of ivory lay in the storehouses of the more wealthy inhabitants, of which many ornaments were made by the natives, and among them the horns which they wore round their necks, and blew in the shrillest manner possible. Carlos told Ajimba of the numerous herds of elephants which they had seen; and he informed them, that he lived far away from where he now was, but had been sent to Assee by the King his master, to trade in ivory. That the travellers had done well to avoid these animals, for if they had even accidentally provoked one, and sometimes a trifle would do it, they would have had no chance of escaping from it or its companions; that nothing but a very strong tree, into which they might have climbed, would have protected them from their fury, for several would have come together, and twisting their trunks round one of lesser strength, pulled it down; and not contented with goring their enemies with their tusks, and throwing them up in the air, they would, when on the ground, have knelt upon them and kneaded them to a jelly.

The friends returned to their hut; and as they sat at work, and Ajimba was absent on his trading affairs, Antonio remarked, that none of the natives whom they had seen seemed to have the smallest notion of taming the elephant. 'No,' returned Carlos, 'nor anywhere else in Africa, I believe. Among other visionary schemes for civilising this country, of which there have been so many, I once heard a gentleman, who was reckoned very clever, seriously propose to convert the Africans by means of tame elephants. His argument was, that when the natives saw the white man master of such an animal as that, they would think his power to be so immense, that they would be more inclined to believe all he said, and follow his instructions. But it is very easy,' continued he, 'to sit in an arm-chair at home and form plans for the good of Africa. I should like to place some of these persons in the midst of a native town, with all its ignorance, its barbarity, its prejudices, its superstitions, its indolence, added to the influence of the fetish, the climate, the scenery, and natural productions, and then they might be convinced what a work of time it must be, even to convert one nation, and by what slow degrees that must be done. Each step must be secured before another is taken; without which no more good will be effected than we have accomplished by passing through the country. One seed must be planted, take root, spring forth, and be well watched before another is sown; one kingdom converted, and endeavours concentrated in that; then a desire will probably be awakened in others, and then they can be attempted in their turns. Above all things, men must be employed, who, by a thorough knowledge of the native character, by patience, forbearance, and their own example, will form native teachers, and send them forth to their brethren. Various things will help the great work,—a knowledge of medicine; a knowledge of music, to which the Africans are so sensible; a sufficient knowledge of useful trades to

direct the efforts of others ; and a facility of expression
in figurative language, so as to bring forward a number
of similes.   But all this is beginning to be felt, so we
will talk about something else.   I do not like the
looks of that fetish man.   Did you see how mysteriously Ajimba whispered "Fetish!" to us yesterday,
as we approached his house, and how savagely the
priest looked at us ?   I wish we had a present to give
him, which perhaps might put him in good humour.
These men are so skilful in poisoning, that there is no
being safe from them.' 'They do not seem to have
any gold here,' said Antonio, 'therefore I suppose do
not care about it ; and our skins would not be of much
value to them, as they can so easily kill the animals
from which we took them.' 'My watch is totally
spoiled,' rejoined Carlos, 'and in my knapsack ; it is
only silver, but Ajimba said yesterday that silver was
often more thought of than gold in some parts, because it is more rare.   I have a great mind to offer it
to this man ; but if I do, what shall I give to the King ?'
'Give him the spade,' suggested Antonio, 'to dig up
his yams ; the implements here are very rude, and
chiefly made of wood ; we could use our Naängo
knives if we wanted to get anything out of the ground.'
'A very good idea,' continued Carlos, 'and we will
consult Ajimba on the subject.'

Ajimba was highly satisfied with the above arrangement ; 'but,' added he, 'do not tell the King you have
nothing better ; say at once this spade is a very good
thing ; and you had better go directly with it, for the
King is now holding a great council.'   To the council
tree the white men now repaired, and presented the
spade in due form.   It was received with an appear-

ance of indifference, but, nevertheless, a boy was ordered to hold it upright, and sit in front of the King; and they afterwards heard that it was carried before him, on his return to his palace, like a mace. The council was stormy, and the Europeans fancied that they were the objects of it; and asking Ajimba, he nodded assent, and told them they would be wise to retire. The King, however, suddenly arose, after a very vehement and indignant burst from the fetish man, which awed the rest into silence; the council was broken up, and the travellers returned to their hut. When their supper was brought to them, Antonio said, 'That fetish man is a dangerous enemy; we ought to put all we are going to take into the rhinoceros cups.' 'You do not believe that story, do you?' asked Carlos. 'Not I,' replied Antonio; 'but poor Wondo did, and thought he had made us the most valuable present that could be procured. At all events we have had many a good draught of water out of them.'

In the morning, when daylight came, Carlos, according to their usual custom, took his prayer-book, and read aloud from it; then both prayed together upon their knees, and as they arose, he, with astonishment, saw Antonio rush to the door and look out. 'What sudden fit has seized you?' asked he. 'I was sure it was that fellow,' said Antonio, returning to his place; I saw his eye through that hole in the wall all the time you were reading, and I caught sight of a piece of his cloth when I put my head out. It was that rascally fetish man.' 'Well,' observed Carlos, 'it does not much signify. I shall ask for a canoe to-day to take us across the river and be off, saving my watch for a case of even greater emergency.

Ajimba says that white men are to be found in that
direction.' On making his desire known to their interpreter, the man shook his head and seemed to be
uneasy; once or twice he was going to say something,
but he then checked himself, and at last went out.
'Do you think we are prisoners?' said Antonio. 'I
hope not,' rejoined Carlos, 'for I am heartily tired of
being here. Perhaps it would be better to try the
effect of my watch.' Accordingly, when Ajimba came
with their breakfast, they told him that they wanted
to see the fetish man and give him their present.
The countenance of the interpreter suddenly brightened, and he then asked if they would go away with
him to his home, which would be the best way to get
to white men. 'To be sure we will,' said Carlos;
and the man immediately left them, as if relieved from
some oppressive care. When he was gone, Antonio
exclaimed, 'I think I can tell you what the animal
is which we are now eating, and which has so often
puzzled us; it is dog.' 'Dog!' exclaimed Carlos,
putting down his spoon. 'Yes,' resumed his companion; 'I saw a lot of dogs yesterday for sale as we
went to the council, and when I passed one of the
huts, an old woman had just finished skinning one,
and was cutting it in pieces, and putting it into a pot.'
'Well,' said Carlos, helping himself a second time,
'there is nothing like necessity for conquering all prejudices concerning food. Dog is very good eating in
this country at any rate.'

The fetish man obeyed the summons conveyed to
him by Ajimba, and seemed to be much softened when
Carlos offered him the watch; but when the latter
wound it up with the key, and it ticked for a few

R

minutes, he was afraid to touch it. When it stopped, Carlos opened it, showed him the wheels and delicate workmanship, at which the man could not help throwing up his hands with astonishment. Carlos taught him how to use the key; and the enemy retired with his treasure, evidently converted, if not into a friend, into good humour for a time. As he went, Carlos laughed, and said, 'I should not wonder if the imperfections of the watch were its greatest recommendations; and that its going only for a few minutes at a time made its greatest charm.' In the evening each received a present from the fetish man of a very curiously-wrought mat; and the interpreter announced to them that he should start the next morning, having completed his load of ivory, and they might accompany him if they pleased. They joyfully acceded to the proposal, and he then said, 'You must come directly and take leave of the King.'

They followed him, and were ushered into the royal private apartments, which were lighted by torches. They found his majesty reclining on cushions, and surrounded by his wives. No one was allowed to enter with them except the interpreter; therefore they concluded that they were admitted for the satisfaction of the ladies. The latter at first approached them with timidity; one, more bold than the rest, advanced close to them, looked them in the face, and then ran giggling back to her companions. Another and another followed her example, till at last the youngest of all ventured to touch Antonio's hand with the tip of one of her fingers, at which the rest laughed so immoderately that the King became angry. A slave was called in, who appeared to have complete authority over them;

and no sooner did he enter, than they became quiet, and went out in the most orderly fashion. As he turned to follow them, Carlos observed that he had a whip in his hand. The Europeans requested their interpreter to thank the King for all his kindness to them, and then bowing low to the ground, they took their leave. As they went out through the state apartment they saw their spade hung over the throne.

The travellers started the next morning before day-break, thankful to have made their escape from the fetish man; for Carlos, in his voyage along the coast, had learned how much he was to be dreaded, and that if he had determined on the destruction of an individual, it was scarcely possible to avert the mischief. On talking of it with Ajimba, the latter appeared to be unwilling to say much, but hinted that they had done well to leave the place,—'For,' said he, 'this man thought you were two great fetish men yourselves, and was jealous of you; and he tried to make the King believe that you had the bad eye.' 'The bad eye!' exclaimed Carlos, 'what is that?' 'I know,' said Antonio; 'it is the evil eye of my country; we there believe that some persons have the power of injuring you by their looks, like a species of witchcraft. I recollect, when a boy, that my grandmother tied a piece of coral round my neck which was to save me from the spell; but I have long lost it and learned to laugh at it, though I was very much afraid at the time it was given to me. I little thought that I should ever be accused of having the evil eye myself.'

The commodiousness of the canoe in which they now travelled surprised the Europeans, accustomed as they had been to the sharp narrow conveyances on the coast. Although it, and another belonging to Ajimba, were far from being the largest on the river, they were each of them capable of holding fifty persons, and had a covered cabin at the end, which would accommodate three or four, during the heat of midday, at nights, or in a storm, and at the opposite end was an earthen stove, used for the purposes of cooking by day, and which at night, as it was always kept burning, was hung outside on the bows of the canoe, by way of lantern. The slight or secondary rains had commenced, and showers, often accompanied by tornadoes, frequently occurred; at which time the travellers crept under the covering, or took shelter in a village, where the credit of Ajimba, who seemed to be known everywhere, secured them respect and accommodation. As he every day conversed with them, his English rapidly improved; and he told them that he had been to the coast, had seen plenty of white men, who had been very kind to him; that he had been sick there, and that a good white doctor had given him medicine, which had made him well again; and that therefore he loved white men. He added that he was a trader in the service of a king who lived in a town on the side of a great river, and he had been to Assee in that capacity. What he had purchased there was to be taken down the great river to meet the English ships, and be sold to them; and if none of these should come to where they were going, Carlos and Antonio might meet them in one of the canoes.

The banks of the river, generally speaking, were remarkably picturesque; they were occasionally high, and covered with silk, cotton, palm, mimosa, and banyan trees, under which small villages were erected;

and now and then an open plain presented itself, where
herds of wild animals might be seen peaceably grazing ;
among which, as they advanced, they discovered a
small variety of bulls and cows. The forests were of
little extent, but frequently came to the water's edge.
At one place where they stopped, they were a little
startled at the mess brought them for supper. It was
a sort of soup, with the flesh of the animal from which
it was made left in it. On taking up a piece with his
spoon, Carlos felt very uncomfortable, and jogged
Antonio, who exclaimed, 'It's a child!' 'No, no!'
said Ajimba, who had been watching them, 'not a
child, but a monkey.' They could not help remarking
that their appearance now excited but little comparative surprise, which was accounted for by the inhabitants assuring them that they had often seen white
men in the great river. It must be owned also that
the Europeans were now so bronzed in complexion,
that they might very easily have passed for Arabs,
who occasionally approached that part of Africa, and
stragglers from whom were seen even upon the coast.
At last the landscape became more and more flat, and
the only risings which met their eyes consisted of some
hills, with flat tops ; and in a short time they entered
a much larger river, flowing towards the south. They
proceeded up it ; and on the evening of the third day
after that, a loud shouting from the crews of the canoes
told that they were close to the place of their destination. Numbers of persons in small canoes came out
to meet them, rowed round them, talked the whole
time, and after one or two exclamations of surprise,
cordially saluted the white men. The large canoes
were at length moored to the shore, and Ajimba, their

faithful friend, begged them to wait in theirs till he could go and inform the King, his master, of their arrival. In about half an hour he returned with a deputation from his Majesty, inviting them to come ashore; and shouldering their knapsacks, they proceeded through a numerous population, to a house made of cane and mud, and thatched as usual. In this they were installed, were desired to consider it as their own, and were assured that mats and cushions would be brought. On going in they were first in danger of knocking their heads, and then their shins; the aperture was so small, and the threshold so high. As they passed they observed that several of the houses were made of bricks dried in the sun. The streets were narrow and crooked, and patches of long, coarse grass frequently grew at the sides. After waiting for some time, their guide, who had left them, returned and said they must now go and see one of the head men appointed by the King to take care of them. On arriving at the dwelling of the latter, they found a supper of stewed duck and puppies, prepared in a wooden bowl, accompanied by mashed yams, which they ate with their own spoons. A man came in dressed in a large loose dress very much the worse for wear, and said, that his Majesty would see them the next morning. A boy then appeared with a basket of eggs for sale, which were purchased with cowries by the head man. The drink offered to them was a sort of beer made from the native corn; but they preferred water.

Having slept with an unusual feeling of security, the Europeans rose the next morning, and performed their ablutions in two large brass pans full of water, supplied

by their attentive friend ; and having concluded their
morning orisons, they were invited to walk through
the town, after which they were again asked to eat at
the house of the head man, who had the royal orders
to supply all they required as long as they might stay
in his dominions.   Having concluded their meal, they
were then conducted to the market-place, where they
were surprised at the variety of articles exposed for
sale.   Salt was contained in coarse bags made of
grass, and was said to come from a great distance.
Cam-wood, beaten into powder, mixed with clay, and
rolled into lumps like eggs, was there for polishing
and softening the skin ; being rubbed first upon a wet
hand.   Large grass hats, quantities of raw cotton with
the seeds left in, silk cotton, and the down from the
pods of other plants, such as the Asclepiades, and used
for making pillows ; wide garments of silk or cotton
made in the interior, ornamented with needle-work,
which resembled surplices in shape, and were called
tobes; calabashes, some of which were carved; earthenware, country cloths, yams, sweet potatoes, beans,
maize and other corn ; rice ; animal and vegetable
butter, the latter very dirty ; eggs, fowls, onions, fruits
of various kinds, sheep, goats, iron, rum, small quantities of gunpowder, and guns, were all lying on the
ground, and belonged to the native traders.   Here
also the Europeans saw ground-nuts, for which they
had searched during the whole of their journey ; but
not knowing the plant on which they grow, had never
succeeded.

After inspecting all that Ajimba thought it advisable
to show them, his own house included, they were
summoned to go through the ceremony of introduction

to the King. They found him enveloped in a number of dirty-looking tobes, with a huge pair of slippers on his feet, and a red cap upon his head, ornamented with brass buttons. Round his neck and ankles were several strings of beautiful coral, and a number of ivory rings encircled his wrists. He was seated on a throne, made of bamboo, covered with a white cotton cloth ; and a gay carpet was spread before him. He was surrounded by attendants, all wearing tobes, which costume Ajimba had also assumed, in exchange for the cloth which he had hitherto worn round the lower part of his person. His Majesty received the white men graciously ; declared that he had been expecting them for some time ; that he had seen plenty of white men before ; that they were welcome to stay with him as long as they pleased ; that they had better wait for a vessel to go down to the big water, for English ships sometimes came even further up than his country, and would take them back. If not, they would go in a canoe. He liked white men to be with him, and did not want any presents from them. 'That's a comfortable hint,' said Antonio, 'considering that we have nothing to give.' At the end of his harangue, the King put them in charge of Ajimba ; and the head man, whom they already knew, offered them rum and palm wine, and concluded by saying that he hoped to see their faces very often. Carlos desired Ajimba to thank him for his kindness, expressing their happiness at being under his protection, and then took their leave.

Here, then, the Europeans were stationed for at least some time, and both agreed that it would be best to wait a little while for a vessel, which would take them direct to England ; and, in case of being disappointed in such a conveyance, they could then proceed in a canoe to the mouth of the river, where they would be sure to find opportunities of getting home. When, however, they had seen the whole place, which strongly resembled all others in that country, had witnessed several sacrifices of animals to idols, and been present at the *fêtes*, they began to find their life exceedingly monotonous. They seemed, although on the banks of the far-famed Niger, to be almost within reach of their countrymen, and this produced a restlessness which they had not known before. To be, as they thought, so near the completion of their wishes, after all they had suffered, and yet not to attain it, was worse perhaps than when the case was apparently hopeless. Their chief amusement was to watch the canoes and their cargoes, which came to the town to trade, and which were often decorated with little flags at their head, wrought or painted with the most curious devices. Among the objects for barter were small horses, which came from the more northern parts of the country. The Europeans were allowed to roam about as they pleased, and saw much of the domestic manners of the people, which, however, were little different from those which they had witnessed elsewhere. In the quarrels, the universal practice among negroes of butting with their heads, by way of fighting, had always been strange, and they tried to teach them to use their fists. Their instructions afforded a great deal of mirth, and they were surprised at the good humour of their antagonists, when, after being knocked down several times, they would decline further trial, and declare that there was fetish in the white men's fists, yet return to the charge the next day. They, however, took care not to carry this too far, for fear of unwittingly exciting some degree of ill-will; revenge being a strongly marked feature in the negro character. They could not in the least comprehend how they had been expected; and on asking Ajimba, they found him to be equally ignorant. The King and head man, however, persisted in the story, that a message had been received from Obi, the King of Ibbo, to say that two white men were coming, which way they did not know; and that the Queen of England would send a present to any one who would receive them kindly, take care of them, and help them to get back to their own country. 'Can this be intended for us?' said Carlos thoughtfully, numerous suggestions starting into his mind as he reflected upon the message; but he dismissed them by the idea, that two travellers had probably started recently from England.

CHAPTER XV.

THE Filatahs, the great enemies to the tranquillity of the part of Africa where the travellers were stationed, and who pour down upon the defenceless towns, and ravage and destroy everything before them, had not for some time been heard of; and a feeling of security began to pervade the whole district. It was therefore deemed advisable that Ajimba should go and trade further up the river. No European vessel was near, and the expedition was not expected to last more than a few days. Thinking, therefore, that it would be a pleasant change, Carlos and Antonio asked the King's leave to join it; and the permission being granted, they prepared to start. They were told that they must leave their baggage; but when they represented that they had nothing but their clothes, their weapons, and their skins, which they then presented to the King, who seemed pleased with them, they were allowed to take their few possessions. To Ajimba's wife they gave some wooden spoons, which they had made, in consequence of her husband's admiration of the contrivance. Antonio was very loth to leave his dear earthern pot behind; but it seemed a very useless labour to take it, and it was accordingly transferred to the domestic furniture of Ajimba.

All was ready for departure at an early hour in the

morning ; and, the canoe filled with articles of food, raw cotton, ivory, salt, a few guns, some powder and shot, some European manufactures, and cowries, which formed the currency, the party embarked. They stopped at most of the villages on their way, some of which were built so close to the water's edge, that they were frequently inundated by the river when it rose to any height, and were consequently dirty and half in ruins. The inhabitants said that they had been so often conquered and impoverished by the Filatahs, that they could neither repair their houses, nor make themselves comfortable ; for what was the use ? If they did, these enemies would come down on them immediately they possessed anything worth taking, and sell the owners as slaves. In every place they saw ugly and rude fetishes, and only in one did they find a blacksmith's forge, where some knives were in process of manufacture. All along the banks were small fishing huts, each built in an eddy, on four posts. The circular nets, hung from a pole, were baited with bruised yam, fishes' intestines, etc., and were watched from within the hut, which, as well as the lines, was hung with small carved fishes, dedicated to the fetish. The fishes thus caught were cleaned, fastened head and tail together, dipped in palm oil and peppers, and dried over a fire of wood. At length they reached a part of the river which was much increased by the confluence of a mighty arm coming from the east. Into this they steered their course, leaving the Niger flowing between a range of mountains, and after proceeding up it for some time, they came to a smaller tributary stream. This was their destination, and pursuing its course, they found its shores on either side well wooded, but without villages, till they arrived at one called Pottinghia. There they moored the canoes, and carrying their contents to the house of the chief, despatched a messenger from thence to the King of Fandah, requesting his permission to visit him, and, if granted, a further request, that he would send horses for them.

The usual practice of giving a *fête* in honour of the arrival of strangers, was also practised in this village. A fire was lighted, and a noise proceeding from a large drum, formed of a skin stretched tightly over a hollow piece of wood like a cask, and beaten with sticks, summoned the guests, who assembled to dance in some empty huts, frequently joining their voices in a sort of chorus, which, however, soon turned into something like a yell or a scream. The dancers frequently moved round two upright stakes placed in the ground, having fetish or charmed substances on the tops ; while others walked about sedately enough, with pipes in their mouths, only now and then giving a jump, to show that they acted a part in the general festivity. The white men being tired, asked leave to quit the assembly early, and were then conducted to a hut ; but little rest, however, did they find there, it so swarmed with mosquitoes and sand-flies. They had recourse to their usual method of sleeping on their faces ; but this was no protection against the flies, so that they were obliged to sit up in the open air, constantly flapping the large leaves of a fan palm which they had found upon the ground, and which, in some measure, kept off their tormentors. They frequently fell asleep during this time ; but the buzzing and stinging again awoke them, and they could not

help envying Ajimba, who slept as soundly as if there
had not been a mosquito in the world.

Beer and fowls were offered to them the next morning, and they saw horses approach from the King of
Fandah. 'Can you ride?' said Carlos to his friend.
'I have tried two or three times in the course of my
life,' answered Antonio, 'and never met with any
accident.' 'You must now do your best,' continued
Carlos, 'for we must not let these black men think
us incapable of doing what they do, so for your life
don't fall off. Stop—your are getting up on the wrong
side. Don't throw your leg over the horse's head.'
'The rigging is the same on each side,' said Antonio,
and sprang into his seat.

The 'rigging,' as Antonio called it, was most com-
plex ; for the saddle was high, and peaked before and
behind, and the bridle and stirrups were composed of
the most intricate machinery and cordage. However,
when he had once vaulted into his place, his sailor
habits, if they did not give him elegance, gave him the
power of holding fast ; and had the horse kicked,
plunged, or practised any other manœuvre which wayward horses are apt to rely upon, he would have found
it impossible to get rid of his burthen. As to Carlos,
he had been accustomed all his life to riding, and
therefore proceeded without any apprehension for
himself. The country was beautifully varied ; small
copses of the most exquisite foliage concealed streams
of pure water, which they had frequently to cross, and
one of which amounted to a river. It flowed between
two high banks of clay, which were slippery for the
horses' feet, but Antonio was not in the least dis-
composed. As usual, in the native towns of that part

of Africa, the streets of Fandah were narrow and wind-
ing, and the eaves of the houses projected far into
them. The trading party took possession of some
which had been deserted, but they were dirty and
uncomfortable, and the floors of them were stony and
uneven. The Europeans and Ajimba spread their mats
in one which formed part of what is called a dwelling,
being an assemblage of huts; and a message was
sent to the King, to ask permission to visit him. His
Majesty's curiosity, however, was too great to admit of
any delay, and he paid a private visit to the strangers.
Some degree of etiquette was observed; for a box
covered with a mat was offered to him, but he dis-
dained the latter, and had one of the white men's
buffalo skins spread for him; and for a very good
reason, it being the law there, that whatever he sat
upon should for ever belong to him. He was attended
by Mohammedan priests called Malems, and several
officers of state, as well as relatives, who stood outside
the hut. Ajimba being already well known to the
King, presented his friends as having come with him
to make the acquaintance of his Majesty, and see the
trading; adding, that if they liked what they saw, they
would send plenty of white men when they got back
to their own country, and who would bring all sorts of
English goods to Fandah. The royal head nodded
approbation, and a gracious leave was given for the
strangers to see the capital, and pay him a visit at his
own palace. He then departed, taking Carlos' bed
along with him, which in point of warmth was but ill
supplied by a country cloth lent to him by Ajimba;
fortunately, however, the weather was becoming hot.

The King of Fandah had nothing to recommend

him in personal appearance, and was dressed in such an enormous quantity of tobes, that he looked like a bundle of dirty clothes. Round his neck were several charms, sewn up in pieces of leather and silk, which consisted of scraps of the Koran, written by the Mohammedans; besides these, he wore a profusion of beads on his neck, wrists, and ankles, and his pointed red cap was ornamented with tarnished gold lace. He seemed perfectly satisfied with himself, and to think that the strangers were equally so; but the strong odour of civet which issued from him, nearly overcame them, and proved that the little animal which they had thrown away in disgust in the forest would have been precious in Fandah, where it afforded the favourite perfume. It could not, however, take away the smell of dirt and grease which hung upon the tobes, as if they were never washed, and which, in fact, when too filthy to be worn, were dipped afresh into the dye-pots.

The next day the Europeans walked out to see the town, which was insignificant, and half in ruins, with only one broad street, which led to the palace. It had been surrounded by a mud wall, but this was now falling to pieces. On the side most exposed to the rains it had thatched battlements, which made it look something like a fortification, an appearance which was increased by a deep dry ditch and a bridge. In the market-place were a few tailors' shops, where tobes and country cloths were sold; but the provisions lay upon the ground, among which were some disgusting-looking meats, and little dirty heaps of salt from the Chadda, costing about the twentieth part of a penny. Ajimba being supplied with good English salt, sold it to great advantage. Bundles of firewood lay just

outside the market, and the only native manufactures
offered for sale were mats and cloths of a poor description,—the latter made in very rude looms, and
of even a narrower web than usual. On their return,
Carlos and Antonio inspected some dye-pits, formed
of earthen pans placed in holes in the ground, and
having lids to them. A very valuable species of native
indigo furnished the dye. The mordant appeared to
be a kind of potash, but the colour was very apt to
come off. When dry it had a bright metallic lustre,
and each pit contained from fifty to one hundred
gallons of liquid. A smith was at work in his forge,
making pipe bowls of copper. His anvil was placed
in the middle of his hut, and his tools consisted of a
clumsy hammer, a soldering iron, and a file, with
which he scratched patterns on the copper, and
thought his performance wonderful. Carlos made
Ajimba ask him whence that copper came; and he
replied, from Haussa. In fact, they everywhere heard
of Haussa as the great mart for that part of the continent, and most of the traders with whom they had
intercourse spoke the Haussa language, as if it were a
necessary acquirement in conducting their commercial transactions.

Two days after the arrival of the travellers, the King
held a review, and flourished about on a small sorry
horse, so covered with charms, pieces of metal, and
strings, that it was scarcely able to see its way. The
cavalry, to the number of ten, galloped about irregu-
larly, and shook their fists and lances at the King by
way of salute; then some men on foot came to pay
him their respects. These were dressed in white tobes,
and when close to him, suddenly stopped, turned round

S

upon their heels, stamped with their right feet, shook their sticks, and then throwing themselves on their knees, poured sand upon their heads as an act of homage.   Besides the horse soldiers, there were a dozen infantry with guns in their hands, which bid fair to burst when they were fired.   The review over, the Europeans followed the King into the town, where he alighted at a house, the entrance of which was concealed by a curtain, and from whence he issued in a much lighter and more convenient dress than that of his robes of state; but he still kept on a helmet which looked as if it had been made of tin, and resembled a common stew-pan without the handle.

In the evening the white men received a visit from a kind-hearted old woman, who had just arrived from a sojourn among the Filatah shepherds, and who brought with her fresh milk and butter, in which she traded; but she gave the strangers some, who were so forcibly reminded of home by these luxuries, now so uncommon to them, that they could hardly refrain from hugging 'Miss Banjih,' as Antonio called her. The kind-hearted woman seeing their delight, insisted on supplying them daily, although she knew that they could not pay her in return.   After a few days passed in strolling about, and accompanying Ajimba in his trading visits, the friends received an invitation from the head priest, or Malem, to call upon him; and they of course were glad to accept it, Ajimba going with them as interpreter.   They were first led through an entrance-hut, called a Zauli, into a large court, where a number of persons seated on mats, were reading the Koran aloud, and appearing to think that those prayed best who read the fastest, and made most noise. Opposite the entrance was a square mud edifice, and they passed through a low door covered with rude figures of crocodiles, elephants, leopards, and other animals, on one side of which lay a drawn dagger, and on the other a book ; and at first the guests feared there might be some treachery. However, they were received with the utmost gentleness and respect, were asked to sit down on bulls' hides, and cushions were placed for their elbows, covered with red and yellow leather in compartments. In the darkest part of the room was a very venerable old man, sitting on a white bull's skin, dressed in white, and having a long snowy beard. One ray of bright light, darting from the only window, illumined his whole figure ; and motioning to the Europeans to sit close to him, he told them, through their interpreter, that his name was Ibrahim, and that he should be glad to see their books if they had any. Carlos desired Ajimba to tell their story to the Malem, also desiring him to add, that they had but one of their holy books with them, which had been saved through all their dangers and sufferings. Carlos then took the gift of Henriquez out of the leathern bag in which he had placed it round his neck, and handed it to the old priest. On seeing this, all present crowded round to behold the curiosity, which excited much observation ; and when Carlos obeyed the request, that he would read some part of it aloud, and when he and Antonio bowed their heads reverently to the holy names, and concluded by singing one of the psalms with their rich voices, all seemed to be impressed with a feeling of devotion. The Malem made a great many inquiries concerning England, which he considered to be the common country of both; was surprised to hear that so many persons there could read; said that a great many good things came from that place; and that he had often heard his father say he had seen Englishmen, whom he called 'God's people,' in the far east. His manners were full of benignity and politeness, suggesting the word 'gentlemanly,' which was by no means too strong an epithet to be applied to them. When the travellers had departed, he sent them a present of eatables; and as they passed through the court on their return, they saw a number of women, children, and slaves in the surrounding huts, some of whom were probably the wives, children, and grandchildren of the Malem.

There was a square Mohammedan temple in the town made of mud, with a thatched turret at one end, and having a small staircase; but it was never used as a minaret, although probably, in the first instance, intended as such. A number of buttresses supported the walls on the outside, and the low doors (only opened in the times of prayer) led to a corridor, where the faithful counted their beads most devoutly. In some parts of the town were raised platforms, where skulls were placed in rows, said to be those of enemies; but if so, and the enemies killed in warfare did not amount to more than the owners of the skulls, the Fandah battles could not have been very fatal. It is, however, the object of the natives in most parts of Africa to take as many prisoners alive as possible, that they may sell them as slaves.

The people of Fandah were much addicted to wrestling; and some of the head men were very desirous of trying their strength with the white guests;

but the latter prudently declined, for, had they conquered, ill-will might have been produced, and had
they been overcome, it would have diminished the respect felt for their nation.   They received a visit from
the King's head wife, who was a much more agreeable person than the Queen of Naängo.   She was fat
and good-natured ; her hair tinged with indigo, and her
feet and hands with henna ; her eyes were blackened
all round with antimony, procured from the north and
east, and put on with a small stylus.   On her head
was a turban, and round her waist a country cloth,
which hung nearly down to her ankles.   She threw
herself on her knees before the Europeans, who immediately raised her ; but as they had nothing to give,
after laughing immoderately, she with her several attendants soon took her leave.   On their visit to the King
in his palace, the strangers were ushered into a large
court, surrounded by buildings, and having a covered
way ornamented with representations of animals ; and
where they saw the King's favourite slave, an ill-looking boy, who had a number of keys hanging in bunches
from his girdle ; a strange ornament which Carlos had
observed on the coast, and was surprised to find repeated so far inland.   It betrayed a singular idea of
personal decoration, for there probably was not a single
lock in either country to be opened by any one of
them.   It is not safe in Fandah to leave keys about,
as they are immediately purloined for the purpose of
decorating the person.

   The most interesting event which occurred at Fandah, was the holding of a court of justice, at which the
King presided in person.   He sat outside the gate of
his palace in full dress, with boots on his legs, de-

corated at the top with jingling brass-work, resembling
a fender; and, added to his usual decorations, was
the rude effigy of a human face, made of the same
metal, and hanging low from his neck. A large, gay,
European umbrella was held over him, and a boy
stood on each side, holding a fan made of ostrich
feathers, dyed of all colours, which feathers were procured from the eastern parts of the continent. An old
man sat in front wielding a brazen staff, and the elders
and men of consequence were placed around. In
the open space before these, were two men and two
women, sitting on the bare ground; and numerous
persons stood at a distance, who watched the proceedings with great interest. Ajimba explained to his
friends, that the four in the middle were the culprits,
who were accused of robbing the King's yam plantations, and were there to be tried for the crime. Much
discussion evidently took place; but the utmost de-
corum prevailed. The King spoke most; and when
he meditated, the boys covered him with their fans to
conceal him from the gaze of the multitude. The male
offenders did not utter a word; but one of the females,
who was old and infirm, cried very much, and frequently held out her arms as if to implore mercy.
The younger of the two, who was tall and strong,
raised herself upon her knees, and with much animated
gesture, and great volubility, made a long and apparently impassioned speech, to which the King listened
with great patience, but which did not seem to make
a favourable impression, as in a fluent reply he passed
sentence of condemnation. This was much applauded
by the court, but the poor delinquents shrieked with
despair; and the King retired to the innermost part of

his palace, where he always remained when executions were going on. The assembly separated, and none were left except the three friends, who remained to witness the result, and the old man with the brazen staff, who was prime minister and executioner. He summoned two attendants, who took some dark shining leaves, like those of the Portugal laurel, and some bark from an aged tree, now propped up and growing close by, which had been nearly stripped of the latter. These were pounded in a mortar, and then an infusion was made from them, half a pint of which was given to each woman. The poor creatures at first refused to take it, but at last, after casting many a piteous glance around, were forced to swallow it. They were then made to drink a copious draught of water, and afterwards to step over a twisted piece of grass; and were driven backwards and forwards past the fatal tree, each time gulping down more water, till they had exhausted several pitchers full. The old woman was very quiet; but the young one filled the air with her loud wailings and appeals to those present, who, however, did not in the least heed her. Both at first kept up a hurried and agitated pace; then they appeared to totter, as if giddy, and at length they fell. The young woman died first, with her arms stretched out, and the old woman sank by degrees into a stupor, from which she never recovered. The two men were sold as slaves. In the evening of the same day, the King administered justice in a very different manner; for, on visiting the white men, without state or ceremony, he found them beset by a tailor, who was not only importunate for them to buy some tobes, which he valued at an exorbitant price, but tried to rob

them. This so excited his Majesty's wrath that with
a cudgel, which he held in his hand, he dealt such
severe blows on the shoulders of the offender, that he
became almost breathless ; and when obliged to desist
from fatigue, the poor wretch crawled away upon his
knees, thanking his sovereign for his chastisement, but
casting sidelong glances at the Europeans, who laughed
heartily.   .

At length Ajimba had completed his bargains, and
before they took leave of the King, Carlos and Antonio
went to Miss Banjih's house, in which she lived with
another old woman.   It was the neatest in Fandah,
being kept perfectly clean, and the floor of which was
paved with pebbles and pieces of broken pottery. As
she had been so kind to them, Carlos presented one of
his remaining sovereigns to her.   The poor creature
was overwhelmed with gratitude ; for evidently, though
Carlos was far from expecting it could be viewed
in such a light, she thought it was a sort of fetish—
probably because it was taken from the bag worn round
his neck. The donor made her understand that she
must conceal it, as he had no intention of giving one
to the King ; and she, in return, insisted on his accept-
ing a bull's skin, which might replace that taken from
him. The whole party left the King with many expressions of gratitude, gave him some old metal buttons
which the Europeans took from their clothes, and
which appeared to please him ; and promising to
send some white traders to him, they left Fandah for
Pottinghia, by a different route to that which they had
taken on their arrival. The slaves carried the goods,
and the friends bore their knapsacks and weapons,
walking merrily through the most exquisite scenery,

presenting hill and dale, distant mountains, streams
and verdure, picturesque but small villages, patches of
Indian corn, and clumps of shrubs and trees interspersed through a green plain, giving, with the exception of the character of the foliage, the appearance of
a large English park. They could not help remarking
the lightness imparted to the thickest mimosas by the
delicacy of their leaves, which permitted the intensely
blue sky to shine through their edges, instead of the
heavy masses of more northern climates; an effect
which is most difficult for the painter to express.

The party gaily re-embarked, stopped afterwards at
a place where the inhabitants were fishing with nets,
and where there were large fields of mild aromatic
tobacco growing, and then proceeded down the Niger.
On the evening of the next day they saw a violent
tornado approaching from the south, and as it was
getting dark, they thought it better to avoid the fury
of the storm. They therefore moored the canoe to
the western bank of the river, where a group of low
overhanging bushes promised something like shelter.
The goods were covered with the hides which Ajimba
had purchased, and they retired into the cabin, the
slaves creeping under the bushes. As it did not yet
rain, they sat for some time at the entrance, watching
the progress of the storm and were struck with its
awful grandeur, for they had never before seen one on
land in so large an expanse. It so darkened the atmosphere, that they could not see their fingers when
held close before them; then a pale streak of light
appeared in the horizon, which became wider and
wider, and the clouds travelled rapidly towards them;
the wind raged till it deadened every other sound, and

then followed torrents of rain. The river appeared to boil, an effect which they were enabled to observe by the repeated flashes of lightning. They crept in under the slight awning, and, used to such phenomena, were soon buried in a profound slumber, canoe-men and all. From this they were awakened by a violent shaking of the canoe, accompanied by stamping of feet, shrieks, vociferations, struggling and splashing in the water. Ajimba, who was nearest to the aperture, sprang out first, drawing his large knive; but he was stabbed immediately, and fell senseless at the bottom of the canoe. The white men seized their spears and rushed after him; but they were instantaneously deprived of their weapons by the crowd which surrounded them, their hands were tied together, they were dragged ashore over the fallen bodies of their companions, and taken to the top of the bank. In despair they struggled to get loose, and partially succeeding, tried to escape; but they had not proceeded many yards before a bullet entered Antonio's leg; he dropped, and all further attempts at flight were useless. Both were again secured; and their captors took them across the country, and plunged with them into a thick wood, where they were rather pulled, than allowed to walk, over the bushes. The ruffians were dressed in short skirts, fastened round their loins, and a small skin cap upon their heads; their weapons were lances, bows and arrows, cutlasses, and one or two guns. They were of powerful make, and seemed to be remarkably active and warlike.

Carlos and Antonio in the hands of Robbers. —*Page* 261.

CHAPTER XVI.

WHEN they had proceeded to some distance, the robbers and their prisoners halted, and they all partook of some cold, roasted yam. A discussion seemed to arise among them concerning their living prizes; but at length, one who seemed to be their chief interposed his authority, and pointing towards some distant mountains, summoned the whole party to continue their route. The black men took up their plunder, for the canoe had been stripped, and set forward; but after walking a few yards, poor Antonio, faint from loss of blood, fell again upon the ground and was wholly unable to proceed; his leg pained him exceedingly, and fever began to pervade his whole frame. A consultation ensued, which Carlos eagerly watched in the hope of being able to guess the intentions of the marauders. He implored them by signs to leave them both where they were; but they apparently resolved to set out again with him alone, and leave Antonio to his fate. Carlos, however, whose strength was rendered fourfold by his feelings, broke all his bonds, and threw himself on the ground beside his friend. Then, as they tried to drag him away, he fell upon his knees, and baring his breast besought them by his gestures to kill them both rather than separate them. More than one spear was levelled at him; but when these rude men caught sight of the leathern bag round his neck, supposing it to be fetish, their arms were paralyzed, and the weapons dropped. He then joined his hands together and supplicated them, in order to try and soften their hearts; and as they stood irresolute, he stooped, and placing the almost insensible Antonio upon his shoulders, tried to make them aware of his willingness to carry his friend. The men, who were already sufficiently burthened, and who, negro-fashion, carried everything on their heads, would not have undertaken such a task; but they shouted their approbation of Carlos' plan, and motioned him to proceed. They went on for some time, Carlos bravely bearing his precious load; but as the heat of the day increased, his strength began to fail; at last a faintness came over him, and sinking under the weight, both fell to the ground together. Scarcely able to speak, Antonio feebly uttered, ' Save yourself, dear Lacy, and leave me to my fate.' ' Never while I have my senses left,' returned Carlos.

A deliberation took place among the robbers, the result of which was, that with the European hatchet which they seemed to know well how to use, they, by the direction of their chief, cut down some branches of trees, made a litter of them, and placing the wounded man upon it, took it in turns with Carlos to carry him. This was comparatively easy, and on they marched, hour after hour, only resting when absolutely necessary. Through what sort of country they passed, however, the white men could not tell; for Antonio was too ill to open his eyes, and Carlos was too intently watching all his symptoms to look about him. Whenever they came to a stream, he begged a small calabash from one of the men, and moistened his friend's lips with water; and this seemed to be the only thing which kept him alive. At length they entered a town of the usual conical huts, the expedition being received by the inhabitants with shouts of joy and triumph, which subsided in the astonishment and curiosity with which they viewed the white men. Their intrusive prying, however, was repressed by the chief, who appeared to be of considerable consequence among them; and who, placing the Europeans in a hut, left them for a short time lying upon some mats, having placed a guard over them, more to keep off others, than to prevent their escape.

After some minutes of tranquillity, Antonio opened his eyelids, and seeing no one near but Carlos, who was hanging over him in an agony of suspense, faintly said, 'Are they going to eat us, Lacy?' 'No! No! my dear fellow,' answered Carlos, 'I hope not; but we are prisoners among a set of robbers, probably Filatahs. What they will do with us I cannot at all guess—not kill us, I think, or they would have done so before; but we are totally defenceless, and our best plan will be to submit to their pleasure.' The chief returned with another man whom they supposed to be a doctor, for he examined Antonio's leg, pressed it cautiously, even tenderly, to find out where the ball was; and then, shaking his head, left him. He soon, however, returned with a poultice, which he applied, after washing the wound well with water, and bound upon the leg with strips of cotton cloth. Everything which had been stuck into their girdles, such as country knives, spoons, etc., was taken from the prisoners; and having been supplied with a mess of boiled rice, and a large pot full of water, they were once more left to repose. Worn with fatigue and distress of mind, they both slept for a time; but Antonio's wound soon began to give him such pain, that he could not enjoy anything like slumber. It seemed momentarily to increase; and, unwilling to disturb his friend by the groans which might otherwise have escaped from him, he sat up, leaning his back against the wall, and by compressing his lips, tried all he could to stifle even a murmur. Carlos, however, was too anxious to sleep long; and when he awoke, instantly came to his companion and asked him to have some water. After he had swallowed a mouthful, he asked if Carlos thought that the poultice might be removed; for he did not think he could bear it any longer, it seemed so much to increase his sufferings. Carlos instantly took it off, and on examining it, exclaimed, 'No wonder it gave you so much pain, for it is made of those little hot peppers from which we get the cayenne.' Somewhat relieved by the removal of the application, and refreshed by the water, the wounded man again lay down; but fever came on, and he tossed about and raved so much, that his friend could scarcely hold him, and prevent him from doing himself some mischief.

Morning at length appeared, and with it the doctor, who, on examining his patient, again shook his head, and fetching a small lamp of palm oil, a knife, and some thick nut-shells, heated the latter in the manner of cupping-glasses, and placed them on Antonio's temple. On taking them off he was about to make an incision in the raised flesh; but Carlos stopped him, seized hold of the cloth which the man had hung over his arm, dipped it into the water, and bound it round his friend's head. He then made signs for more water and more cloths; the man comprehended and obeyed him, then sat watching the effect, which was that of producing much relief. He again left the hut, brought Carlos some food, and in a few hours returned with a sort of plaster, made, as he showed Carlos, from some emollient leaves, which the latter recognised as belonging to the Hibiscus tribe of plants. The native doctor appeared to feel much compassion for his patient, and was earnest in his endeavours to do him good; for nothing softens the black man's heart so immediately as illness. The cold applications were constantly renewed, and at length Antonio slept soundly.

Carlos was fed; both were left for the night; and the next day, Antonio was not only able to sit up, but had the entire possession of his senses. 'How shall we get from hence?' said he. 'Shall we ever extricate ourselves from these wretches?' 'Stop till you are well of your wound,' answered Carlos; 'you could neither run fast nor far just now; but I hope you will shortly be as well as ever, and as strong upon your legs as upon the various occasions in which we have had to save ourselves by the help of our heels.'

'Could we but get this ball out!' continued Antonio, looking at, and pinching his leg. 'Look, Lacy, here it is, on the side opposite to the hole; if we had but a knife to cut the skin with, it would roll out of itself.' 'They have not robbed me of my sailor's knife,' said Carlos, 'for they know nothing of trouser pockets hereabouts. But I am afraid it is not very sharp.

T

Poor Ajimba had promised to set it as soon as we got back to his home. But I am afraid he was finished in that horrid affair on the river. Next to Wondo he was our kindest and best friend, and I shall always think of him with affection.' Antonio stretched the skin over the bullet, Carlos contrived to make the incision, and out it flew to the opposite side of the hut. They showed it in triumph to the doctor when he reappeared, who was exceedingly astonished. He looked at the leg, then at the bullet, but could not comprehend how it had been extricated—for Carlos had again pocketed his knife—and saying 'Fetish!' left them. 'If it were but possible to escape,' said Antonio, 'I am sure I should be able to walk in a few days;' but the prisoners were much too narrowly watched and surrounded to render any scheme practicable which they could form in their destitute condition; and they knew too well the absolute requisites for sustaining life in a wild country, not to shrink from encountering the risk without them.

As soon as Antonio was able to walk, although in consequence of limping a little he was obliged to use a stick, the chief made signs to both Europeans to follow him outside the hut. There he bound a cord round the neck of each, and fastened them together. He then started with the addition of four attendants, and they marched after him. Several days elapsed; the journeys at first being short on account of Antonio, and food was supplied by the attendants. The Europeans did not enter any village, but remained on the outskirts while two men at a time were sent to purchase what they wanted with cowries. As Antonio recovered his strength, the distances performed each

day became longer, till they reached a plain at the
foot of some detached mountains; and there lay a
large city, composed of much better-looking houses
than any which the travellers had yet seen. They
stopped short of it, however, all night, sleeping as
usual in the open air, and were the next morning
taken to a river, where they were ordered to bathe;
their skins were rubbed, their hair smoothed with a
coarse native comb, their hands were bound behind
them, and they were marched into a large market-
place, where they took their stand among a great
many others, who, like them, were going to be sold
as slaves. On casting their eyes around, they saw a
display of wealth and industry for which they were
not prepared. Natives with cloths round their waists,
or short petticoats, were bustling about in all directions; then came their masters with caps on their
heads, their feet thrust into highly-wrought sandals,
and their figures enveloped in handsome cloths, put
on toga fashion, or in tobes; and besides these were
Mohammedans, with ample tunics and turbans. The
appearance of the Europeans created considerable
surprise, and many were the questions put to the
man who had them in his possession. His answers
appeared to be always the same, and his gestures
seemed to imply that they came from a distance.
Several persons, apparently of consequence, offered
to buy them; but their price was rejected. 'I should
think,' said Antonio, 'that they are asking a great
sum for us; I hope we shall not be separated.' This
probability had not struck Carlos before, and the
paleness which immediately overspread his countenance showed that he suffered from it. Anguish was

written there, and he pressed still more closely to his friend. Slavery itself was comparatively slight to this; and with intense anxiety, both awaited the result of each bidding. At length the crowd which had gathered round them opened, and made way for a Moor, whose rich, brocaded silk dress and jewelled turban bespoke the man of consequence. Many of those around prostrated themselves before him, and others made a salaam to the ground. He stopped and looked at the white men with keen curiosity, and continued to gaze at them the whole time that the slave-trader was telling their history. Then the Moor, scornfully uttering the word 'Nassareen,' evidently asked what he was to give for them; their master answered, a little bargaining ensued, and at length, calling an attendant, the Moor desired him to pay a certain number of cowries out of a bag which he carried, and then bidding him take the man with him, probably to deliver to him the remainder of the sum, he ordered that the newly-purchased slaves should be led to his house. 'Thank God!' exclaimed the two friends at the same moment, ' we shall be together;' and, with a light step, they almost joyfully followed their guide even into slavery.

The dwelling of the Moor consisted of a large square court, surrounded by highly-ornamented buildings, but thatched in the usual manner. Through that which faced the street, and which was open in front, the white men passed into the court, crossed it, and going through another, were lodged in a small apartment, which looked into a third court of very diminished proportions. Into this room they were thrust, unbound, and then left; a rude wooden bolt being let down, which fastened the door on the outside; after which, the steps of the man to whom they had been entrusted were heard to retreat across the outer court. In a few hours the bolt was withdrawn, and rice and water brought to them. The whole night was passed in suspense as to their fate; another meal was supplied, mixed with a very glutinous and highly-flavoured soup, made from snails. 'They mean to treat us well, however,' said Antonio. 'I am not sure,' said Carlos, 'for I think we have fallen into the hands of powerful Mohammedans, who will be spiteful to us, if it be only because we are Christians.' As he said this, several men entered, stripped them of all they had on, and gave them in exchange a narrow strip of cloth to twist round their loins. Only the bag remained which contained the prayer-book, and to retain this Carlos struggled, and then entreated; but it was of no use; he was overpowered and unheeded, and he thought that only one thing could be worse than losing this, which was parting from his friend. The escape from the latter, however, reconciled him to everything; and the moment this thought suggested itself, with a look of gratitude to heaven, he quietly submitted. 'I am afraid this is a bad omen,' observed Antonio; 'now that book is gone, I shall feel less protected than ever.' 'Nay,' rejoined Carlos, 'that is superstition. Have we not the words, and the spirit of the words, in our hearts? We can say all the prayers and psalms without the book, for we have repeated them in many a dark night; and if we could not, we should be heard in our own words. Resistance would but bring destruction upon us, and therefore we must be patient in all things, even as our Great Master was before us.

Courage then, Antonio!' So saying, he followed the men into the little court, where were two wooden stakes, to which he and Antonio were tied, and made to beat corn incessantly. The moment they relaxed, a man, who stood by, struck them with a whip which he held in his hand, and which was composed of many lashes. During the great heat they were unbound, and suffered to lie down in their room; but when the sun began to decline, they were forced to resume their labour, from which they were only again released at nightfall. After a few days their patience and docility seemed to make some impression; they were allowed to work without being bound to the stake, and their food was also a little improved, from being allowed to mix a little fruit with their rice. It was, however, hard labour; and although grateful for its being no worse, and that they were allowed to pass their nights at least in repose, the hopelessness of their situation, and the confined view of their little court, began to prey upon their spirits. So long used to exercise in the open air, they became oppressed, and almost for the first time in their lives had headaches.

A long weary month was passed in the monotonous routine of sleep and beating corn, when the white slaves were summoned to their master, who, seated in the verandah of his house, smoked his long pipe, and viewed them with a malignant expression of countenance. He desired that a coarse tunic should be brought to each, and then that their heads should be shaved, a turban being substituted for their natural covering. 'Good-bye to my beautiful locks,' said Antonio. 'And to mine too,' added Carlos with a sigh, 'of which my dear Kathleen used to be so proud.'

'They will grow all the stronger for it afterwards,' re-joined Antonio; 'and if we are always to wear these turbans, we are certainly better without hair. But I wish I knew how to get into favour with that ill-looking master of ours.' 'I would do anything but turn Moham-medan,' resumed Carlos, 'and which, if I am not mis-taken, they are now going to ask us to do. Be firm Antonio.' 'Never fear for me,' replied his friend; 'I should have profited but little by all your lessons, Lacy, if I were not ready to meet death rather than deny my religion.' As he said these words, the Koran was pre-sented to each; but they turned their heads away, and tried to express that it was useless to ask them to accept it. The chief looked angrily at them; the most threatening gestures were used; but finding that all was ineffectual, he ordered them back to their mono-tonous employment.

Carlos and Antonio submitted to all their priva-tions without complaint, and the experiment of induc-ing them to become Mussulmans was repeated several times with the same want of success; and at length they were taken from their court, fastened to black slaves, and sent to cut and carry wood and water from the neighbouring forest. These offices, though intended as a great degradation, were infinitely more agreeable than that which they had just quitted. Their strength, their willingness, their forbearance towards their companions, whom they frequently assisted, and their general good-humour, procured them many friends, and they endeavoured to acquire some of the languages which they heard spoken around them. Most of all, however, did they desire to learn Arabic, and no word of it which they recognised as such did they suffer to pass unheeded. The slaves, as they came in procession to the town with their burdens, often uttered a monotonous chant, with which to beguile their way. 'Let us astonish them,' said Antonio to his friend, 'with some of our music. If we please their ears, as we have done those of others, they may be more inclined to think well of us.' Carlos complied, and taking advantage of a pause in the negro chant, they both began ; and before they had finished a verse, the wondering natives were listening with breathless interest. They continued as they passed through part of the town, where such sounds were never before heard, and where all left their employments as the procession passed, to hear and to admire. This practice was repeated again and again at the request of their brethern in bondage, till it became a settled thing to flock to the foot-way which they took, and wait and listen to Sidi Baba's white slaves as they went home. The exercise cheered the singers themselves ; and as they did not mind toil in the open air, the breezes from the neighbouring mountains, and the free use of their limbs, restored them to a portion of their usual vivacity.

At length Sibi Baba himself was informed of their proceedings, and summoned them to his presence to give a proof of their powers. He affected to hear them with indifference, but the impression was evidently favourable. By degrees their condition was ameliorated ; they were earlier summoned home ; they were allowed to wear full trousers, handsome tunics, and sandals, and were frequently ordered to entertain their master, and sometimes his guests. Once or twice, too, they thought they heard a rus-

tling behind the curtain of a doorway, which told that
the ladies of the harem were also allowed to listen.
Practice gives power, and Antonio's gondolier habits
of improvization extended to Carlos, so that their
songs became inexhaustible, and it was difficult sometimes, even for the performers, to keep their gravity,
as they uttered the most absurd inventions in the
rhythm of several languages. A buffo song, alternately grave and comic, and in which Antonio took
the latter part, and both finished by rapid utterance,
as they sang together, was an universal favourite,
especially as they, in some sort, acted the story.
Even the solemn Moor himself would relax his stern
features into a smile, and stroke his scanty beard
between his fingers, while his followers laughed till
the tears trickled down their cheeks. This was generally the closing melody, and was an easy manœuvre
on the part of the singers to get away when they were
tired; for the disorder which ensued, generally caused
the Moor to end the entertainment; but he seldom
failed to send the performers afterwards something
good for their supper.

Having selected some wood in the forest which
they thought would suit their purpose, they begged
to be allowed the use of a knife each, and having
won the heart of Aboosee, the superintendent of the
slaves, their request was secretly granted. Being
further allowed a lamp of palm oil, they in time produced a bowl and platter, on which they carved
flowers and animals in high relief, and which they
presented to the superintendent himself, in return for
his repeated indulgences. He did not, however,
dare to keep them, and, perhaps, having a kinder

motive, carried them to his master. They obtained his approbation. The white men no longer remained hewers of wood and drawers of water; they were moved into a larger apartment, where they received much more air and light. They were allowed to select what logs they pleased, and, under the superintendent's eye, were permitted to purchase whatever they wanted in the market-place, thus improving their tools; for though there were none made expressly for their art, yet they found some which, by a little contrivance, were altered so as to suit their purpose. All this, however, had its attendant evil,—they were generally kept so closely at work, that their health at first suffered from the confinement; but their extreme temperance and resignation were their best friends; and next to these, Aboosee, who, whether known or not to his master they could not tell, now and then indulged them with a ride on horseback.

Such rare talents could not long remain hidden, and the King one day angrily sent for Sidi Baba, and asked why he too should not hear and witness the powers of the extraordinary slaves. In order to appease him, the Moor presented him with some of their carving; but this only created a desire for more, and by no means satisfied his ears. They were therefore summoned in too peremptory a manner to be denied. They were ushered into the presence of an immensely fat old man, enveloped in tobes, with a cap on, covered with gold, and an enormous gold chain round his neck. Their performance excited a sensation of delight throughout the whole court; and if he had dared, the King would have retained them both as his own; but it was not policy on his part to

offend the powerful Sidi Baba. His demands, however, for their company were so incessant, that Sidi
Baba was displeased. At length he hit upon an
expedient which kept them more with him, which
was, that of ordering them to make a large stool
for the King, of the soft yellow Sessa wood, which
was to be highly decorated; and pretending that
they were too busily employed for his Majesty to
come often, he thus contrived to secure them almost
entirely for himself.

Thus passed a second rainy season, which more
than completed the two years which had elapsed since
the Europeans had left Liverpool. They saw nothing
of the surrounding country; for the more valuable
they were, the more jealously they were watched.
At length the stool was completed; it was supported
by two lions at rest, or what heralds call *couchant*,
whose heads peeped from beneath the seat, and
served for handles, while the paws formed the slab
on which stood the seat. In front, and at the back,
hung the most beautiful flowers of the country. The
whole was polished with the rough leaves of a species
of Grewia, which were found in the forest, and which
were also used by the natives for the same purpose.
The Moor condescended to express his approbation,
and presenting the stool in due form on the King's
fête-day, announced his intention of journeying on
business to the south. The King asked again whether
he might purchase the clever slaves; but he was again
refused, and preparations were made for immediate
departure. Carlos and Antonio were ordered to take
especial care of their tools, and carry them with them;
and the former thought this a good opportunity of

trying to regain his prayer-book. He asked Aboosee
to solicit this favour from their master; but the superintendent shook his head mysteriously, and told him
it was impossible.

All was ready for starting, and the caravan slowly
wound its way through the city and the neighbouring
forest. A guard of men, with bows, arrows, and
lances, dressed in short white tunics and caps, pre-
ceded the whole cavalcade. Then came the chief
slaves on horseback, among whom were the white
men, who were followed by the officers in pay;
then Baba and the harem and children, all on
horseback, each woman carefully veiled, accompanied
by her own attendants. These were entirely surrounded by the Arab guard, riding Arab horses, and
armed with lances, cutlasses, and muskets, and
dressed in short tunics and turbans, with a large
robe called a burnous, which served them as a
wrapper by day and a bed by night. At the heel of
all came the common slaves and attendants, taking
charge of the baggage horses, and themselves carrying burthens.

The delight of the Europeans at again finding
themselves in a wild country was great; it seemed
to promise home and freedom, and their spirits rose
accordingly. The route lay across mountains, which,
however, were not very high; over rivers, plains, and
rich savannahs, and through forests of great magnificence; and in all there was something like a track,
for no one seemed to be doubtful of the way, and the
foremost rode on as carelessly as if there had been
a high road. They were bound for Yahndi, the capital
of Dagwumba, where the Moor had promised to go

and organize the affairs of the Mohammedans who had
settled there ; he being a high priest and lawgiver of
the tribe of Ali.

The march was long and wearisome, because it
was not possible to go very far in the course of the
day on account of the women ; some of whom appeared to the Europeans to be very fat, and were
lifted like bundles from their steeds by their own
allotted servants. They encamped every night, and
the ladies were secured in the large tent of Sidi
Baba, round which the Arab guard was always on
duty. The slaves slept in the open air, which was
not at all disagreeable to Carlos and Antonio. The
two latter were narrowly watched, for fear they should
attempt to escape, but they had no intention even of
trying. They knew they were going to the south,
which was all in their way, and as they had always
heard of Dagwumba as a place which held extensive
intercourse with other nations, they hoped there to
find some opportunity favourable to the views which
they never ceased to entertain, of ultimately reaching
home. By this time they spoke Arabic fluently, and
forming a sort of friendship with some of the Arab
guard, could not help being struck with their superior
bearing and deportment ; verifying the expression of
a celebrated English traveller, who calls the Arabs,
' the aristocracy of savages.'

The cavalcade never ventured into large towns,
but always encamped at a little distance from them.
Sidi ·Baba, however, when he had business there,
frequently absented himself for a night ; and the
inferior slaves constantly accompanied the superintendent to make purchases of food. On one of the

occasions of Baba's absence, the guard was picketed as usual; the moon was clear and bright, but the night was hot, and Carlos was strolling about the camp in order to try and find a cooler place to lie in than that which had been allotted to him. In the course of his perambulations he came in contact with the outposts of the Arab guard, where he found one of the men writhing with pain, unable to remain at his duty, and yet not daring to leave it. 'Go,' said Carlos to him, 'and lie down for a short time: our dresses are alike; give me your arms, and I will stand in your place.' The man hesitated; but he became worse and worse, and at length was obliged to trust the white man to remain in his stead. Carlos had not been long at his post before the horses, which were not far off, became agitated; and the live stock was restless and uneasy. This made him still more watchful, and seeing that his firelock was in good order, he stood ready to meet the foe, which his long experience in wild beasts told him was approaching. The camp was not far from a large forest, whence issued two lions. The outlying scouts being negroes, who sleep anyhow and anywhere, even when standing upright without support, were probably fast asleep, and the animals advanced. One of them was shot by a soldier of the Arab guard, and retreated, leaving traces of his blood along the path, and the second was shot through the heart by another of the same body. The whole camp was in an uproar; but the danger being over, all returned to quiet and order. Yusuf, the sick man, came back to his post, much relieved from his pain, but in an agony of alarm, for fear he should have been found

out, and not having dared to leave his hiding-place,
for fear of discovery, while so many were stirring;
but all was safe. Carlos returned his weapons, and
went back to his own lair, after telling him what had
occurred. When Sidi Baba reappeared at the camp
the next day, the circumstance was related to him. He
inquired after the two men who had fired the success-
ful shots: the first was easily found, and received a
handsome present; but where was the guard who had
killed the second lion? He was seen standing over the
body of his foe, as one of the slaves was stripping the
skin off. He was summoned to his master's presence,
who praised him and offered him a reward; but Yusuf
refused, saying, that he did not wish for any recom-
pense. 'Then, I make you chief of the guard,' said
Sidi Baba, 'for the present captain leaves me to-day
to remain in the town with my brother, who has
begged for him.' The Arab made his most respectful salutation, was immediately installed in his new
office, and the skin of the lion was presented to him
to hang upon his saddle as a trophy.

The caravan again started; and soon after, as the
horsemen became mingled together, Yusuf took an
opportunity of whispering to Carlos, 'Christian, you
are my brother; to you I owe all that I am now.
Had I remained at my post I must have died, for I
was too ill to have fired my gun. You have had all
the danger, and I the reward, and yet you do not tell.'
'No!' returned Carlos; 'all men are brothers among
Christians. I shall never tell.' 'And I shall always
remember,' added Yusuf. From that moment the
influence of Yusuf was often felt by the Europeans;
better horses, with more commodious trappings, were

given to them to ride ; many a delicious mess was sent from the Arab fire at the time of the bivouac-ing, which, as slaves, they had no right to expect. When the Christians were called upon to sit at the door of Baba's tent, to amuse him and his wives with their songs, Yusuf, who also liked to hear them, whispered many an encouraging kind word in their ear, without exciting suspicion.   But they knew he was obliged to be very cautious for fear of awaken-ing jealousy ; or there were other times, when, owing to his apparent indifference, they might have fancied themselves forgotten by the man who owed everything to Carlos.

It was on this journey that the Europeans learned to like the Gora or Gooroo nuts, which the slaves gathered in the forests, and which were often distri-buted through the whole caravan, as a means of secur-ing health, and of correcting the badness of the water, which they were sometimes obliged to drink.   A little time after they had been steeped in it, the liquid be-came perfectly sweet and pure in its flavour.   The natives constantly chewed them, and Carlos and An-tonio at last conquered their repugnance to their astringent properties, and began, in their turns, to think them necessary to their comfort.   They saw the trees on which they grew, and found their leaves to be large and broad, and the pod which contains from seven to nine beans, about the size of a chestnut, but flatter, was about eighteen inches long.

Signs of civilisation appeared, and a superior degree of cultivation opened upon the travellers as they ap-proached Yahndi, showing unequivocal signs of the vicinity of a large and important city.   They encamped

on the outskirts of a wood, through which a broad
path had been made, and was carefully kept. A
deputation was sent to the town to announce the
arrival of Baba to his brother Moors, who, already in
expectation of his coming, had prepared quarters for
the accommodation of his numerous company. It was
probably the last morning which they should pass in
the bush, and the Mohammedan ordered that solemn
thanks should be given for their safe arrival. The
ablutions being performed, cow-hides were spread for
all the inferior worshippers, and a rich carpet was
placed on the ground for Baba, on the eastern side of
the tents. The sandals were taken off, and all prostrated themselves; their faces in the supposed direction of Mecca. The service began by the call to
prayer, and was ended by loud chanting, the burthen
of which was the sentence 'God is great,' in which
praise none could more fervently join than the Christians, but who kept aloof from the rest of the worshippers, saying their own prayers.

The morning meal was eaten, and Sidi Baba placed
himself at the door of his tent, where he had not been
long seated, when two men on small horses galloped
up to the camp at a furious pace, in company with
the two Arabs who had been despatched to Yahndi.
They dismounted, and Baba giving them permission
to approach his presence, they, under the guidance
of Yusuf, followed him inside. They bore a letter
wrapped in red silk, which they delivered with many
prostrations; and immediately after reading it, the
Moor gave orders to Yusuf to put the whole caravan
into motion as speedily as possible. He was obeyed,
and before they had proceeded far they were met by

U

a whole body of Moors, accompanied by the firing of muskets, the blowing of horns, the beating of drums, and other noisy demonstrations of joy. The cavalcade divided and formed a sort of lane, through which those from Yahndi passed, and paid their homage to the powerful Mussulman who was come to visit them. The welcome was returned by the usual salutation of ' Peace be with you,' and each man then fell in with the order of the procession as he best could ; those of the most consequence keeping close to Baba, with whom they entered into conversation. The Europeans now and then fancied they were alluded to in it, as the speakers occasionally turned in their saddles, and shading their eyes with their hand, gazed earnestly upon them.

The whole population of the city seemed to have assembled to gratify its curiosity ; and it was very difficult for the horsemen not to tread some of them under foot ; but, avoiding the principal streets, the procession was conducted to the Moorish quarter, where each horseman was ordered to lead his steed to a long row of stables provided for them, and to see to it himself. The ladies were lifted from theirs, and their children carried carefully after them. They waddled through the entrance-room into the court, and disappeared from public inspection.

The position of the white slaves was by no means improved by their removal to Yahndi ; for the same occupations were assigned to them of carving and singing, the same jealous watchfulness was observed towards them, perhaps even in a greater degree ; and they were never suffered to walk out except under the care of their superintendent, or occasionally with one

or two of the Arab guard, when the logs of wood provided for cooking did not present them with that
which they required; but they certainly took care to
be very difficult to please, that they might oftener enjoy change of scene. This, however, was soon de-
feated, for the intelligent natives began to comprehend
what they wanted; and, well acquainted with the trees
around them, soon brought the choicest morsels to the
dwelling of the Moor, delighted to have found a new
material with which they could trade. Some of these
were so hard and firm in their texture that they completely turned the edge of the fine tools which the
Europeans employed; on others they could not make
any impression at all. With several species they were
already acquainted, especially the bamboo, which had
so nearly spoiled their hatchet in the forest, from the
quantity of flint which it contains; but many were new
and beautiful, not only from colour, but veining; and
one sort was so soft and fibrous, that it was perfectly
useless. They inquired what it was, and were told
that it came from a very large tree, not very lofty,
but having widely spreading branches and broad
leaves; that it would not even burn, and that it had
only been presented to the carvers by way of experiment. The travellers easily recognised the Baobab
in this description, and thought it one of the inexpli-
cable secrets of nature, why this enormous mass of
vegetable matter should comparatively afford so little
advantage to man or beast.

Aboosee and Yusuf were the only persons who were
admitted to converse with Carlos and Antonio; but
the latter came so seldom, that he was evidently afraid
of exciting suspicion. Their singing, however, was

often put in requisition for the entertainment of their master and his guests. For a time they performed with spirit, and nods of approbation and presents were bestowed upon them, the latter of which, however, they were obliged immediately to deliver over to Aboosee or Yusuf, even if they were merely eatables. It would have been a wretched life if they had not possessed a source of enjoyment which was only known to themselves. The window in their apartment opened on to the roofs of others; and at the end of one of these was the large bough of an enormous tree. By creeping out of the window, and clinging to the neighbouring thatch, they contrived to reach this bough, and by means of it place themselves in the midst of the tree itself, from which they had a view of the whole town and its vicinity. At a distance were mountains, and the rest of the country bore the same features as those they had so lately witnessed. Small forests were interspersed through the plains, and gentle risings prevented monotony in the latter, presenting the English park-like appearance which they had so often seen in Africa. Immense herds and flocks, and a small breed of horses, grazed all round, mingled with antelopes and swine. Beyond these elephants were seen occasionally to issue from the forests, but not venturing near the city. Now and then the gnu was to be seen among the antelopes, and easily distinguished from the peculiar carriage of its head. They cautiously inquired concerning it of Aboosee, and were surprised to find that it bore the same name there as that which distinguishes it in the southern parts of the continent.

CHAPTER XVII.

THE houses of Yahndi were most of them extremely well built, and consisted of various apartments round a series of courts, the principal entrance to which, being the usual open reception-room, faced the street. The lower and outer portions of these rooms were constantly washed with red ochre; the upper were covered with the most elaborate patterns, formed in relief with pliant wood, and washed over with white clay. The roofs, supported by square pillars, were sloping, made of palm leaves, and having rafters of bamboo inside, which were blackened and polished. The street rooms were halls of audience for men of consequence. The doors within were richly carved and coloured with various pigments, procured chiefly from vegetable substances.

Numerous caravans were constantly arriving at and leaving the city, giving a high idea of its commercial relations. All the natives who were not Mohammedans had three long deep scars under the eye; while those from the neighbouring country had three on the cheek-bone, and one below the eye, which was horizontal, and which were said to have been made while the person was young, and an infusion of bitter herbs poured in to make him strong. The cognomen of the sovereign was Innana, and he had been converted to Mohammedanism.   The lower classes, however, were pagans, and lived in bell-shaped houses.

The whole merchandise of north-western Africa flowed into that immense market; and as their tree was not far from it, and they were sometimes taken stealthily into it by Aboosee, on condition that they did not speak to any one there but himself, the white slaves were enabled to ascertain what articles were exposed for sale.   Their variety and frequent beauty often excited their admiration, and the dresses for the Ashantis, among other things, particularly attracted their attention.   Those for the captains consisted of sleeveless jackets of red cloth, so covered with scraps of the Koran, esteemed as charms, and called safies, that none of the original material could be seen, except when the wearers used any violent gestures, at which time they flapped up and down, and displayed the colour underneath.   These safies were sewn up in cases of variously-coloured silks, and were a great source of wealth to the learned Moors who wrote them.   The value of a jacket thus covered was equal to the price of thirty slaves, and it was supposed to render the wearers invincible.   This belief might be easily confirmed, as the captains of the Ashanti army never mingled in the battle itself, but kept in the rear, in order to direct and turn back any soldiers who might try to run away.   The caps for these commanders were formed, it was said, of black and brown eagles' plumes; but the latter looked much more like dyed ostrich feathers.   They were ornamented in front with gilded rams' horns, were fastened under the chin with bands of cowries, and the tops waved about with much grace and majesty.   The trousers were short and full—made either of muslin from the east, or white cotton, woven in Dagwumba. The boots, formed of red leather, came half-way up the thigh, and were fastened to a broad black belt round the waist with fine chains of iron. They were decorated at the top with cows' and horses' tails, and strips of leather, all of which were considered as amulets ; and round the ankles was a string of small brass bells, which jingled as the wearers walked. Single cow's and horse's tails were destined to hang from the arms, and were charmed by the fetish.

All the leather, for every purpose, and of every kind, was prepared and dyed in Dagwumba, and was remarkably soft and pliant. Of it were made saddles, bridles, and other trappings for horses and bullocks, which were occasionally rode by the Moors ; bags, caps, cushions, which were ingeniously tinged with various colours, and ornamented with patterns made by thinly paring off the upper surface, and exquisitely stitched together ; the sheaths and handles of daggers, quivers, and sandals, the latter of which might be alsmot termed woven, for the leather was cut into very narrow strips, and plaited over the surface, or inserted into very small holes made with a sharply pointed instrument in a solid mass of leather, so as to resemble stitches. The black caps and belts for soldiers were made of pig or elephant skin.

The cloths of Dagwumba were formed of many breadths sewn together, the widest of which measured only three inches and a half across. The cotton which was used for them was spun chiefly by women, with a spindle ; and the loom, constructed of bamboo, was simple almost to rudeness. The patterns were chiefly stripes; but there was a peculiarly beautiful white cloth, worn by the negro kings on their fetish day, and which, when painted all over in black patterns, with a fowl's feather dipped into a liquid made of the bark of a tree, and fowl's blood, was used as mourning. Aboosee one day took the white men to see the operation, when they found the cloths spread upon the ground, and the men who painted them on their knees, beginning the design at one corner, and crawling backwards as they filled up the space. The devices were most fanciful, but they did not appear to be symbolical. In those of the houses and doors, Carlos was surprised at finding vestiges of Egyptian characters and symbols. The cloths worn as togas were frequently of immense size, and silk was often introduced into the web, which was procured from the silks brought by the Moors, and unravelled for the purpose. Threads of gold were occasionally inserted, also derived from eastern silks. Numerous were the dyes made from native substances, chiefly vegetable; and among them was one of a bright blue, derived from a plant called Acassie, which had a red flower, and broad pointed leaves; the latter were bruised in a wooden mortar, spread out on mats to dry, and kept in masses. When used, a certain quantity was put into a pot with water, and suffered to infuse for six days; it was then strained and returned to the pot, when the material was steeped in it. If to be of a deep colour, it there remained for six days; but if intended to be of a light blue, it was left only for three days; and in each case was perfectly fast without a mordant. A great deal of cotton was dyed before it was woven. Thread was made from aloe and pine-

apple leaves, flax from various plants; and the sheep
of the neighbourhood supplied wool, which was converted into coarse blankets.

The pottery ot Yahndi, generally red in colour, was
frequently of a beautiful and classical shape, and
polished by friction; the patterns on it were cut out
while they were soft, and filled up with white clay;
the pipe-bowls are of the most fanciful forms. There
was a rarer sort of earthenware of a deep black, and
most brilliant polish, but which was brittle in texture.
The working of gold surprised the Europeans; it was
frequently so delicate and elaborate. None of this
metal was found in Dagwumba, but it came in large
quantities from the south-west in the shape ot lumps
or dust. In the former instance it was procured from
pits, and in the latter washed out of the sand. The
model of the device was first made in bees' wax, which
was carefully enclosed in wet clay and charcoal, mixed
together, which formed a mould of the wax figure.
To this was attached a small cup of the same materials,
to contain the gold, and put into the earthen furnace.
where the wax melted in the mould, and the gold in
the cup; the whole was then turned, and the latter
ran into the hollow left by the former, through a small
perforation. When cool, the mould was broken into
pieces, and if the articles were not perfect, the whole
process was repeated. The gold was coloured with
red ochre, and boiled in a mixture of that substance,
water, and salt, and it was then cleansed by brushing
and rubbing. Silver was occasionally wrought in the
same manner, which was chiefly supplied from the
western coast, and brought to Yahndi by the traders.
The forges were blown with rude bellows, and the

smiths had an anvil of iron or stone. The ore of the former was melted in earthen furnaces, came from a distance, and was made into numerous articles, from the enormous broad, flat swords, the blades of which were perforated like fish trowels, to needles, the size of those used for making carpets in Europe. Gong-gongs, or hollow funnels, used as warlike music, were also made of this metal, and struck with bars of the same, as well as a sort of castanet, lance-heads, and bullets, when there was no lead to be procured. The latter was brought from the north, or sold in small bars on the leeward and windward coast. The weights were made of brass, in the forms of birds, beasts, articles of furniture, etc., and the material came from Europe in the shape of rods.

Umbrellas, chairs, stools, and other household furniture were made by the native carpenters, although rudely. The former were enabled to open and shut by means of strings, in the most ingenious manner, but were very apt to get out of order. They were frequently of enormous size, like canopies, covered with the gayest-coloured cotton cloths, and frequently bearing some device upon the top. The musical instruments were drums, formed of the hollow trunks of trees, and covered with skin at the top only; violins, such as the travellers had already seen; rattles made of gourds and filled with pebbles; flat sticks, a sort of wooden dulcimer, played with little round wooden hammers, and rendered more full in tone by hollow calabashes hung underneath; sankos, which were wooden boxes, covered with deer skin, the strings carried across a bridge on to a long wooden neck, tuned by being shifted into a series of notches, and to which a whizzing noise was thought a charming addition, by means of a porcupine's tail, which vibrated as the strings were struck ; a very softly sounding flute of sweet tone, made of reed, having only three holes, and covered with leopard skin and red cloth ; and large horns of elephants' tusks, which, according to the imagination of the performers, uttered sentences, such as, 'I pass all kings in the world,' and which were in reality so modulated as to emit varied but constant sounds, which were immediately recognised by the hearers. It was curious to see how little relief was introduced into the carving of these ingenious people. Sometimes the surface of the wood was charred, and the black cut away till the white part appeared in patterns ; sometimes there were mere scratches, filled up with white clay, probably a sort of gypsum. The ivory carving was most forcible ; but even this was extremely rude when the human figure was attempted. The performances, therefore, of Carlos and Antonio were thought wonderful, and they might have made themselves rich, had not their master monopolized all their productions, except the few which they presented to those who showed them kindness.

The toilet was not forgotten in the market of Yahndi. Ornaments of the same sort of mother-of-pearl as they had seen on the idols in the Niger, were now found by the travellers to come from the enormous snail shells which abounded hereabouts, and the animals of which they also ascertained to have supplied the gelatinous soup so often given to them. Small stamps, or blocks of ivory, were cut into delicate patterns, which, when dipped into liquid white clay, formed coquettish marks on the cheeks of sable beauties; beads of all kinds, some of which were of splendid coral; curious combs, large bodkins for the hair, paint, rings of metal, chains of gold and grass, antimony in ornamental cases for blackening the eyelids, vegetable butter, and palm oil, made into cosmetics, and highly perfumed with musk, and other odoriferous substances, such as gums, were all exposed for sale; and with them were the richest India silks for the wealthier portion of the community, handsome tobes, tunics, vests, silk scarfs, turbans, morocco slippers, fans made of ostrich feathers, which were dyed of every colour, and had ivory handles; razors, knives, scissors, rude iron locks manufactured in Haussa, and even small packets of writing paper, and the reed pens and thick ink used by the Moors.

That portion of the market destined to the sale of provisions was of great extent. Meat of various kinds, such as venison, kid, beef, veal, mutton, both of goats and sheep, pork, etc., were either dried or fresh. Good salt was rather scarce, as was also dried fish. Snails, both fresh and smoked, were plentiful, as well as a small sort of tortoise, much esteemed. The fruits struck the travellers as being nearly the same as those which they had already seen; but added to those were some peculiarly fine oranges, which they were told grew wild in the bush. The colour of their peel was of a delicate green, often turning into a pale yellow; they had but few seeds, and the pulp was of a deep orange, with a flavour which Antonio pronounced to be even finer than that afforded by the oranges of Italy. There were papaws too, which Aboosee told them to eat with lime juice; Erasma, that highly flavoured astringent fruit of one of the Eugenias, and also what the Europeans on the Gold Coast call the miraculous berry, because, when eaten, it makes everything which is taken for some hours afterwards taste sweet. Of peppers there was an immense variety; and Antonio could not help shrinking with the remembrance of his pain, when he heard that they were not only used as a condiment, but applied to all local inflammations. There was also an extensive variety of tomatas. The prickly pear, or fruit of the Cactus opuntia, was sold to afford juice to the poorer sorts of pine-apple; ground nuts, wild figs, and huge watermelons, were in profusion. The yams and sweet potatoes were remarkably good, as well as the cassava, plantains, and bananas, evidently showing the results of cultivation; the first of these were said to be eight months reaching maturity. There were many kinds of corn, either uncooked, parched, or converted into foofoo, or kankeé, each of which was a sort of paste; and among the great delicacies were dried locusts, which had an acid flavour. Carlos, however, could not be prevailed on to taste these, as they too strongly reminded him of the large cockroaches which had so often annoyed him on board the ‘ Hero.’

Some medicines were to be found at the stalls, such as senna, and the Malaguetta pepper, which forms one of the universal remedies of Western Africa; it is the seed of the lesser Cardamom, and is given for internal pains, as well as bruises, sprains, swellings, etc., and children are rubbed with it to make them strong. A species of vine was used for ophthalmia, and the leaves of the beautiful tree called the Melia azedarach, with its bunches of lilac blossoms, and its naturally perforated seeds, were given as a tonic; no use, however, seemed to be made of the castor-oil plant, which there grew to the height of thirty feet. Natron was sold for putting into the water which was given to cattle; and sal-ammoniac, to be mixed with the mild native tobacco, which grew in quantities in the neighbourhood, in order to render it more pungent when used in the form of snuff.

The poisons seemed to be numerous, and derived from vegetables. That used for arrows was composed of the juices of plants, to which were added the tails of scorpions, heads of snakes, and venomous parts of other reptiles, mixed with many incantations over a fire, and the arrows then dipped into the liquid. The operator was not allowed to eat or drink during the time of preparation, but was obliged to keep constantly stirring the mixture, and shaking castanets over it.

Carlos was surprised to find that the Moorish children were inoculated for the small-pox; but the negroes would not suffer theirs to undergo the trial, although this disease makes dreadful ravages among them. He was still more surprised to find that the Moors drank both wine and spirits. Cowries formed the universal currency, but there was much barter.

The confined life led by the Europeans at last affected their health very seriously. Their carvings remained long in hand, instead of being promptly finished, as formerly; their songs were listlessly sung, and they appeared to be sinking into apathy. Their master ordered their portion of food to be lessened, then that they should be flogged; but neither punishment, thanks to Aboosee, was severe. At last the

Moor became convinced that they were ill, and he asked what would cure them. To this they replied, that they had all their lives been accustomed to breathe the fresh air, and to take strong exercise; and that now they were deprived of these, they should die. Consequently, Baba allowed them to ride out three times each week with his Arab guard, in all respects dressed like them, in order that they might not be distinguished from them by the populace, for he thought it a bad example for Christian slaves to be indulged. The white men hailed this shadow of liberty with delight, not only as a means of regaining health and vigour, and as an amusement, but eventually, as opening the way for their escape. They rode chiefly on the plains near the town; but occasionally, in their sports, when exercising their horses, the whole guard would disperse through the forests, and as Yusuf always kept with Carlos and Antonio, he, when they were separated from the rest, took especial pains to point out to them the different routes which led from Yahndi; his favourite theme, however, was Sallagha, which he said was a large place. They performed the various evolutions taught them by the Arabs, and succeeded so well, that Yusuf thought they ought to be enrolled among the guard; but when he proposed it to his master, and urged the good qualities of the slaves, the Moor wholly differed from him, and sternly refused.

Sidi Baba, who had hitherto been kind and complaisant to Yusuf, was now completely altered, not only towards him, but to every one around him. He very seldom summoned the white men to sing to him in the evening, and a weight of care overshadowed

his brow. He frequently sent messengers on secret
journeys with letters, and was continually having con-
ferences with the King, or holding private conclaves
with the Mussulmans. The Europeans questioned
their superintendent as to the alteration in their
master's demeanour ; but he only shook his head, and
refused to answer. They heard the ringing of metals,
and were convinced that there was some unusual
bustle and agitation. To their great grief, they were
suddenly deprived of their equestrian exercises, and
were more closely shut up than ever. Their tree now
became doubly precious to them, and the first night
they mounted into it, after a long interval, they saw
by torch-light numbers of soldiers in various parts
of the town. Some were on horseback, who wore
turbans and tobes, others had caps and short tunics ;
and the dress of the infantry was a piece of white
cloth round the loins, a pointed black leathern cap
with a short fringe of the same material, belts, and a
pouch of knives, which, with bows and arrows, formed
their accoutrements. A guard seemed to surround
the city, and they were convinced that this wealthy,
but not warlike capital, was threatened with invasion.
They no longer teased Aboosee with questions, and
secretly hoped that some circumstance might occur
in the confusion of war, which would lead to their
emancipation.

Night after night the friends mounted into their
observatory, and as often saw an increase or confirmation of the sight which had given them their first
suspicion ; besides which, they perceived that the
cattle were now kept nearer home, and entirely removed from the north-west, in the direction of some

high mountains. Occasionally, as the Moorish servants passed under the tree in conversation, they
heard the word 'Kong' uttered ; and they therefore
concluded that the King of Kong had declared hostilities against the King of Dagwumba. Many were the
consultations which they held together, and the plans
which they formed in order to get away ; but a sort of
hesitation arose in Carlos' mind as to the honour of
the proceeding. He deemed that it would be much
more upright on their part to offer to fight for their
master, and to ask to serve in the Arab guard, instead
of running away when danger was coming. Antonio,
however, deemed this Quixotic, and said, that at that
rate they should never regain their freedom ; 'for,'
observed he, 'the more useful we are, the more will
they wish to keep us. If we had once pledged our
word to fight, we must keep it ; but as we have done
no such thing, and have not promised anything at
all, I think we may perhaps, when the bustle comes,
by means of the tree, and passing for Arabs, whom
we now resemble so much, both in dress and complexion, get through the army in that way, and be
off.' 'But we cannot go without arms,' observed
Carlos. 'We shall surely be able to get some in the
field,' replied Antonio. 'At all events do not let us,
by binding ourselves, lose any opportunity that may
present itself.' Carlos could not help agreeing with
him that this was but common sense, and that their
best policy was to keep quiet, and watch patiently for
the favourable moment.

For some days the prisoners had observed an unusual expression and manner in their superintendent,
and fancied that some new misfortune was hanging

x

over them.   Restless, and full of foreboding apprehensions, they determined to get into the tree, although,
as it was not moonlight, they could not see very far.
Perhaps, in the darkness, they might venture to drop
down, and steal into the streets, where they might
pick up some news, and pass for Arabs; for they
knew that the guard went about at night unarmed,
except with daggers.   Accordingly, after their last
evening meal had been given to them, and the bolt
of their door had been let down, showing that
Aboosee had left them for several hours, they crept
out, and gained the tree in safety.   Carlos, however,
who was foremost, suddenly stopped, and whispered
in English, 'There is some one else in the tree, I
hear breathing close to us; have you your cutting
knife with you?'   Antonio answered in the affirmative.
'Be ready then,' continued Carlos; 'but be sure not
to strike till you are obliged to do so in self-defence.
Perhaps it is a spy come to look into the Moorish
quarters.'   The friends paused for a moment in silence,
their hands upon their knives, when they heard a
voice gently utter the names by which they were
known among the Arabs.   They did not answer, and
the voice continued, 'Fear not, brothers; it is only
Yusuf come here on purpose to speak with you.   Do
you think I never saw you in the tree?   Do you
think Aboosee did not know that you got into it?
We have often passed under it when we knew that
you were sitting over our heads; but we were only too
glad that you could get even a small pleasure.   We
loved you too well to tell our master; and now I am
going to show you that I can be grateful, and do all
for my friends.   Ever since you were sick, I have

thought you might want to see your country, as I
always do when I am in a town. I wish I could take
you with me to my own people, and show them to
you; then put you into a ship to go back to your
brothers. Perhaps you may die if you do not soon
see white men, and I have long made a plan for you
to be free. War is coming, and Sidi Baba is too
much troubled to think about you. The King of Kong
is going to fight the King of Dagwumba; he dare not
kill our master, but he may take his gold, his slaves,
and his clothes away; and he knows that the Dagwumba people cannot fight well. We are now trying
all we can to teach them, and we guards take them
out on horses, and pretend to be the enemy, and
attack them; and we go about night and day to show
them that they are not to be surprised. To-morrow
night you can go too, and nobody will see you. Get
up into this tree soon after Aboosee has brought you
your supper; eat well, for perhaps you will have to
ride many hours before you can eat again; then come
to the tree, slip down and go towards the stables.
I will be ready to meet you with the horses, and all
things which you will want. If any one sees us all
together, he will think that I am going to send out
my men,—keep quiet all day. If Baba wants you, say
you are sick. You need not bring anything with you,
but put on your Arab dresses.' So saying, he descended to the ground and left the friends, bewildered
with the prospect which he had placed before them.
They regained their apartment with beating hearts,
where sleep scarcely visited their eyes, and where
they hardly dared to talk of the future even to each
other, it seemed so full of uncertainty as well as hope.

Aboosee brought them their breakfast. He seemed unhappy, and looked mournfully at them; he spoke but a few words, though he lingered longer about them than usual; but he at last left them to their work. It so happened that they were just about to finish two cups, which were to be presented to the King by their master; and by using great diligence they completed them both. They gave them to Aboosee when he visited them at night, begging him to give them to Sidi Baba. They then presented him with some trifles for himself and his children, entreating him to accept them as a proof of their gratitude for all his kindness to them. Contrary to his usual habit of refusing all presents from them, the good-hearted man took the boxes with tears in his eyes, put them into the basket in which he had conveyed their supper, and carrying the cups in his hand, went away with a mere acknowledgment of the head, for his heart seemed too full to speak. He gave one last look as he opened the door, then, hastily shutting it after him, made more noise than usual in fastening the bolt, as if to convince them that they were safe from his interference. Their shutter closed with a hasp inside, which caught as it reached the framework, and one outside; they made it secure, as if they were closed in for the night, for at such times even over-precautions are taken. Then assuming all the composure they could command, they climbed along the roof next to them and swung into the tree. There they waited for the moment when all was quiet; invoked the blessing of God upon their scheme; and then, dropping from branch to branch, leaped from the lowest on to the ground. They pro-

ceeded towards the stables, near which they found
Yusuf, who, in a low voice, said, ' All is ready ; put on
these arms, which are those you used to have when
you rode with the guard ; the horses are saddled ; a
bernous, a bag of cowries, and some provisions hang
upon each, for you and the horses ; they will want a
little corn.   Ride fast all night and all day ; stop not,
except to feed them, and let them drink a little ; you
can eat in the saddle.   You know well how to use
your arms.   I give them to you, for they are my own.
Here is gold to buy what you want when you come
nearer to the sea.   Nay, take it,' he added, seeing
Carlos was about to refuse it, ' it is all your own.   I
have sold the carvings which you have made for me,
and saved all that my master has given me of the
presents made to you, for I knew you would want it
when you went away ; put it into your sash as well as
these daggers.   My master, when he finds you are
gone, may send the Arabs out to look for you ; but I
will take care that they shall not find you ; indeed,
they all love you too well to catch you.'   Saying this,
he put their bows and arrows upon them, slung a
musket at the back of each, girded on a pouch with
powder and balls, and giving each a spear, added, as
they approached their steeds, ' If you like to send
back your horses, let them loose and they will find
their way home, after you have ridden far enough.
When they come without you, perhaps Sidi Baba will
think you are killed.   Lose no time anywhere.   All
who see you here will take you for some of us ; but
if any should ask who you are, as you pass the last
line of soldiers, say that you are men of Ali.   You
know how often I have told you which is the path to

Sallagha; follow that, and when you come to the town, put the sign of peace upon your spears.' He then gave them a white scarf, and proceeded with his instructions. 'Pass through Sallagha as quickly as you can, and try that they shall not stop you, for there are Moors there. If they do, say that you are come from Sidi Baba, to take a letter to Sidi Hamed, at Koomassie;' and he then put a piece of paper, directed in Arabic, and wrapped in a piece of red silk, into Carlos' hand. 'When you get to Koomassie,' continued he, 'after passing through Sallagha, although you will find white men there, do not stay, but go on to Igwa, where you will see plenty of your own tribe, and plenty of ships to take you home. I shall go back to my own country when I can; and if you know any one coming to Misr, tell them to ask for Yusuf Ibn Ali, and perhaps they will see me, and I shall know if you are safe and well. You are both my brothers,' exclaimed he, with much feeling; but turning to Carlos, he added, 'It is to you that I owe so much; therefore, change turbans with me.' Carlos complied, and warmly returned the embrace given by the noble-hearted Arab, whose last words were, 'Ride softly through the town, gallop afterwards till you get to the forest; do not fear for the horses, they will go like the wind, and never tire. May God and the Prophet be with you !'

CHAPTER XVIII.

OBEYING the injunctions of Yusuf, Carlos and Antonio gently rode through the town; every apprehension being deadened by the absorbing feelings of affection and regret at parting with this excellent friend, and admiration for his noble conduct. They knew that he exposed himself to some risk for' their sakes, and would have given much to learn that he was exempted from punishment on their account. They hoped, however, if he should be found out, that dismissal would be all the infliction imposed on him; for the guard which he commanded would not see him suffer without rising into rebellion; and Yahndi was not in a condition to admit of internal disturbance. They did not, however, feel as certain of the impunity of Aboosee; but as they had not had any communication with him, they flattered themselves that he, too, might not be severely visited. They passed the outer picquet, answering the challenge as instructed by Yusuf; and in a few minutes pushed their horses on at their utmost speed. After about six hours' hard riding, they felt the poor animals flag a little, and somewhat slackened their pace till they found themselves in a small wood. Here they bathed the feet of their steeds in a little stream, as also their own heated foreheads, gave the beasts a handful of corn each, and then rode on again at a tolerable speed. They proceeded in the same manner all day, till they came to a large forest of fine oaks richly loaded with acorns, through which, however, there was a road. From this they retreated behind the trees, where they unsaddled their horses, fed them, and suffered them to lie down. They opened their own bags of provender, into which they had hitherto only dipped their hands ; and besides the corn meal which had supported them during the last twenty-four hours, found some dried meat. These were the two most nourishing things possible ; and, indeed, the armies of those countries will subsist for days on the corn alone. Swallowing just enough to allay the pangs of hunger, they in an hour were again upon the road. As daylight appeared, they occasionally met parties of natives, who hailed them kindly, and to whom they returned the usual peaceful Arabic salutation. They rode on the whole of that day ; and at night, after a short repose, with their heads resting on their horses for pillows, they prepared for walking. They left their steeds, as they thought, sleeping ; but had not proceeded far when they heard them running and neighing after them. It cost them much not to take them on with them ; but they knew they could not keep them at Cape Coast, if they ever should reach that place, for these animals will not live there ; they could not leave them in charge of any one at Sallagha, or Koomassie, for that would be to betray themselves ; and, at all events, they would most probably not be able to ship them for England, even if they conquered all the obstacles of their route. They stood irresolute for a few minutes, the horses pushing their noses on to their shoulders ; but Carlos at last exclaimed, 'The matter is soon settled by recollecting that they are not ours to take, and consequently we have no right to them.' 'No,' said Antonio, who longed to have the horses, 'nor to these dresses, perhaps.' 'I think that is a different case,' returned Carlos, 'considering that the Moor took away everything which we had; no matter how old, it was all we possessed; besides which, we served him long and faithfully.' They then remounted their horses, rode them to a turning in a wood, then fastening them to a tree by their bridles, which they knew they could easily break, they left them, and walked on as quickly as they could. They, however, frequently turned round to ascertain if the animals had made their escape; but they never saw them more.

So little had the Europeans walked of late, that they found their powers in this respect much diminished, and they were foot-sore before night came; but they had on soft leathern boots, which greatly protected their feet, and their sandals were slung at their backs, to be used when these should be worn out. They rested during the heat of the day, and had just thrown themselves down upon the ground, when they started up and went on again as fast as possible. 'That must have been an emigration of large red ants,' said Carlos, 'and they sting dreadfully. There is also a black ant besides this, of which we must take care. I have been told, also, on the coast, that there are tarantulas in the woods. I never thought of them before, but these ants put me in mind of them. One morning, when I was at Cape Coast, I looked into the space round which the soldiers'. barracks were placed, and there saw a large moving ridge of these insects close to their door, and over which the men carefully stepped when they wanted to go in and out. I was told that they were ants on a journey ; and, in fact, in two hours there was not one left.   About the same time the Governor assured me, that he had been fairly driven from his bed-room one night by myriads of minute black ants, not larger than a pin's point, all of which were gone before morning ; and it was he who described the tarantulas with their thick legs, and bodies covered with hairs.'   ' Are the tarantulas here venomous ?' asked Antonio.   ' I believe so,' answered Carlos, 'worse than they are said to be in your country.   I wonder we never had any brought in with our wood from Yahndi.   They say no one recovers from their bite ; but that may not be true. However, there are neither ants nor tarantulas just here, that I see, although there is much moss to conceal them ; so let us rest ourselves, for I am quite foot-worn.'   When refreshed, the Europeans rose and proceeded, and, to their great satisfaction, found a profusion of oranges on their way, which cooled them very much, and of which they put as many into their provision bags as they could carry.   At night they resumed their old practice of sleeping in a tree ; and the next day found their frames much more accustomed to their now novel exercise.   They avoided stopping longer at any of the villages through which they passed than to purchase provisions, and took care not only to have their cowries and pinches of gold-dust ready, but to tie the white silk scarf on to their spears as they approached.   No one, however, attempted to molest them ; and, as to other dangers, ' it was hard, indeed,' Antonio said, ' after passing three years in Africa, and much of that time in wandering through countries never before trodden by man, if we did not know how to take care of ourselves now.' So saying, he laid himself down snugly on the bough of a tree. 'Nevertheless, there is a sufficient number of wild beasts here,' observed Carlos, 'ready to snap us up; though I expect we have taken our leave of lions. That snake with horns was not a pleasant novelty, and makes me think that cockatrices really exist. The woman whom we met told us that that large town, a little way off, was Sallagha; and, as I think we had better pass through it early in the morning, before those rascally Moors shall be stirring, I shall get to sleep as quickly as I can.' As he pronounced these words, he, too, composed himself, but both were shortly awakened by a loud laugh. 'I never heard that before,' exclaimed Antonio, starting up; 'what is that? It is just like the laugh of a madman. I suppose there are black as well as white madmen?' 'I should think so,' answered Carlos; 'but now I remember, we have never seen a black idiot. I do not doubt that there are some; but they cannot be common, or we must have met with them. Hark! the sound is coming nearer.' It was followed by the bleating of a sheep and the lowing of a bull, which puzzled Antonio exceedingly. 'For,' said he, 'I did not see any of those animals near us.' 'Then it must be a hyæna,' observed Carlos. 'I have been told that these beasts imitate others very cleverly, in order to draw them nearer to make them their prey, and that they can laugh like men; in fact, that they can perfectly counterfeit the mingled sounds of

voices. I shall not disturb the fellow, it is so droll to
hear him.'

When the travellers descended the tree, long before
dawn, the hyæna scampered away as fast as it could,
for it is a very cowardly beast, and they started for
Sallagha. They had calculated well; for, after the
first two days, their limbs recovered their former elas-
ticity, and they were able to estimate their walking
powers as usual. None but the poorer classes were
stirring when they reached the town, who looked at
them with considerable astonishment. Of one woman
they purchased a draught of sweet milk for a few
cowries ; also some eggs, which they persuaded her
to boil for them in a pot which she had upon her fire.
After that they did not stop till they had left the
city far behind them. ' If I mistake not,' said Carlos,
' Sallagha was the place which Yusuf most feared for
us ; nevertheless, I do not think we ought to relax
our exertions till we have reached Koomassie. Now,
too, we walk as well as ever we did, and do not
require much rest.' The only new feature in the
country which lay before them, was the beautiful
coral trees, which they could not help stopping to
admire, as their scarlet blossoms hung from their
frequently bent and gnarled branches almost destitute
of leaves. They did not employ their arms in procuring food, as the villages were so frequent, and they
were well provided with the two currencies—cowries
and gold-dust. As they approached Koomassie, however, they found the latter prevail ; and having no
weights, were obliged to give it out in pinches, taking
care not to display their whole stock, in case they
might incite any one to follow and try to rob them.

Carlos finds his Prayer-book.— *Page* 309.

They always met with fowls and eggs; and oranges and other fruits were plentiful in the forests.

'It is long since we had a comfortable bathe,' said Antonio, the next day, as the travellers came to a little river; 'suppose we swim across at the widest part, just where those beautiful little kingfishers, with their blue wings and heads, and their scarlet breasts, are darting about, above that exquisite white pancratium; we will carry our arms and clothes above the water.' They stripped, and having fully enjoyed the proposed luxury, were resuming their attire, when Carlos exclaimed, 'How provoked that old Sidi Baba would be, if he were to see how our hair is growing again; our heads are already quite European, and our curls just the same as ever. I think yours, Antonio are even stronger. But avast there, that's my turban.' 'It is heavier than mine,' observed Antonio, giving it back to his friend. 'So it is,' added Carlos, weighing them both in his hand, 'yet they look very much alike in size and material. I wonder what Yusuf has done to his.' So saying, he felt it all over, and found a hard lump between the folds. 'What can this be?' he continued; and taking out his knife, undid a few long stitches which he saw inside, pulled the folds asunder, and out fell his beloved Prayer-book. Truly, there it was in its leathern case, unharmed, with the identical string for fastening it round his neck, and which had been so rudely undone by the orders of Sidi Baba. The Europeans looked at each other with astonishment and delight; Carlos' heart was at first too full to speak, but he kissed the treasure with fervour, and both falling on their knees, not only thanked God, but read their favourite psalms and gospels, and joined their voices in a hymn of praise to their great Preserver. His emotion having subsided, Carlos exclaimed, ' That Yusuf is a princely fellow, it must be allowed ; but how could he get at the Prayer-book ?' . 'Perhaps,' said Antonio, ' he saw it in his master's room, to which he had free access, and secreted it for us when Baba was too busy to think of or miss it. I hope he will not suffer for his kindness to us.'

The wanderers again started with lightened hearts and such vigour, that their bodies seemed to be mere pieces of machinery, put in motion by and obeying their energetic will ; and never did they walk such a distance as on this day. Yusuf was the constant theme of their conversation and praise. 'You may be sure, however,' observed Antonio, ' that Aboosee helped him, and knew his whole plan.' ' To be sure he did,' said Carlos. ' Do you recollect the silent farewell he took of us ? Who will say that we have not met with friends in Africa, in every grade of civilisation, from the man-eater to the Mohammedan ?' 'Except the Filatahs,' returned Antonio. . ' No, not excepting the Filatahs,' continued Carlos ; 'you forget the doctor who was so tender over your leg, and seemed to pity you so much, in spite of his pepper poultice.'

The next morning early, on emerging from the forest in which they had passed the night, and where they had seen some beautiful tree-ferns which they at first mistook for young palms, and whose fronds were frequently covered with moss, they came upon some plantations, the neatness and richness of which be-tokened their approach to a large city. These they crossed, and as they again came to a belt of trees, they met with a stream of water, full of apparently

tame fishes, with flat heads, the colour of eels, and the
largest of which was eighteen inches long. They
crossed this by wading and jumping, and then they
heard a sound which seemed to electrify them.
'Hark!' said Carlos, catching hold of Antonio, and
holding his breath. Both listened, and heard the
tinkling of a bell. 'It must be Koomassie!' cried
Carlos; 'and that is the bell to call the Moors to
prayer. Let us avoid the town and pass through the
outskirts while they are at their devotions.' They
turned a little on one side, and as they crossed an
opening, saw a neat low building of European appearance, and several windows in front. The bell became
more and more distinct. 'This is surely a place of
Christian worship!' exclaimed Carlos, and both, with
the same conviction, rushed forward to enter it. The
recollection, however, of their unusual appearance,
and of their arms, for a moment stopped them. They
tied the white silk upon their spears, waited till the
congregation seemed to be assembled, and had fallen
on their knees in prayer, and then silently and reverently taking off their turbans, they glided in, and
stood in the most obscure corner which they could
find, behind all the others. The officiating minister
was standing on a raised platform, and his complexion
showed that he had a slight claim of affinity with the
dark inhabitants of sunny climes; but he was gentlemanly, pious, and intelligent. The Morning Hymn
was sung; and when the sweet, manly voices of the
wanderers echoed through the building, he started,
paused for a moment, looked round with astonishment, but suddenly recollecting himself, he proceeded
with the service. The prayers were almost entirely

Y

those of the Church of England ; and the white men
joined in them with hearts overflowing with gratitude
for the mercies vouchsafed to them, and not the least
for again finding themselves among Christians. Their
responses, in perfect English, fell upon the minister's
ear. He felt reassured by them, and from that moment
proceeded with perfect confidence. The prayers over,
he pronounced an extemporary discourse in language
suited to his audience, who mostly understood the
English tongue when adapted to their peculiar minds,
and filled with similes drawn from the familiar objects
around them. He was heard with the deepest attention ; and every now and then that toss of the head
which the negro so entirely calls his own, and which
is so expressive, could be seen, and which was a sign
that the individuals who practised it comprehended
and subscribed to what they heard. The ceremony
concluded with a short prayer and a blessing. The
natives rose from their knees and departed, each, on
going out, looking with astonishment at the strangers,
and immediately on reaching the outside, whispering
their observations and conjectures concerning them.
Carlos and Antonio followed, but lingered near the door
of the building till the minister came out, when they
saluted him, and he instantly walked up to them, saying,
'Are you Charles Lacy and Antonio Pietri?' It was
now their turn to be astonished ; but on answering in
the affirmative, the reverend gentleman offered his
hand, and warmly bade them welcome. 'How can you
know us?' exclaimed Carlos. 'I will tell you in a
more fitting place,' answered the minister. 'The sun
is hot here ; and besides, we are exposed to observation. Come to my house and you shall hear all.'

They obeyed, and in a few minutes were safely installed in the dwelling of the Wesleyan minister, for
such he was. He insisted on their partaking of his
dinner, which was awaiting his return from church ;
and although filled with curiosity to hear what he
could tell them, they did not like to interfere with his
habits, and forbore for a time to make further inquiries. The meal over, he wished them to take some
repose ; but they assured him they were not tired, and
would rather hear some explanation of his acquaintance with their names. He then complied with their
request, and told them that circular letters had been
sent by the English Government to all the settlements
on the western coast of Africa, written in as many
languages as Europeans could command ; and orders
were given with them, that, when possible, they should
be forwarded to the interior. These stated that two
men, belonging to the 'Hero,' of Liverpool, having
been abandoned by the rest of the crew after the
death of the Captain, on the shores of the Bight of
Benin, it was supposed possible that they might still
be alive, and in need of assistance. The Government,
therefore, would handsomely reward any one who
should aid or protect them, and further their return to
England ; a reward was also offered to any one who
would give certain information concerning them.
This official document was signed by the English
Colonial Minister, and a copy of it given to the
Wesleyan, accompanied by a private letter to him
from Henriquez, stating, that although he feared he
must abandon all hope of ever seeing his beloved
brother again, still as he had never received any
certain account of his death. he could not, and indeed

ought not, to desist from using every endeavour to recover him, or, at least, to arrive at the truth. He therefore made it his earnest request to Mr. F., that he would leave nothing undone, while in the interior, to forward his wishes, promising cheerfully to meet any expense whatever which might be incurred in the search. The tears rushed into the eyes of Carlos as he again beheld his brother's handwriting, and thus received a fresh proof of his undying affection; but this explained all that they had heard on the Niger, the inquisitive glances which the Moors of Yahndi had cast upon them, and several hints which they now recollected, but which passed unheeded at the time. His reflections were, however, interrupted by their kind entertainer, who said, 'Afternoon service is about to begin. Will you rest here, or attend it with me?' They preferred the latter; and laying aside all their warlike paraphernalia, they again went to hear God's word; and when the duties of the day were over, their host begged for a recital of their adventures. They only gave him a short narrative; but the night was far advanced before they had finished their imperfect sketch of their wanderings and sufferings. Their account of the people on the Niger made the minister hope that some impression might be shortly made upon them, to wean them from the fetish, and convinced him that pagans would be more easily converted, over whom Mohammedanism did not exert its sway. When the wanderers described their surprise and emotions at first hearing the bell toll for prayers, their unwillingness to admit its possibility, and their fears leading them to ascribe it to the Mussulmans, together with their

ecstasy when they found their hopes realized, by beholding a place in which Christians, even in the
midst of the heathen and the wilderness, called upon
the God who had been so merciful to them, the good
man was quite overcome. Recovering himself, however, in a short time, they all three joined in solemn
thanksgiving, and retired to rest.

Not even the feeling of security, and the desire for
repose, could deter the travellers from joining in the
early orisons of their host; and these over, he said,
'A message must be immediately sent to the King
from us all, to inform him of your arrival. I do not
doubt that he is already aware of it, because nothing
passes without his knowledge; and of course so unusual an event has been the topic of conversation in
every house in Koomassie, from the palace to the
poorest hut. You must, therefore, ask the royal permission to pay your respects as you pass through the
town. I would have sent yesterday, but I did not
choose to break through the strict observance of
the Sabbath, and—whatever may be my opinion of
attending to works of necessity—appear to let anything interfere with my holy duties. Watched and
reported as I am, I am obliged to be particularly
careful, that no inconsistency should be visible in my
conduct which would immediately be detected by these
shrewd observers. Now, however, it becomes a duty
to communicate with the King, for he deserves every
respect which I can show, for his kindness in allowing
me to preach the gospel here. I should advise, much
as I should like to keep you with me for a few days,
that you should return to the coast as fast as possible;
not only for fear of losing any opportunity of getting

back to your friends, but because there will be a very unpleasant day here shortly, during which I always shut myself up completely, to express my abhorrence of the circumstance.   Two criminals are to be sacrificed to the fetish; for I am sorry to say these dreadful ceremonies are not yet abolished.   Thank God, however, they do not now amount to hundreds as formerly; and I hope that true religion is fast taking the place of idolatry and superstition.   There are Moors here, and they perhaps might raise a question in the King's mind, whether he ought not to detain you as the slaves of Sidi Baba, white though you may be.   Should he just now be in a good humour, you will easily get off; if not, we must have patience; and at the worst, we can but send to Cape Coast, and ask the Governor there to interfere.'

The messenger was despatched while the travellers breakfasted, and soon after an answer came from the King, conveyed by two men, one of whom carried a very large golden sword, to which was fastened a pint decanter of the same metal.   They said that his Majesty would like to receive the white men in state, if they were not in too great a hurry; but that if they wanted to go directly, he would see them in his palace in two hours; that he was glad they had come to his town, should like to do what Queen Victoria wished, and pay them honour for her sake; that they must think of all they wanted, and ask him for it, and no one else; and he would give them men and hammocks to take them down to Cape Coast.   The Europeans immediately returned for answer, that they preferred seeing his Majesty in private, as they had so little time to stay at Koomassie, and would, if he pleased, present themselves at the palace in two hours.

Punctually at the appointed time the travellers and their friend asked admittance at the gate of the royal residence ; but considerable delay took place before they could be permitted to enter beyond the outer court, it being the idea of these monarchs that such delays increase their consequence. There was evidently some preparation making for their visit, for a number of persons hastily passed and repassed, and among others were some little boys with curious caps on their heads, the tails of which hung down their backs. On seeing them, Antonio exclaimed, 'Look, Lacy, these boys are wearing the skins of those funny little beasts of which we have seen so many in the bush.' 'They are pangolins,' said Mr. F., 'and those are the King's criers, who constantly enforce silence in all great palavers (or discussions) by making a clamour themselves. But here comes Akimpon, the King's ironer, to take us in ; his office is to smooth the King's clothes, and I think you will say that he is a good specimen of the Ashanti court manners.' A noble-looking man, with a very courteous demeanour, then made his appearance, and bowing respectfully, bade the strangers welcome in the King's name, and said that his Majesty was ready to receive them. He politely begged them to follow him, showed no signs of curiosity or surprise at their appearance, but led the way through several courts, all arranged in the manner of the palaces of the interior, except that the buildings here were highly decorated and frequently ornamented with gold. Seated in a black and gold chair, at one end of the innermost court, was the King of Ashanti, surrounded by his linguists, his principal chiefs, and his and their retainers, in all amounting to several hundreds. He was about forty years of age, of pleasing appearance and deportment, and wore a handsome cloth. All the court had on the same costume, variously ornamented; boys with elephants' tails and fans of ostrich feathers stood around; and rich golden ornaments decked the persons of the courtiers, which amounted to some hundred pounds in value. This profusion of the precious metal presented a more magnificent spectacle than the Europeans had yet seen; but everything else reminded them strongly of Yahndi. It was with great satisfaction that they did not perceive any turbans, or Moorish caps, among the crowd. On approaching, they took off their turbans, thereby distinguishing themselves from the Mussulmans. The King was polite and dignified, but, unlike his ironer, he looked at them with intense curiosity, and asked why they wore those clothes, so different to those of white men in general. To this they replied by means of their friend and interpreter, that their own had been either worn out, or taken from them, and they had been glad to get what they could. He then asked them where they had been; and they answered, over rivers and mountains, through plains and forests, sometimes living in the bush, sometimes in towns, and at last they had sought his powerful protection, and begged that he would allow them to depart the next day. To this he made no reply; but expatiated on his own consequence, and willingness to oblige the Queen of England. He then dismissed them, and they left him in some uncertainty as to his intentions towards them. This, however, could not be helped, and they well knew all the delays and petty obstacles which these barbarous monarchs delight in practising.

The Europeans had not long returned to their quarters, when the King sent them a present, consisting ot a pig, a sheep, some yams, plantains, palm and ground nuts, and some gold. In the evening, as they sat talking with their friend, one of the linguists came with a special message, requesting them all to proceed to the palace immediately, for the King very much wished to talk to them alone. This summons, coming as it did through so important a person as the linguist, rather startled them; but they instantly obeyed, and following the courtier, found his Majesty in a private apartment, well lighted with palm oil, reclining on mats and cushions, attended only by two of his ministers of state, including his messenger, and apparently somewhat agitated. He told them that he wished to be their friend, and then desired them to tell him everything. They felt that he was sincere, and Carlos acting as spokesman, and making the narrative as short as possible, began with the motives which they supposed had induced Gray to abandon them, and ended with their arrival at Koomassie. The chief difficulty lay in the desire not to compromise Yusuf, who might be reported to Sidi Baba by the Moors. Carlos therefore merely stated that they had descended from the tree one night, taken the horses they had been accustomed to ride, together with the gold and cowries which they had procured by their earnings, and the arms which had been given to them, and started. Of their Prayer-book he said nothing, because that must have betrayed their friend. As the narrative proceeded, the King's feelings were strongly imprinted on his countenance. He seemed most indignant at the desertion of the travellers, al-

most started from his chair when he heard it, and said
that he did not think white men could have behaved
in that manner. He was positively agitated at the
history of the Kaylees; and when their escape from
them was told, he sank back upon his cushions as if
relieved. He was delighted with the account of the
Naängo people, and exclaimed in English, 'Very good,
very good!' At the adventure with the Ingheena
he laughed heartily; was interested by the description of Fandah; was angry with the Filatahs; and
when it was related how the white men were sold
as slaves, and how the Moor had treated them, his
attention was redoubled, and he never took his eyes
off Carlos till he had come to a conclusion.

When the speaker had ceased, the King assured him
that he knew he had told the truth; but that some
persons in Koomassie thought they were still slaves
who had run away with some of their master's property. But he would not hear of white men and
Queen Victoria's servants belonging to anybody but
herself; therefore they had better go away the next
morning early, and he would send them provisions for
the road. Thanking his Majesty very gratefully, the
Europeans took their leave, and returned home by
torch-light.

Long before the sun had risen, the sable monarch
kept his word. He sent them an ample supply of
gold to pay their expenses, two very handsome cloths,
two leopard skins, two cushions, two stools, some provisions, a slave to wait upon them 'for ever,' carriers
whom they were ordered not to remunerate, and a
messenger of his own, bearing a gold-headed cane, to
walk before them, and show that they were under his

protection, accompanied by a desire that they would tell their sovereign how much he was their friend. In return for this, Carlos sent his ring to the King, and Antonio the two remaining sovereigns, all of which had lain safely in the bag, as a proof of their gratitude, requesting the Wesleyan minister to explain to him that these had been returned to them with the Prayer-book without saying how; and after receiving the blessing of their kind host, they started immediately, not doubting that the royal anxiety for their absence was most likely occasioned by his fear of Moorish influence, and that his hurrying them away was a proof of his kindness.

CHAPTER XIX.

THE first place reached by the travellers on their way to Cape Coast was Framfraham, and at noon they came to Edgewabin, where, in presence of the chief, they formally declared their slave to be free, at which the young man appeared to be delighted. They told him he was at liberty to go where he pleased; but he, falling at their feet, begged them to take him with them to their own country, promising to be a faithful servant all his life. His account of himself was that he was called Corintchie, and had been originally made prisoner of war; as such he had been taken from country to country, and sold and resold, till he had wholly lost sight of all belonging to him; that he had expected nothing less than torture and death at the ensuing sacrifice; the crime he had committed having been an endeavour to escape from a severe master, who, in revenge, had given him to the King to be killed, and therefore he had no one but the white men to whom he could look for protection.

The next day the party reached Fomunnah, which they found all in commotion, from an accident which had taken place during the night. A poor little girl about ten years old had been sleeping in a room by herself with the window open, through which a leopard had leaped and tried to drag her away. The cries of the child alarmed the other inbabitants of the house; and the animal, frightened in his turn, made his escape as he entered, by the window, leaving his victim dreadfully wounded. The Europeans saw her, found a triangular piece of the scalp torn off, the shoulder lacerated, and the throat had two incisions, which resembled those made by a knife. None of the hurts were mortal, but the little sufferer died of exhaustion in two days. Among the mulattoes who crowded to the spot was a woman, who had some fearful scars on her shoulder, and she was shown to the white men as having extricated herself from the claws of one of these ferocious beasts. She had been walking near the forest with her child at her back, when a leopard sprang upon her side; she did not lose her presence of mind, and the hope of saving her infant giving her strength, she hit the panther so violently about the eyes, that the astonished animal let go its hold, and made its escape, leaving her much torn, but she had had sufficient strength to bear the shock. The father of the poor little girl declared that he would set a trap for the leopard the next day, and kill it, paying a fine to the fetish man for doing so; that it had already committed great havoc in the neighbourhood, and ought to be destroyed. On in quiring of the chief of the village for an explanation of the fine, he told the travellers that the leopard was a sacred animal in that country, and that whenevei any one killed a beast of this kind he was obliged to pay some gold dust to the fetish man, and give him the head of it wrapped in a piece of white baft, a species of cotton manufacture. This chief regaled

the strangers with monkey soup and palm wine, and
the next day, passing over the hills of Adamsee, and
through the forest, they halted a while, and settled
themselves for the night at a small croom or village,
not far from the Prah river, where a wild hog having
been killed, they found plenty of provisions for themselves and their attendants.   They observed, however,
that their host, who was the chief man of the place,
did not eat with them ; and on asking him why, he
replied that hog was his fetish, and therefore he never
ate it.   On requiring further explanation, he added
that the people of Fantee and Ashanti were divided
into families, each of which had a peculiar fetish, which
being worshipped, they could not eat, such as eggs,
fowls, milk, etc. ; but that there was a much larger
division among them, such as the Buffalo family, the
Panther family, the Corn-stalk family, the Servant
family, etc., for which they could not assign any reason.

The Europeans were surprised at finding that they
walked much better, were much more easily satisfied,
and much more willing to make light of trifles than
those around them, and hoped that they had received
a lesson of content which would never be forgotten.
They crossed the river in a rude canoe, and stopped
at Berracoe ; on the noon of the following day at
Fessu ; and on the ensuing morning at Mansue,
wondering at the quick succession of villages.   At
this place the chief received them with much honour,
and hoped, when they came again, they would find
him with a chapel and a missionary.   He fed them
sumptuously ; and Antonio observed that they fared
much better than many kings of the interior.   At
Yancoomassie, the Caboceer, or captain of the croom,

entreated them to remain with him for a few days; but
they were too anxious to get on to admit of any delay,
and the nearer they came to the coast, the greater
was their desire to reach it. Pushing on therefore by
the shortest possible path, although it was the most
overgrown, and only allowing their people the necessary rest at Doonqua, they on the following morning
appeared on the heights by Igwa, or Cape Coast.
There was the beautiful ocean again before them, and
it was a sight which could not fail to arrest their steps:
they paused, and stood leaning on their spears, to
contemplate it with mingled feelings of affection and
sadness. For a few minutes they were completely
overcome with the intensity and number of thoughts
which rushed upon them; but they were startled from
their reverie by a booming noise, which rolled towards
them, and made the hills and forests echo, while
volumes of smoke shut the scene from their view
'It is a salute,' said Carlos, 'the arrival of a man-of-
war, or perhaps some birth-day.' Their attendants
were enchanted; and when the clouds from the guns
cleared away, they saw the standard of England un-
furled, and waving over the principal bastion of the
castle; while another floated from the war-brig which
was at anchor in the roads. They pressed forward,
and were met outside the town by the Governor, his
officers, the resident missionaries, the merchants, the
principal natives, and, in fact, almost the whole population, shouting and huzzahing, waving their hats
and handkerchiefs, and making every demonstration
of joy. This salute, then, had been fired in honour
of them; this, then, was their reception by their
white brethren; and toil, wrong, suffering, and even

slavery, were forgotten in the keen delight occasioned by this welcome.

It seemed that a little urchin had stolen away from the town at which they had passed the previous night, and, from that irrepressible love of gossip which forms part of the negro character, had given the first intelligence of the safety and presence of those who had been mourned as among the dead. Scarcely believing the news, the king of Igwa had communicated it, however, to the Governor, and he to the Captain of the war-brig: each ordered the guns to be got ready, in case it should prove true; and, telescope in hand, stood watching the path from Koomassie. The messenger with the gold cane was recognised, also the Arab-looking youths, all as the boy had represented, and, no longer doubtful, both sea and land were made to rejoice.

Clothes, money, presents of every kind, would have been showered upon the travellers by the generous Europeans; but they insisted on checking such bounty, saying that they had all they wanted, for they had plenty of gold; and, in fact, their picturesque dress so fully developed their vigorous forms, now reaching a rare perfection, that no one seemed willing that they should alter their costume. However, the cold periodical wind from the desert, called by the natives the Harmattan, began to blow, and so chilled them, that though unwilling to deprive their friends of that which they could not replace in Africa, they accepted cloth jackets and trousers, selected from the wardrobes of the Europeans. The Captain of the war-brig would gladly have given them a passage home, but he was not to return for several months. Such, however, was the general interest excited by them, that the master

of a Liverpool trader offered a free passage not only
for themselves, but their servant.   But this they would
not at first hear of, and Carlos pledged himself for the
payment on their arrival; but Captain Turner said
he would answer for his owners, and that they would
only be too happy to afford them every accommodation.   He had often heard of Colonel Lacy, and their
disappearance had been frequently mentioned in his
presence; but the subject had been dropped for some
time, and he believed that their friends had now given
up all hopes of ever seeing them again.   Further par-
ticulars he was unable to state, for when the 'Hero'
had reached Liverpool he had been absent: that she
should ever have come home was a matter of surprise
to all.

No one who has ever visited an English colony can
refuse to bear testimony to the generosity and hospitality of its inhabitants.   They make their guests feel
that they themselves are the obliged parties; they
think that they never can do enough for the stranger;
and the only drawback is, that they are not able to
act upon even a larger scale.   There may be gossip-
ing, there may be jealousies, as in every small community; but these fade away before the liberal, delicate,
and untiring kindness with which they not only receive,
but retain their visitors, let the nation be what it will.
Carlos and Antonio experienced all this in its fullest
extent; for everything was placed at their command.
They ostensibly lived with the Governor; but each
officer and each merchant thought himself injured if
the travellers did not partake of a feast at his house;
and they would have been killed with good cheer,
had they not made it a rule from the first, to live as

z

nearly as possible as they had done in the wilderness.
It was some little disappointment, however, to their
entertainers to find the travellers so very abstemious;
but they could not help acknowledging it to be the
wisest plan, and they determined to be doubly profuse in their own persons. Relishes, dinners, break-
fasts, and toasts, went on a great rate, but more
solid things poured in upon the travellers. Specimens
of every portable native produce and manufacture
which could there be procured, were offered for their
acceptance; but when the articles were of value, as in
the instance of gold workmanship, they felt they had
no right to accept them. They saw, however, that the
donors would have been hurt at their refusal, and could
not but receive with gratitude what was so cheerfully
bestowed. Among these ornaments were bracelets and
collars of gold, rings, ear-rings, clasps, brooches, etc.;
most of which were copied from European models, and
executed with a delicacy and finish which surprised
them as much as the quantity, which seemed to be
inexhaustible. They inquired as to the localities
whence the metal was procured, and found that, all
along what is called the Gold Coast, the soil teems
with it: sometimes it is to be had by merely washing
the earth, which is everywhere trodden under foot; at
others it lies in veins near the surface, and the natives
dig it up in lumps. It is generally embedded in quartz,
which is ground with the metal and then washed from
it. Occasionally, however, the lumps can be separated
entire; and one was shown to the travellers which
weighed fourteen ounces. The tools used by the
natives are the rudest possible, and they dig till the
pits fill with water, and which are never deeper than

twenty-four feet. The people of Ahanta and Warsaw are wholly ignorant ot any means of extracting this water; therefore they make another pit, and work it, till it in its turn becomes inundated. All this takes place at no greater distance from the sea-shore than twenty-five miles, among a peaceable people; and it surprised Carlos that no enterprising individuals should have endeavoured to form mines there, and with the assistance of a few intelligent Englishmen merely to direct, and a body of Kroomen, who could each be changed at shorter or longer periods, turn these rich deposits to profit.

Among those who most heartily welcomed Carlos to Cape Coast, and in fact Antonio for his sake, was the kind mulatto woman, who lavished upon them all she could command. She was never tired of hearing their adventures, and they often sat talking to her by the hour together, wondering at her excellent sense and shrewd observation, and from her obtained much information which was valuable to them in after life. She not only gave them gold trinkets, but the beauti ful skins of the Diana monkey, with their rich streak of brown down the back, also those of the long-haired black monkey, and some bracelets of very small gold and coloured glass beads, strung by herself in com- plicated patterns on pine-apple thread, and which, she said, they must keep for their wives, when they had them, to make them think of their friend Sarah. Carlos promised, at any rate, never to part from them, any more than the aggry bead, which he showed her with pride still lying in safety in the little bag. On inquiring the fate of Mr. Mortimer, the travellers found that he had partially recovered, having during the last few weeks been nursed by this kind-hearted woman, who would have ornamented even polished society by her dignity, grace, natural talent, and disposition. He had left the coast in a trading vessel, of which he took charge, and had been heard of since that, by a present which he had contrived to send to his benefactress.

The merchants changed the cowries and gold-dust of the travellers into English money, clothed their servant, and undertook to stock them with necessaries for their voyage. Such loads of preserved guavas, tamarinds, ginger, erasmas, pepper, plantains; such loads of fresh fruits, among which was the mammee apple, which had been introduced from the West Indies. Everything that was good and rare in the vegetable or animal world was sent on board the 'Nancy;' and so far was the kindness carried, that seeds and bulbs for the hothouse of Colonel Lacy, butterflies, birds, and quadrupeds for museums, and beautiful live birds as pets, were freely given; in short, the whole place was ransacked, even to some of the salt from the salt-tree up the Volta. The attention, however, which most gratified the travellers, was the joint work of the Governor and the merchants. It was an assemblage of European articles for the King of Ashanti, whose conduct all agreed had been excellent, and well deserved acknowledgment.

Two days before the departure of the guests, as they were walking through the streets of the town, a black man started when he saw them, looked at them very intently, passed them again and again; but accustomed as they were to be stared at, they at first did not heed him. At length, however, they stopped to see what he meant, when he threw his arms round Antonio,

exclaiming, ' My friends, my friends !' Willingly did
each European embrace him in his turn, for it was
Ajimba, who they thought had been killed on the banks
of the Niger. His delight was so excessive, that a
crowd began to collect round them ; therefore they
asked permission to take him into the house of a friend
close by ; and when his joy had a little subsided, he
told them his story. He said that the Filatahs often
came to the river-side and robbed the canoes, but he
had not imagined there would be the slightest danger
of meeting with them in such a storm as that which
had compelled him to stop; that he lay for some
time senseless—how long he did not know, for when
he recovered he found himself nursed and taken care
of by some kind people from a village not far off;
that several of his crew had survived, but others had
been killed ; that the wound in his breast had taken a
long time to get well ; and, in fact, that he had never
been able to breathe properly since that time, and was
now at Cape Coast to find a good white doctor who
might make him better; that the King his master
was dead ; and when he had lost his protection, the
people of the town, who had been related to the
murdered canoe-men, often reproached him as being
the cause of their death ; therefore he had taken his
wife and children, and all he possessed, and traded
up and down the river ever since ; that he had seen
the good missionaries at Badagry, and heard them
preach, and wished very much to settle near them, and
learn to pray to God ; for he had thought of that ever
since he had seen and heard the white men pray and
read from their book ; and he wished his children to be
taught. ' But,' continued he, ' my wife Beeah is here

and she will be glad, too much, to see your faces. We all thought you were killed and thrown into the river, as we could not hear of you again, and we were almost sick to think of it.' He then suddenly darted out of the room, exclaiming that he was going to fetch Beeah. In two minutes he returned, and the woman with him, who was overjoyed at beholding her friends again. She took something from under her cloth which had been concealed there, and gave it to the travellers; and great was their surprise and delight at seeing the rhinoceros' horn cups once more, which they had always prized so much for Wondo's sake. Ajimba told them that they had been found in the corner of the cabin after the canoe had been plundered by the Filatahs, and had been taken great care of by Beeah, as she would not even let him use them. 'When I first met you in the street,' added he, 'I thought you so like my old friends, that I was astonished too much; but when I heard you speak, I knew my heart was right.' Carlos and Antonio warmly thanked the good man for all his friendship, and his wife for their precious relics, in which they could almost have fancied there was some charm, so unexpectedly were they restored. They presented Ajimba to the merchants, who promised to give him a preference in their trading concerns, and employ him whenever they could, and said they would interest the missionaries in his behalf. They promised also to get his children admitted into the schools, and seemed determined that no one who had been kind to the wanderers should go unrewarded.

At length the parting moment arrived, when it was impossible to enumerate the embracings, the shakings

of the hand, the assurances of friendship, the promises of correspondence, the anticipations of visits to
England, the expressions of gratitude, the desires for
future health and prosperity, such as never before distinguished the setting out of two travellers.   Everything
was stowed away in the vessel for them.   The live
stock was on board ; even goats for supplying milk ;
and large was the party which, in canoes, accompanied
them to the deck of the homeward-bound vessel.   The
orders were given to weigh anchor, the Government
chaplain pronounced a blessing ; and as the 'Nancy'
left her moorings, loud cheers from the gentlemen in
the canoes followed her progress ; while those who
departed in temporary sadness, stood gazing on their
generous friends till they were lost in the distance.

The 'Nancy' steered south-south-west till she came
to about two degrees south of the line, where she for
some days rolled about in an entire calm.   The sails
flapped about, the heat was intense, the Europeans
were glad to resume their tunics and turbans, and
began to think that the scene there was as monotonous
as that between their four walls at Yahndi ; the men
became cross and listless, and greatly preferred the
white squalls, which occasionally drove them on,
although they never came without giving the watch a
complete drenching.   The travellers found their captain intelligent and good-humoured, and possessing
the usual frankness and simplicity of the sailor.   He
had such a horror of the western coast of Africa, that
nothing but the necessity of leaving the owners of the
'Nancy,' had he refused to come, would have induced
him to venture near it.   Neither he nor any of his
men had slept once ashore ; and as his crew had sailed

with him for several years, they were in such habits of discipline that they never thought of disobeying his commands. Hiring a party of Kroomen the first time he met with them, all service connected with the land was performed by them and himself; and he believed that none of his men had been induced to take more than their usual allowance of grog, therefore he had not lost a single life since he had started. 'If once they get ashore,' said he, 'they are lost men. I knew a good ship with one of the finest set of men ever seen, amounting to twenty-eight in number, including the captain, and she returned to the port of Liverpool with only three of them left. When the case was inquired into, it was found that the men began to drink and go ashore even at Goree, and continued to slip off at every opportunity.' Carlos could not help thinking of his own painful experience, and that this was but the history of the 'Hero.' 'I do not mean to say,' continued Captain Turner, 'that my plan will certainly secure life, but I am sure that it affords the best chance, till some better way of treating the fever is discovered. Those who do survive it frequently feel the effects of it, and the remedies against it, the whole of their remaining lives. A lady of my acquaintance, who was on the coast for some time, had ague for twenty-four years after her last attack; and only when she was almost sinking under it, changed her system of treatment. This change, however, cured her, and she has never had the ague since.'

With such discourse Captain Turner beguiled the wearisome feeling of remaining almost stationary day after day; and among his anecdotes were those of

pirates, who used frequently to infest those seas. ‘ I
knew,’ said he, ‘ the master of a vessel, who, standing
out to sea, as we have done from Cape Coast, was
boarded by some of these ruffians, whom he had no
power of resisting. They put all the crew under
hatches ; then, taking the captain from the place in
which they had confined him, insisted on knowing
where he had stowed away the gold which they supposed formed part of his freight. It so happened that
he had not any, but they would not believe him ; so
they beat him, stripped him to his shirt and drawers,
and hid him in one of the cabins. They then killed a
fowl, sprinkled its blood upon deck, took out the mate,
showed it to him, told him it was that of their captain,
whom they had killed because he would not confess
where he had put the gold, and would serve him in
the same manner if he did not discover where it was.
The mate persisted in the same story of there being
none on board : he was hidden in his turn, and the
second and third mate were threatened with a similar
punishment ; but as they all used nearly the same
words, the pirates left them, taking provisions and all
they could lay their hands upon. The only thing that
the poor captain could do was to steer for Accra,
where he could not go ashore till some of the officers
there sent him some clothes. The vessel was freighted
again, and set sail ; she reached home in safety, but
her captain never recovered the treatment which he
had received, and died shortly after. A very common
trick of these pirates was to leave only the barest
allowance of rice and water, or old biscuit, and to
take away even the charts and compasses. The
vessel thus stripped, and no one on board able to

steer accurately, was inevitably destroyed, unless she
fell in with a friendly ship, which was more fortunate
in having escaped the plunderers.   The pirates were
so powerful that they attacked large ships, and always
behaved worse when any attempt at resistance was
made; but the increased number ot cruisers, it it has
not prevented the slave trade, has in a great measure
cleared the seas of them ; and this is fortunate, as they
often combined slavery with their other lawless proceedings.'

At length the wind set in from the south-east, and
gaily did the 'Nancy' spread her sails and fly over the
surface of the water, till a little interruption of a few
days came ; then she got into the track ot the north-
westers, and after that steered direct for home.   That
home seemed to be almost at hand when quantities of
the weed called the *Fucus Natans* so surrounded the
ship, that she seemed scarcely able to make her way
through it.   The travellers knew by this that they
were in the Gulf Stream, and hooked up quantities of
the weed.   The berries of it they pickled, and the
numbers of tiny mollusca which clung to it they put
into spirits for the curious.

The Azores were passed with a mere glimpse of
Fayal, and at length a boat full of men dressed in
frieze coats appeared in the open sea ; and they knew
that they were not far from the Scilly Islands.   It just
held the four sailors, but her gunwale was almost in
the water ; and when Carlos beheld the sturdy sons of
England, he could not help contrasting them with the
slight and delicate forms which he had left behind
him, even among the Europeans on the coast.   It is
true that among the natives he had seen some who

might have been models for Hercules, especially in
the thickness of the nape of the neck.   This peculiar
feature in the negro always accompanies the antique
busts of that hero, and Carlos had been much struck
with it; but these magnificent-looking men were
heavy as if they could conquer by weight, while the
large men of England generally bespeak an active as
well as gigantic race.   The brawny and bare chests of
the two who plied the oars met every blast, and were
wet with spray; every vigorous pull was a matter of
yards, totally different to the quick short stroke of the
paddles in the hands of the pliant Kroomen.   But
the boat itself, though sound and solidly built, was as
liable to capsize as the long slender canoe formed of
the hollow trunk of a tree.   These men had come out
with newspapers, and to collect intelligence from the
in-coming ships; but unwilling that their names should
precede their arrival, Carlos begged Captain Turner
merely to state that they were passengers for Liverpool, and the men left them without further questions.
Another boatful came to meet the 'Nancy' with fresh
fish, butter, and eggs, and as soon as they had disposed
of their cargo returned to port, which probably was
near the Land's End.

Up Channel went the 'Nancy,' as if eager to
gladden the hearts of friends at home with her long-
wished-for burden.   'You bring me good luck,' said
Captain Turner to Carlos.   'I never before came so
fast up Channel.   I hope it is a good omen for us all.'
The mountains of the Emerald Isle opened on the
one hand, on the other the blue hills of Wales; and
as the wanderers stood on deck eagerly watching for
the well-known landmarks, they entered the mouth of

the Mersey. Carlos' emotion became almost insupportable, and he retired to the cabin, where, hiding his face in his hands, a thousand apprehensions, which had never suggested themselves before, now tarnished his joy. 'If any of his dear ones should be dead?' Even the loss of Mrs. Lacy, once so detested, he felt would be sufficient to mar his happiness; but if death should have visited any one still nearer? He dared not ask himself the question, and felt as if he could not breathe. Nor was Antonio without a large portion of anxiety. He had no relatives, no friends to meet beyond the common tie of companionship; his all, his world, was centred in Carlos. Would he be always the same to him that he had been in the wilderness? He himself was a wiser and better man than when he had started from the spot to which he was now returning, and had been chastened by no common trials. He had been the inseparable and intimate friend of one who was infinitely superior to him in education and habits; and he now looked to his former life with the conviction that he could never endure to return to it. He shrank from again coming in close contact with the careless, if not the impious; and elevated as his mind had been by Carlos' instructions, and the wonders of creation which had been laid open to him, he turned from such society with a sickening of heart which he had never before felt. But he had no hope of emancipation from it, excepting through the friends of Carlos; and would they receive him, would they admit him among them, uneducated as he was? He could not be their servant; but would they permit him to be their associate? And if they did, how was he to get his living? Such were his reflections as he leaned over the side of the vessel, apparently watching for the pilot, who was coming off in a small boat in order to take the vessel into port.

As for Corintchie, his curiosity was intense; but, negro-like, he did not betray any surprise. He had seen the measured action of the oars in the boats, as they plied round the ship at Cape Coast, for Captain Turner had not suffered canoes to approach; he had seen the ocean; he had seen a ship for the first time, and noticed them only by tossing up his chin. He had been ill at sea, and thought he was going to die; but instead of leaving him to get well as he could, both Carlos and Antonio had soothed and comforted him. He became consequently much attached to them, but he had not expressed it. No, he had been a slave, and his expansive feelings had been withered. Now his teeth chattered with the cold; but he stood patiently waiting till Carlos should look up, and give directions how to dispose of the things which they had had in daily use. The latter was roused from his reverie by his friend, who entered the cabin, saying, 'My dear Lacy, the pilot and the Custom-house officers are on board, and we must make some arrangements for going ashore. We shall be in Liverpool by the afternoon, and then, I suppose, we must separate.' 'Separate!' repeated Carlos, starting up; 'what do you mean? You and I can never separate, unless it be from your own choice. What could you do—where would you like to go without me, Antonio?' 'You forget,' resumed the latter, 'that your friends may not be of the same opinion as you are, and that they may not be inclined to love me because you do. You

cannot expect them to receive a common sailor'—
'Then they shall not receive me,' interrupted Carlos.
'Hear reason,' continued Antonio; 'I have often
thought of this in my voyage home: it is not what I
would do, but what I must do. I shall seek my discharge immediately from the owners of the "Hero,"
receive my arrears of pay, and then look out for employment of some sort.' 'I charge you,' resumed
Carlos, 'by all we have suffered together, to tell me
candidly what your wishes are.' Antonio remained
silent, but looked down, for his eyes were full of tears.
'Will you not tell me?' rejoined Carlos, taking his
hand. Thus urged, Antonio replied, 'I have but you,
Lacy, in the world; and where you are, there would I
wish to be; but'— 'We will never part!' exclaimed
Carlos hastily. 'I promise you that; so all is settled.
And now let us tell Corintchie what to do.'

CHAPTER XX.

IN the presence of a Custom-house officer, the travellers selected what they intended to carry ashore. Captain Turner promised to take care of everything else, till they should claim it, and come to pass it through the duty office. A boat was alongside ; they took a temporary leave of their friend, stepped into it, and made for the quay. As they went along, Carlos said, ' I cannot go at once to Wavertree, for fear there should be any bad news for me there ; so we will proceed to the Institution, and hear from my good friends the Browns if all be well.' Rapidly paying the boatmen, they jumped ashore ; and all three, carrying the luggage, threaded the bustling streets of Liverpool, Corintchie scarcely having time even to wonder, from the difficulty he felt in following his masters, and getting through the crowd. The good inhabitants of this great commercial city are too much accustomed to foreign men to spend much time in gazing at strangers ; and although most of them turned their heads as the bronzed passengers, with their black servant carrying weapons, passed hastily by them, they offered no interruption. The door of the Institution was shut, and Carlos, springing up the steps at one bound, thundered at the knocker. The Sergeant, wondering at the loud summons, opened it, and for a moment stood to hear

what the visitors wanted. Carlos looked him full in
the face. The Sergeant gave a scrutinizing glance;
his hand dropped from the door; but he still hesitated. At that moment Kathleen crossed the hall,
and gave a scream. Carlos could no longer restrain
himself. 'Kathleen! my dear Kathleen!' he exclaimed, and rushing past the Sergeant, clasped her
in his arms. The old soldier could not be angry, because he was so much astonished; and when he saw
Kathleen return the hug which she had received, the
truth flashed across him, and before the kissing was
over he had seized hold of Carlos' hand, and was
weeping over it with joy. 'Ah, Master Carlos!' said
Kathleen, 'we thought you were dead. But how altered
you are!' 'Are all well at Wavertree?' asked Carlos,
almost dreading the answer. 'Every one,' said the
Sergeant. 'Mr. Henriquez, and the Don, and some
friends, dine with the Colonel to-day, for you know it
is his birthday, and we shall be there in the evening.'
'Thank God!' exclaimed Carlos with fervour. 'Are
these the friends who have taken care of you, Master
Carlos, in that wild country?' asked Kathleen: and
then came the necessary introductions. 'No,' said
Carlos, 'not exactly that, though to one I owe
much. This is my fellow-traveller, who has been
everywhere with, and everything to me; and this
good fellow,' continued he, pointing to Corintchie,
'would follow us home, and be our faithful servant.
But we must go to the Colonel's directly. Will you
get me a car, Sergeant?' But here Kathleen stole
away, and in a minute reappeared with her string of
children, who were unwillingly dragged out to be
shown to the strangers, and were particularly averse

to look at the black man. Carlos noticed them all, remarked how they were grown, and asked whether they were as well-behaved as ever; but having sufficiently admired them, in order to gratify the mother, his impatience returned, and he again asked for a carriage, and then turning to Antonio, said, 'I have a great fancy to see if they will know me in my Arab dress, and that is why I brought it and yours ashore. I would not tell you till I knew who was alive to greet us. So let us put them on.' Kathleen showed them into a room, which Carlos almost deemed unnecessary, considering that he had been so long with people who did not dress at all; and while the Sergeant sought for a vehicle, the travellers fully equipped themselves, tucking their betraying curls as well as they could under their turbans. 'You know,' said Carlos, as he issued to the wondering gaze of the Sergeant and his wife, 'we could not walk in this fashion through the streets.' 'I should think not,' said the old soldier, smiling. The two friends entered the car, and Corintchie was placed in safety on the box by the coachman, with many injunctions not to fall off; and as he closed the door, the Sergeant exclaimed, 'Master Carlos is just the same, always full of his tricks and surprises; but how beautiful he is, although he is so dark! He is taller than Master Henriquez. I am sure they will never know him.' 'Do you think so because you did not?' observed Kathleen. 'I knew him directly.' 'So should I if he had spoken,' resumed the Sergeant, half piqued. 'Ah! I am sure,' continued Kathleen, 'his brother will see directly who it is.'

It was with difficulty that Carlos prevented himself

from thrusting his head out of the window as he passed each familiar object, and his moderation arose more from the danger of knocking off his turban than any self-command; but he constantly called Antonio's attention to the well-remembered scenes. As for Corintchie, as he afterwards confessed, to be outside this 'horse house,' which was the name he gave to the car, seemed so perilous, that he clung fast to the first thing which he could lay hold of, and did not attempt to answer any of the questions of the inquisitive coachman, though his stock of English was very good. At length the carriage drew up at Colonel Lacy's gate. 'Drive in,' said Carlos impatiently, 'and stop at the door;' and as the man obeyed, an arm, naked to the elbow, with the short-sleeved tunic, was thrust outside, ready to turn the handle at the moment of arrival. The windows of the dining-room looked on to the drive, whence Henriquez saw that something unusual approached; and as he sat at table, the glimpses which he had of turbans and dark men puzzled him exceedingly. He turned extremely pale; for never having in his heart felt sure of Carlos' death, he always imagined that every strange figure which met his eyes would bring him news of his lost brother, even though it should be the confirmation of his worst fears. Unwilling to disturb the guests present, he sat perfectly still, watching the approach of the carriage and the bare arm, and, in spite of himself, felt disappointed, for Carlos never would come in that way, he thought. The latter darted out of the conveyance, rang violently at the hall bell, flung some silver to the coachman, ordered Corintchie to bring everything out of the carriage, and when the servant opened the door, rushed in without permission, followed by his companions. The man stood bewildered at this sudden invasion, and Carlos, recollecting himself, made signs to Antonio—for he could not speak—to follow him ; then, walking into the dining-room, stood in his singular costume before the astonished company, with his eyes fixed upon his brother. Henriquez rose, but stopped as he saw another figure enter, who was in the same extraordinary dress. However, when the black face of Corintchie appeared, the idea of Africa presented itself, and with as much self-control as he could assume, he walked up to Carlos, saying, 'If you know anything of Charles Lacy, I beseech you to tell me.' A smile passed across the features of the foremost Arab, and although the mouth was concealed by the moustache, the eyes betrayed the identity, and, to the astonishment of, every one present, the spear fell from the hand of the stranger, and the brothers were locked in close embrace. Tearing himself, however, from the arms of Henriquez, Carlos sought those of his benefactor, exclaiming, ' My father ! my best friend ! ' Mrs. Lacy, too, whose heart had been quite softened by the letter from Sierra Leone, instead of taking the hand which Carlos respectfully held out to her, threw her arms round his neck, and kissed him with unaffected joy. There was still another candidate for family greeting, and a dignified old gentleman, who had beheld the scene with deep emotion, said to Henriquez, ' Recollect that I too have a share in your happiness ;' and gently folding his arms round the astonished Carlos, exclaimed, 'Welcome, my long lost nephew !' But this was not the time for explanation, and Carlos there-

fore returned the salutation upon trust.   The other
guests crowded round with their congratulations, and
there was a complete stop to the ceremony of dinner.

Antonio had all this time stood a silent spectator of
the scene; not a feeling of regret at his own isolated
position entered his heart, not a single feeling of
jealousy that he should be omitted in the general joy;
not a single spark of envy, that his fellow-traveller
should have so many to greet him, seemed to enter his
head; and he was, perhaps, as delighted as any one
present.   But Carlos had not forgotten him; and the
instant he could free himself, presenting his friend to
Henriquez and the Colonel, he said, 'This is my friend
Antonio, my preserver, my comforter, my constant companion!'   And then poor Antonio was overwhelmed
in his turn; and how long the excitement would have
lasted it is difficult to know, had not Colonel Lacy's
servant stepped forward and said, 'If you please, sir,
shall I take the black man into the kitchen?'   Orders
were given to install Corintchie instantly in the best
quarters in the servants' apartments, where a good fire
seemed to restore his bewildered faculties to their
natural place; and as he spoke tolerable English, he
was soon in a condition to satisfy the curiosity of the
domestics, who plied him with questions.

Colonel Lacy, after receiving the refusal of the
travellers to eat, proposed that all should adjourn to
the drawing-room, and hear an outline of Carlos'
adventures, saying that they would make up their
deficiencies at supper.   This was hailed by all present
as the best possible arrangement; and on crossing the
hall the pretended Arabs laid aside their accoutrements,
and even their turbans, and wrapping themselves in

their bernous, they seated themselves, and were immediately surrounded by the whole party, who were eager to hear. Colonel Lacy and Henriquez sat so as to contemplate the dear face which they had so long yearned to behold; and while other listeners articulated sounds of wonder, compassion, and almost alarm, the fulness of their joy admitted of no utterance. Sergeant Brown and his wife, who by this time had reached Wavertree, were summoned, as having nearly as strong a claim to hear as any one present, and modestly took their seats behind the richer but not more warm-hearted and rejoicing guests.

A mere summary of proceedings of course was all that could be given at the time; but as Carlos was the narrator, Antonio rapidly rose in the esteem of every one present; and before his friend had ceased, he was installed in the minds of his hearers as one who was henceforth to form a part of the family circle. Nature will make her demands, as the travellers had often found to their cost: at the present moment, however, it was convenient to listen to her; and when supper was announced, they felt that food was necessary. Curiosity satisfied, conviviality ensued. Corintchie stood behind the chair of Carlos in due form, displaying all the knowledge of waiting which he had picked up at Cape Coast, and from the steward of the 'Nancy.' The only drawback upon the general hilarity was the abstemiousness of the new guests, who could not return in kind the frequent toasts which were given in their honour; but with heartfelt emotion they joined in good wishes for the Colonel, who, in his reply of thanks, said that he had, in the return of his beloved boy, received the best birthday present which the world could produce.

At length it became time to separate, and a sort of debate took place as to the sleeping arrangements for the travellers; they insisting upon it, that a carpeted floor was quite luxurious for them. 'You forget,' said the uncle, gently interfering, 'that I have a right to accommodate my nephew and his friend. I have already sent a message to my housekeeper to get beds ready, and the carriage is at the door, so we had better at once go home.' Colonel Lacy acceded, and, on taking leave, promised to breakfast with the party the next morning. They entered the vehicle, and gave Corintchie a bernous to keep him warm as he sat outside. Carlos, who was now prepared for all sorts of surprises, inquired after many old friends, not stopping till he had entered the gate of his new abode, which proved to be a large and handsome house, surrounded by pleasure grounds, and all the appurtenances of wealth. 'Who am I,' thought he, 'that this good old gentleman should call me nephew?' On entering the hall the bedroom candles were ready; the servants were assembled to salute their master's newly-found relative; and the uncle, turning round to Carlos, exclaimed, 'Welcome, my dear boy, to your real home; and not less welcome are you,' added he, holding out his hand to Antonio, 'for it is yours also.' Then wishing them a good night, he retired to his apartment.

Henriquez accompanied his brother and friend to their rooms, which communicated with each other, and where Antonio, thinking that Carlos would wish to talk more unreservedly than if he were present, was about to go to his and shut the door; but Henriquez stopped him, saying, 'Do not go, Antonio; I am sure you will like to hear what I have to tell Carlos.

Henceforth you are identified with him in my mind, and therefore what I say concerns you almost as much as it does him ; so, if you are neither of you too sleepy, you shall hear my history.' Sleep was the last thing wished for by all three ; and Henriquez began his narrative, saying, 'I need not tell you all the distress and agony we felt on the arrival of the " Hero" without you, Carlos, but proceed at once to say, that after she left you she had been spoken at sea · by one of our war-cruisers, who found her under the command of the villain Gray, who stated that most of the crew had died, and that he had brought her far out into the Bight of Benin as fast as possible, to save the rest. An officer went on board, and on questioning the man, found him wholly incapable of navigating the vessel. He therefore sent a midshipman from the war-brig who was competent to the task, and who, with the assistance of the Kroomen, got her as far as St. Mary's, in the Azores, whence, obtaining more hands, he brought her safely into port. He immediately communicated with us, and told us that one day, on looking over the captain's, the surgeon's, and your things, in order to make an inventory of them, he found a piece of paper thrust into the log-book, on which was written, "We are two men on board who know all, but we are afraid of one in this ship. The captain, surgeon, mate, and steward are all dead ; but Charles Lacy and Antonio Pietri were left by Gray in an island in the Bight, and we do not know what is become of them. You must not betray us, or he will be revenged on us.' The midshipman very wisely did not show that he was in any way suspicious ; but narrowly watching Gray, was convinced that he was a bad fellow. He therefore consulted with us, and the owners of the " Hero," what was to be done with him. We brought him before a magistrate, and easily detecting the writers of the anonymous letter, who were a Scotchman and an Irishman, we brought them up as witnesses. They deposed, that as they lay sick in their hammocks, they overheard Gray arrange a plan with one of the crew, whom he had either intimidated or bribed to get rid of you and Antonio the next day. He said he knew you would go ashore to bury the captain, and even threatened to destroy you ; but his accomplice, who afterwards died, would not hear of this. They said that Gray had always hated you, but why they could not tell. They were unable in their weak state to cope with so ferocious a person as he seems to have been, and too closely watched by him to warn you of the wretch's intentions ; they therefore tried to soften the heart of his comrade, and so far succeeded as to be able to crawl out and collect the things which you found in the boat, and which were put in by the more merciful of the two rogues, unknown to the other. In consequence of this evidence, Gray was imprisoned for some time, and since his release he has gone to America, and not been heard of since ; the two witnesses are respectably employed through my means.

'I know not,' continued Henriquez, 'whether this intelligence was not worse than the certainty of your death would have been, for we fancied every horrible fate for you which could be imagined. There was, however, always a sort of hope within my heart, which never died till that portion of your boat, which you mentioned last night as having drifted away, was picked up by one of the cruisers, all of whom were constantly looking after you along the coast; and then I confess that I lost courage. It was not right, however, to leave anything undone which might tend to your safety, till the fact of death was ascertained. Colonel Lacy went to London, procured the order from the Colonial Minister which you saw, and I wrote to the missionaries and merchants. I thought I should never hold my head up again, and in order to give me change of scene, which was thought desirable, the gentleman in whose employment you left me as a clerk, requiring the transaction of some business in Cadiz, and knowing that I spoke Spanish, proposed to send me there; and as the Colonel acquiesced, I would have gladly accepted the offer, had I not been unwilling to leave him so depressed as he was; but he insisted, and I went. I gave great satisfaction, and my health and spirits were both improved, not only by the journey, but by the occupation which an errand of such importance gave me. On my return I found Colonel Lacy so dreadfully dejected, and grown so thin, that I feared I was about to lose him also, and blamed myself for having gone. He continually reproached himself for having suffered you to go to Africa, accused himself of having exposed you to perhaps worse than death, and would not be comforted. I was again requested by my employers to revisit Spain; but I would not consent unless the Colonel would accompany me, for I could not again leave him, and knew by experience the good results of such a change. After much persuasion he yielded to my entreaties, and on our arrival we both lived with the correspondent of the house, who treated us most hos-

pitably. My stay there was prolonged far beyond my
expectations, and while waiting for the arrival of a
cargo from the Levant, we all went to stay a few days
at the country house of our correspondent. Here we
became acquainted with a Spanish gentleman, who was
a near neighbour, and who, from the moment he saw
us, took such a fancy to both the Colonel and myself,
that he asked us to stay with him. I could not accept
the invitation ; but the Colonel did, and in the course
of conversation our benefactor accidentally remarked
that I was a Spaniard by birth, and the curiosity of
Don Andreas being excited, he asked who I was.
The story was soon told, and when concluded he
mused for some time, and then said, " I lost a
beloved sister with her husband and two boys in the
war about that time. Don Gaspar de la Rosa, for so
my brother-in-law was named, espoused the liberal
cause, although of noble birth, and served in the army
of the Christinos. His wife and children went everywhere with him ; but they all disappeared, and I never
could get further tidings of any of them, except the
fact that he had been seen to fall in the field. It
would be a strange coincidence if your two boys
should prove to be my nephews. I have always
looked upon Henriquez as your son ; but his countenance interested me from the first moment I beheld
it, and his features seemed familiar to my eye. Yes !
he certainly is like·poor Gaspar, although I have
often dismissed the idea as foolish and romantic. I
am a lone old man, now getting into years ; and
should be glad to find some tie which might make
my old age happy."

'Dates were compared, the persons of our father

and mother were described, an old servant questioned, who said my likeness to Don Gaspar had struck her also, but more than that, my voice and carriage. I was sent for; the ring which I always wore was said to resemble one which had been in my father's possession, and which you recollect the Sergeant took off his finger; the other ornaments were obtained from England, and recognised by the servant, and our parentage was established.

'Satisfied with my identity, Don Andreas would have made no further inquiries; but the Colonel, determining not to leave anything undone, actually repaired to the spot where he had buried the bodies, and persuaded my uncle and the old nurse to go with him. With great difficulty he found the place, but plains are not often disturbed in that country. Some of the neighbouring people were paid for clearing away the bushes and digging up the ground; and the remains were actually discovered. Of course there was but little left; but the colour of my mother's hair was remembered by the nurse, and identified with that found in the grave. The clothes fell to dust when touched; but a metal plate, belonging to a military cap, was still perfect, and on it was scratched the name of "Gaspar de la Rosa." All doubts now vanished; the remains were taken to consecrated ground, and wealth, rank, and family were restored to me. I hope I may be forgiven, however, for having at first looked on them with a feeling amounting to indifference; for you, Carlos, were not to share them with me. This, however, was but an ungrateful return for the blessings which thus flowed upon me, and I strove to rouse myself from such a sickly state of mind.

My uncle wished me to remain with him in Spain, and to claim the property which had been my father's. But I could not separate myself from my best friend; and, moreover, I had a secret feeling that in Liverpool I was on the spot where the first news of you was likely to arrive. I had no difficulty in obtaining my inheritance, to which my uncle added what he called his sister's portion. A life of idleness was irksome to me, and I dreaded its effect upon my character. I had begun my career in commerce, and it interested me. My uncle felt the force of what I said, and consented to my becoming a merchant on a large scale; and the extent of my affairs had put me in communication with all parts of the world. One-half of the property has been carefully saved for you, Carlos, and you may use it as you please, either in conjunction with me or any one else; or you can live upon it. I endeavoured at first to divide my time between England and Spain; but I soon found that this did not answer. I never was away from the former, but I found that my presence had been required; and at length my good uncle consented to take up his abode here entirely, and I had no longer any reason to absent myself. This is our house, and of course yours also, as well as everything which I possess. At another time we will deliberate upon the future; but morning dawns, and you ought to be in bed; to-morrow we will talk further.' 'My excellent Henriquez,' said Carlos, 'how much better you have always been than I ever was! But I have been well chastened, and hope I shall never forget the lessons I have received. I have been a wayward, spoiled child; but now I will be your pupil, and you shall find me docile and obedient for the rest of my life.'

Carlos and Antonio both undressed ; but no sooner had the former sunk into the soft feather bed, than he started up again, and rolled himself on to the floor. Antonio, after making the experiment for half an hour, exclaimed, 'I shall be suffocated if I stay here,' and followed his example. As to Corintchie, he thought his accommodations the most luxurious he had ever met with, and did ample justice to the first bed in which he had ever slept. In about three hours the travellers rose perfectly refreshed, and threw open the windows for air. They strolled into the park and into the stables, longed to have a ride upon the beautiful horses, but thought it would be indecorous to indulge their wild propensities just now, and recollected that they must behave like civilised men. They returned to their rooms and made a more careful toilette, put on the European clothes which had been given them at Cape Coast ; but they could not endure as yet to tie up their throats. The dark glossy curls of Carlos, therefore, were seen to steal on his neck ; and when he met his uncle at the breakfast table, Don Andreas started, but welcomed him with a warmth which far exceeded that of the preceding evening, saying, 'This is the likeness I longed to see ; this is indeed the child of my dear Isabella, and she is perpetuated in him. I am a happy old man,' continued he, 'to have two, nay three, such fine young men to take care of me, and grace my table ;' and as Colonel Lacy walked in to share the meal, he observed that the group was complete.

The first operation when breakfast was over was to send for the tailor, and by the next day the young men, including Corintchie, were presentable. The precious treasures from Africa were passed through the Custom-house, and some of them given to Colonel and Mrs. Lacy, and the Browns ; and as calmer moments succeeded to the deep emotions which all had felt, the commonplaces of life came under consideration. Carlos willingly obeyed the wishes of his friends by sharing his brother's occupations ; and as it pleased God to bless their endeavours, they were the channel through which many blessings flowed upon their fellow-creatures. Commerce with the western coast of Africa was a principal feature in the transactions of Carlos, in the hope of benefiting a country in which he took an undying interest; and when he reflected on the immense riches of that beautiful land, and the universal spirit of traffic which pervades its inhabitants, he hoped that sooner or later its natural productions would wholly supersede the degrading and inhuman slave-trade, which stamps it with the seal of barbarity.

The increasing consequence of the brothers, and Carlos' experience in one quarter of the world, gave weight to their opinions with men high in the service of their adopted country; and their suggestions being acted upon, were most important to the welfare of their sable brethren : for it is the fashion either to depreciate the negro character too much, or estimate it too highly ; and few persons view it with that moderation which ensures justice. Convinced that the enormous quantities of calomel, colocynth, quinine, etc., with occasionally profuse bleedings, in cases of fever, only increased the danger, Carlos suggested that other systems of medicine should be tried, till the baneful effects of the climate were ameliorated, and white men found that they could live in Western Africa. Hand in hand with those efforts walked Christianity. Men were educated purposely to enlighten their countrymen, whose complexions and constitutions were partially or wholly tinged with negro blood ; and they by degrees carried the blessings of revealed religion into the heart of the continent. Among these was the son of Wondo, for whom Carlos sent, and who was joyfully entrusted to his care by the father. The education of these men was liberal in solid things ; and along with one or two of the arts of more polished life, they were always taught any eminently useful occupation for which their talents fitted them.

All the individuals who had been kind to Carlos, and who survived, sooner or later tasted of his bounty; and some years afterwards he was even happy enough to serve his friend Yusuf, and secure his assistance in importing Arab horses. Corintchie proved a most valuable servant, preferring to remain in the capacity which 'kept him in constant communication with his beloved masters, but whose example of piety and fidelity had much influence over those of his countrymen who came in contact with him.

Antonio,—the generous, devoted Antonio,—who shared the affections of the whole circle into which he had been received, and who was an especial favourite with Mrs. Lacy and her children, never married, but spent his whole life with Carlos. The brothers settled a sum of money upon him, which made him wholly independent; but this did not make him idle. He tried by industry to supply the deficiencies of his

early education, and became the confidential superintendent, the second self of the merchant brothers,
attended to all their shipping concerns, and secured
respect for them and for himself in every class.

If Don Andreas had been asked which of his
nephews he loved the most, it would have been impossible for him to have supposed that he had any
preference ; but there was a tenderness in his manner
towards Carlos, of which he was himself unconscious,
but which Henriquez perceived only to increase his
own love.   Nor was he less gratified at the reputation
which his brother had secured, even though his personal attendance was commanded in the highest
quarters.   To the solicitations of learned bodies who
sought for his contributions, Carlos was glad to answer
by communicating all the knowledge he possessed ;
but he found it very difficult to check the accumulated
entreaties of the fairer sex that he would give them
his autograph, or make a sketch for their scrap-books.
At length, however, some new wonder came, and the
collectors left the African traveller in peace.   The
children of the Browns flourished under the auspices
of the brothers; and when Colonel Lacy, in his
declining years, looked around, and saw how his
endeavours had been blessed, he rejoiced in the hour
when the cry of the wailing orphans met his ear,
and he had obeyed the impulses of his heart, by
adopting for his own the excellent Henriquez and
little Don Carlos.

MORRISON AND GIBB, EDINBURGH,
PRINTERS TO HER MAJESTY'S STATIONERY OFFICE.

4 M—G/83—D.

A CATALOGUE OF
BOOKS FOR THE YOUNG,

OF ALL AGES,

SUITABLE FOR PRESENTS AND SCHOOL PRIZES,

ARRANGED ACCORDING TO PRICES,

FROM HALF-A-GUINEA TO SIXPENCE EACH.

PUBLISHED BY

GRIFFITH, FARRAN, OKEDEN & WELSH

(SUCCESSORS TO NEWBERY AND HARRIS),

WEST CORNER OF ST. PAUL'S CHURCHYARD, LONDON.

E. P. DUTTON AND CO., NEW YORK.

A

20M. 9/87.—V. T. & S.

BOOKS FOR THE YOUNG.

Arranged according to Prices.

7/6   *Seven Shillings and Sixpence each, cloth elegant. Illustrated.*

Alice's Wonderland Birthday Book. By E. STANLEY LEATHES and O. E. W. HOLMES.

Child Elves. By M. G.

The Looking-Glass for the Mind. With Cuts by BEWICK. An Introduction by CHARLES WELSH.

Wanderings of a Beetle. By E. P. WARREN.

6/-   **KINGSTON'S SERIES OF SIX SHILLING BOOKS.**

Twelve Volumes. Each containing from 450 to 550 pages, well Illustrated by the best Artists. Imperial 16mo, cloth elegant, bevelled boards, gilt edges.

Hurricane Hurry.

Master of his Fate. By A. BLANCHE. Trans. by Rev. M. R. BARNARD.

Middy and Ensign. By G. MANVILLE FENN.

The Missing Ship; or, Notes from the Log of the *Ouzel Galley.*

Paddy Finn: The Adventures of an Irish Midshipman.

The Three Midshipmen.

The Three Lieutenants; or, Naval life in the Nineteenth Century.

The Three Commanders; or, Active Service Afloat in Modern Times.

The Three Admirals, and the Adventures of their Young Followers.

True Blue; or, a British Seaman of the Old School.

Will Weatherhelm; or, The Yarn of an Old Sailor.

Won from the Waves; or, The Story of Maiden May.

Young Buglers: A Tale of the Peninsular War. By G. A. HENTY.

6/-   *Six Shillings each, cloth elegant, with Illustrations.*

The Bird and Insects' Post Office. By R. BLOOMFIELD. (Or paper boards, price 3s. 6d.)

Flyaway Fairies and Baby Blossoms. By L. CLARKSON.

Golden Threads from an Ancient Loom. By LYDIA HANDS.

His Little Royal Highness. By RUTH OGDEN.

Journey to the Centre of the Earth. By JULES VERNE.

Little Loving Heart's Poem Book. By M. E. TUPPER.

Mabel in Rhymeland. By EDWARD HOLLAND, C.C.S.

Mamma's Bible Stories. 3 Vols., in cardboard box.

The Vanderbilts and the Story of their Fortune. By W. A. CROFFUT.

5/-   *Five Shillings each, cloth elegant. Illus. by eminent Artists.*

All Round the Clock. By H. M. BENNETT and R. E. MACK. 4to, Boards.

Belle's Pink Boots. By JOANNA H. MATTHEWS. Gilt edges.

The Day of Wonders. By M. SULLIVAN. Gilt edges.

Dethroned; A Story for Girls. By the Author of "Girlhood Days."

Extraordinary Nursery Rhymes; New, yet Old. Small 4to.

GRIFFITH, FARRAN, OKEDEN AND WELSH,

Five Shillings each—continued.

Favourite Picture Book (The) and Nursery Companion. Compiled anew by UNCLE CHARLIE. With 450 Illustrations by ABSOLON, ANELAY, BENNETT, BROWNE (PHIZ), SIR JOHN GILBERT, T. LANDSEER, LEECH, PROUT, HARRISON WEIR, and others. Medium 4to, cloth elegant (or coloured Illustrations, 10s. 6d.).

₊ This may also be had in Two Vols., cloth, price 3s., or coloured Illustrations, 5s.; also in Four parts, in paper boards, fancy wrapper, price 1s. each, or coloured Illustrations, 2s. each.

First Christmas. By HOFFMANN.

From May to Christmas at Thorne Hill. By Mrs. D. P. SANDFORD.

Gladys Ramsay. By Mrs. M. DOUGLAS. Crown 8vo.

Goody Two Shoes. In a Fac-simile Cover of the Original, with introduction by CHARLES WELSH.

Harris's Cabinet: { The Butterfly's Ball. | The Lion's Masquerade. / The Elephant's Ball. | The Peacock at Home. Or in Four Parts at 1s. each.

History of the Robins. By Mrs. TRIMMER. Small 4to, gilt edges.

Little Margit. By M. A. HOYER.

Little People of Asia. By OLIVE THORNE MILLER.

Merry Songs for Little Voices. Words by Mrs. BRODERIP. Music by THOMAS MURBY. Fcap. 4to.

Nothing Venture, Nothing Have. By ANNE BEALE.

Patrañas; or, SPANISH STORIES, LEGENDARY AND TRADITIONAL.

The Pattern Life. By W. CHATTERTON DIX.

Pictures and Songs for Little Children.

Queen of the Meadow. By R. E. MACK.

Queer Pets and their Doings. By the author of " Little People of Asia."

Wee Babies. By IDA WAUGH and AMY E. BLANCHARD.

Five Shilling Series of
TALES OF TRAVEL AND ADVENTURE.

Crown 8vo, well printed on good paper, and strongly bound in cloth elegant, bevelled boards, gilt edges. Each volume contains from 300 to 400 pages of solid reading. Fully illustrated by eminent Artists.

The Briny Deep. By CAPTAIN TOM.

From Cadet to Captain. By J. PERCY GROVES.

The Cruise of the Theseus. By ARTHUR KNIGHT.

The Duke's Own. By J. PERCY GROVES.

Friends though Divided. By GEO. A. HENTY.

Hair-breadth Escapes. By the Rev. H. C. ADAMS.

Masaniello. By F. BAYFORD HARRISON.

Mystery of Beechy Grange (The). By the Rev. H. C. ADAMS.

Perils in the Transvaal and Zululand. By the Rev. H. C. ADAMS.

Rival Crusoes (The). By W. H. G. KINGSTON.

A Search for the Mountain of Gold. By W. MURPHY.

Five Shillings series—continued.

A Soldier Born. By J. PERCY GROVES.
In Times of Peril. By GEO. A. HENTY.
Who did it? or, HOLMWOOD PRIORY. By the Rev. H. C. ADAMS.
Who was Philip? By the Rev. H. C. ADAMS.

THE BOYS' OWN FAVOURITE LIBRARY.

3/6

Twenty-seven Volumes, price Three Shillings and Sixpence each.

Each volume contains from 300 to 450 pages of solid reading, well illustrated by the best Artists. Crown 8vo, cloth elegant, gilt edges.

Mark Seaworth. By W. H. G. KINGSTON.
Hurricane Hurry. By W. H. G. KINGSTON.
Salt Water. By W. H. G. KINGSTON.
Out on the Pampas. By G. A. HENTY.
Peter the Whaler. By W. H. G. KINGSTON.
The Three Admirals. By W. H. G. KINGSTON.
Early Start in Life. By E. MARRYAT NORRIS.
Fred Markham in Russia. By W. H. G. KINGSTON.
College Days at Oxford. By Rev. H. C. ADAMS.
The Young Francs-Tireurs. By G. A. HENTY.
The Three Midshipmen. By W. H. G. KINGSTON.
The Fiery Cross. By BARBARA HUTTON.
Our Soldiers. By W. H. G. KINGSTON.
The Three Commanders. By W. H. G. KINGSTON.
The Three Lieutenants. By W. H. G. KINGSTON.
Manco, The Peruvian Chief. By W. H. G. KINGSTON.
Our Sailors. By W. H. G. KINGSTON.
John Deane. By W. H. G. KINGSTON.
Travel, War, and Shipwreck. By Colonel PARKER GILLMORE.
Chums. By HARLEIGH SEVERNE.
African Wanderers. By Mrs. R. LEE.
Tales of the White Cockade. By BARBARA HUTTON.
The Missing Ship. By W. H. G. KINGSTON.
Will Weatherhelm. By W. H. G. KINGSTON.
True Blue. By W. H. G. KINGSTON.
The North Pole, and How CHARLIE WILSON discovered it.
Harty the Wanderer. By FARLEIGH OWEN.

THE GIRLS' OWN FAVOURITE LIBRARY.

3/6

Twenty-seven Volumes, price Three Shillings and Sixpence each.

Each volume contains from 300 to 400 pages of solid reading, well illustrated by the best Artists. Cr. 8vo, cloth elegant, gilt edges.

Guide, Philosopher, and Friend. By Mrs. HERBERT MARTIN.
Her Title of Honour. By HOLME LEE.
Michaelmas Daisy. By SARAH DOUDNEY.
The New Girl. By Mrs. GELLIE.
The Oak Staircase. By M. and C. LEE.

THE GIRLS' OWN FAVOURITE LIBRARY.
Three Shillings and Sixpence each—continued.

3/6

For a Dream's Sake. By Mrs. HERBERT MARTIN.
My Mother's Diamonds. By MARIA J. GREER.
My Sister's Keeper. By LAURA M. LANE.
Shiloh. By W. M. L. JAY.
Holden with the Cords. By W. M. L. JAY.
"Bonnie Lesley." By Mrs. HERBERT MARTIN.
Left Alone. By FRANCIS CARR.
Very Genteel. By the Author of "Mrs. Jerningham's Journal."
Gladys the Reaper. By ANNE BEALE.
Stephen the Schoolmaster. By Mrs. GELLIE (M. E. B.).
Isabel's Difficulties. By M. R. CAREY.
Court and Cottage. By Mrs. EMMA MARSHALL.
Rosamend Fane. By M. and C. LEE.
Simplicity and Fascination. By ANNE BEALE.
Millicent and Her Cousins. By the Hon. A. BETHELL.
Aunt Hetty's Will. By M. M. POLLARD.
Silver Linings. By Mrs. BRAY.
Theodora. By EMILIA MARRYAT NORRIS.
Alda Graham. By EMILIA MARRYAT NORRIS.
A Wayside Posy. By FANNY LABLACHE.
Through a Refiner's Fire. By ELEANOR HOLMES.
A Generous Friendship; or, THE HAPPENINGS OF A NEW ENGLAND
     SUMMER.
A Country Mouse. By Mrs. HERBERT MARTIN.

Price Three Shillings and Sixpence each.
Elegantly bound, and illustrated by the best Authors.

3/6

Bird and Insects' Post Office (The). By ROBERT BLOOMFIELD.
     Crown 4to, paper boards, with Chromo side (or cloth elegant, 6s.)
Bunch of Berries (A), AND THE DIVERSIONS THEREOF. By LEADER
     SCOTT.
Castles and their Heroes. By BARBARA HUTTON.
Child Pictures from Dickens. Illustrated.
Clement's Trial and Victory. By M. E. B. (Mrs. GELLIE).
Daisy Days; a Colour Book for Children. By Mrs. A. M. CLAUSEN.
Every-day Life in Our Public Schools. By CHAS. EYRE PASCOE.
In Time of War. By JAS. F. COBB.
Joachim's Spectacles. By M. and C. LEE.
Lee (Mrs.) Anecdotes of the Habits and Instincts of Animals.
     ,,   Anecdotes of the Habits and Instincts of Birds, Reptiles,
             and Fishes.
     ,,   Adventures in Australia.
Lily and Her Brothers. By C. E. L.
Little Chicks and Baby Tricks. By IDA WAUGH.
Little May's Friend. By ANNIE WHITTEM.
The Little Wonderbox. By JEAN INGELOW. A series of Six Vols.

3/6

Three Shillings and Sixpence each—continued.

My Friend and My Enemy. By PAUL BLAKE.
Nimpo's Troubles. By OLIVE THORNE MILLER.
Old Corner Annual for 1888. Illustrated.
Perils of the Pacific; a Tale of the Sea. By ROBERT BROWN.
Reached at Last. By R. H. CUTTER.
Restful Work for Youthful Hands. By S. F. A. CAULFIELD.
Sermons for Children. By A. DE COPPET.
Talks about Plants. By Mrs. LANKESTER.
Two Stories of Two. By STELLA AUSTIN.
Under the Mistletoe. By LIZZIE LAWSON and R. E. MACK. 4to, boards.
Unwelcome Guest. By ESME STUART.

2/6

THE "BUNCHY" SERIES OF HALF-CROWN BOOKS.

Crown 8vo. Cloth elegant, bevelled boards, gilt edges, fully Illustrated by the best Artists.

African Pets. By F. CLINTON PARRY.
Bunchy. By E. C. PHILLIPS.
Bryan and Katie. By ANNETTE LYSTER.
Cast Adrift: the Story of a Waif. By Mrs. H. H. MARTIN.
Daring Voyage across the Atlantic. By the Brothers ANDREWS.
Dolly, Dear! By MARY E. GELLIE.
Every Inch a King. By Mrs. J. WORTHINGTON BLISS.
Family Feats. By Mrs. R. M. BRAY.
Fearless Frank. By MARY E. GELLIE.
A Gem of an Aunt. By Mrs. GELLIE (M. E. B.)
Gerty and May. By the Author of "Our White Violet."
Grandfather. By E. C. PHILLIPS, Author of "Bunchy."
Great and Small. By Miss HARRIET POOLE.
Growing Up. By JENNETT HUMPHREYS.
Hilda and Her Doll. By E. C. PHILLIPS.
House on the Bridge. By C. E. BOWEN.
Hugh's Sacrifice. By CECIL MARRYAT NORRIS.
Mischievous Jack. By O. E. L.
Nora's Trust. By Mrs. GELLIE (M. E. B.).
Our Aubrey. By E. C. PHILLIPS.
Punch. By E. C. PHILLIPS.
St. Aubyn's Laddie. By E. C. PHILLIPS.
Ten of Them. By Mrs. R. M. BRAY.
"Those Unlucky Twins!" By ANNETTE LYSTER.
Two Rose Trees. By Mrs. MINNIE DOUGLAS.
The Venturesome Twins. By Mrs. GELLIE. Crown 8vo.
Ways and Tricks of Animals. By MARY HOOPER.
We Four. By Mrs. R. M. BRAY.

Two Shillings and Sixpence each—continued.

Boy Slave in Bokhara. By DAVID KER.

Boy's Own Toy Maker (The): A Practical Illustrated Guide to the useful employment of Leisure Hours. By E. LANDELLS.

Choice Extracts from the Standard Authors. By the Editor of "Poetry for the Young." 3 vols. (2s. 6d. each.)

Cruise of Ulysses and His Men (The); or, Tales and Adventures from the Odyssey, for Boys and Girls. By O. M. BELL.

Girl's Own Toy Maker (The), AND BOOK OF RECREATION. By E. and A. LANDELLS. With 200 Illustrations.

Goody Two Shoes. A Reprint of the Original Edition, with Introduction by CHAS. WELSH.

Holly Berries. By AMY E. BLANCHARD. Coloured Illustrations by IDA WAUGH. 4to boards.

Ice Maiden AND OTHER STORIES. By HANS CHRISTIAN ANDERSEN.

Lesson Notes. By STAFFORD C. NORTHCOTE.

Little Child's Fable Book. Arranged Progressively in One, Two, and Three Syllables. 16 Pages, Illustrated. *Cheap Edition.*

Little Gipsy. By ELIE SAUVAGE. *Cheaper Edition.*

Little Pilgrim (The). Illustrated by HELEN PETRIE.

Model Yachts, and Model Yacht Sailing: HOW TO BUILD, RIG AND SAIL A SELF-ACTING MODEL YACHT. By JAS. E. WALTON, V.M.Y.C. Fcap. 4to, with 58 Woodcuts.

My Own Dolly. By AMY BLANCHARD and IDA WAUGH.

On the Leads. By Mrs. A. A. STRANGE BUTSON.

Sea and Sky. By J. R. BLAKISTON, M.A. Suitable for young people. Profusely Illustrated, and contains a Coloured Atlas of the Phenomena of Sea and Sky.

Science in the Nursery; or, Children's Toys. By T. W. ERLE.

Wild Horseman of the Pampas. By DAVID KER.

Two Shillings and Sixpence, cloth elegant, with Illustrations by Harrison Weir and other Eminent Artists.

As Yankees see us. By LEANDER RICHARDSON.

Animals and their Social Powers. By MARY TURNER-ANDREWES.

A Week by Themselves. By EMILIA MARRYAT NORRIS.

Babies' Crawling Rugs, and How to Make them. By EMMA S. WINDSOR.

Christmas Box.

Christmas Roses. By LIZZIE LAWSON and R. E. MACK. 4to, boards.

Christmas Tree Fairy. By R. E. MACK and Mrs. L. MACK.

Cleopatra.

Funny Fables for Little Folks.

2/6

Two Shillings and Sixpence each—continued.

Granny's Story Box. With 20 Engravings.
Jack Frost and Betty Snow ; Tales for Wintry Nights and Rainy Days.
London Cries. By LUKE LIMNER.
Madelon. By ESTHER CARR.
Margaret Kent. An American Story.
Odd Stories about Animals : told in Short and Easy Words.
Percy Pomo ; or, the Autobiography of a South Sea Islander.
Secret of Wrexford (The). By ESTHER CARR.
Snowed Up. By EMILIA MARRYAT NORRIS.
Tales from Catland. Dedicated to the Young Kittens of England.
Talking Bird (The). By M. and E. KIRBY.
Three Nights. By CECIL MARRYAT NORRIS.
Tiny Stories for Tiny Readers in Tiny Words.
Trottie's Story Book : True Tales in Short Words and Large Type.
Tuppy ; or, THE AUTOBIOGRAPHY OF A DONKEY.
Wandering Blindfold ; or, A BOY'S TROUBLES. By MARY ALBERT.

NEW ILLUSTRATED QUARTO GIFT BOOKS.

Wreck of Hesperus. By H. W. Longfellow. Small quarto, cloth bevelled, stamped in gold and colour.

Uniform with the above.

The Village Blacksmith. | Keble's Evening Hymn.
The Sweet By-and-Bye.

COMICAL PICTURE BOOKS.

Two Shillings and Sixpence each, fancy boards.

2/6

Adventures of the Pig Family, The. By ARTHUR S. GIBSON. Sixteen pages Illustrations, oblong 4to, boards.
The March Hares and their friends. Uniform with the above. By the same author.

The following have Coloured Plates.

English Struwwelpeter (The): or PRETTY STORIES AND FUNNY PICTURES FOR LITTLE CHILDREN. After the celebrated German Work of Dr. HEINRICH HOFFMANN. Thirtieth Edition. Twenty-four pages of Illustrations (or mounted on linen, 5s.).
The Fools' Paradise. Mirth and Fun for Old and Young.
Funny Picture Book (The); or, 25 FUNNY LITTLE LESSONS. A free Translation from the German of "DER KLEINE ABC SCHÜTZE."
In the Land of Nod; a Fancy Story. By A. C. MARZATH.
Loves of Tom Tucker and Little Bo-Peep. Written and Illustrated by THOMAS HOOD.
Spectropia ; or, SURPRISING SPECTRAL ILLUSIONS, showing Ghosts everywhere, and of any colour. By J. H. BROWN.

GRIFFITH, FARRAN, OKEDEN AND WELSH,

THE HOLIDAY LIBRARY.

A Series of 15 Volumes for Boys and Girls, well illustrated, and bound in cloth, with elegant design printed in gold and colours, gilt edges. The size is Foolscap 8vo, and as each volume contains upwards of 300 pages of interesting tales of all descriptions, they form one of the most attractive and saleable series in the market.

Price Two Shillings, each volume containing Two Tales,   **2/-**
well Illustrated.

LIST OF BOOKS IN THE SERIES.

Vol. I.	Sunny Days. Wrecked, Not Lost.	Vol. VIII.	Children's Picnic. Holiday Tales.
„ II.	Discontented Children. Holidays among Mountains.	„ IX.	Christian Elliott. Stolen Cherries.
„ III.	Adrift on the Sea. Hofer the Tyrolese.	„ X.	Harry at School. Claudine.
„ IV.	Alice and Beatrice. Julia Maitland.	„ XI.	Our White Violet. Fickle Flora.
„ V.	Among the Brigands. Hero of Brittany.	„ XII.	William Tell. Paul Howard's Captivity.
„ VI.	Cat and Dog. Johnny Miller.	„ XIII.	Amy's Wish. New Baby.
„ VII.	Children of the Parsonage. Grandmamma's Relics.	„ XIV.	Neptune. Crib and Fly.
		„ XV.	What became of Tommy Geoffrey's Great Fault.

Two Shillings, cloth elegant, Illustrated.

Captain Fortescue's Handful. By C. MARRYATT NORRIS.
Children's Gallery. Four Parts, price 2s. each.
Elsie Dinsmore ⎫
Elsie's Girlhood ⎬ By MARTHA FARQUHARSON.
Elsie's Holidays ⎭
A Far-away Cousin. By K. D. CORNISH.
How to Make Dolls' Furniture AND TO FURNISH A DOLL'S HOUSE. With 70 Illustrations. Small 4to.
Illustrated Paper Model Maker. By E. LANDELLS. In envelope.
Mademoiselle's Story. By MADAME RYFFEL.
Mamma's Bible Stories. First Series. FOR HER LITTLE BOYS AND GIRLS.
Mamma's Bible Stories. Second Series.
Mamma's Bible Stories. Third Series. Illustrated by STANLEY BERKELEY. The three Volumes can be had in a handsome case. Price 6s.
Scenes of Animal Life and Character. FROM NATURE AND RECOLLECTION. In Twenty Plates. By J. B. 4to, fancy boards.
Seeking His Fortune. Uniform in size and price with above.
Two and Two; OR, FRENCH AND ENGLISH. By Mrs. SEYMOUR.
Wonders of Home, in Eleven Stories (The). By GRANDFATHER GREY.
Young Vocalist (The). Cloth boards. (Or paper, 1s.)

Price One Shilling and Sixpence each.

Babies' Museum (The). By UNCLE CHARLIE. Paper boards.

Children's Daily Help. By E. G. Bevelled boards, gilt edges.

Directory of Girls' Societies, Clubs, and Unions. Conducted on unprofessional principles. By S. F. A. CAULFIELD.

Little Margaret's Ride to the Isle of Wight ; or, THE WONDERFUL ROCKING-HORSE. By Mrs. F. BROWN. Coloured Illustrations.

Our Wild Swan and other Pets. By HELEN WEBLEY PARRY, Author of "An Epitome of Anglican Church History." With coloured illustrations by HARRISON WEIR. Price 1s. 6d.

Rivals of the Cornfield. By the Author of "Geneviève's Story."

Seasons' Songs and Sketches. 4 Vols. small quarto. Price 1/6 each.
    I. Spring. II. Summer. III. Autumn. IV. Winter.

Taking Tales. In Plain Language and large Type. Four vols.
May also be had in 2 vols., 3s. 6d. each ; and in 21 parts, cl. limp, price 6d. each.

ANGELO SERIES OF EIGHTEENPENNY BOOKS.

Square 16mo. Cloth elegant, fully Illustrated.

Angelo ; or, THE PINE FOREST IN THE ALPS. By GERALDINE E. JEWSBURY. 5th Thousand.

Aunt Annette's Stories to Ada. By ANNETTE A. SALAMAN.

Brave Nelly ; or, WEAK HANDS AND A WILLING HEART. By M. E. B. (Mrs. GELLIE). 5th Thousand.

Featherland ; or, How THE BIRDS LIVED AT GREENLAWN. By G. M. FENN. 4th Thousand.

Humble Life : A Tale of HUMBLE HOMES. By the Author of "Gerty and May," &c.

Kingston's (W. H. G.) Child of the Wreck ; or, THE LOSS OF THE ROYAL GEORGE.

Lee's (Mrs. R.) Playing at Settlers ; or, THE FAGOT HOUSE.
———————— Twelve Stories of the Sayings and Doings of Animals.

Little Lisette, THE ORPHAN OF ALSACE. By M. E. B. (Mrs. GELLIE).

Live Toys ; or, ANECDOTES OF OUR FOUR-LEGGED AND OTHER PETS. By EMMA DAVENPORT.

Long Evenings ; or, STORIES FOR MY LITTLE FRIENDS. By EMILIA MARRYAT.

Three Wishes (The). By Mrs. GELLIE (M. E. B.).

The CHERRY SERIES of EIGHTEENPENNY BOOKS. 1/6

PRESENTS AND PRIZES FOR BOYS AND GIRLS.

Thirty-six volumes, well illustrated, small 8vo, clearly printed on
good paper, and strongly bound in elegant cloth boards, gilt edges.

Adventures in Fanti-land. By Mrs. R. LEE.
African Cruiser (The). By S. WHITCHURCH SADLER.
Always Happy; or, Anecdotes of Felix and his Sister.
Aunt Mary's Bran Pie. By the Author of "St. Olave's."
Battle and Victory. By C. E. BOWEN.
A Child's Influence. By LISA LOCKYER.
Constance and Nellie. By EMMA DAVENPORT.
Corner Cottage, and its Inmates. By FRANCES OSBORNE.
Distant Homes. By Mrs. J. E. AYLMER.
Father Time's Story Book. By KATHLEEN KNOX.
From Peasant to Prince. By Mrs. PIETZKER.
Girlhood Days. By Mrs. SEYMOUR.
Good in Everything. By Mrs. BARWELL.
Granny's Wonderful Chair. By B. F. BROWNE.
Happy Holidays. By EMMA DAVENPORT.
Happy Home. By LADY LUSHINGTON.
The Heroic Wife. By W. H. G. KINGSTON.
Helen in Switzerland. By LADY LUSHINGTON.
Holidays Abroad; or, Right at Last. By EMMA DAVENPORT.
Lucy's Campaign. By M. and C. LEE.
Lost in the Jungle. By AUGUSTA MARRYAT.
Louisa Broadhurst. By A. MILNER.
Master Bobby.
Mudge and Her Chicks.
My Grandmother's Budget. By Mrs. BRODERIP.
Our Birthdays. By EMMA DAVENPORT.
Our Home in the Marshland. By E. L. F.
Parted. By N. D'ANVERS.
Pictures of Girl Life. By C. A. HOWELL.
School Days in Paris. By M. S. JEUNE.
Starlight Stories. By FANNY LABLACHE.
Sunnyland Stories. By the Author of "St. Olave's."
Talent and Tatters.
Tittle-Tattle: and other Stories for Children.
Vicar of Wakefield (The).
Willie's Victory.

1/-

THE HAWTHORN SERIES OF SHILLING BOOKS.

PRESENTS AND PRIZES FOR BOYS AND GIRLS.

Forty-two volumes, well illustrated, small 8vo, clearly printed on good paper, and strongly bound in elegant cloth boards.

Adrift on the Sea. By E. M. NORRIS.
Alice and Beatrice. By GRANDMAMMA.
Among the Brigands. By C. E. BOWEN.
Amy's Wish : A Fairy Tale. By Mr. G. TYLER.
Cat and Dog; or, Puss and the Captain.
Children of the Parsonage. By the Author of "Gerty and May."
Children's Picnic (The). By E. MARRYAT NORRIS.
Christian Elliott ; or, Mrs. Danver's Prize. By L. N. COMYN.
Claudine; or, Humility the Basis of all the Virtues.
Crib and Fly : the Story of Two Terriers.
Daughter of a Genius (The). By Mrs. HOFLAND.
Discontented Children (The). By M. and E. KIRBY.
Ellen, the Teacher. By Mrs. HOFLAND.
Eskdale Herd Boy (The). By LADY STODDART.
Fickle Flora and her Seaside Friends. By EMMA DAVENPORT.
Geoffrey's Great Fault. By E. MARRYAT NORRIS.
Grandmamma's Relics. By C. E. BOWEN.
Harry at School. A Story for Boys. By E. MARRYAT NORRIS.
Hero of Brittany (The) ; or, The Story of Bertrand du Guesclin.
History of the Robins (The). By Mrs. TRIMMER.
Hofer, the Tyrolese. By the Author of "William Tell."
Holiday Tales. By FLORENCE WILFORD.
Holidays among the Mountains. By M. BETHAM EDWARDS.
Johnny Miller. By FELIX WEISS.
Julia Maitland. By M. and E. KIRBY.
Life and Perambulations of a Mouse (The).
Memoir of Bob, the Spotted Terrier.
Mrs. Leicester's School. By CHARLES and MARY LAMB.
Neptune : The Autobiography of a Newfoundland Dog.
Never Wrong; or, The Young Disputant; and It was only in Fun.
New Baby (The). By the Author of "Our White Violet."
Our White Violet. By the Author of "Gerty and May."
Paul Howard's Captivity. By E. MARRYAT NORRIS.
Right and Wrong. By the Author of "Always Happy."
Scottish Orphans (The). By LADY STODDART.
Son of a Genius (The). By Mrs. HOFLAND.
Stolen Cherries (The) ; or Tell the Truth at once.
Sunny Days. By the Author of "Our White Violet."
Theodore ; or the Crusaders. By Mrs. HOFLAND.
What became of Tommy. By E. MARRYAT NORRIS.
William Tell, the Patriot of Switzerland. By FLORIAN.
Wrecked, not Lost. By the Hon. Mrs. DUNDAS.

Price One Shilling each—continued.

Easy Reading for Little Readers. Paper Boards.
Fragments of Knowledge for Little Folk. Paper Boards.
The Nursery Companion. Paper Boards.
The Picturesque Primer. Paper Boards.

These Four Volumes contain about 450 pictures; each one being complete in itself, and bound in an attractive paper cover, in boards (also with coloured Illustrations, 2s.)
The Four Volumes bound together form the "Favourite Picture Book," bound in cloth, price 5s., or coloured Illustrations, gilt edges, 10s. 6d.

The Butterfly's Ball (reproduced). With an Introduction by CHAS.
The Elephant's Ball. Ditto.   [WELSH.
The Lion's Masquerade. Ditto.
The Peacock at Home. Ditto.

The Child's Duty.	**Meta in England.**
Cock Robin. Sewed.	**Mr. Fox's Pinch for Pride.**
Courtship of Jenny Wren. Sewed.	**Three Fairy Tales.** By PAN.
Fairy Folk. By E. LACKY.	**Whittington and his Cat.**
Goody Two Shoes. Cloth.	**The Wreck.**
House that Jack Built. Sewed.	**Young Communicant's Manual.**

Babies' Museum (The): OR, RHYMES, JINGLES, AND DITTIES FOR THE NURSERY. By UNCLE CHARLIE. Fully Illustrated. (Or paper boards, 1s. 6d.)
Bible Lilies. Scripture Selections for Morning and Evening.
Cowslip (The). Fully Illustrated cloth, 1s. *plain.*
Daisy (The). Fully Illustrated cloth, 1s. *plain.*
Dame Partlett's Farm. AN ACCOUNT OF THE RICHES SHE OBTAINED BY INDUSTRY, &c. Coloured Illustrations, sewed.
Fairy Folk. By E. LECKY.
Fairy Gifts: OR, A WALLET OF WONDERS. By KATHLEEN KNOX. Illustrated by KATE GREENAWAY. Fancy boards.
Fairy Land. By the late THOMAS AND JANE HOOD. Fancy boards.
Female Christian Names, AND THEIR TEACHINGS. A Gift Book for Girls. By MARY E. BROMFIELD. Gilt edges.
Flowers of Grace. Scripture Selections for every day.
Hand Shadows, to be thrown upon the Wall. Novel and amusing figures formed by the hand. By HENRY BURSILL. Two Series in one. (Or coloured Illustrations, 1s. 6d.)
Lufness. A Sequel to the Wreck. By ETHEL.
Nine Lives of a Cat (The): a Tale of Wonder. Written and Illustrated by C. H. BENNETT. 24 Coloured Engravings, sewed.
Peter Piper. PRACTICAL PRINCIPLES OF PLAIN AND PERFECT PRONUNCIATION. Coloured Illustrations, sewed.
Primrose Pilgrimage (The): a Woodland Story. By M. BETHAM EDWARDS. Illustrated by MACQUOID. Sewed.
Rhymes and Pictures ABOUT BREAD, TEA, SUGAR, COTTON, COALS, AND GOLD. By WILLIAM NEWMAN. Seventy-two Illustrations. Price 1s. plain; 2s. 6d. coloured.
Rosebuds and Promises. A Little Book of Scripture Texts.

1/-

One Shilling each—continued.

Short and Simple Prayers, with Hymns for the Use of Children. By the Author of "Mamma's Bible Stories." Cloth.

Short Stories for Children about Animals. In Words of One Syllable. Fully Illustrated by HARRISON WEIR.

Christmas Carols. For Children in Church, at Home, and in School. Words by Mrs. HERNAMAN, and Music by ALFRED REDHEAD. Twenty-two Carols. Price 1½d. each; or complete in paper cover, price 1s. 6d. each in Two Volumes; or in One Vol., cloth, price 3s. 6d. The Words only, price 1d. for each Series. List of the Carols :—

1. Jesus in the Manger.	12. The Prince of Peace.
2. The Birthday of Birthdays.	13. Carol for Christmas Eve.
3. The Welcome Home.	14. The Babe of Bethlehem.
4. Carol to Jesus Sleeping.	15. The King in the Stable.
5. The Lambs in the Field.	16. The Infant Jesus.
6. Carol for the Children of Jesus.	17. The Holy Innocents.
7. Christmas Songs.	18. Epiphany.
8. Round about the Christmas Tree.	19. A Merry Christmas.
9. Old Father Christmas.	20. The Christmas Party.
10. We'll Gather round the Fire.	21. Light and Love.
11. Carol we high.	22. The Christmas Stocking.

Upside Down ; or, TURNOVER TRAITS. By THOMAS HOOD.

Whittington and his Cat. Coloured Illustrations, sewed.

Wreck. By ETHEL.

Young Vocalist (The). A Collection of Twelve Songs, each with an Accompaniment for the Pianoforte. By Mrs. MOUNSEY BARTHOLOMEW. (Or bound in cloth, price 2s.)

9d.

Price 9d. each, elegantly bound in Paper Boards, with Covers in Chromo-lithography.

THE TINY NATURAL HISTORY SERIES
OF STORY BOOKS ABOUT ANIMALS FOR LITTLE READERS.
ALL PROFUSELY ILLUSTRATED BY THE BEST ARTISTS.

Especially adapted for School Prizes and Rewards. In one way or another, the books either impart knowledge about Animals, or inculcate the desirableness of treating them with kindness.

Little Nellie's Bird Cage. By Mrs. R. LEE, Author of "The African Wanderers," &c.

The Tiny Menagerie. By Mrs. R. LEE, Author of "The African Wanderers," &c.

The Dog Postman. By the Author of "Odd Stories."

The Mischievous Monkey. By the Author of "Odd Stories."

Lily's Letters from the Farm. By MARY HOOPER, Author of "Ways and Tricks of Animals."

Our Dog Prin. By MARY HOOPER, Author of "Ways and Tricks of Animals."

Little Neddie's Menagerie. By Mrs. R. LEE, Author of "The African Wanderers," &c.

Frolicsome Frisk and his Friends. By the Author of "Trottie's Story Book."

Wise Birds and Clever Dogs. By the Author of "Tuppy," "Tiny Stories," &c.

Artful Pussy. By the Author of "Odd Stories," &c.

The Pet Pony. By the Author of "Trottie's Story Book."

Bow Wow Bobby. By the Author of "Tuppy," "Odd Stories," &c.

The above 12 vols. in Cardboard Box with Picture Top, price 9s.

Only a Kitten. By MAUD RANDALL.

GRIFFITH, FARRAN, OKEDEN AND WELSH,

6d.

In 21 Parts, cloth limp, fancy binding, with Chromo on side.
Price 6d. each.

TAKING TALES FOR COTTAGE HOMES.
Fully illustrated.
N.B.—Each Tale is Illustrated and complete in itself.

1. The Miller of Hillbrook: A RURAL TALE.
2. Tom Trueman : A SAILOR IN A MERCHANTMAN.
3. Michael Hale and His Family in Canada.
4. John Armstrong, THE SOLDIER.
5. Joseph Rudge, THE AUSTRALIAN SHEPHERD.
6. Life Underground; OR, DICK THE COLLIERY BOY.
7. Life on the Coast ; OR, THE LITTLE FISHER GIRL.
8. Adventures of Two Orphans in London.
9. Early Days on Board a Man-of-War.
10. Walter, the Foundling : A TALE OF OLDEN TIMES.
11. The Tenants of Sunnyside Farm.
12. Holmwood; OR, THE NEW ZEALAND SETTLER.
13. A Bit of Fun, and what it cost.
14. Sweethearts: A TALE OF VILLAGE LIFE.
15. Helpful Sam. By M. A. B.
16. Little Pretty. By F. BAYFORD HARRISON.
17. A Wise Woman. By F. BAYFORD HARRISON.
18. Saturday Night. By F. BAYFORD HARRISON.
19. Second Best. By F. BAYFORD HARRISON.
20. Little Betsy. By Mrs. E. RELTON.
21. Louie White's Hop-picking. By Miss JENNER.

N.B.—The first Twelve parts may also be had in 4 volumes, 1s. 6d.
each vol, and 2 volumes, 3s. 6d. each vol.

THE PRIZE STORY BOOK SERIES.
A Series of Six elegant little books for children from five to seven
years of age, price 6d. each.

2. The Sand Cave.	4. So-Fat and Mew-Mew away from
1. The Picnic.	Home.
3. So-Fat and Mew-Mew at Home.	5. The Birthday.
	6. The Robins.

THE CHRISTMAS STOCKING SERIES.
A new Illustrated Series of Gift Books, with coloured cover and
  Frontispiece. Six volumes, price 6d. each.

The Christmas Stocking.	Kitty Clover.
From Santa Claus.	Robin Redbreast.
Under the Christmas Tree.	Twinkle-Twinkle.

6d.

OUR BOYS' LITTLE LIBRARY.

PICTURES AND READING FOR LITTLE FOLK.

A Series of Twelve elegant little volumes in Cloth extra, with Picture on front, price 6d. each. The 12 vols. in a Box, price 6s. Every page is Illustrated.

They are especially suited for School Prizes and Rewards.

1. Papa's Pretty Gift Book.
2. Mamma's Pretty Gift Book.
3. Neddy's Picture Story Book.
4. Stories for Play Time.
5. The Christmas Gift Book.
6. The Prize Picture Book.
7. Little Jimmy's Story Book.
8. Bright Picture Pages.
9. My Little Boy's Story Book.
10. What Santa Claus gave me.
11. Tiny Stories for Tiny Boys.
12. Little Boy Blue's Picture Book.

OUR GIRLS' LITTLE LIBRARY.

PICTURES AND READING FOR LITTLE FOLK.

A Series of Twelve elegant little volumes in Cloth, with Picture on front, price 6d. each. The 12 vols. in Box, price 6s. Every page is Illustrated.

They are especially suited for School Prizes and Rewards.

1. Nellie's Picture Stories.
2. Stories and Pictures for Little Troublesome.
3. Little Trotabout's Picture Stories.
4. Birdie's Scrap Book.
5. Stories for Little Curly Locks.
6. Bright Pictures for Roguish Eyes.
7. Daisy's Picture Album.
8. Wee-Wee Stories for Wee-Wee Girls.
9. May's Little Story Book.
10. Gipsy's Favourite Companion.
11. My Own Story Book.
12. Pretty Pet's Gift Book.

THE HOLLY SERIES OF SIXPENNY TOY BOOKS.

With original designs by IDA WAUGH. Exquisitely printed in bright colours, and issued in attractive and elegant covers. Verses by AMY BLANCHARD. Price 6d. each.

The following is a List of the Books in the Series.

1. Holly Gatherers.
2. Little May.
3. Horatio Hamilton Harris.
4. Our Boys.
5. The Christmas Carol.
6. Our Pussy Cat.

Ah Chin-Chin ; HIS VOYAGE AND ADVENTURES. By F. CARRUTHERS GOULD.

4d.

THE BLUE BELL SERIES.

A new Illustrated Series of Beautiful Gift Books, containing numerous Pictures and Coloured Plates in each. Six vols., price 4d. each.

Little Blue Bell.
Oranges and Lemons.
May-time and Play-time.
Sweet as Honey.
Good as Gold.
Summer Days and Winter Ways.

OUR FATHER'S GIFTS.

A Series of Four beautiful little Books of Scripture Texts for one month. Illustrated, 48mo size, 4 Vols. 4d. each.

His Loving-kindnesses.
His Good Promises.
His Testimonies.
His Covenants.

GRIFFITH, FARRAN, OKEDEN AND WELSH.

www.ingramcontent.com/pod-product-compliance
Lightning Source LLC
Chambersburg PA
CBHW051525100726
47898CB00005B/1577